ADVANCE PRAISE FOR
ELIZABETH AND MARILYN

"Wonderful . . . I loved this. Julie Owen Moylan is a writer you can always trust in the way she portrays women. They are believable, flawed, complex, and fascinating. Their motivations and loves, the way they grapple with meaning and their callings is all sensitively done; I love the way she shows the parallels between the two women."

—Georgina Moore, author of *The Garnett Girls*

"A vibrant imagining of the inner lives of two iconic women in the year of their storied encounter . . . thoroughly enjoyable."

—Charmaine Wilkerson, *New York Times* bestselling author of *Black Cake*

"Two women struggle with the pressures of fame, work, and marital problems while living close to each other during one eventful summer. This is a brilliant concept, and Owen Moylan has pulled it off perfectly, capturing the voices, vulnerabilities, and inner lives of two icons of the twentieth century. I couldn't put it down."

—Gill Paul, author of *Jackie and Maria*

"Exploring the inner lives of two of the most famous people of the twentieth century with tenderness and compassion, *Elizabeth and Marilyn* brilliantly illuminates the women behind the myths."

—Carole Hailey, author of *The Silence Project*

"An immersive and emotionally complex portrait of two brilliant women under unimaginable pressure . . . Brava!"

—Caroline Lea, author of *The Glass Woman*

"We think we know these iconic women, but Owen Moylan reveals them in a whole new way. . . . Atmospheric, glamorous, and fun . . . a hugely enjoyable read."

—Jodie Chapman, author of *Another Life*

"Gorgeous, glamorous, and moving . . . Julie Owen Moylan reimagines Elizabeth and Marilyn with her trademark ability to get under the skin of complex female characters. . . . Brilliant."

—Anna Mazzola, author of *The Book of Secrets*

"A unique premise, perfectly executed and utterly addictive."

—Louise Beech, author of *This Is How We Are Human*

BY JULIE OWEN MOYLAN

That Green Eyed Girl

73 Dove Street

Circus of Mirrors

ELIZABETH AND MARILYN

ELIZABETH AND MARILYN

A NOVEL

JULIE OWEN MOYLAN

BALLANTINE BOOKS
NEW YORK

Ballantine Books
An imprint of Random House
A division of Penguin Random House LLC
1745 Broadway, New York, NY 10019
randomhousebooks.com
penguinrandomhouse.com

A Ballantine Books Trade Paperback Original

Published in the United Kingdom by Michael Joseph, Michael Joseph is part of the Penguin Random House group of companies.

ISBN 979-8-217-09373-1
EBOOK ISBN 979-8-217-09374-8

Printed in the United States of America

1st Printing

BOOK TEAM: Production editor: Andy Lefkowitz • Managing editor: Pamela Alders • Production manager: Jane Sankner • Copy editor: Mark McCauslin • Proofreaders: David Goehring, Rebecca Maines, and Tess Rossi

Book design by Ralph Fowler

Adobe Stock illustrations: sorrapongs (newspaper background), ganesh_502 (frontispiece and part openers), MdRanju (leaf ornaments)

The authorized representative in the EU for product safety and compliance is Penguin Random House Ireland, Morrison Chambers, 32 Nassau Street, Dublin D02 YH68, Ireland. https://eu-contact.penguin.ie

Life—
I am of both your directions
Somehow remaining hanging downward
the most
but strong as a cobweb in the
wind—I exist more with the cold, glistening frost.
My beaded rays have the colors I've
seen in a painting—ah life they
have cheated you

Marilyn Monroe

I declare before you all that my whole life, whether it be long or short, shall be devoted to your service.

Queen Elizabeth II

ELIZABETH
AND
MARILYN

London, October 29, 1956

Hello again, dear listeners, it's your old friend Ida Lapine, your resident American columnist living right here in London, England. I am standing outside the Empire Theatre in Leicester Square, where any minute now we expect to see the two most famous women in the world arriving for this royal film premiere.

I can tell you that all the stars are glittering here this evening, but there is only one name on everyone's lips. Yes, dear listeners, this is the night when America's very own Marilyn Monroe will be presented to the Queen of England. Can you imagine that?

I'll be reporting live on every single detail of that meeting. What does a girl wear to meet the Queen? We're about to find out because we can surely only be minutes away from seeing Marilyn herself. She's right here in England making a movie with none other than Sir Laurence Olivier, and I understand that she's been living in Windsor all summer. We'll try to ask her what she thinks of England when she gets here. Of course, we all know that timekeeping is not her strong suit, so let's hope she won't be keeping Queen Elizabeth waiting tonight. That would never do.

Before Marilyn arrives, let me set the scene for you. Make yourselves comfortable at home and let Ida Lapine bring all these exciting events right into your living room.

It's a chilly evening here in London. The cold darkness is beautifully illuminated by the lights of this grand old theater. A honey-yellow glow beams out at the crowd of people that is gathered here. There must be several hundred onlookers, all clutching their coats around them to keep out the slight spots of drizzle in the air. Young and old, men and women—they've all come along hoping for just one peek. They may be cold, but that won't stop them waiting to catch sight of the most famous movie star in the world and the Queen of England. A frisson of excitement races through this crowd every time we see a sleek black car pull up outside the movie theater. And I have to confess, my dear listeners, that I am as excited as can be for what this evening may hold. I'll be going inside the theater to watch the performance and to report on the stars as they line up to shake hands with the Queen. What an honor and a thrill that must be!

Now, to the best of my knowledge, I don't believe these two women have ever met before, but I did find out an interesting tidbit for you, dear listeners—did you know that Marilyn and the Queen are exactly the same age? Born just months apart, they both recently turned thirty. Isn't that something?

Tonight's showing of *The Battle of the River Plate* in the presence of Her Majesty Queen Elizabeth II will aid the Cinematograph Trade Benevolent Fund, so a great cause and a wonderful evening ahead of us. Now, I don't know about you, but for all the great and the good that are gathered here this evening, I just want to know one thing—what will Marilyn find to say to the Queen and what will Queen Elizabeth think of Marilyn Monroe? Oh, to be a fly on that particular wall!

Well, let me tell you this—Ida Lapine is here to bring you every morsel of news that she can get her hands on. Don't go anywhere, dear listeners—keep your dial tuned to this station because I do believe that I see a black limousine pulling up just outside the Empire Theatre, and if I am not very much mistaken that is Marilyn Monroe with her new husband, the playwright Arthur Miller. I think I can see a glimpse of blond hair in that rear window. Is it her?

The crowd is surging forward a little, trying to get a good view. Every photographer in the world seems ready to pop their flashbulbs. We are all waiting for that door to open and for Marilyn Monroe to step out of the car . . .

PART ONE

NORMA JEANE

1956

I hate night flights. There's something so lonely about everyone sleeping when you're wide awake. Yesterday I was excited to go to London, but that was Marilyn. She's fearless. I should know because I created her. I made her out of all the parts of me that know how to pretend. I wish I could be like her all the time, but once I got on the plane it was just me and the thoughts of all the things that could go wrong.

That stewardess keeps looking at me every time she passes by our seats. Sly, checking glances when she thinks I can't see her. I know what she's doing. It's always the same. They all want to see Marilyn—to compare themselves to her.

Sometimes they'll say it out loud when they think I can't hear them. "Oh, I thought she'd be taller . . . or different somehow." Their faces are always puzzled because they can't understand why the woman in front of them looks the same—yet somehow she's not the same woman at all. I guess it's because Marilyn lives up there . . . on a movie screen. The truth is I slip her on and off like a fur coat. Those faces searching for her only find me: Norma Jeane . . . Mrs. Arthur Miller.

Arthur is fast asleep in the seat next to mine. His face carries that worn creased look I love so very much, and for a moment I just sit back and look at him. His dark hair curling around his ears, the slight tan of his skin, and the folds around his mouth. I'm just crazy about him, and the best part about it is that he loves me too. He shifts slightly in his seat, moving closer to me as his fingers come to rest on my hand. A tiny gleam of light from the galley glints off his wedding ring, and I thread my fingers through his, wanting to feel the truth of it. He's my man forever and ever.

The plane dips a little and my stomach gives a nervous flip at the thought of landing in England. My mind begins to chew over the movie that I'm making there and whether it will be any good. It's the very first film for Marilyn Monroe Productions, and suddenly I let out a small nervous sigh. This has to work—I can't afford for it to go wrong. And it's not just me—Arthur has a new play opening in the West End, so there's a lot riding on this trip for both of us.

But I'm excited too. The two of us have been looking at pictures in magazines, and at night, Arthur and I talk about all the things we'll do on our English honeymoon. I keep imagining a quaint little cottage where we'll live, the kind with a thatched roof and tiny windows like you see in the movies. I can already see myself baking pies for my man when I'm not working.

Well, I'll try—I've never been much of a cook. And we'll take long romantic walks in the rain with our arms wrapped around each other, and every day Arthur will love me more and more. I have everything that I ever wanted. And this time I know I have the right guy.

That stewardess passes by our seats again, but this time she doesn't look. Maybe she's seen enough to tell all her friends about the night she worked the TWA flight from Idlewild to London Airport with Marilyn Monroe on board.

Once she moves away, I lay my head on Arthur's shoulder and nuzzle in, smelling the sweet earthy scent of his skin. His white shirt is soft against my cheek and I can feel the warm rhythmic shift of his breathing.

At the beginning of last year, I was so very miserable and desperate to leave Hollywood to start over somewhere else. I couldn't have believed how my life would change. I feel like a fairy godmother suddenly showed up and granted me all my wishes in one go—the man of my dreams and the chance to control my own movies—doing the work that I want to do. I have it all now!

A small giggle escapes from somewhere inside me and Arthur turns away, his head resting back against the seat as his mouth falls open. I must have slept a little during the night—I took a Nembutal when I got on board. It made me kind of dozy in that nice way you feel when you're a kid. But just like every other night my eyes suddenly opened wide and I was awake again.

At least the bad dreams didn't come.

Everyone else is fast asleep, and the only signs of life are the stewardesses whispering in the galley and padding softly up and down the aisle to see if Marilyn Monroe snores or maybe even drools in her sleep. I think the answer is no, but you can't be sure—I mean, if I'm asleep then I hardly know what I'm doing. Anyway, I hope they all get something to go back and tell their friends about.

"Hey, what time is it?" The sound of Arthur's voice startles me. He leans forward in his seat and rubs his hands over his face, trying to push away all traces of sleep, before fumbling in his shirt pocket for his thick black-rimmed glasses.

"I don't know—it's getting lighter outside so we can't be far away now," I whisper softly.

The same stewardess appears right by our seats as if we've summoned her there. "Can I get you some coffee, Mr. Miller?" She smiles, bright and wide, like a Girl Scout trying to sell us cookies. She wants us to remember her. Arthur doesn't even glance up. He's grumpy first thing in the morning, but she wouldn't know that.

He mumbles, "Yeah . . . coffee."

And then Girl Scout turns her big smile on me. "Miss Monroe . . . sorry, Mrs. Miller, can I get you something?" Her eyes are wide blue pools, drinking me in. I don't like being looked at this way when I get nervous. I always feel as if people will go away disappointed in some fashion.

"Oh . . . I would very much like a glass of warm milk," I tell her. I hate to be a nuisance, but I like what I like.

"Of course . . ." she replies, only too glad to help now.

"Wait—I'd like two eggs beaten into a glass of warm milk and with a dash of sherry if you have it."

Arthur pulls a face, but it's my breakfast drink of choice and I won't apologize for it—and anyway it's good for you. Someone told me that dairy makes your bones strong. The stewardess is still standing there, her smile slightly faded as she thinks about what I just asked for. Then she nods and goes off to the galley while Arthur and I try to face the day. He puts his hand on my knee and squeezes it gently. Then I feel the warmth of his lips on my cheek and I breathe him in—every last drop.

"Happy?" he says.

"Sure am," I say as our hands entwine, and my heart feels fit to burst.

The plane makes a sudden turn, the wing on our side dipping down toward the sea, and I push aside the little curtain that covers our window. It's daylight outside. The night is over and from today I'm going to be living in England for four whole months.

Suddenly a bolt of fear shoots right through my body like an arrow and I have to remind myself that I wanted this more than anything. I try to block out the feeling and remember it was only eighteen months ago that I walked out on 20th Century-Fox. The parts were junk—one dumb-blonde role after another—and I knew I could do more than that. So I took a chance and ran away to New York, before issuing a list of demands to the studio. Norma Jeane might constantly doubt herself, but when I'm Marilyn, I know what I'm worth.

Director approval. Project approval. The right to make my own movies with my very own production company. Then I sat back and waited . . .

The thing about making a big deal about something is that when you finally get what you want, it really has to go well. And here I am in charge of Marilyn Monroe Productions along with my business partner, Milton, and now we're all on our way to film a movie with one of the greatest actors in the world.

The fear shifts and tangles inside me, forming tight knots in my stomach and my chest until my hands begin to tremble.

I can do this. I can.

This is *my* movie, I tell myself. It's not like any of the others. I chose Sir Laurence Olivier to make it with me, and I get to call the shots . . . but if this goes wrong, I don't know what I'll do. I take a deep breath, the way my acting coaches tell me to. *Find your center. Breathe in calm and breathe out the fear.* The breath going in feels sharp and jagged like I've forgotten how to breathe properly, but I keep on going and eventually that stillness drapes right over me.

It's all going to be okay.

I *am* going to work with the greatest actor in the world and everyone will see that I'm not just some dumb blonde.

And I'm really not. I've studied so hard—all those days and nights at the Actors Studio. The first time I crept into that room I kept the collar on my black coat turned up to hide my face. I sat right at the back. I was trying so hard to hide away. The place was full of so many wonderful actors and I didn't think I would ever fit in there, but the minute Lee Strasberg began speaking, I could feel the truth of his words rippling right through me. I wanted to learn everything he knew.

In the beginning, the other actors were kind of awkward

around me. I guess they had opinions about Marilyn Monroe the movie star, but eventually we started hanging out, drinking coffee after class, or going out for drinks. I was scared to death of acting in front of them, but one day I did a scene from *Anna Christie* and all those great actors just sat there applauding me. Cheering me on like I was one of them. The thought of it makes a wave of calm flush right over me and the fear subsides.

There's really nothing to be scared of. I've got everything I need right here.

Girl Scout arrives with a silver tray carrying Arthur's coffee and my glass filled with eggnog. She places them down on our tray tables and I thank her, but this time something clicks into place deep inside me and I give her the full Marilyn treatment. A thousand-watt dazzle and I know the story she will tell her friends—*Oh yes, I waited on Marilyn Monroe and she was just like you'd imagine*—because all she can see now is what they all see. A halo of platinum hair and a movie-star smile. Top lip pulled down to hide the fact that the tip of my nose is just a little too close to my mouth. People do impressions of me talking that way but I don't mind. It's kind of cute. It's better than nobody knowing who you are is what I think.

I sip my eggnog, drinking the creamy mixture slowly. The little dash of sherry helps to calm my nerves about the whole situation. Arthur swallows down his coffee in two big gulps and then goes off to find the bathroom.

Turning around, I can see Whitey Snyder just a few rows back, gathering his makeup case and checking everything. I catch his eye and he gives me that old Whitey look that he's been giving me for the past ten years, the one that tells me everything will be fine. He raises his eyebrows to see if I'm ready for him, and I nod.

Look out, England, here I come!

"Ready?" Milton asks. He's nervous too: I can tell. We've gone over and over this movie—every single detail—yet we're both scared to death. Neither of us has ever produced a movie before, and we don't know a thing about working in England, but we're sure going to give it everything we've got.

I gaze up at Whitey, who is dusting my face with powder. His long, thin face with his long, thin nose. Slicked-back dark hair. He always gets this little crinkle in his brow when he's concentrating, like he's painting the *Mona Lisa* or something. It's only me, but he treats it just the same as a work of art. He's one of the nicest guys I know, and I feel my breath calm at the sight of him.

He stands back to check that everything is where it should be. No lipstick on my teeth or mascara flakes on my cheek. Only perfection will do. Like me, he knows that when people see Marilyn for the first time it has to take their breath away.

"Do I look okay?" I whisper to Whitey, knowing he will say something that will flick the switch.

"You look like a queen. You go out there and handle yourself with dignity. They're lucky to have you." He gives me that warm smile and the nod that means I'm ready.

I stand up and smooth down the front of my beige jersey dress. The heel of my cream Ferragamo shoe catches a little as I walk toward the exit.

There's a cool breeze blowing in from the open door, and a woman suddenly arrives with a bouquet of pretty white flowers for me. She is standing there in a brown dress, flushed like she's been running, and I have no idea who she is. The woman hesitates before handing the flowers over with her mouth flapping open and closed as she just stares at me, her eyes wide as if she's had an electric shock.

"Thank you very much. They're beautiful," I say, beaming at her, before moving across the aisle to put my hand on Arthur's waist. "I guess we should get going."

He frowns and that familiar furrow appears between his brows as he slips on his white jacket and takes his leather briefcase from the overhead locker. His face is still creased with sleep as he towers over me. "There must be a hundred photographers out there." Arthur looks at me accusingly for a split second as if I invited them.

"I tell you what: you grab the bags and we'll make a run for it," I whisper, and he laughs while his fingers gently stroke my face.

"We have twenty-seven pieces of luggage, Marilyn. I don't think we'll be able to run very far."

"A girl needs clothes to wear. I guess I'll just have to face the press, then."

He softens at this and plants a lingering kiss on top of my head and drinks me in for a long moment. "You're so goddamn beautiful, Mazzie. What did I do to deserve you? I can't wait to get settled into our new home and start our honeymoon. I love you, precious girl. You're my angel."

"Oh, Papa . . . me too." His eyes light up when I call him that, and Arthur folds me into his chest and hugs me tight. I just want to stay right here, feeling safe and loved.

Behind us, someone makes a polite coughing noise, and I know they're waiting for me. Taking a deep breath, I pull away from Arthur and lean over to grab my tan leather handbag from my seat, hooking it over my elbow. He smiles at me and I run my fingers along the folds of his smile, and along his jaw. The bouquet of flowers has gotten a little crushed between us, but I drape it across my arms as Whitey throws a cream raincoat across my shoulders. This beige dress is tight in all the right places and I stand a little straighter, licking my lips as my eyes grow wide with fear, but it's too late to back out now. I hide my eyes behind a pair of dark sunglasses and take another step toward the door.

London, please be good to me—I send up a tiny prayer and take a deep breath. The same arrow of fear bolts through me as I nervously lick at my lips again, then stop because my lipstick will be wiped off and Whitey will be annoyed if I ruin his creation.

The press photographers are not waiting for me anyhow. She's the one they've come to see. I can already hear them calling out her name: "Marilyn! Marilyn!"

I take another deep breath and that switch inside is flipped. "Let's go," I say, and step out of the airplane.

The air outside is cool even though it's July, but there are pools of water on the ground as if we just missed a summer shower. The air smells of fuel and damp, and I pose for a moment on top of the plane steps alongside Arthur and turn on that smile.

Suddenly all the fear melts away—she's here now. There's a moment where my spine straightens even further, my mouth opens into *that* smile, and I'm not the same woman any more. People are calling out my name—they love me and I love them right back.

I let go of Arthur's arm. It's all gray clouds and the gray faces of the crowd as far as I can see, but I walk down the steps and wiggle my way across the tarmac.

"Hello, boys!" I say as I breeze past a group of guys in overalls. I think they're supposed to be refueling something, but they're just standing around, their mouths hanging open as I walk by. I start to laugh. Marilyn has this crazy effect on people.

In the distance, I see Sir Larry and his wife, Vivien, waiting to welcome us. He looks just as handsome as when I met him in New York. Dark-haired with deep blue eyes and such a nice face.

Larry greets me with a warm kiss on my cheek. He's very polite, but his eyes are roving in that way I've come to recognize as he takes in the "tight in all the right places" beige dress. When we had dinner in New York, he was so very lovely to me. We had talked all about the Terence Rattigan play and how we might turn it into a movie. I'd play the showgirl who meets a handsome prince and finds herself in his palace. We'd produce the film together and Larry would direct it, in addition to playing the Prince Regent of Carpathia.

As we were finishing our desserts, I gushed about how thrilled I was to be acting with the great Sir Laurence Olivier. He leaned right across the table and, with a mischievous little twinkle in his eye, said, "My dear, you're a very great comic actress and I'm sure to fall madly in love with you in this role." I just adore him—he's my ideal leading man. I just hope we come across well on film because you never know if it will work until you see people on the screen. The camera never lies.

Now Larry gives me a warm and inviting smile. "It's very nice to see you again, my dear. Did you have a good flight? Not too bumpy, I hope."

"It was pretty smooth actually. It's so nice to finally be here," I say, smiling right back at him.

"Well, they've set up some sort of area so we can say a few words for the press if you don't mind? Just a quick stop. We'll do the proper press conference tomorrow at the Savoy Hotel."

"Sure . . . I don't mind." As I speak, I can feel Arthur's shoulders sagging with displeasure by my side, but we aren't going to get out of here without saying a few words. The two men greet each other warmly as I turn to Vivien and kiss her cheek. "Congratulations on the news about the baby. I'm so envious. I really want that for Arthur and me once we wrap this movie." I giggle like we're all girls together, but she just glares at me with those sharp gray-green Scarlett O'Hara eyes and gives me a tight smile.

"Thank you," she says coolly. For a moment, I feel a little disappointed. She's such a wonderful actress and I admire her so very much. I had even imagined us becoming great friends while I was in England.

I don't know whether Vivien is upset that she didn't get to play Elsie in the movie after her rave reviews on stage, or she thinks that I'm flirting with Larry when I have my own man that I'm mad about. This happens quite often with other women. I guess they think I'm going to steal their man or make them feel bad. People only see Marilyn and imagine all kinds of things about her. Nobody sees the real me underneath the blond hair and red lipstick and wiggling walk.

Anyway, Vivien can like me or not. I just have to concentrate on getting this movie right.

I thread my arm deliberately through Arthur's and smile as if I don't have a care in the world. The press pack throngs around us as we push our way through to the four chairs that are laid out in a corner of the lounge. It's really too small for the number of people, and I notice they have set out microphones, which I hate. I either speak too loudly into them or get the awful whistling noise that makes everyone put their hands to their ears. I don't want to use them and I say so. For a moment everyone looks at me like I'm crazy, but it's bad enough having to answer a million questions when you're tired and jet-lagged without worrying about microphones.

Someone rushes to take them away and we all squeeze into our chairs waiting for the parade of questions to begin.

"What are you most looking forward to about being in England, Marilyn?"

"I'd like to see as much of it as I can, including that little guy with the bow and arrow in Piccadilly." I widen my eyes and broaden my smile and the guys in the press laugh. I know how to make men laugh. It's a well-rehearsed act, and I feel a flush of pleasure at all the smiling faces. Arthur's face breaks into a weary grin, and Larry chuckles at my answers, while Vivien wears that tight smile on her lips.

"Do you know where you'll be staying tonight?" one guy yells out from the back of the crush.

"No, I don't actually. I'm sure they'll find me a bed somewhere." And we all laugh again.

"What do you think of England?" another faceless shout from the crowd.

"I've heard a lot about it and I think it's wonderful. I'd like to really get to know it and meet people. Maybe even your Queen." They all laugh again, but I *would* really like to meet her. We're the same age, although I can't imagine ruling a whole country at this age. I can barely manage to get out of the bathtub some days.

Then it's over and we are hustled away into a shiny black car and driven through the damp gray streets toward Windsor. That's where they've found us a house. We told them we wanted a proper English house just like the ones we'd seen in magazines.

Our little honeymoon cottage where Arthur and I can be alone.

The car speeds along the narrow country lanes, and through the window I can see lots of green fields, but the houses are so small. It's like a movie set—we could be on the Fox backlot pretending to be driving through the English countryside, except it's not a movie. I'm really here.

I start looking out for a thatched cottage with little windows and chintz curtains—maybe a log fire for chilly fall evenings. Dreaming about coming home from the studio every day and curling up on the couch with Arthur. Being the best wife that any man has ever had. Since Arthur's divorce came through, it's been a whirlwind and we've barely had a moment to ourselves. First he was under investigation by that awful committee who wanted him to name any communists he knew, and then we were rushing to get married in time for this trip. It's perfect timing with his new play opening and my movie starting production, but so far we haven't really had a moment to get used to married life. England will be lucky for us, though—I just know it.

Suddenly the car slows down and turns into a long gravel driveway with a large white wooden gate that's been left open. Everywhere I look there are tall green trees leading up to the house. I try to get a better look by pressing my face against the window and then I see it. . . .

The house is not at all what I was expecting. It's like some kind of mansion and not a quaint little cottage at all.

Swallowing my disappointment, I smile at Arthur, but I can see him frowning as he takes it all in. It's a very big house, and there are so many windows it's hard to count them all. I stare at the front of the house. It's very pretty with some kind of climbing plant trailing all over the front door and beautiful pink roses peeking out from behind dark green leaves, but it's not the English honeymoon cottage I had in mind.

We dreamed of being alone, just the two of us, but this house is way too big for one person to take care of . . . and that means there will be staff.

Back in New York, I lived in a small apartment without anyone to help me and I've always liked it that way. It's private, you know. Nobody watching you all the time or leaking things to the press that shouldn't be leaked.

As we pull up outside, I see a large number of people waiting to greet us in the doorway. My heart sinks at the thought of them being around us all day long. There's even a butler. . . .

Suddenly the tiredness catches up with me. I don't want to answer any more questions or take a tour of the house. But everyone wants to say this is the day they took Marilyn around her English house or brought her tea in her English drawing room. I can feel Norma Jeane shift deep inside me. She wants to lie in a tub of hot scented water until her skin prunes. She wants to sleep naked under fresh sheets with her thighs pressed against Arthur's hips, feeling him nuzzling the back of her neck.

Before I can even take a breath or introduce myself to the staff, the press pack arrives. They scramble out of their little gray cars and here we go again. "Can we get a shot of you and Arthur? Can you look right at him, Marilyn?" they call out, insisting we turn this way and that.

I strike a pose outside the front door of our new home. "Welcome to Parkside House," somebody says.

My arm wraps around Arthur's waist, clinging to him like a life jacket in a stormy sea. I smile so hard that my face aches. I say again and again how pleased I am to be here. Yes, I love the house. Yes, I can't wait to start work with Sir Larry on our movie. Yes, I love England already. Yes, I'd like to buy a bicycle to get around Windsor. Yes. Yes. Yes.

I beam up at my handsome husband, who is towering over me in his smart white jacket. He is tolerating this dog-and-pony show because he loves me. In that moment I answer yet another reporter, "Yes, we're very happy. He's my man and I adore him."

Arthur gazes down at me as if I just handed him the whole world on a plate.

"Well, if that's all your questions, gentlemen, I think we'd like to have a quiet evening alone. After all, we're still on our honeymoon."

The press men give a knowing laugh, and I say our goodbyes. We have to do it all again tomorrow at the Savoy Hotel—more questions and more answers. How many ways can I find to say that I love England and I am looking forward to making this movie?

Marilyn is flickering away like an old lightbulb as I close the front door on them all.

LILIBET

1956

Margaret is waiting in my drawing room, smoking a cigarette and looking her usual glamorous self. My sister has a way with her that I don't possess, and she knows it only too well.

"Hello, you," I say, leaning over to kiss her cheek.

"Oh, we are a bit matchy . . ." Margaret bobs a reluctant curtsy and eyes me with a slightly petulant look on her face, as if it is my fault. We are wearing exactly the same open-toed white shoes with matching handbags and elbow-length white gloves, although our dresses are different, as are our hats. I'm wearing a sea-green floral dress with a ruched waist while Margaret is in pale lemon silk with a matching feathered hat. She does rather remind me of a little bird about to take flight, but I don't say so.

"Oh well, I expect people will be much more interested in the bride than us," I say as we begin to walk briskly along the wide corridors of Buckingham Palace. We would play games in these great halls as little girls. I can clearly remember chasing Margaret past the paintings of our great-great-grandmother at her own coronation. Queen Victoria came to the throne at such a young age. She's only eighteen years old in that painting, nine years younger than I am in my coronation portrait. I can't begin to imagine what it must have been like, taking on this responsibility at that age. I still don't feel old enough in some ways, and I've been doing the job for four years now, although it feels even longer.

Out of the corner of my eye, I can see members of staff hastily backing out of doorways as they see me coming. "I do so hate it when they do that," I mutter almost to myself, but Margaret doesn't miss a word of it.

"Do what?" she asks as we rush down the grand staircase toward the front entrance where the car is waiting.

"People scurry out of my way when they see me coming. It makes me feel most peculiar, as if I'm not really a person but some terrible ogre that they mustn't encounter. I am just an ordinary human being after all." I sound more irritated than I am, but I find that tone is creeping into my voice most days at the moment. One does feel quite alone in this job at times.

"Well, you *are* the Queen, so not really an ordinary human being." Margaret points this out as if it is some sort of character flaw on my part, and for a second, I am reminded of a winter's day in our nursery when Margaret made me so very furious that I tipped an entire pot of dark blue ink all over her head. I am rather tempted to do it again some days. A sly smile flits across my face as I conjure up the image of my little sister standing there with her blond curls dripping dark blue ink, while Crawfie, our governess, ran around squealing. I'm sure I was severely punished for it, but now I can't entirely recall what happened to me, or how long it took to wash all that ink out of Margaret's golden hair.

"Where's Philip today? How come he's not taking you to this wedding?" Margaret asks testily. She's quite sensitive about the topic of weddings at the moment, and I would have asked somebody else to accompany me, but I did think it might cheer her up a bit. She's always complaining that I never have time for her these days, but it's not personal—I don't have time for anything except my duties.

There are appointments every twenty minutes or so, and my diary is not my own. Whole hours of hand-kissing with ambassadors, countless visits to places, and all the while making small talk with people. Then every single day the endless red boxes of government papers for me to go through. It's just as well I'm a fast reader or they wouldn't see me at all. Just the past fortnight I've held a state visit for the King of Iraq, and countless investitures, plus, of course, I have my weekly meeting with the prime minister, Mr. Eden. He's a strange, twitchy man and I do wonder sometimes if he's quite well. I very much miss the wise counsel and support of my dear Winston, but things change quite regularly in politics. One just has to get used to it. The people want what they want, at least for a short time.

"He's in North Wales at some slate quarry today," I reply with a little snap.

"Oh, poor Philip, how dull." Margaret thinks everything is dull. I'm sure she'd be happier if life were just one long party, but actually Philip is very interested in slate quarries. He was explaining some intricate part of what he was going to see over dinner last night.

As we approach the front door it is whipped open by a footman in a red jacket with shining brass buttons and polished shoes. He informs the driver that we're off to St. Margaret's in Westminster while my sister and I settle back in the car; it sweeps out of the black iron gates of the palace and proceeds down the Mall. We fall silent for a moment, and I'm reminded of the profound awkwardness that lies between us. We were always easy companions as girls, but the past few years have filled that space with resentment. As I married Philip and began to live my own life, my sister found herself falling in love with my father's equerry, Peter Townsend. He was a handsome war hero, and Margaret a young and beautiful princess. I liked Peter tremendously when he was working for my father, although I would be lying if I said that I didn't have concerns about the age difference between him and Margaret. And, of course, the fact that he was divorced.

I cast my mind back to that awful day, sitting opposite my sister and seeing the anguish on her face when I said, "The thing is, Margaret, you can't marry Peter and keep your title and privileges. That's not my decision. It's the decision of the government and . . . well, of the Church. It's because of the divorce. I'm so sorry."

Margaret looked at me, her face completely stunned. "But we did everything you asked. We waited and waited. You promised me it would all work out."

"I'm very sorry," I whispered, having nothing that I could possibly say to make things better.

"But I love him, Lilibet. You can't ask me to give him up. I won't do it. Please do something to help us." Her voice pleading—begging me to help her. "Please . . ."

"There's nothing I can do. The decision is final." The words sounded so cold even to my ears, but inside my heart was breaking for her.

It's been a year now, and I can tell that Margaret still blames me for the way her life has turned out. There are also times, if one were to be perfectly honest, that I resent the fact she has the freedom to fill her days as she pleases, while I most certainly do not. If I had her life, I like to imagine I'd head for the hills of Scotland and spend my time riding horses and walking the dogs quite happily. But Margaret prefers to spend her evenings at an endless round of society parties and her days nursing her sore head.

The car crawls along toward the church in Westminster and, as I don't wish to fight with her, I try to put on a pleasant smile and think of something to say that won't provoke yet another argument.

"How's Mummy?" I ask, even though I spoke to my mother just an hour ago on the telephone.

"As well as can be expected given she's lost her husband, her home, and her job, I suppose," Margaret snaps at me so quickly that it seems to take even her by surprise. I don't know what to say in response. It's been four years since my darling papa died, yet they all seem unchanged by the passing of time, the feelings as raw as ever. None of that is my fault, yet I seem to be blamed for it, as if I have caused all of our lives to be uprooted and changed irrevocably.

I miss him terribly. He's the one person whose advice I would dearly love, and now I understand only too well why he always looked so terribly burdened. Some days I would creep along the corridor and stand outside his office. When we were young girls, he had our rocking horses placed just outside his door so that he could hear the gentle rhythm of our riding and our childish laughter, I suppose. And we in turn could hear him—his language often becoming quite salty, as he was frequently infuriated.

Occasionally the door would open and he would spy me lurking there and wave me inside. I would happily stand there watching him wrestling with his official papers, and from time to time he would look up and give me a little wink as if we were engaged in a secret mission. "One day this will be your desk," he would say, and then, as my face bunched into a little frown, he would burst out laughing. "Oh, don't look like that, Lilibet—not for very many years yet. You'll be as old as I am."

I think we all believed that—certainly Philip and I had hoped so. I saw us bringing up our family first and Philip having his naval career for many years. Of course, my dear papa died so very young and here we all are. My mother has been relegated to a lesser royal overnight and has moved out of Buckingham Palace and into Clarence House, which she shares with my sister, while I feel very much as if I've been cast in the role of a queen and am now expected to perform eight shows a week in the West End with full costume and no days off.

"I'm sorry, Lilibet. That was uncalled for. I'm in a filthy temper today and I don't know why." My sister can be perfectly infuriating, but as her sharp blue eyes meet mine, I can see the well of sadness that these days lives permanently behind her rather grand facade. She gives my hand a little squeeze, and as we draw up at St. Margaret's Church, we are peaceful once again. "Mummy's fine . . . you know how she is. Making the best of it, as we all are," she says as we eye the wedding guests chattering away on the steps of the church.

The car door is opened, and just as I am about to step out, Margaret spies one of the guests wearing an elaborate frilly dress in dark gold with a matching hat. There are so many ruffles and bows that the woman is quite overcome by them.

"What is she wearing? My goodness, that woman is a walking cream puff. How perfectly awful," Margaret exclaims with horror and I have to wrestle my face into its usually composed expression to greet people.

The bride looks quite beautiful in her white lace dress. The weather is splendid and just in time, as it was raining earlier and it has been a rather dismal summer so far. The happy couple beam at us on the way back up the aisle as the organist thumps out a hymn that swells around the church, and I see that Margaret's eyes are sparkling with tears. For a moment I feel such great pity for her poor broken heart and would do anything to make her feel better.

"Are you all right?" I whisper to her with a sympathetic smile.

Margaret watches the bride shining with joy as she clutches her new husband's arm, and just for a second, I can see terrible pain etched across my sister's face. Before I can do or say anything, she composes herself and the look is gone. We follow on behind the bride and groom as they glide back up the aisle and out into the beautiful July afternoon.

I squeeze my sister's arm gently while all the attention is focused on the newlyweds, who are beaming with delight as they pose together on the steps of the church.

"This won't be forever, Margo. You'll make a beautiful bride one day and very soon. I'm sure the right chap is out there waiting for you." The minute the words leave my lips I know that it is entirely the wrong thing to have said to my sister. Her face turns sharply toward me as if I've wounded her.

"I've already met the right chap, as you so delicately put it, but if you recall you wouldn't let me marry him because the Crown must always come first."

"It wasn't my decision, you know that," I say in a hushed whisper, as I really don't want anyone to see that we're arguing. I don't know what she expects from me. After all, I am head of the Church in this country and have to abide by its teachings. I keep my smile bright and wide and my eyes on the bride and groom. Margaret doesn't respond, and so we spend the next few minutes ignoring each other but smiling and shaking hands with an assortment of guests, saying, "Hello, lovely to see you . . ." over and over again.

I'll make it up to her. We're going to Scotland together next month, and then she's got a tour of East Africa. It will give her some much-needed time away from Britain and hopefully a moment to shine in her own little spotlight. We are all willing her to get over Peter, and she has no shortage of eligible young men wanting to date her, but Margaret is bored by them. I wish I could magically find someone she could love and who would love her back. I do so want her to be happy. I want all my family to be happy.

The funny thing is that nobody ever asks me if I'm happy.

Philip glances across the table at me, although the greater part of him is wholly invested in this new dinner dish. He still retains the same charming boyish quality I remember from the very first time I laid eyes on him. I was a shy and rather awkward thirteen-year-old, certainly not wanting too much attention or to be studied carefully, as if I were an archaeological treasure or some such thing. Yet Philip, even on our first introduction, stood there, so tall and blond with his keen blue eyes piercing in their curiosity. And so he has remained ever since our first meeting. He has a mercurial quality that's difficult to contain—always moving toward something. Chasing the new, yet not for the sake of it but rather to understand how he may employ it to help people.

All of this is a marvelous trait except when employed in the confines of a palace where nothing significant has changed in one hundred years. Nothing could frustrate him more. Today he has driven the cooks mad by insisting on a new dish with a recipe he picked up on his travels. I smile encouragingly because I want him to be happy and inwardly give a delicate sigh, as any complaints about Philip wanting to try something new inevitably reach me.

"This is delicious, darling, won't you try some?" he says, willing me to give it a go.

"No, you know I don't like anything too rich." If I'm being perfectly honest, I much prefer the kind of plain food I ate as a child, but I can't help indulging Philip in his passion for new foods. He's lost so much in his life, and this is such a small thing, but it makes him happy.

"You really should try some. I think you'd like it." He wrinkles his nose up as he smiles at me. His whole face lights up with the pleasure of his discovery. He's in a terribly good mood today, which is more than I can say for myself. Margaret is avoiding me, I fear, and although we spoke on the telephone earlier today, it was very stilted.

"No, thank you. You know I prefer plain food."

"And chocolate . . ." he says with a grin, knowing full well that is my weak spot.

"Well, yes, I rather like chocolate things. Is that so bad?" I give him a quizzical look and then temper it with a slight smile, as I don't want to fall out with anybody else this week. The upset with Margaret is playing on my mind, and I wish that I could wave a magic wand and give them all what they need to make them happy. Margaret to have the love of her life and live happily ever after, Philip to have his naval career, and Mummy to have my dear papa back. For a moment I consider how wonderful that would be, for then I wouldn't have this job. Philip and I would be living happily in Malta with our children, having so much fun in our quite ordinary Navy life. We might even have had another baby by now, and just think how lovely it would have been for Charles and Anne growing up there instead of being stuck inside this palace with a mother who is always too busy and a father who is growing increasingly resentful of her job. My mind flits between the different scenarios—the two of us walking along the beach together at sunset or having quiet dinners with other Navy couples far away from palaces and duties. I am quite lost in memories until I become aware that Philip is still talking to me.

"It must run in the family. Is that why we all have that same birthday cake time after time? What happens if someone doesn't like chocolate cake? You could have a change, you know. Just because Queen Victoria did something doesn't mean that you all have to follow on. That's the trouble with this place. Because someone once had a thought, everyone thinks that that is the only thought now possible and then nothing ever changes. The men in gray suits in this place fight me over every last thing—even a new recipe."

A shadow of annoyance falls over his face and I resist the temptation to defend the courtiers and their ways. Not all tradition is bad, nor is it necessary to change things merely for the sake of it. He pushes his food around his plate, then loses interest in it altogether and sits back in his chair with a mixture of satisfaction and, as usual, the urge to move on to the next thing in his day. Philip is like quicksilver and I often wonder how we rub along together, as I am mostly not like that. I try to keep the peace, smoothing things over as I go along. Although I do have a bit of a temper when pushed too far, as he knows only too well.

"It's just a family tradition, that's all, and it is a very nice chocolate cake. You'll be seeing it again very soon for Mummy's birthday party at Windsor, but you don't need to eat it if you'd prefer not to. The kitchen will make you another cake, Philip, if you desperately want one." I sound exasperated and yet I'm not particularly irritated with him. We both feel trapped in this role that neither of us was ready for. The past four years have been hard for him, but they've also been hard for me—something that he doesn't always recognize.

I feel as if I've become two distinct people. The loving woman whom he married, and mother to our two beautiful children, and of course the person doing this job. Sadly, on most days there is no Lilibet Windsor to be found—there is only Elizabeth, and she has little time to play with her children or spend time with her grieving family. There is nothing that I can do about it.

Philip doesn't react to my snapping, but instead takes another mouthful of his discovery, and a look of sheer delight crosses his face. He has such a great curiosity, and I envy him a little for his ability to appear so fascinated by the workings of a jet engine, or a tin mine, or a new recipe. He seems so genuinely enthused by everything, and then at other times he is extremely frustrated and angry at being kept from the things that he loves to do. I had hoped that by setting up his outward-bound scheme for children he would find his purpose, and it seemed he did for a while. But it's not enough to keep him occupied, and my husband is a man who needs a mission in life.

"By the way, did you read the newspapers? We have a new neighbor." Philip has a devilish grin on his face that I rather like.

"Well, of course I read the newspapers every day. Whom are you talking about?"

"The film star—Marilyn Monroe . . ."

"What about her?" I reply, somewhat puzzled at the turn this conversation is taking.

"She has moved to Windsor . . ." He leans forward conspiratorially, and over his shoulder I can see the footman's lips twitch in a smile.

"Windsor? What on earth for?" I really don't know the first thing about her, and we haven't watched any of her films, but of course I have seen photographs. Like most Hollywood people she appears rather larger than life and impossibly beautiful. I can't imagine for one minute how she might find Windsor.

"She's making a film with Laurence Olivier. She's moved here with that playwright Arthur Miller. They're married now."

"Oh . . . well, I do hope she enjoys her stay. I expect our rather damp summer will come as a shock after California. Isn't it renowned for its sunshine?"

"She'll get used to it. It should brighten up Windsor a bit anyway. You should ask her to the castle for tea," Philip says, and he actually winks at me across the table. I'm not sure if he's just teasing me or if he seriously expects me to invite her.

"What for? I imagine she's quite busy making her film. I'm sure she wouldn't be the slightest bit interested in us." I don't know whether that's true or not, but I'm not entirely convinced by Philip's motivation in this conversation.

"So we can see what she's like in real life. It would certainly be a story for my gentlemen's lunch club." He sounds a bit too enthused about his idea for my liking.

"If you want to meet Miss Monroe, then you can invite her to tea. I'm not in the habit of extending invitations to people because my husband wants to see what they look like in real life or to brag to his gentlemen friends," I say with a mock severity as I know he is toying with me.

Philip bursts out laughing. "Ha! Can't blame a chap for trying."

I start laughing too, because he's quite ridiculous sometimes, but the world would be a terribly bleak place without him to tease me out of my bad moods some days. The footman who was smirking earlier begins to clear our plates. As I take a sip of my wine, Philip suddenly leaps up from the table and leans over me.

"Where are you going?" I say, but my words are muffled by his fleeting kiss as he strides toward the door.

"We're having drinks this evening for one of the chaps who's getting married."

"Philip!" I cry out. There were things I wanted to discuss with him about Mummy's birthday party, but he's already gone.

I sit there for a moment carefully folding my napkin and pondering what to do with the rest of my evening when I suddenly become aware that I am no longer alone.

"Your Majesty . . ." My private secretary, Michael Adeane, gives a little bow as he stands in the doorway looking most grave.

"What is it, Michael?" My heart sinks at the sight of his face, as it's always a sign of bad news incoming when he looks this way.

"Downing Street is on the telephone, ma'am. It seems that

Colonel Nasser has gone ahead with his plans to nationalize the Suez Canal. He's threatening to block all of our ships. The French are furious, and obviously so are we."

"Oh dear. Then I'd better speak to the prime minister." My heart sinks, and I feel a nervous clench of my stomach. Conflicts make me feel quite sick, and for the second time in the past few days, I wish that my father were here. He would know what to do and say at this moment. We obviously can't allow Colonel Nasser to block the Suez Canal, but I feel such awful dread at the thought of sending young men to fight for their country's interests should it come to that. Of course, it's the government's decision to act, but those young men die in my name, and I can't bear it. I simply can't. Whenever some serious conflict occurs in the world, I can feel the old men in the government and the courtiers in the palace watching me—weighing me to see if I'm up to the task of leadership. Am I my father's daughter or just some young woman with her head filled with trivial nonsense? Well, I am my father's daughter, but I can't help it if I hate conflict. These old men are rarely the ones who have to shake hands with the grieving families and wish them well. Looking into the eyes of mothers who have buried their sons is a terrible thing, and their agony is not something that I would ever take lightly. No medal in the world could make up for losing Charles or Anne. Even the thought of it makes my heart ache.

As I walk toward my office, the dogs scatter about my feet, racing up and down the corridors as we go. "Susan! Sugar! Come now," I shout as two of them almost succeed in tripping up a passing footman. They are the only things in the entire world other than horses who neither know nor care that I am a queen. I'll always be Lilibet to them.

As the dogs and I make our way along the corridor I cast a critical glance at the priceless artwork that adorns the walls. There are times I feel as if I am the most expensive caretaker in the world—after all, none of it is really mine. I am looking after it on behalf of the nation while making sure that a dictator doesn't come to power and sell it all off for gold. There are some wonderful pieces in the collection, but if one were to be perfectly honest, there is a good amount of it that I'd prefer not to be hanging on my walls. I much prefer a good English landscape, although Philip likes to tease that I would cover the walls with portraits of dogs and horses if I had my way. He's not entirely wrong.

I very much dislike living in Buckingham Palace, if the truth be told. It's rather like being imprisoned in a delicately gilded cage, although it has seen better days, I'm afraid. The palace is surprisingly tatty in places and quite overrun with mice on the lower level, which is something that most people wouldn't imagine. We have a man who goes about the place with sticky traps to catch them all.

As I turn the corner, I find a large section of the floor covered in a workman's cloth, as part of the plaster has crumbled. Two men in white overalls seem somewhat surprised to see me.

"Good evening," I say, and sweep past them so quickly they barely have time to bow their heads.

Sometimes I like to dream about how lovely it would be to live somewhere private, just Philip and our children, where we were not constantly being observed. For all the convenience of being waited upon, there is always the thought that we are being judged—and not always favorably.

The door to my office is opened for me by a rather short, squat footman whom I don't recognize. He must be new, and I nod briefly as I pass him. He eyes me as if I'm not quite what he was expecting. Don't I look like a queen? People are always staring, and I do wonder what it is they are looking for. I imagine they find me quite ordinary—which I am—yet I am also anointed to carry out this sacred duty, and I intend to do this job to the very best of my ability, however difficult it may be on occasion.

Sliding into my chair, I pick up the telephone and brace myself. I try to deepen my voice in order to sound more authoritative, straightening my shoulders out, even though he can't see me.

As I twist the telephone cord through my fingers, I notice that the evening newspaper has been left out on my desk. There's a photograph of Marilyn Monroe at London Airport wearing dark glasses although there is almost certainly no sunshine to speak of. How very peculiar. Folding it away, I clear my throat and try to focus on the job at hand.

"Prime Minister . . ." I say.

And I recognize Mr. Eden's calm drawl as he replies, "Your Majesty, I'm afraid we have a rather serious problem developing with Egypt. . . ."

NORMA JEANE

1956

For a moment when I open my eyes I don't know where I am. Everything about this white bedroom seems strange and unfamiliar. Outside the window, a dense gray mist is curling against the glass panes and the daylight seems so gloomy. Then I remember that I'm in England.

Arthur's hand slips across my belly and pulls me closer. I can smell his cologne mixed with that musky just-woken-up scent that I love. His other arm wraps around my shoulders as his fingers reach for mine. He has such long, elegant fingers. It was one of the first things I noticed about him when we met.

I'd gone to one of those dull Hollywood parties with some guy who'd abandoned me to talk to all the important people the minute we walked in the door. Then someone introduced me to Arthur, and the two of us ended up sitting together in a corner of the room. His eyes were staring at me so intensely it made me shiver. Dark brown soulful eyes filled with longing. Yet there was something so solid about him. He was like a cool drink when you have a fever.

"So what do you do when you're not working?" he asked, like he was really interested in the answer.

"I love to read books—all kinds. I like to know about things and the only way is to read as much as I can," I replied, and straightaway he wanted to know what I was reading. It was a book about Abe Lincoln because I've always had a thing about him. Arthur then recommended a biography and we just talked and talked all night long, like we were old friends.

After a while, I got so comfortable that I kicked off my black suede heels and tucked my legs right up underneath me on the couch. One of the straps on my blue satin dress was hanging down off my shoulder, but Arthur was looking right in my eyes, listening to every word I said.

And then the funniest thing happened. My foot was hanging over the edge of the couch and he quietly reached across with those long elegant fingers of his and touched my toes. He carried right on talking to me—yet at the same time his fingers were holding on to my little toe. He didn't make a pass or anything—just sat there with my little toe in his hand.

It was five years before our paths crossed again, but I never forgot that first meeting. Now we're married and this is forever. I just know it is, even if it's my third time making those vows—can you believe that?

My body feels heavy with jet lag and the bed so cozy and warm that I don't want to move. I have no idea what time it is. It's hard to imagine the whole world waking up at different times and living their entire lives while the other half are still sleeping.

Somewhere downstairs there are so many people: the butler, the housekeeper, a cook, a maid, a gardener. Someone at the studio has even arranged for a security guard to keep watch over us. Mr. Hunt used to be a police officer and he doesn't smile at all. When we were introduced, he insisted on calling me "Mrs. Miller" even though I told everyone to call me Marilyn. I felt a little like a criminal being inspected by him, and I'm going to do my best to stay out of his way. I don't want to be watched over and spied on all the time, even if they are all perfectly nice people. At least here in our bedroom, Arthur and I can shut out the world.

I love my public, but then at other times I just want to be alone and have nobody notice me. I could do that in New York but I'm not so sure about England.

"Shall I go see if I can find us some breakfast, Mrs. Miller?" Arthur whispers into my ear as I curl into him.

I reach for the hand that is still resting on my belly and tangle my fingers through his. "Not yet." I can feel his breathing quicken as his other hand reaches for my breast. There's all the time in the world this morning.

Whitey is plastering something under my eyes to hide the dark shadows before applying a light dusting of face powder.

"Almost there . . ." he says, knowing that I'm impatient to be done.

"If only people knew that you keep Marilyn's face in your makeup case, Whitey," I say with a laugh.

"It's all you, baby. You make my job easy. A little powder and paint and there she is."

He's done and I slip into a black sleeveless dress with a dark net middle. You can see right through it but I think it's classy. It's not like stripper see-through. More of a hint. I complete my outfit with black shoes and a pair of white gloves that finish below the elbow. Running my fingers through my hair, I tease little platinum strands into position as Whitey gives me his seal of approval. As I look up, I can see Arthur's face—he disapproves. "What's the matter, Papa?" I ask, trying to tease a good mood out of him. He doesn't want to go to yet another press conference or to lunch at Claridge's with the Oliviers. He wants to stay home and write. He's frowning at me again.

"Is that see-through?" His tone makes it sound like I'm wearing nothing but tassels on my nipples rather than an elegant black dress. "Honey, you want people to get to know the real you. You don't need to show flesh to impress them."

"It's just a little net. That's all." I sound defensive and I really don't want to fight over it, but I have been dressing myself for a long time now. This is Marilyn. She wants to be taken seriously, but she can't go around dressed like a nun.

"I can impress people with my work and dress the way I like to look." I wind myself around him—my fingers curling through his dark brown hair. "Let's not fight about it."

Maybe the memory of us rolling around naked before breakfast softens his response. "I'm just looking out for you, baby. I want everyone to see how talented you are," he whispers in my ear as I press myself against his chest, running a finger along his shoulder and tracing the line of his jaw until he gets that look in his eyes again. The look that means he wants me—he adores me. All is well.

We're interrupted by the housekeeper tapping on the door. "I'm so sorry to disturb you, but there are photographers gathered outside and they'd like to take some pictures in the garden."

"Tell them I'll be right out. Thank you." I smile at her and try to look friendly, but I've already forgotten her name, which is embarrassing. There are so many names to remember that I keep getting them wrong. Mixing up the cook with the maid—I just keep smiling and hope they don't notice.

We make our way outside, and for the first time I really look around at where we are. It's a pretty country garden, luscious with greenery and beautiful flowers, although my God this country is so damp. I haven't seen a patch of blue sky since we landed. People keep telling me that it's a bad summer and it is usually much better weather than this in July. Just my luck, I guess. The photographers yell their instructions and snap their pictures as I pose and smile until my face aches and Arthur grows impatient. Then we make our excuses and finally we're allowed to leave.

Our driver, John, is waiting in the Humber to take us to the Savoy Hotel. As we bundle into the car, I see a bunch of schoolkids standing on the slats of the white gate at the end of the driveway yelling "Marilyn!" I give them a big wave and they all wave back. They're adorable. The ringleader has fair hair—kind of reddish blond. He could be my little boy with his gap-toothed smile—big and bright. Kids are so nice. They don't pretend to like you—they just do it.

John promises to take us past the Queen's castle on our way through Windsor and then past her palace once we get to London. I didn't even know she had a castle. I can't imagine what it must be like to live in something so grand. I wonder if she remembers everyone's names. The car purrs around the turn at the end of the lane and then I can see a castle looming in the distance. It's just like out of a fairy tale.

"Is that it?" I cry out, but of course it is. How many castles can you have in one town?

"That's Windsor Castle." John has the whole history down pat. He wants to give me the full tour, and I want to let him, except I promised Sir Larry that I would be on time and we are probably a little late already.

"And the Queen lives there?" I can't imagine it, but we're practically neighbors.

"She's usually there on the weekend. See that little flag on top of the tower? That means she's in residence."

That little red and gold flag is how they can tell if the Queen is home. I wouldn't want such a thing. Why would you want people to know where you are all the time?

"You know your house at Parkside backs onto the Great Park. You can get there through your garden gate." John glances at me in the rearview mirror. He seems pleased with himself that he's able to give me this information.

"The Great Park?" I ask. Honestly, they give things such grand names here. Everything is a Great something.

"That's the parklands that surround the castle. There's the Great Park and the Home Park. You'll often see the Queen and the Duke at horse events or polo matches there. She likes to ride on Saturdays and Sundays or walk her dogs."

I squeeze Arthur's arm. "Do you hear that? We're neighbors with the Queen of England. I'd like to meet her. Do you think they'd let me?"

"I expect she's a little busy for us, honey," Arthur says in that way he has of talking to me like I'm a kid he has to correct, even though I've been running my own life for a long time now. Never mind. I'm still going to ask around—after all, I'm not nobody. Besides, we might have a lot in common. We're both in the spotlight. Maybe she puts on the Queen like I put on Marilyn in the morning. I'd certainly like to compare notes. Who knows?

The car hums along until we reach London. I like the way everything looks here. Great pillars of sandy- or cream-colored stone and enormous wide buildings with flags flying from the top of them. Then we turn a corner and crawl along a street. Rain glistens on the paving stones and there are houses with black front doors and elegant long windows. Polished brass door knockers and iron railings with little steps leading down to rooms that are under the sidewalk. The windows look as if they're filled with heavy ruffles of velvet in gold or red or dark green.

Everything seems so solid and old like it's been right here for hundreds of years and it will be here long after we've all gone. Then we turn and John drives us right past Buckingham Palace. It looks like a big gray-white wedding cake stuck in the middle of London. I like the castle much better—if I had to choose one to live in.

We drive on past stores and office blocks. Theaters with their neon signs. And brightly colored restaurants—their windows filled with customers drinking tea. When we stop at a red light, I watch a young man reading a newspaper as he eats all alone. Everywhere I look, there's kind of a gloominess, a melancholy, but also great beauty.

I'm going to love it here—I can just tell.

The car makes a slow turn and glides to a halt outside the Savoy as a man in a smart red uniform, wearing a top hat, whips open our car door and helps me out. Flashbulbs pop all around me and for a moment I'm blinded by the lights. Then someone says, "This way, Miss Monroe," in an elegant English voice and ushers me inside. Everyone is so polite here. It makes me feel like a great lady to be treated so nicely. There we go with the "great" again.

As I walk into the room in the Savoy Hotel, Larry is pacing the floor impatiently, a cigarette clamped in his mouth. When I take my seat, he leans right over me, whispering impatiently in my ear, "Oh, my dear, you're very late. I've been desperate for you to arrive as I do so hate being stuck with this lot on my own." Drawing a breath, I glance first at him and then at the press pack: all of them are looking a little sullen as I've kept them waiting.

"I'm sorry, everyone. We were delayed by your own people wanting more pictures. I don't know how many pictures of Marilyn Monroe it's possible to have in the world, but I guess you needed a few more." Everyone laughs and the tension dissolves. I smile warmly at Larry and am pleased to see that he is looking happier. I have charmed him again—at least a little, I think.

The questions come thick and fast. "That's quite some dress," someone remarks, and I throw my head back and sit up straight.

"Well, it's not my idea, but it certainly is my midriff," I say, and then realize that they're all staring at it. Some of the guys from the *Daily Sketch* newspaper present me with a blue-and-white bicycle to ride around Windsor, and I certainly shall do that, but I'm not sure how we are going to get it back to Parkside, as it won't fit in our car. The press guys are good sports and tell us they will personally deliver it; I'm sure they will—in exchange for some photographs, I expect, but it's still sweet of them.

I sip a cup of tea and accept the offer of a cigarette from Sir Larry to calm my nerves. I always get a little anxious with so many journalists and much prefer to talk to them one at a time, but they don't like that. It takes too long.

They ask me about being a newlywed, and I search the room to find Arthur standing to one side, watching me. As our eyes meet across the room, I tell the reporters, "I've never been happier," and it's true. Arthur looks both proud and embarrassed at the same time. He loves everyone to know that he's my guy, but I know he'd prefer it if he never had to see another press pack again. We gaze at each other for a long moment and I feel happiness bubbling up inside me. I have everything I've ever wanted. I just have to try to hold on to it.

Someone asks how I'm going to keep my private life separate from my movie life. It's a good question, and I tell them that it's up to a person to keep things private. I'm not going to answer questions about things that belong to me—or to us, now.

A thin-faced man with greasy hair sitting right in the front row asks me about my acting studies. He looks so serious, and from the tone of his voice I guess he writes for one of those important newspapers. I tell him about the Actors Studio in New York and how hard I've studied to learn my craft. He asks me if there's one role I'd like to play, and I say, "Why, yes, I'd like to play Lady Macbeth." Which is true. They seem surprised that I even know who Lady Macbeth is, but I've read a lot of plays and classic literature. A girl can read books and wear lipstick, but these guys don't think that. Anyway, I believe Lady Macbeth gets a bad rap—just because she's kind of sexy and dangerous. That part I keep to myself, because they're snickering at my answer. Even Sir Larry gives a kind of smarmy smile. I feel a flush of irritation and my jaw tightens, although my smile doesn't falter. They all think it's ridiculous for Marilyn Monroe—the dumb-blonde tits-and-ass actress—to play their beloved Shakespeare, but I might surprise them all one of these days.

"I think Lady Macbeth is a strong woman who finds herself married to a very weak man. I can imagine that's quite challenging, and I'd love a chance to play her like that."

The room goes silent for a moment as they take in what I said. Their mouths gape a little in shock. They might underestimate me, but I did all kinds of scenes back in New York, and that's pressure, my friends—going deep inside to find the character with the likes of Marlon Brando watching you. I'm still annoyed at the reporters, but my smile gets wider and brighter. I don't care if these guys think I'm stupid. The people I wanted to respect me really thought I did good work and that's all that counts.

Then it's time to wrap it all up, but not before someone asks me if I'm still only wearing Chanel No. 5 in bed now that I'm here in England. With these temperatures I'd probably freeze to death, I think, but I don't say that part out loud.

"Maybe I'll try Yardley's Lavender over here and see how that works out," I reply. It's time for the final question, and the thin-faced man asks what I intend to do with my time when I'm not filming. I tell him straight about all the galleries and museums and plays and concerts that I'd like to experience while I'm here. He thinks he's being clever and slips in a question about whether I like classical music.

"I like Beethoven," I tell him, and it's true. I went to concerts at Carnegie Hall, and I could feel the music like a wave smashing into me. I'm not going to explain that to this man, though.

"Oh, really?" He raises a skeptical eyebrow. "And which number concerto is your favorite?" I feel stupid for a second because I don't know the answer, but I won't let him make me feel small because I do really like the Beethoven that I've heard. So, I set my face at him and give him the old Marilyn smile. The English press seem kind of snide, and I wonder if they talk to the Queen like this or treat her like she's some stupid dame. I guess they wouldn't dare. Men always think it, though, even when they don't say it out loud, in my experience.

"Well, I'm not very good with numbers, but I'd know it if I heard it." They laugh, but this time they're laughing with me, and so I get to my feet to signal that it's over. We've finished all our press duties, and now I can get on with exploring London and making this movie. Arthur is beaming at me. He wants me to succeed and prove to all these guys that I'm not just some dumb blonde. When we're at home we sit and talk about art and literature for hours on end.

I can look like Marilyn and do all kinds of different work. Why do people always want me to be one thing or the other?

The next morning the blue-and-white bicycle arrives at our front door. The press guys who deliver it don't even ask for another picture. "Welcome to England," they say.

It puts me in a good mood until my publicist, Alan, arrives with the morning papers. The pictures from yesterday all look good, but some fashion editor has written a whole piece calling my clothes dowdy and tired. She says they aren't elegant and that you could see a spare tire through the netting of my black dress. The nerve of her! I'm so mad that I screw up the newspaper and dump it in the trash. In the other newspapers next to the photographs from our press conference they have all printed pictures of the Queen.

She's wearing a floral dress and a pretty hat with white gloves and open-toed white shoes. I guess that's how they want me to look—kind of neat and buttoned-up. I wonder where she buys her clothes. I'll ask Alan to find out. I keep a list of things I need him to do for me. Every day I am going to add "arrange tea with the Queen" to his list and see if he can do it. I might even buy a floral dress and hat if that happens.

LILIBET

1956

The car sweeps along the driveway that leads to Windsor Castle and I feel myself exhale with the relief of a weekend here. The dogs lie contentedly at my feet. Susan places her warm nose against my foot, and I lean down to tickle her behind her ears. I received her for my eighteenth birthday, and she was quite the loveliest present I've ever received. She accompanies me almost everywhere, and even came on our honeymoon. As Philip and I were driven away from the palace, I secreted her away at the bottom of the carriage, covered with an old rug so that nobody knew she was there.

I'm still fretting a little over my recent conversations with the prime minister. That man makes me feel quite stupid at times.

"What do you intend to do about this Suez situation?" I asked him.

"We're going to withdraw all the pilots, ma'am," he said. "And then we wait. . . ."

Without thinking I blurted out, "Pilots? But I thought the Suez was a canal," and I swear that I could hear him stifle a laugh.

"Boat pilots, Your Majesty. They're highly skilled men who

take the ships through the complicated twists and turns of the canal, and without them, Colonel Nasser will have no choice but to give in." He said it in a tone of voice that suggested it was beneath him to have to explain it to me.

Of course they would be boat pilots—it had been a very long day, and I just wasn't thinking. But there was no need for him to treat me as if I'm quite so silly. At times like these I so miss Winston. He never made me feel like a fool.

"And what will happen if your plan doesn't work, Prime Minister?" I asked, trying to recover my composure.

There was a long, haughty pause before he said, "My plan will work, ma'am. I'm completely confident that we will bring Nasser to his senses."

The way he responded made me feel as if he were my headmaster and I was merely some errant pupil. The memory of it makes the anger swirl around in my chest again, and I shake my head with such violence that one of the dogs sits up straight and begins to bark.

I can't wait to get inside and change my clothes before going for a brisk walk across the park away from urgent papers and telephone calls or the prying eyes of servants always watching and waiting for something. Windsor feels like a lovely respite from the constant busyness of Buckingham Palace with its endless parade of visitors and appointments.

Then later on this evening the entire family will gather for Mummy's birthday. She's fifty-six tomorrow and already a widow with no role to speak of.

Royal life can be so terribly harsh on the remaining partner—not only do you lose your loved one, but in a split second you find yourself demoted. No longer the most senior female member of the family, she now has to remember to curtsy and let me go before her. It's a most unnatural way of behaving and it's taking its toll on our family members, who are all still missing my father terribly. Poor Mummy, it must be very difficult, and I am making an extra effort to visit as often as I can, but it's never enough. She's so very lonely without my father, as they were such a team.

The soldiers stand to attention outside their little sentry boxes as the car comes into view, and then the door opens and we all pile out—a very tired Queen and her assortment of dogs all very glad to be home. Philip is arriving later, as his meetings have run over. He will keep people talking and won't be satisfied until they've explained all the inner workings of something to him.

This evening is a family dinner for Mummy and tomorrow a proper party so that all her friends and relatives can celebrate her. She does so love to be the center of attention, and I don't begrudge it at all, especially now she is so alone. All the parties in the world wouldn't make up for losing Philip, so I do understand how she must feel.

"Good afternoon, Your Majesty. Would you like some tea sent up?" My faithful dresser, Bobo, is waiting for me in my dressing room, replete with all the downstairs gossip when I'm ready for it. She was my nursemaid when I was born; she was a young woman when she joined us, and now her hair is gray and her face is lined. We are the closest of confidantes, and I simply couldn't imagine my life without her. She's the only person outside of the family who is allowed to call me Lilibet . . . although she rarely does so.

"No, thank you, Bobo. I'll get changed and then take the dogs out for a bit. Has anyone else arrived yet?"

"The children are in the nursery with Nanny, and I believe Princess Margaret is accompanying Queen Elizabeth, and they should be here shortly. The Waterloo Chamber is all set up for dinner, and the menu is as you agreed. Will there be anything else?"

"No, I'll have a quick check on the dining table on my way out. I think we'll have drinks in the Crimson Drawing Room and then go through to dinner," I say as my clothes are expertly unzipped and unbuttoned so that I can step out of them. In a matter of minutes, Bobo helps me into a tweed skirt and jacket, with stout walking shoes and a silk headscarf tied firmly under my chin. Her fingers straighten my collar while I stand patiently waiting to be released.

"I won't be long. Tell Nanny I'll be up to see the children as soon as I get back, would you?"

"Yes, I'll tell her, don't you worry." Bobo finishes off with a final button and I rush away, back down the stairs toward the Waterloo Chamber.

It's a very nice room, full of dark wood paneling with the most gloriously ornate ceiling. The walls are covered in portraits of the Duke of Wellington celebrating his victory against the French, while the long formal dining table has been beautifully laid out with fresh flowers and several large silver candle holders. The cutlery is gleaming and the crystal glasses sparkle under the lights. I walk the length of the table checking that everything is in place, and when I'm satisfied, I turn to the two footmen standing guard by the door and nod my approval.

"Everything looks splendid. It's a little chilly in here, though, so maybe we could find a heater of some sort? Nobody needs to freeze over dinner because we're having a terrible summer."

"Yes, Your Majesty." The taller of the two scurries away to search for an electric fire, and I run down the stone steps to the front door, pausing only at the little alcove where we keep a selection of towels to wipe muddy paws and a basket filled with doggy treats. I fill the pockets of my tweed jacket with as many dog biscuits as they will hold and set off out of the door, the corgis trotting obediently behind me.

Striding away from the castle and into the park, I feel my shoulders relax. For a few brief moments it's just me and the dogs scampering around my feet. Although, out of the corner of my eye, I catch a glimpse of my detective following at a discreet distance. One is rarely completely alone.

The dogs leap up, sniffing at my pockets for their biscuits. I twirl around, holding an old rubber ball just out of their reach, and then I throw it as far as I can. They chase after it until Susan manages to retrieve it and the entire pack comes racing back toward me. Kneeling down, I open my hands and allow them to take their treats, patting and fussing them all as they lick my face and nudge at my pockets, wanting a little more. We play for several minutes until the dogs begin to tire.

In the distance, over the top of the tower, the sovereign's standard has been raised. The flagman stands on top of that tower from the minute the palace telephones to say that I'm on my way. He watches through a pair of binoculars no matter what the weather for the first sight of my car and then hoists the standard up the flagpole so that everyone can see the Queen is now in residence. There is no hiding place when you're the monarch. Wherever I go, my little flag is flying.

Taking a deep breath, I try to mentally prepare myself for the evening ahead, searching for ways to smooth over any difficulties with Margaret and to ensure that Mummy has a lovely birthday. Margaret and I have spoken only once on the telephone since the wedding, and she was very cool with me, so I can only assume that I have not been forgiven.

"Sugar!" I call one of the dogs who has wandered off, and the pack of us reluctantly head back toward the castle.

Both Charles and Anne are deeply engrossed in a large jigsaw puzzle that has been set up on a low table in one corner of their nursery. Nanny Helen is fussing around them, checking that Anne doesn't need a cardigan, as the late afternoon has brought a slight mistiness and yet more rain.

For a moment I stand at the nursery door watching my children and feeling my heart fill with love, followed by a stab of guilt. When I think back to my childhood, my memories are nearly all happy ones, and the time spent with my parents each day, playing and laughing at our games, was very much a part of that. I do worry for Charles and Anne that they won't have enough memories with me when they grow up.

"Hello, you two," I call out to them, and their little faces light up at the sound of my voice.

"Mummy!" they both cry out, and Charles gives his tiny bow and Anne bobs her little curtsy before they rush into my arms.

"Now then, this looks like a very complicated jigsaw puzzle. I think you need to find all the edges first. That usually does the trick." I pick a small piece of sky from the table and offer it to Charles.

"Nanny Helen, could you bring the children downstairs just before seven o'clock to see their grandmother and wish her a happy birthday for tomorrow."

Nanny Helen is a tall, austere-looking woman with a rather sour expression most of the time, but she is utterly devoted to our children. She does not like changes to their routine, however, and drives the kitchen quite mad sending back plates of food and asking for things to be redone for them.

The woman gives me a pained look, so I quickly interject, "I am aware that will disturb your evening routine; however, it is their grandmother's birthday tomorrow and she would very much like to see them this evening." I offer up a silent prayer for a peaceful conclusion.

"As you wish, ma'am," Nanny Helen says, as reluctantly as it's possible to sound without being downright disobedient.

"Good . . . now then, you two. Tell me all about your day." I sit myself down on the window seat and gather my children in—one on either side of me. Charles is in his navy blue shorts and little white shirt with his hair neatly combed into a side parting, while Anne wears a primrose-yellow summer dress that matches her blond curls. Their little warm bodies nestle into me, and I can smell the sharp aroma of their shampoo mixed with that very particular smell of young children. It's my favorite scent in the world, and I run my fingers through their hair and breathe it in for a long moment.

"I learned a new song on the piano," Anne says earnestly, "but my hands are too small to play it quickly." She stretches out her tiny fingers and thrusts her palms practically into my face.

"Oh dear . . . you'll have to wait for them to grow a bit, won't you?" And the three of us giggle to ourselves.

"It's nearly my birthday, and I'll be six . . . My hands might be bigger then, don't you think?" Anne looks quite serious about it, and I plant a playful kiss on the palm of her hand.

"I expect so. And what have you been up to, Charles?" He is staring out of the nursery window, looking rather lost in thought. He's growing into a little man now. It seems only the other day that he was born and now he's very nearly eight years old. Time passes so quickly.

"I had an arithmetic test," he says with a grimace.

"Oh dear . . . that doesn't sound like fun." I study his face for a moment. I do worry about what's in store for him. This job and the crushing weight of it, with all it entails, landing on the shoulders of my dreamy-eyed son.

"It wasn't fun, and I don't think I did very well," he mutters as a tiny frown appears on his brow.

"I wasn't terribly good at arithmetic either, but if you practice, then it does get a little easier." I put my arm around him and offer a small kiss to the center of his head in consolation.

"I suppose so," Charles says, but I can tell that he's not so sure, and it reminds me of the terrible lessons that Margaret and I sat through—counting the seconds before we could be set free to run around outside.

"I must go and get ready for Granny's dinner now. I'll see you two later." We exchange brief kisses and I let them slide off the window seat and return to their jigsaw puzzle.

As I reach the nursery door, I turn and take a final look at my children. There is never enough time for us . . . and I love them so dearly.

Several hours later, the children are both in bed and we are all dressed in our finery drinking cocktails in the Crimson Drawing Room. Margaret looks lovely in a peach chiffon gown, while Mummy is in her favorite pale blue silk. She has a gin and Dubonnet in one hand and is gesturing toward one of the cabinets in the room, talking animatedly with the family of the Duke of Gloucester, who are all gathered around her.

Philip is looking very handsome in his black dinner jacket and is deep in what looks like a very jolly conversation with Princess Alexandra. He's happy and smiling, and I let out a small exhale of relief to see him having a good time.

A passing footman approaches me carrying a single glass of gin and Dubonnet on his silver tray, which I gratefully accept. I take a sip and glance over at Margaret, feeling that I really ought to make amends for my clumsy attempt to cheer her up the other day, but she doesn't catch my eye, so I head straight for my mother.

"Hello, Mummy, many happy returns," I say, kissing her on her cheek.

"Lilibet, darling! You really need to speak to Margaret. She's been in the most awful mood since that wedding. It's been weeks now. What on earth did you say to her?"

"I was trying to help and clearly it backfired. I'll talk to her." Taking another sip of my cocktail, I feel my spirits sink at the thought of it. A slight ache begins at my temple and my neck feels quite tense. I try to relax my muscles a little to ease the pressure but the ache continues.

My mother's sweet face is etched with concern and she is as

usual relying on me to do the right thing and smooth it over. "Well, do it before we sit down to dinner, would you? I'd like to have a lovely weekend without there being any tension, and you know how sensitive Margaret is to her current situation."

"Yes, I do. All right . . ." There is no way to avoid dealing with my sister this evening, and so I paste on my most compliant smile. In the past four years, I've learned to speak diplomatically to a wide range of people, yet none has caused me more problems than my own sister. Taking a deep breath, I greet relatives on all sides of me as I head straight across the room toward the window where Margaret is now standing alone smoking a cigarette.

"Am I to be forgiven?" I say gently as our eyes finally meet. "You look lovely, by the way. Peach is a good color for you."

"Flattery will get you everywhere," Margaret says with a smile that doesn't quite reach her eyes. She's still cross with me, but it goes beyond what was said at the wedding. This is more of a general resentment that I have a husband and the top job and she is the "spare." The day of my coronation I remember Margaret looking so very sad, and when I asked her about it she said, "I feel as if I've lost my only sister and dearest companion."

"You haven't lost me. I'm still your sister. Nothing can change that." I gave her arm a little comforting squeeze, but she wouldn't be cheered by my words and I'll never forget what she said in response.

"Yes, but before we were the same, and now, I'm nobody . . . and you're the Queen."

Her words stunned me into silence. The idea that one thing had caused the other. Me being a queen meant she was a nobody—at least in her mind.

Now Margaret takes a long drag of her cigarette and stares gloomily out of the window. There is a beat of silence before I say quietly but firmly, "I am terribly sorry if I upset you. I only want you to be happy—more than anything I wish for that, but there is a limit to what I can do. You must see that?"

Margaret fixes me with her steely blue eyes and says quite furiously, "Oh, Lilibet, I've lost my only chance at happiness, as well you know, while you've got everything that *you* wanted."

I feel a tiny sting as her words register. As if I could ever have wished for any of this. I exhale a long, miserable sigh, as we really are going around in circles. Every conversation ends the same way.

"We can't keep going over this, Margaret. It's not my fault that I have a husband and you weren't allowed to marry the man of your choice." I am pleading with her to let this go, once and for all, but her expression is that of the stubborn little girl I shared a nursery with. She exhales a deep puff of cigarette smoke quite deliberately in my direction, knowing full well that I detest it.

A tiny blaze of fury scatters across my sister's face and her tone is icy cold: "While we're on the subject of *your* husband, you might want to pay a little more attention in that direction. There's a lot of chatter in our circles about Philip and his gentlemen's lunch club. It seems he and his private secretary, Mike Parker, are getting quite the reputation for their behavior."

The shock of her words leaves me reeling, and I can feel a boiling anger erupting deep inside, as she fully intends to wound me. "What kind of behavior? I don't know what you mean," I say sharply.

"Let's just say they are seen a little too often in the company of other women." Margaret's lips purse as her spiteful words cut me deeply, and out of the corner of my eye, I can see Philip across the room still laughing in his carefree way with Alexandra. Any pity I felt for my sister's plight dissolves into a cold fury.

"You shouldn't listen to cheap gossip, Margaret, however unhappy you may be." And with that I walk away with my head held high. Inside I feel completely bruised that she should want to hurt me so, and a flash of pain at the thought of this rumor being true. He wouldn't do that . . . yet my mind too easily conjures up a world where there might be more to it. My lips tremble for a second as I watch Philip pouring his easy charm over my family and I feel a very real sense of dread that everything is about to go wrong. . . .

NORMA JEANE

1956

Taking a deep breath, I walk into a cold, narrow room at Pinewood Studios and find a long wooden table filled with strangers. Nothing makes me happier than hanging out with actors—really watching one another discover our characters and getting to know the cast.

These things are usually casual affairs, so I've arrived wearing my old black cigarette pants and one of Arthur's white shirts, with the cream raincoat that I'm going to be wearing forever given how bad the summer is here. I've given Whitey a day off, so I'm bare-faced, with hair that's only had a comb dragged through it. Nobody will care; after all, we're all actors together. I feel a buzz of excitement flood right through me. This is where the real work begins.

Standing in the doorway I take a look around. At first, I only recognize Larry, and yet all these people seem to be talking over each other as if they're old friends, and I suddenly feel like the new girl at school.

I slip quietly into the nearest chair and take out my script. Larry is sitting right at the head of the table wearing a pale gray sweater over the top of his shirt and tie. Eventually, he glances down the table and smiles thinly at me while continuing to chat away with a woman on his left. There's a tingle of nervousness deep down in the pit of my stomach as I wait for him to introduce me to everyone, but he doesn't say a word.

I think the older lady at the other end of the table is Dame Sybil Thorndike, one of the greatest English actresses alive. I'd so like to go over and greet her, but I don't dare. Maybe when there's a break, I'll get to say hello to her.

Another man I don't know breezes into the room and kisses everyone, even me, although he doesn't seem to recognize me.

"Hello, darlings," he says, and then they're all laughing and joking about the last time they worked together. From what I can gather, it was a play that didn't go terribly well. They are chattering about someone who forgot their cue or got a line wrong in an important part of the play, and I can feel my heart fluttering like I've got a little bird trapped inside my chest as the palms of my hands grow sticky. Their voices are very fancy, and they all use a kind of shorthand that I don't understand.

One man says loudly, "Do you remember that terrible girl? Awful Ophelia at the Vic," and I have absolutely no idea who or what he's talking about, but they all laugh.

I try smiling at the people sitting across from me, but they just nod politely and then look away again. I thought once the press stuff was done and we got to work, it would be like it was at the Actors Studio, with everyone being more casual in their dress and talking like actors do about their characters and such. Yet everyone seems to be wearing their good suits and gossiping among themselves.

Then suddenly a hush descends over the room, and I glance up to see that Larry is looking at us.

"Welcome, everybody. I'm sure we all know each other, so let us begin. Most of you will be familiar with *The Sleeping Prince* from the stage play by Terence Rattigan, with me as the prince and my darling wife playing the showgirl, of course."

Someone across the table begins to applaud, and I'm not sure whether I should join in or not. I knew that Larry and Vivien had played those roles on stage and that he had also directed the production, but I didn't see it, so I just try to smile until he carries on talking.

"Thank you. There have been some changes, of course, as 'the movies' are quite different to the theater." Larry makes quotation marks with his fingers when he says "the movies," which I find strange. I mean, we're here to make a movie—maybe it's a British thing. . . . I get the impression that Larry doesn't like movies very much, or at least he thinks movie people are not proper actors. I guess they all think acting only happens on a stage in front of an audience. I bite my lip. I wonder if he feels that way about me. . . .

"Darling, you can say that again," the man who had kissed everyone when he entered the room interjects, and everyone laughs.

"Now, now, everyone. Settle down. Let's start reading, shall we?"

And so we begin. It's a Cinderella-type story really. Girl working as a showgirl in a theater meets a handsome prince and gets invited to his palace. Elsie Marina is the showgirl—that's my part—and Larry is my leading man. Elsie seems like a girl you don't need to take seriously, but she turns out to be wiser than all of them.

I know this girl inside and out, but when it comes to my lines, I can feel my throat closing around the words. All I can think about is the way they all gossiped about people they didn't think were any good, and for a moment my nerves get the better of me. I whisper my line, but Larry stops me impatiently. "Try the line again, my darling. A little more oomph maybe."

"I can't hear her . . . can she speak up? I missed my cue," a woman sitting next to Larry says with a sigh.

I clear my throat, take a deep breath, and stumble through

my line. He nods as if to say that will do for now, but he doesn't seem pleased. It's only a read-through, though. Everyone else seems to be performing for one another as if we've got an audience here. I remind myself that I don't need to be good at a read-through. I need to be good when we shoot it. That's what counts, after all.

The words keep tumbling out of my mouth and although I keep sipping at my glass of water, my tongue feels big and parched. My voice comes out too soft or too shrill and at times my old stutter comes back as I trip over the lines. I try to reach for Marilyn inside me—she'll know what to do and how to deal with these people—but I can't seem to summon her.

I can't find the character of Elsie the showgirl either. All the times that I read through the script at home, I felt that I knew this girl so well. I could do her funny mannerisms and get her little laughs just right. Yet today I sound as if I've never seen these words before. My hands are trembling as I turn the pages and I feel hot and stupid. I get a shooting cramp in my belly like a fist clawing at my insides, and I have to bite my lip with the pain of it. It's the last thing I need. I can't stop being me long enough to play someone else today.

The pages of the script keep turning and turning. When I'm not in the scene my eyes drift around the table, watching them all and trying to put names to faces by the roles that they're playing. Dame Sybil pronounces every word like she is a grand empress of some exotic empire, and I could listen to her all day. At one point I get so carried away watching everyone that I miss my next line entirely. Larry skips right over it and goes straight to his own line without missing a beat, although he gives me kind of a scolding glare as if I'm a small child who's peed on the floor.

He was so very charming when I first met him in New York, I was sure we would work well together. Yet here he's going so fast I can hardly keep up with him. He seems to be showing off a little—commanding the room. I feel like he wants me to know that these are *his* people, not mine. Although maybe he's a little nervous too. I try to think more kindly of him and focus on the lines.

As my fingers curl the corner of the final page, I give a long silent sigh of relief. That's all for today and we are free to leave. But then I remember that rehearsals begin tomorrow and the thought makes me feel sick. If every day is going to be like this, then I don't know what I will do. This movie just has to work out. If it's a flop, then I'll never live it down. The stupid blonde who bought the rights to a play, produced the movie, brought on board the world's greatest actor to star and direct it—I'll get the blame for it all. I suddenly get a flash of all these great English actors sitting around a table gossiping about it, and a stab of panic pierces my heart.

I take a breath. I'll come back tomorrow and make sure Larry knows this is my movie too. I'm sure that things will seem different in the morning. We'll all get to know one another and it will work out fine.

Gathering up my things, I throw the old raincoat over my shoulders. "Good-bye, everyone," I say quietly, but they are all laughing so loudly about something that they don't pay any attention.

As I step outside the room, I suddenly hear Dame Sybil say loudly, "That was very nice, but why didn't Marilyn come?"

Then Larry says, "But that *was* Marilyn, my darling," and they all laugh again.

The next few days are a blur of rehearsals, dress fittings, and meetings before we start shooting. We've decided that Elsie Marina's main dress will be a white mermaid-style ball gown. It's silk with sheer organza sleeves and a sweetheart neckline, which I think flatters my figure—although I do worry that my stomach bulges a little at some angles. The words of that nasty fashion editor ring through my mind—a spare tire indeed! I need to look out for it, though, as I don't want it on camera. Jack, our cinematographer, is coming over to the house later, and I'll need to mention it to him, along with the usual stuff about my best side.

The dress is covered in seed pearls, rhinestones, and beads, so the light should capture everything beautifully. There's a purple wrap to go over the white dress that is a pretty ruffled thing. Of course, with costumes they don't always behave like you think they will when you start shooting and moving around the set, but at least Jack is the kind of person who will listen to me. He's a brilliant cinematographer, but I know how to get the best out of my looks on-screen. I can always visualize how I will look and decide instantly if something is right or wrong for me. It's just something I understand how to do. Photographers have all told me over the years that I can do things in front of a camera they didn't even think of. I imagine the lens like an old friend—someone who sees only the best in me. That makes it easy to show the parts of myself that my old friend will love. Of course, movies are different from modeling, but I've been doing this for a long time now, and I know what I need.

If I look good, then I can relax and just focus on trying to capture Elsie's character. I've been driving Arthur mad this week by doing my acting exercises every day with Paula, my coach. She stands around peering at me through her thick lenses, with her hair scraped back in her usual bun, yelling in that broad New York way she has: "No, darling . . . like a bird in flight. Light . . . light . . . light."

Poor Arthur—half the time he doesn't know if I'm being Marilyn or Elsie. The trouble is once I think I've got into the heart of Elsie, I want to stay there for a good long while. Some actors just put their character on and off like a costume, but I can't do that. I need to believe that she's real.

All my characters have been real to me. I find the things they love or the things they're scared of, and that's how I breathe life into them. It's the only way I know how to work. You have to tell the truth up there on the screen. When your face is twenty feet high, the audience can see any lies very clearly, and I hate to lie to people. I guess, growing up like I did, I came across too many people who lied to my face. All those foster families saying I'd have a home with them forever—usually right before they kicked me out or chose another kid over me. I have to feel that everyone around me is being truthful, or it makes me crazy—like I can't trust anyone or I'm walking on shifting sands.

I've thought about Elsie Marina night and day. She's just like me, I guess. The way I used to be before I got signed by the studio, back when I had nothing to lose. Every day was a hustle. Elsie just wants a better life, and then she meets a real-life prince. Who wouldn't make the most of that?

When I read through the script again last night, I thought some of her lines needed to be changed. I'm going to mention it to Larry before we start shooting because I really think I can make them land better here and there if they're shorter. It's easier to remember that way and most of the acting work can be done with a tiny gesture or a little smile. I can walk across a movie set and say more with a wiggle or a giggle than ten pages of dialogue. A lot of directors don't understand that—or they don't want to understand it. But like Lorelei Lee said in *Gentlemen Prefer Blondes*, "I can be smart when it's important, but most men don't like it." That was *my* line. I insisted we put it in the script, and it's a good line too.

I feel Larry is as impatient to start shooting as I am. I thought we'd spend more time together, talking about our movie, but he likes to make decisions as a director and tell me later. I'm starting to see that we're very different people in the way we work. He likes to do a lot of rehearsing, which I generally don't, but at least I know who everyone is now, even if all we do is smile and chat about the weather. As it turns out, the British can have whole conversations about a cloudy morning. Anyway, thank heavens it's a friendlier cast than it first appeared at the table read. I've been working hard to charm them all—smiling at their jokes, even if I don't understand half of them, and trying my best to fit in. Dame Sybil was mortified that I'd been at the table read and she hadn't recognized me. She was expecting Marilyn in full costume, and they haven't stopped teasing her about it yet. She's been very sweet to me, though. Even Larry has complimented me on my scenes once or twice, which is nice.

Of course, rehearsals always feel fun and relaxed because the clock's not ticking and we're not burning through film. Everything is going well, though—let's hope that continues when the camera starts rolling.

The drawing room at Parkside is a large room covered in a pretty chintz wallpaper with matching drapes and comfortable couches. We even have a piano in one corner of the room, and along the far wall there are elegant glass doors that open out onto the garden. From there you can sneak through into the park without anyone seeing you, which I appreciate very much.

Arthur waves to me through the window. I watch his long back leaning over his bicycle as he tightens the chain, his index finger hooked around a cigarette as usual. He keeps stopping to suck smoke into his lungs, but as soon as he bends over the bicycle, he has to keep pushing his glasses into place because they slip down his nose.

Today we're going riding through the Great Park. It will be nice to spend some time alone together, just the two of us. He's been keeping busy by writing and spending hours on the telephone arranging things to do with his play while I'm rehearsing, but when I come home, we're always surrounded by other people. I take another peek through the window to make sure that Mr. Hunt isn't checking up on me, as I like to escape from his beady eye whenever I can. He's probably gone down the driveway to tell those kids off again, as they stand on our gate calling my name for hours on end.

After slipping on my shoes, I head outside to find that Arthur has set up our bicycles ready for our adventure. We push them through the garden gate and out onto the path that leads into the Great Park. Straddling my blue-and-white bicycle, I push off with my right foot and for a moment I wobble as if I'm going to fall off the thing. It's harder than it looks.

"Are you okay?" Arthur laughs as we teeter away, looking none too steady. I haven't ridden a bicycle since I was a kid and it shows.

"I think so . . . aah . . ." I cry out as my wheels skid to the side, but I manage to just about keep my balance.

The unsteadiness continues for quite some time, but then something finally clicks into place, and before long we're rattling over the stony pathway as we ride faster and faster. On either side of the path are bright green trees and bushes with the beginnings of blackberries. A small gray squirrel darts alongside us for a second before disappearing into the undergrowth. I can hear Arthur laughing—a boyish howl of delight. I laugh too. This is so much fun.

"Pa . . . we're flying!" I shout to him.

Arthur yells back, "Yeah!"

There's nobody to see us and the two of us shoot down the pathways without a care in the world. By the time we head back, my face is aching from laughing so much.

"See, that was fun." Arthur grins hard at me. He's usually so serious about everything that to see him like this makes my heart melt. England is good for us—I knew it would be.

"Hey, now we're pretty good at this, how about we try riding through the town?" I suggest. "I was thinking about those kids who hang out at the entrance to our house—maybe we could buy them some candy. They're so sweet."

"I don't know if we're ready for roads, but I'm game if you are. You'll be the sweetest thing in the candy store, that's for sure."

He tries to lean over and kiss me, but the bicycle wobbles so precariously that I dart away, yelling "Catch me if you can" over my shoulder.

Our bicycle ride was just lovely, and we found the nicest candy store in town. The English call it a sweetshop. Isn't that cute? It's one of those old-fashioned places with all those big jars filled with bright colors. Half of the candy had such funny English names like "licorice all-sorts" and "sherbet lemons," but most things I recognized as the same kind of stuff we have back home. After a lot of deliberation, I ended up buying bags of peanut brittle for the children at the gate.

I loved peanut brittle when I was their age, and they all seemed delighted when I turned up carrying a dozen little white bags of candy. They're real nice kids and they all yelled, "Thank you, Marilyn," as we pushed our bicycles back up the driveway to our house. Arthur said I'm a natural with them. We can't wait to have a family together once this movie wraps.

When we got back to the house, I took Arthur up to our room and made him strip me naked. Just stood there giving him that hungry look while he unbuttoned my shirt and slipped my pants off. Arthur likes Marilyn this way—naked, for his eyes only. I whispered that I love my papa in his ear in the way that drives him wild, and he flipped me right onto the bed. We were giggling so much, and then of course we weren't laughing at all . . . but I don't care if the whole house heard us. In fact, I wanted them to. Let them all spy on us. We're honeymooners, after all.

Later on, Jack came to dinner and we talked through what to look out for on set. He came all dressed up in a dark wool three-piece suit, and as usual he was sucking on his tobacco pipe. Talking quickly, Jack pausing only to light or relight his pipe, the two of us soon found a common language—the language of the camera—and I felt right at home with him. I talked about how sometimes the skin on my hands can show up red on film. I'd love elegant white hands like other movie stars, but all those dishes I scrubbed in the orphanage left their mark, I guess. He was so nice about it that I even told him I was worried about my stomach sticking out, so we developed our own secret code word. Whenever he says "Tom" I'll know he means I need to suck in. Now that's a pal!

After dinner I took a Nembutal with a glass of champagne to help me sleep. If I don't get my eight hours, I'll look like death in front of the camera. Tomorrow is a big day and it has to go well.

I am going to show them all what Marilyn Monroe can do.

LILIBET

1956

I am standing in the middle of my dressing room, wearing a rose-pink robe and waiting for Bobo to set about her work of putting me together for the day. She bustles into my room carrying a smart pale green dress with a rather lovely paisley print. It's one of my favorites at the moment and always makes me feel quite put together.

"Good morning, Bobo. How are you today? And more importantly, what's the latest news?" There is a budding romance belowstairs between one of the maids and one of our cooks. So far there is very little to report, except a lot of long, lingering looks and a fair bit of sighing, but Bobo is convinced that a proper courtship may be on the way, and we are both quite heavily invested now.

"Disaster, Your Majesty. We think that he may have another girl away from the palace. He was seen walking along the Tottenham Court Road arm in arm with a young lady on his day off. Needless to say, the news hasn't gone down well. . . ." Bobo stretches her mouth wide in horror at the prospect of another woman on the scene and then rolls her eyes at me.

"I imagine not. Shame. We had such high hopes for a palace

wedding. We haven't had one for quite some time." I slip off my robe as Bobo unrolls my stockings for me. Slipping them on, I fasten them onto my suspender belt, while my mind ponders what Margaret said to me the other night at the party.

I'm sure she was just striking out, but part of me can't help but worry about it. The idea that Philip is going about town with other women pierces me right to my core. I couldn't bear it if it were true.

Bobo holds the paisley green dress for me to step into and she quickly pulls it up, waiting only for me to place my arms in the sleeves. There is something deeply comforting about having someone who has been with me since I was a baby. I'd trust Bobo with my life. She really is the most loyal person.

Buttoning up my dress, she then gives a little tug on the skirt to make sure that it falls properly. "There we go—all done. We're doing the pink dress and matching coat for the opening of the factory this afternoon, and I've given the blue gown you wanted to wear a nice press, so that will be ready for this evening," she says, standing back to admire her handiwork.

"Oh yes, I'd almost forgotten about that." It's a rather long day, with a morning reception for South American diplomats and then an evening reception for charity workers from all over the country. "Right, well, that will do for now. I'll see you later when hopefully you'll have better news for me on our downstairs romance." I give Bobo a mischievous smile and we both laugh.

I slip out of my room and walk quickly along the corridor toward my private office, where Michael will be waiting to go through the correspondence. There are simply thousands and thousands of letters sent to the palace addressed to me. Of course, I can't possibly answer them all, but we do select a handful and I write back to those people thanking them for their good wishes or congratulating them on their achievements.

"Hello, Michael. What have we got today?" I settle into my chair and wait for the countless number of letters that require my signature or further instructions.

"Good morning, Your Majesty." Michael bows his head solemnly and flips open the large leather diary to go through our day. "I thought we'd start by reviewing what to expect from the two receptions today. This morning it's just a bit of handshaking and a short speech that I've drafted for you; then the diplomats will be whisked away for a fine lunch at the Foreign Office," he says with a smile as he hands me a typewritten speech for my approval.

I trace the words with my pen, checking for any errors, and then hand the document back to him. "That's fine."

"And then this afternoon is just the usual ribbon-cutting and 'I declare this new factory open' sort of thing. On to this evening . . . it's a drinks reception, so just a bit of mingling. No speech required for that one," he says with another little smile, as he knows that will please me.

"Right. That all seems straightforward. Shall we crack on with our correspondence?" I am keen to get through the mail as soon as I can because I fear that there may be a lot of government papers in my red box today, and it will be a rush to get it all done before the South Americans arrive.

The morning has flown by and I haven't managed to get through even half of my red box papers so far, but there's no time now as I have to go and make this speech to the South American delegation. I walk quickly down the corridor and slip through the secret doorway into the White Drawing Room. I quite enjoy appearing from nowhere as it were—for you can't tell by looking that there is a doorway there at all.

Before entering the room, I take a long breath and put on my "Queen Face" as Philip likes to call it. It's a sort of shield, so nobody can see what you are really thinking or what you are really like, which is the way I prefer things. They can have a little glimpse of me, but that's all.

As the doors open wide, I take in the throng of dark-suited men. They are all chatting in small groups, until suddenly a hush descends over them as I walk into the room, where the foreign secretary, Mr. Lloyd, is waiting to introduce me. I place my handbag strategically over one arm, knowing that if I shift it to my other arm, one of my staff will notice the signal and seek to rescue me.

Offering my hand to one man after another, I try to think of something meaningful to say to them in the short time that's available. I am a shy person by nature, not really given to small talk. It's difficult to meet so many people for such a brief period of time.

An enormous man with great long arms presses my hand quite firmly, as if I might disappear should he ease his grip on me. Mr. Lloyd is forced to distract him by introducing him to our ambassador. Sometimes my hands can become quite bruised during a day when there is a lot of handshakes, even when I'm wearing gloves, for some people do manage to squeeze far too tightly.

Then I make a short speech to welcome them all in the spirit of friendship and cooperation. I'm not the most natural of public speakers—my voice sounds quite wrong to my ears. High and girlish without the gravitas of a leader. But one does one's best. It's a strange thing to be a queen who is a bit shy with strangers and detests making speeches.

What I am, though, is steadfast and neat. And they are good qualities in a person, I believe, and occasionally underrated. The ability to see something through is important, and I learned that from my father.

Eventually the reception draws to a close, the diplomats are whisked away to the fine lunch, and I am free to escape back to my office to work on my red box papers.

. . .

A footman comes into my study and spreads a narrow white cloth to protect the floor as the dogs instantly stir themselves. They are scattered around my desk, with Sugar and Susan lazily sleeping at my feet as I unlock my red box full of government papers to sign.

Another footman follows behind carrying a tray filled with several bowls of dog food and water, which he then proceeds to lay across the white cloth in a neat row. The smell of food instantly alerts the corgis to the prospect of lunch, but they all wait for my command before racing over to eat.

I sigh. This morning has felt endless, and I am still quite upset with Margaret. Every time I think of her, my neck tenses and I develop an ache right up through my temples. We didn't speak again for the entire weekend, and it came as a relief to be back at my desk in Buckingham Palace.

There is no training manual to be a queen. The role seems so terribly far away from you, and then it turns out you were merely one breath away from it all along. There is the terrible moment of being informed that your beloved father has died—followed by the realization that you will never hear his laugh again, or see him beam with pride watching you undertake some small achievement.

He will never grow old, nor will he see his grandchildren turn into a young man and woman. There may be grandchildren that he will never get to meet. And at that awful moment, with the full understanding that your darling papa has died, you are expected to instantly turn into this other person. A queen. The head of this state and of the empire beyond its borders.

The footmen clear away the dogs' lunch and I am alone again. My train of thought—and, it must be said, my embarrassing moment of self-pity—is quickly interrupted by Philip bounding into the room with his usual impatient stride, barely able to wait for someone to open the doors. I do wish he would slow down a little, although he's wearing his gray suit and a pale blue shirt that makes his eyes sparkle, and I can't help an admiring glance at my rather dashing husband as he strides toward me.

"Hello, you. This is a surprise," I say with a bright smile. "I am rather busy, though, as I've got to get through this lot and then go and open a new factory in Lewisham."

"Oh . . . what kind of a factory?" he says, giving a quick bow of his head as he leans across my desk.

"I didn't actually ask that. I'm sure someone will tell me before I get there," I say warmly while gazing up at him. "Now what can I do for you?"

"I've had the most marvelous idea about my tour. . . ." He places a kiss on top of my head and flops into the chair on the other side of my desk. "Rather than fly straight home from Australia after I open the Olympics in November, what about I carry on with my tour on board *Britannia* and visit Antarctica? There are some other places too that we could add on. The Falklands—all kinds of British territories that we never visit. I mean, if I'm to go on this blasted royal tour then it makes sense to visit as many places as possible—really get out there and see things."

He has that pleading tone to his voice, trying to convince me, when he knows that I will of course give in to him. There is simply nothing laid out for him to do and so he must invent a job for himself. It is ironic that when a king has a queen, then she will have an allotted role to carry out, but the reverse is not true. Everything that Philip has become involved with so far has ended up very much annoying somebody whose family role it has been for a thousand years.

"Well, it does sound like a good idea but how long would it take to cover the other places? I mean, you're already going to be away for several weeks." I am trying my best to sound calm at the prospect.

His face is flushed with excitement, and I get the smallest pang inside my chest at the thought of being without him for months on end. I've tried to put Margaret's horrible gossip to the back of my mind. Philip is quite steadfast—after all, he waited for me for such a long time. And I'm sure that he is trustworthy. Yet there is something about vicious gossip that leaves a little hook inside you that can't be ignored.

"That's the thing, Lilibet . . . I'd be away for Christmas." His voice softens as the full impact of his words lands.

"Oh . . . I see." And I *do* see that it's necessary for us to be out and about meeting people. But for us to be apart for months, especially at Christmas?

I want to say no. I want him to be home with his family, not gallivanting halfway around the world—even if it is for a good cause. But then I look at his face, which is so bright and happy at the prospect of an entire world to explore, while his eyes are shining in anticipation . . . and I wonder if he will miss me at all.

"The children will miss you terribly," I say, and it's true, but underneath I am more worried about how I will manage without him. Taking breakfast alone, instead of having Philip's keen chatter as we compare diaries or talk about what's in the newspapers that day. His little bursts of laughter or irritation when he finds something ridiculous. He's such a constant presence, always offering me his advice and support. And I love sitting down with him for dinner, where he makes me laugh and jollies me along if I'm in a bad mood. It will be very hard without him.

And how will he feel? What if he perhaps realizes that his happiness lies in making a life away from me? And how will we keep in touch?

There are so many questions running through my mind, but one look at him tells me that there is only one answer I can give. "All right, then. You go on your extended tour, and I'll hold down the fort here," I say as cheerily as I can manage.

His eyes fix upon me. "Thank you. You won't regret it. For the first time I feel as if I can actually do something useful here. I can go to places that you can't visit. There must be a lot of people in the world who will never get a glimpse of their queen, but maybe that can be my role. I just want to feel that I'm doing my bit, Lilibet. I hate to be idle."

"I do know that, and I want you to make the job your own. And when you return, I'm going to see about making you a prince of this realm. You gave up your title to marry me, and I feel it only right that we restore you to that rank."

Philip's face grows tender for a moment, and then, having got what he came for, he leans across my desk, grabs my face between the palms of his hands and plants a wet kiss on my lips. "That's for you," he says, grinning in that devilish way. "Right, I'm off. . . ."

"Aren't you staying for lunch? Where are you going?" I ask, still feeling the warmth of his lips on my mouth.

"It's Thursday!"

"Ah, the infamous gentlemen's lunch club," I say, but my tone is too sharp, and Philip is instantly alert.

He eyes me curiously. "Infamous? How exactly are we infamous?"

I am now regretting raising the subject, but I try to keep my tone as light as possible.

"It seems that people are talking—well, gossiping really, about your lunch club and whatever it is that goes on there. . . ." I hesitate, unsure exactly what it is that I'm supposed to be accusing him of. Being seen in the company of women isn't a crime, and I didn't ask Margaret for the details of her gossip, as I was so very wounded by the idea. But now I wish that I had. I can tell by the set of his mouth that he's very much irritated by what I've said.

"Who is gossiping?"

"I don't know. . . . People. It has come to my attention that some people are talking about your club and what goes on there. It is very secretive, after all."

"Why are *you* raising this? I mean, they say all kinds of things about us. It's their sport, isn't it? Gossiping about those of us in the public eye. Making out that they are privy to information about our private lives when none of them are." Anger flashes across his face. He's such a stubborn man and really doesn't like to be told what he can or cannot do.

"I'm just informing you that there is gossip and, well . . ." My voice trails off as I really don't know where to go next. All I want is for him to put my mind at rest—to tell me that I'm being quite ridiculous, and it is merely an innocent meeting of some old friends.

"I fully expect that strangers with dull lives will gossip about us. They have nothing better to do. What I don't expect is that my own wife should be raising this tittle-tattle with me. For goodness' sake, Lilibet . . . What on earth has come over you?"

"If it's all just idle gossip, then you can say so and I'm sure that will be that."

There is a moment of silence as Philip gives me an icy glare, then gets to his feet and walks out of the room.

Why is it that every conversation I begin these days ends up making things worse? I wish I'd never mentioned it, and I very much wish that Margaret had kept any silly gossip to herself instead of using it as some kind of missile.

Once Philip leaves, I sit alone at my desk for several minutes, clasping and unclasping my hands and staring at the large red box with the latest briefings on the Suez crisis yet unable to concentrate on any of them.

NORMA JEANE

1956

It's the middle of the night when I wake up in such a wild panic that I can hardly breathe. The awful dreams have started again. I was trapped inside a small room, and I couldn't get out no matter how hard I tried. There were ugly devils everywhere I looked, with their strange evil faces, and I couldn't escape them. They were grabbing me and hurting me until I woke up with my heart pounding in my chest and a cold sheen of sweat all over my body.

I don't know what time it is, but I have to get some sleep or I'll be fit for nothing on set. I try to snuggle closer to Arthur, but he flings an arm out and turns away from me.

Now I'm wide awake, lying in the dark, stewing in my own fear. Of all the nights to have a bad dream it had to be tonight. Maybe I should take another Nembutal—although I don't want to be too sleepy on set. Tomorrow I want to show Larry that I know what I'm doing.

I take a deep breath, trying to calm myself, but each time I close my eyes, I see those devilish faces leering and spitting at me. I don't know how to stop these nightmares. Nothing seems to work, no matter what I do. Tears begin to spill down my cheeks. If this movie fails, I'll have to go back to Hollywood and take any part they will give me. It will be an end to what I've fought so hard for—to get some control over my work. I can't let that happen—I just can't.

The morning breaks with some weak sunshine and I feel like death, but I've made it to the set pretty much on time. The white dress is a little tighter than I'd like, but it moves well and Jack gives me a nod to tell me that it looks good through the lens. I am so tired, though, and I keep tripping over my lines, which is making Larry a little frustrated with me. I don't mean to hold things up, but I need to feel Elsie's character, and I can't at all. She's such an innocent and fun person, and there's no trace of anything light and hopeful inside me today. When I feel good, I can rely on my old friend, the camera, and sense it all working, but on days like these, nothing can help me.

We take a break, and I head back to my dressing room to gulp down some coffee. Something needs to wake me up a little.

Paula leans over me. "Like Coca-Cola," she says, meaning my acting needs to be fizzy and light. I'm trying to get there when someone taps on my dressing room door.

"They're ready for you, Miss Monroe," a man's voice calls out.

I exhale, using my fingers to give my face tiny slaps. "Wake up, Marilyn," I say to myself in the mirror. "You can do this."

Whitey flicks over my face with some powder to blot away any shine before fixing my lipstick, and I'm good to go. "You look beautiful, honey," he whispers.

I take a deep breath and set off down the corridor back to the set. The crew is gathered around the lights and the cameras as we'll be redoing the scene between Larry and me in his room at the palace. They've done such a good job with the set that I can truly believe he's a prince and I'm a showgirl. "Fizzy, like Coca-Cola," I remind myself under my breath, setting my face with

Elsie's smile. I can do this. I know this girl. She's poor but she's excited by life, and now this big fat opportunity has landed right in her lap. I've *been* this girl . . . I just need to remember my lines and it will all be fine.

Larry strides over to me, smiling with his eyebrows raised as he takes hold of my hands. "You look positively delicious. Now, Marilyn, just say the lines exactly as we rehearsed." His tone is a little patronizing, but I'm sure he means well. He probably finds acting so easy that he just wants to help everyone else. I look up at him and he squeezes my hands to reassure me. "Ready?" he says, and I nod.

For a moment I capture Elsie. I knew I could do this! Oh, she feels so light and fun that I want to slide right inside her skin and live my whole life as her. My eyes widen as Larry calls for "ACTION." I hear my cue and open my mouth to speak—but then my mouth goes dry and I stumble over my words. When I try it again, my tongue trips up over the line but in a different place this time.

No matter what I do, I can't seem to make the words come out right. Everyone is staring at me as we cut yet again and reset.

"ACTION!" We do it over again, and this time I really thought I had it, but Larry calls, "CUT!" in a frustrated voice. "Darling—that's the wrong line."

Oh . . . of course. We made a change and I'd forgotten that we had. I give him a pleading smile and we reset. Larry takes up his position by the camera and calls for "ACTION" again.

I take a long breath and open my mouth to say my line. It comes out fine, but it's just Marilyn speaking meaningless words because I can't feel Elsie inside me anymore.

Larry smiles again. "Wonderful, darling! We'll set up for your next scene. Why don't you go and sit down and we'll call you." He raises his hand and kind of waves me away, but I stay in place.

"Wait, I want to go again," I say softly. Larry's face flares with irritation and I do feel bad for causing him a problem, but I'm right about this and this movie has to be good. We can't just make do with any old scene.

"What's the problem, darling? You said the line. We shot you saying the line. That's it." His voice has an edge to it that I haven't heard before. But he has to understand that this will be better for our movie. I know what I'm doing.

"No. I couldn't feel the character. It wasn't Elsie saying the line—it was me. The audience will know if it's not truthful. You have to find the truth inside to say the lines," I explain.

He releases a great sigh of exasperation and shakes his head. "Is this the method they taught you in New York? It's really not necessary, darling. I've been acting for many years and trust me—you can just speak the line and it's perfectly good." He wants me to agree with him but I can't. I *know* he's wrong. I can't do this movie if I can't be truthful. He has to see that.

"That's not how I like to work. Could we just break for a minute so I can talk to Paula? She helps me when I can't find my character." Out of the corner of my eye, I can see her hovering behind the camera, staring at me with her big owllike gaze, waiting for my call.

"My darling girl, we're running late, and we really need to crack on with the other scenes. Time is money. . . ."

"I don't mean to be a nuisance, but I don't want to move on. I can do that scene better—I know I can." My eyes are pleading with him. I won't let this go. This is my movie, after all.

Larry nods his head reluctantly. "Why don't we try it one more time? See if that does the trick." He strides away toward the camera.

"ACTION!" he calls, and we do the scene again, and it's still wrong. I'm trying to feel light and fizzy, but inside there's nothing but more misery piling up.

"Can we stop, please? This isn't working. I need to talk to Paula," I say quietly.

"Darling, you're thinking about it too much," Larry snaps. "Just say the line, my dear, and the feeling will come. I'm sure of it." I sense my confidence crumbling away as Marilyn begins to disappear and soon all that will be left is shy, awkward Norma Jeane.

I want to protest, but I do as he asks, stumbling over the line because I'm not in character and the line is useless if I can't be Elsie. The scene is worse than when we began and I don't know what to do about it, other than go through my exercises with Paula and start over.

"I'm sorry—can we take a break?" I ask. I need to try to get back inside Elsie's mind.

Larry's face turns a deeper shade of red as if he's furious. Walking slowly across the room, he comes to a halt right in front of me. "Marilyn, stop thinking and just try to be sexy."

Everyone can hear him speak to me that way and I feel as if he's slapped me right across the face. I might have preferred it if he had hit me, for then I'd know what to do about it.

He thinks I'm nothing. Just a sexy doll in a costume who he wants to order about. This is just like all those studio guys who want me to play dumb blondes in the same old way, time after time. Tears prickle behind my eyes, but I won't let him see me cry. I feel the full power of Marilyn lighting up inside me now. The damn cheek of this man.

I glare at him. An awful hush has fallen over the set. Larry exhales a small sigh, then his face softens and he grasps my hand. I relax a little. He's sorry and he's going to apologize. He just got frustrated. That can happen on a movie set. He didn't mean to speak to me that way. We all want the same thing here.

I gulp back my tears and I smile at him. The full Marilyn dazzling smile—so bright you can't see what I'm really thinking—and I wait for him to say that he's sorry. But instead, he leans down and whispers in my ear, "I think we should wrap for today. Better luck next time."

"All right." I wait for him to follow up with his apology, my smile fading when it doesn't come.

"That's a wrap, everyone. See you next week." Larry begins to walk away, but then suddenly turns back as if he's forgotten something, which of course he has. I'm ready to hear his apology now, although I would have preferred that the crew heard it too, but men can be proud sometimes. I'm willing to forgive and forget, though. After all, we're all under pressure here.

He looks at me curiously with his head tilted to one side and then he smiles, his most charming smile, and says, "Just one tiny thing. Darling, your teeth are coming up a little yellow on camera. Try some baking powder and lemon juice—that usually does the trick."

The shock of his words renders me speechless, and I just stand there with my mouth hanging open, gaping up at him. And then he turns and walks away as if I've been dismissed. The nerve of that man! All I can think of is that I've got three more months of this, and I won't let him treat me this way. He has no idea who he's dealing with because Marilyn Monroe is nobody's fool.

If he wants a fight, then I'll damn well give him one.

LILIBET

1956

"What on earth are those sandwiches?" Margaret asks with her eyes wide as she lights up a cigarette and exhales a cloud of smoke all over the tea tray.

"They're jam pennies—you remember them. We used to eat them in the nursery, and I rather enjoy one or two of them with afternoon tea." It's a childish thing, I know, but I've always had a passion for these tiny round sandwiches with their delicious layer of strawberry jam, and I had hoped it might sweeten Margaret into remembering that we are sisters after all. She grimaces at the sight of them as if I've mortally offended her in some fashion.

"I don't suppose we could have a gin instead?" she says.

"Well, it's a little early, but I can get you a drink if you'd like one."

"And are you going to join me?" My sister sits back on the sofa exhaling another cloud of smoke with an impatient look on her face. She's wearing a coffee-colored cashmere cardigan with a pair of matching cigarette pants and a brightly colored silk scarf tied around her neck. Her eyes look sharply curious as if she's waiting for me to say something that she knows will irritate her.

"No, not for me. I've got my meeting with the prime minister later on and I need a clear head for that. But you go ahead." I don't want to antagonize her by appearing to suggest that it's an inappropriate time for her to be drinking gin, but whatever I say these days I get that same disdainful glare.

Moments later she is settled with a gin and tonic, while I abandon my jam penny sandwiches, feeling quite chastised at serving up nursery food to my own sister. I'll save them for Charles and Anne once Margaret has gone. At least they'll enjoy them.

"The reason I asked you here is . . . that is, I wanted to clarify a few things. . . ."

Margaret is immediately alert—eyebrows raised and her lips pursed in readiness.

For days I've been trying to figure out how to begin this most awkward conversation, but I need to know precisely what rumors Margaret has heard about Philip. The only way is just to begin, I suppose.

"I invited you to tea so we could have a proper talk. What you said the other day at Mummy's party . . . about Philip." I fix her with a determined glance, my heart beating a little too quickly. There is part of Margaret that wants to lash out at anyone with an ounce more happiness than she possesses at present. I know she's utterly miserable, but it does make life very difficult, as we are all walking on eggshells around her. Normally I would try to ignore her caustic little barbs, but this one has rather struck home, and now that I've upset Philip, it is up to me to get to the bottom of it. One can't put one's head in the sand if people are gossiping. We need to nip it in the bud, as it were.

Straightening up, I take a sip from my teacup. "You said that some people were talking about Philip . . . gossiping and such. And I need you to tell me who is doing so and exactly what they are saying."

Margaret seems surprised; her mouth hangs open a little, and for a brief second there is neither a cigarette nor a sip of her gin to fill the space.

"You must see how damaging this kind of gossip can be. Not just to me personally or to Philip but to the monarchy. An institution that, like it or not, you are very much a part of. So . . ." Biting my lower lip I wait for her to respond to her cue.

Margaret releases a slow stream of cigarette smoke. "I was at a dinner party and one of the guests knows a member of Philip's lunch club. There was nothing very specific—just a lot of 'boys will be boys' type of innuendo." Her eyes flicker away from mine and she takes a long sip of her drink followed by another lungful of cigarette smoke.

"You said that he was seen around town with other women." I can hardly bear to say the words out loud.

"That's the rumor. . . . I don't know if it's true."

"I see. So, in essence there's nothing concrete to report and yet you chose to treat that silly conversation as if my husband were guilty of doing something wrong. And furthermore, your concern was not your beloved sister, but instead you simply saw it as an opportunity to *wound* me. I know that you're still upset with me, but I didn't think that this would make you want to hurt me." I see a tiny flicker of shame cross her face as her cheeks flush crimson.

"Lilibet, honestly . . . it was a casual comment and I thought you should know. For all I know, they're holding Roman-style orgies at their lunch club every Thursday. The tone of the conversation at that dinner party did rather lead one to believe that it wasn't entirely a choice of lunch dishes on the menu. There is chatter about Philip and especially that friend of his, Mike Parker—they are seen about town a little too often."

"Philip is perfectly entitled to visit his friends and have a private life without my own sister insinuating that he is up to no good," I say coldly.

"I'm not insinuating anything. I'm telling you, as my sister, that people are gossiping about your husband."

I feel an awful tightness in my throat as if I'm going to cry. I am completely furious with Margaret, yet only too aware that the day after tomorrow we shall all be aboard the royal yacht *Britannia* heading to Scotland and spending the next month in each other's company.

"It was nothing more than idle chatter and you might have more consideration in future, that's all. These things can be hurtful."

I hope this will be the end of the matter, other than any apology I may need to make to my husband. But Margaret is not one for backing down.

"Well, I'd want to know if my husband were the subject of talk around town."

I can feel my composure cracking and a cold fury building. "Philip has always been like a brother to you. Yet since Peter . . . you seem to have taken against him, as if he's done something to hurt you, and that's not the case. You're being very unfair to Philip, and to me."

The sulky petulance vanishes in an instant and Margaret stares down at the floor. "It was just an offhand comment at a dinner party, and there wasn't time to respond. I didn't wish to draw more attention to it by making a fuss. I'm sorry if you think that I've let you down. Honestly, I don't imagine Philip will care at all. If anything, he might feel his reputation is rather enhanced by this gossip. And of course, if it's not true, then no real harm has been done."

A little stab of stubborn anger boils silently inside my chest and I cannot let go of it. We could make up right now. I could tell my sister that we will let bygones be bygones, but I am not a terribly forgiving person if someone crosses me. It's not a quality that I am proud of, but it is nevertheless a quality that I possess.

"This isn't about *his* reputation. It's about mine. The idea that I am such a dull and awful wife that of course he should seek pleasures elsewhere as 'boys will be boys,' as you so delicately put it. It's never about the man and his actions. It's always about the very clear implication that the wife is simply not up to it."

"Oh, that's just ridiculous. . . ." Margaret splutters.

But it's the truth. What really hurts is that they think I am so lacking in the qualities it would take to keep someone like Philip interested in me. I must admit that once or twice I've wondered myself. We are in many ways quite different people. I know they look at me and think: *Well, of course he must have other interests because she must be deathly dull to live with.* She is made up of nothing except her silly ideas of duty. She is not a woman who could tantalize or that one could truly love—she is merely a queen.

To my horror I feel a single tear trickling down my cheek and I wipe it away quickly—but too late, as Margaret has already seen it.

"Lil, I am truly sorry. Let's not fall out over some silly gossip." My sister reaches across the divide between our chairs and takes my hand.

"It's not the silly gossip that has hurt me. It's very much the fact that my own sister wanted to wound me with it. I'm not responsible for your unhappiness, Margaret. You have to stop blaming me."

"I *don't* blame you—but you do have to admit that I was promised things with regard to Peter and then it all came to nothing."

She's correct that I did promise her that everything would be fine, but I was following official advice that turned out to be wrong. The government asked her to wait and separate from Peter for two whole years, which she did, albeit impatiently. I told her she could marry him once the two years were up, only to find they would need permission from Parliament because of his divorce. They gave her an ultimatum—a choice between Peter and her royal position. But we have been over this again and again.

"And I may remind you that you had a choice. We didn't stop you marrying the man you professed to love. You *chose* to keep your royal title and position rather than marry Peter. Those are the facts of the matter. You could be living happily with Peter in some other country right this minute, but instead you are *here* . . . gossiping about *my* husband."

The minute the words leave my mouth I know that I've gone too far. Margaret's face is white with shock and she stabs out her cigarette in the ashtray. Almost without thinking, I take one of the jam penny sandwiches and pop it into my mouth.

PART TWO

NORMA JEANE

1936

"Norma Jeane—string bean . . ." one of the boys at the end of the dining table yells at me when I sit down. I've grown tall for my age, and my legs look too long for my body. Everyone else is still regular-sized, so it's just one more thing that makes me a freak around here. I don't say anything back. Sometimes I can't get the words out properly. My mouth gets frozen and the sentence gets stuck at the back of my throat. I know what I want to say, but it won't come out of my mouth. The other kids tease me, so it's better if I don't speak.

The dining room is a large, high-ceilinged room with maybe a dozen long white tables scattered around it. There are six or seven chairs set out at each table and the kids all sit in the same places for every meal. This is partly so the matrons, who all stand around in their starched white dresses watching us, can see that we're all where we should be and keep a count. There are four girls and two boys at my table. The boys are much younger—only five or six years old—but the girls are around my age. I'll be ten years old on Monday. I can't imagine being ten years old already, but that's very nearly grown up. The rest of my life stretches out like a long road.

Aunt Grace says that even though I'm in the orphanage now, it won't be forever, and my future is bright. I don't think I believe her, though, because people are always promising me good things, but they never seem to happen. Anytime I get settled with a nice family, the next thing I know I'm packing up my little suitcase again because they decided to take another kid instead of me or they didn't like the way I looked at them. You can't win when you don't belong to anybody. I'm everybody's problem, but nobody really cares. I want to believe Aunt Grace, but she's the one who put me in this place.

One morning I woke up in my little bed with its pink and white quilt that's got a dark stain in one corner because it wasn't new when Aunt Grace got it. The sun was shining through the windows and I thought I might go outside and sit under a tree to read a book after breakfast. Aunt Grace made eggs for us both, and she was the same as always with me, smiling and making jokes as she drank her coffee. When I said that I wanted to go out into the garden and read my book, I saw her face change. Then she said that there wasn't time for that because we were going on a little trip together, and I should get washed and pack my suitcase.

Well, I couldn't even imagine where we were going, but I carefully folded up my skirt and blouse, placing them inside my bag. Grace is a good driver, but she doesn't talk much in the car, so I started humming little songs under my breath as we drove along. I was busy watching the buildings when Grace pulled up in front of the Los Angeles Orphans' Home. At first, I thought she was visiting someone there, but the next thing I know she took my little suitcase out of the trunk. I started screaming, clutching the door handle of the car like my life depended on it. I was yelling, "I'm not an orphan. I've got a mama." But Grace pulled my fingers off her car door and the staff came out and shuttled me inside.

It must have been lunchtime when we arrived because the

matron took me straight into the dining room. Every kid in that room stared me down for what felt like the longest time, and then the matron gave me a little push between my shoulder blades into this chair. They put a plate of something in front of me and I can't even remember what it was. I didn't eat a bite. My throat felt so tight and full of fear that I couldn't eat or speak a word. I could hardly see the rest of the room for the tears in my eyes, but when I wiped the back of my hands across my face, I saw that Grace was gone and I was left all alone.

Forever is a long time. "It won't be forever," she said when she came to visit on the weekend, but eight months feels like forever. Eight months of doing chores—washing dishes and cleaning floors for pocket money. I've washed a hundred plates in one go until the skin on my hands turned red-raw.

"You'll soon make friends," the matron told me, but it's not true. Not real friends, anyway. Sure, there are girls who I talk to sometimes, but I won't let anyone get too close to me now. It's better this way. That's what I think. I like people in books better, like Nancy Drew, who's smarter and more clever than all the grown-ups. The girls in books are nicer, and they're the kind of people you might be friends with if they lived in your town. They wouldn't make fun of you for growing too tall or for not being able to get your words out sometimes. I'm reading an English story now about a horse called Black Beauty, and I just love it. I've never been on a horse.

The dining room in the orphanage is too noisy for me. I like to be quiet and just lie around on my bed thinking about stuff. Some days I try to imagine what my father looks like, and whether he might come and find me. I make up names for him and things that he likes—which are mostly the things that I like. At other times I don't even know what it is that I think about, but my mind just whirs away like a little machine while I stare up at the ceiling.

I like to hide away with a book or play the piano downstairs.

Mostly I stare out of the window at the RKO tower blinking away and imagine what it must be like to work in a film studio like my mother and Aunt Grace. My mama was a film cutter before she got sick. If I close my eyes, I can remember her face, but it's like a photograph—it doesn't really move or talk to me. Just her hair and her eyes and the way her mouth parted before she was about to smile. It's like my mind took a picture of her somehow, and it's the only one I've got. That's funny to think of your mind taking pictures of people, but I guess it does.

I don't remember her saying sweet things to anyone except God, but that may be because I was always being bad. She said I was a liar, and the devil takes liars for his own. Night after night I dream that the devil has come to get me. Awful dreams that make me wake up in a cold sweat crying. I've had them a long time now . . . ever since that day. . . . Some sins you can't wash away so easily—like what happened in that room with Mr. K.

One day my mama went right out and bought us a house on Arbol Drive. A beautiful house too and right up close to where the movie stars live in Hollywood. I don't know how she did it, but it was a dream come true. She made it all nice and even bought a white piano for me to play. We were so happy there—at least for a little while. My mama took in some nice people as boarders to help pay the bills. We had a few paying guests, but Mr. K was her favorite. Always neat and tidy in his gray suit with a gold watch in his pocket and paid his rent on time.

One day I was folding laundry and carrying the towels upstairs to the linen closet to help my mama out because she got all anxious about things sometimes. I could hear her crying at night when she felt blue, and I tried to make her feel better by being as good as I could be.

I was always offering to run errands for the boarders. "What can I get you?" I'd ask, and they'd send me to the store to buy them extra shoelaces or hard candy. Sometimes they'd give me a nickel for going, and I could save them up to buy something just for me.

That day, though, I was putting the towels away in the closet on the landing when Mr. K called out to me. He wasn't a very tall man, and his face was always flushed red. Mostly I remember his fingers were kind of crooked, like they wouldn't straighten properly. He's one of those men who had a strange way about him and never really looked at people when he smiled, but I'd run errands for him before, happily taking his nickels—so that day I just stepped inside his room and smiled eagerly.

"Where do you want me to go, Mr. K?" I asked him quietly. Inside I was already waiting for the list of things to remember from the store, because you've got to make sure you don't forget anything or you won't get your money. I remember thinking that his face looked funny—kind of sweaty and more flushed than usual. My feet were barely even inside his room when quick as a flash he slammed the door shut behind me and turned the key in the lock. At first I thought he was playing a game, and I laughed that little-girl laugh because I didn't know any better.

"Now you can't get out. . . ." he whispered, breathing hard, and I knew right then that he wasn't playing a game. My heart began hammering away inside my chest as he grabbed hold of me. Two big meaty paws sweeping around my waist and pulling me down on to his lap. I started struggling and kicking him like a crazy thing, but he was too strong for me. Pinning me down and touching me under my skirt with his crooked fingers.

What happened next, I can't think about.

"Here's a nickel, Norma Jeane, why don't you buy yourself an ice cream?" he said afterward, like I'd just run an errand for him. He lifted his lips into a smile, but it wasn't a real smile at all. My mouth just hung open, staring up at him as if it had been a bad dream—but I knew I hadn't dreamed it. My legs were shaking so hard. My bones melting away into nothing. I couldn't speak or move. He'd unlocked the door now, but my legs couldn't make my feet walk through it. All the time he just stood there, tightening his belt buckle on his pants, smiling down at me as if nothing had happened.

The nickel felt as if it was burning the palm of my hand, and I began to tremble so violently that I couldn't stop myself. I wanted to scream, but my throat wouldn't let a sound out of my mouth.

Then, before I knew it, my arm went back and I threw the nickel right in his face.

I ran as hard as I could straight down the stairs to my mother. "I have to t-t-tell you s-s-s-something about Mr. K," I stuttered, trying to hold back my tears because I knew it was important to get the words out right, but my breath felt funny and they came out all wrong. I had to tell her before he came down the stairs.

I got my words lined up and I spoke them clear as day. When I turned around, Mr. K was standing in the doorway, listening to me with that stupid smile on his face, shaking his head as he looked right at my mama. "Don't be cross with her," he said. "I wouldn't give her a nickel to go to the store for me. Norma Jeane, it's a terrible sin to tell such lies. You should know that at your age."

I stood there waiting for my mama to do something but she just glared at me like I was all wrong. Suddenly her hand came out of nowhere, whipping through the air, and slapped me hard across my cheek. "Don't you dare say a word about Mr. K," she told me. "He's my best boarder. You're just a little troublemaker."

My cheek turned bright red as the slap stung my skin. Tears tumbled down my face as I began to cry and shake, but my mother just stood there with her arms folded and her mouth set tight. My throat closed around all the words that needed saying.

They got sealed away somewhere and my mouth wouldn't release them.

The next day was Sunday and we went to church. When it came time for the sinners to confess their wicked deeds, my mama pushed me out of the pew to go and repent for my lies. "You have to learn to tell the truth. The devil takes liars for his own," she hissed at me.

I started trembling from head to toe as I stepped forward, one foot in front of the other. All the sinners were clustered at the front of the church on their knees—wailing and crying as everyone begged the Lord to forgive them. I tried to tell people that I wasn't a liar, but nobody could hear a little girl crying, with all their grown-up sins being confessed.

When I turned back to look at the congregation, their heads were all bowed, praying for our salvation.

A couple of rows back I could see Mr. K in his blue Sunday suit, his gold watch sitting in his vest pocket, his eyes tightly closed, his crooked fingers wrapped around his Bible, and his lips praying loudly that we might be forgiven our sins.

Three months later they locked my mama away in the asylum.

"Norma Jeane—string bean!" the boy yells again. The matron claps her hands and announces that dinner is over, and I begin to carry the dishes through to the kitchen and take my place at the sink. The water is boiling hot, and the soap suds make my skin itch. I can feel tears filling my eyes, but I won't cry. I can put another nickel in the little pot where I keep my coins; I earn plenty of nickels from washing dishes or cleaning things here. One day Grace says she'll be able to give me a proper home, but for now I'm all alone.

Standing out on the sidewalk in the dusty afternoon heat, I scan the road for a black car. There are blue cars and gray cars sweeping past me, but no sign of a black car.

Aunt Grace is late. Maybe she's forgotten that she promised to take me to the movies and afterward for something to eat. She's not really my aunt, but she is my mother's best friend. They worked together in the film studio, and Grace has so far kept her word to take care of me. Of course, it's difficult for her, as often the men in her life don't want a kid around, and so here I am living in the orphanage, even though I'm not an orphan.

There are worse things than being an orphan, I guess. When your mother goes crazy there's nobody to explain to you what's going on. They whisper about her at night—the men who care about Aunt Grace. They say, "That kid will turn out like her mother." They mean crazy like her mother, but I'm not going to let anyone lock me away. The asylum is not a place to visit when you're a kid. It's filled with the sound of weeping and screaming, like all the misery in the whole wide world lives inside those doors. Maybe when people get too much sadness inside them, they can't hide it anymore, and the rest of the world hates to see sad people being sad, so they put them away behind high walls and locked doors. My mother thinks she's a nurse and they let her wear a white uniform as long as she doesn't try to touch anyone. She just likes to wander around checking on things as if she's in charge of them. I guess it's harmless.

I walk back up the path toward the orphanage so I can check the big clock on the wall right inside the front door. I really hope Grace hasn't forgotten because I'd like a day out and she can be fun.

I don't know if she's remembered that it's my birthday on Monday, and I hate to remind people. They give you a birthday cake in the orphanage so people can sing as you blow out the candles, but it's not a cake you can eat: the inside is full of dust. I don't like my birthday. It makes me sad—another reminder that other kids have a mama and a daddy who throw them parties with presents and real chocolate cake. I don't even care about the presents and the chocolate cake, but it might be nice to have parents who celebrate the day you were born. Nobody has ever cared much about the day I was born. Even my mama never made much of a fuss about it. I guess it reminded her of my daddy—whoever he was. That's what being born outside of marriage does for you. Everyone pretends they don't know how you got here.

The clock ticks away and I wander back onto the sidewalk feeling a sticky heat running down the back of my blouse. Then suddenly in the distance I see Grace's little black car racing toward me, and I feel a flood of relief as she draws up outside and waves me to hop in beside her. I'm so pleased to see her that I forget all about the fact that she's late.

"Norma Jeane, I swear you are growing every time I see you," she hollers at me through the open car window. I hate being tall for my age. I'm already much taller than the boys in the orphanage, so I'd really like to stop growing right now. I can't stand the way they tease me, but I don't say anything, I just give her a lopsided grin and say, "Hi, Aunt Grace."

On the seat beside her is a small pink box tied with a blue ribbon, and my heart leaps inside my chest. She's remembered my birthday! As I open the car door and slide in beside her, she plucks the box off the seat and gives me a big, wide smile. "Happy Birthday, Norma. This is for you," she says, placing the pink box on my lap.

The little box feels hard in my hands with sharp edges and I want to rip open the paper, but I'm not sure if I'm meant to open it now or wait until Monday. I stare up at Grace for a moment until she says, "Go ahead. It won't matter if you open it early."

I tear off the ribbon and the pink paper, and all the time my mind is trying to imagine what might be inside. It's not a very big box, so maybe something small and pretty. Something that I can have just for myself. I'm wearing the same blue skirt and white shirt that I always wear. I've got another set exactly the same. Nobody believes in buying things when you're growing taller every day, but the other kids make fun of me because I always look the same. When I grow up, I'm going to have pretty dresses in all the colors that I like best.

The lid of the box lifts up easily, and inside is a yellow hair slide with tiny jewels on the end that sparkle in the light. It's the loveliest thing I've ever seen, and I throw my arms round Grace's neck. "It's beautiful. Thank you, Aunt Grace." Even as I'm thanking her, I'm gathering up a handful of my hair and sliding the clip into place. Grace opens up her compact so I can see myself, and I smile a real wide grin because I look pretty in her mirror.

Before I can say another word, Grace has started up the car and we're pulling out of the street and leaving the orphanage behind for a whole day. When we get downtown, Grace parks and we walk across the street to a candy store, where she lets me buy a whole bag of peanut brittle. Then we walk arm in arm to the movie theater, where Grace buys us two tickets, and in we go.

There's something about the darkness of the movie theater that I like. You can see everyone's faces when they're laughing or if they're scared by the movie. Sometimes I like to watch the audience as much as I like to see the picture. We slide into the end of a row. Grace lets me sit on the aisle seat and I bite off a sticky corner of my peanut brittle. It leaves my fingers covered in toffee so I wipe them on my blue skirt when Grace isn't looking. The news reels finish, and we settle down in our seats for the main event as I touch my yellow hair clip just to remind myself that this is a good birthday and I'll remember this one.

The movie features the Three Stooges playing pranks on one another, and they make me laugh out loud. I can't take my eyes off the screen, and my cheeks ache a little from laughing so much. With a mouth filled with peanut brittle and Aunt Grace laughing along beside me, I wish every day could be like this. I don't want to waste time thinking too much, though, because I'll spoil today if I'm busy worrying that on Monday when I wake up it will really be my birthday, but I'll be surrounded by a bunch of kids teasing me and a dusty old cake that you can't eat.

I feel a blackness open up inside my chest where I keep my lonely ache. It aches all the time, like if you'd hurt yourself and the bruise got pressed on. Suddenly the movie doesn't seem so funny to me anymore. Afterward, Aunt Grace will drop me off in her little black car and go back to her life, because when it comes down to it, there's nothing about me that makes anyone want to love me. Nobody has ever really cared enough to put me first. Every time I got moved along to a new foster family, I thought maybe they would look at me working hard, helping out with the chores, or being as nice as I could be and think *That little girl could be part of our family,* but they never did. They just cashed their five-dollar checks and treated me like I was nothing.

Looking around at the audience, I can see that every single face is watching the people up there on that big screen. I can't even imagine what it must be like to work in the movies. I don't mean like my mother or Grace cutting film—I mean being up there on the screen with everyone looking at you and paying attention. The audience members are staring as if there's nothing else in the whole world that matters except the people on that screen—even Grace, who is smoking a cigarette, but all the time her eyes are wide and shining. They never leave the screen for a second. I could walk out of here right now, and I swear she wouldn't notice until the lights came up.

I help myself to another piece of peanut brittle, but this piece is too big and has sharp edges that hurt my tongue, so I slip it into the palm of my hand and sit there with the candy still warm from my mouth until the movie finishes.

"Would you like to get some ice cream?" Grace asks me when the lights come up. All around us people are standing up and shuffling back outside into the daylight. I nod, but really all I'm looking for is somewhere to get rid of the sticky peanut brittle as it's still lodged inside the palm of my hand. Grace puts her fingers between my shoulder blades and steers me out into the lobby of the movie theater, past the popcorn stall and the place where they sell boxes of chocolates.

Suddenly I see a poster on the wall of the lobby advertising "Coming Attractions." It's a woman with golden hair and a handsome dark-haired man. I can't walk another step because there is something about that movie poster that I don't want to stop looking at. The woman looks like an angel. I've never seen anyone with hair that color. My mouth falls open, and my hands go limp as the sticky peanut brittle falls to the floor without me even noticing at first.

"Norma, what are you doing? Come on, it's getting late. We need to scoot if we're going to get ice cream before I take you back." I hear the words, but I'm still gazing at this angel woman on the poster. I reach out a sticky finger and gently trace the outline of her golden hair.

Grace laughs but not in a nasty way. "Oh, that's Jean Harlow—the Blond Bombshell."

"What's a blond bombshell?" I ask, but what I really want to know is if that's her real hair.

"It's because she makes a bomb go off in men's minds." Grace laughs again and then grabs me by the arm and gently pulls me outside into the late May sunshine. All the way home I think about women making a bomb go off in men's minds and whether that's a good thing. I wonder how they would even do that, but I'm not going to ask. It feels like information that is dangerous to know. Yet part of me wants to understand.

My stomach is full of ice cream and peanut brittle, but my mind is chewing over something else entirely as I see the familiar sign for the Los Angeles Orphans' Home. Aunt Grace pulls up outside the orphanage and leans across me, opening the car door so that I can get out.

"I'll see you real soon, Norma. I'll let you know when I'm coming to take you out again," she says, but I can tell that she is already somewhere else. Late for a date maybe.

I slam the car door shut and wave good-bye, but she doesn't bother to wave back, and the car jerks away from the curb and races away.

As I walk back up the path that leads to the orphanage, I start to think about the movie and all the people in the audience with their eyes as big as saucers, laughing and smiling. I'd like someone to look at me that way—like I was somebody that really mattered.

When I reach the door, I turn around and catch a glimpse of the RKO radio tower in the distance. Then it hits me right out of the blue . . . when I grow up I want to be in the movies just like that angel woman.

LILIBET

1936

The windows at 145 Piccadilly overlook St. George's Hospital, and as the late afternoon is full of wintry darkness, the little lights shine out into the cold air from every room. I like to watch the goings-on in the street below and imagine the poor patients lying in their hospital rooms while I am here in our nursery with Margaret. There is an icy lace beginning to form on the outside of the glass, and I imagine that the passersby will have clouds of frosty air around them as they breathe. It's very cold out there, but inside we have a coal fire burning away and a lovely plate of jam penny sandwiches with a fruit cake for our tea.

"Come away from the window, Lilibet," Crawfie, our governess, says with a sigh. "Sit nicely now, girls, and have your tea. Then you can go down and see your parents."

The promise of our usual games with Mummy and Papa is very much the highlight of our day, for we don't see many other people. We go for our walks or play in Hamilton Gardens, and on occasion I'm allowed to take my shilling pocket money to Woolworths to buy things.

I like to watch how people are just going about their lives, which seem so very different from ours. Every morning the brewer's horses trot down the street all loaded up with their wooden barrels of beer, and the man driving them is so old that he looks as if he might topple off his carriage at any time. Yet he is able to carry an entire barrel on just one shoulder, which goes to show that one should never judge someone by how they look, for people can be surprising.

Reluctantly I leave my little perch in the window and all the interesting sights of Piccadilly and sit at our table just in front of the fire, which is already laid with two plates painted with blue flowers. In the middle of the table is a silver cake stand and at the bottom of it are several small sandwiches, of which my favorite are the tiny round circles filled with strawberry jam. Margaret sits next to me, swinging her legs back and forth under the table, and comes very close to kicking me at times. She's a terrible wriggler and is unable to keep still no matter how many times she's scolded.

"Stop it, Margaret," I say, but she just crams a jam sandwich into her mouth and pulls a face at me. She can be very annoying, and today in particular she is blaming everything that goes wrong on her imaginary friend, "Cousin Halifax."

"Oh, that wasn't me," she will say adamantly. "I wouldn't do that. It must be Cousin Halifax that took your crayon," or, "It was Cousin Halifax who spilled paint on your watercolor pad." It's most infuriating, and obviously it was her and she will never admit it.

After we've eaten as many sandwiches and pieces of cake as we like—which for me was just three jam pennies and one slice of cake, but for Margaret I counted up at least four jam pennies and two slices of cake because some days she can be a greedy little thing—we wash our hands and faces before going downstairs.

Crawfie likes to make sure that we are all neat and tidy before Mummy and Papa see us in the evening. Of course, often we are a bit scratched and messy after a long day doing lessons in addition to playing games in the gardens, but our parents never seem to mind. Papa says it's good for us to get out in the fresh air, while I don't think that Mummy really cares at all about our lessons as long as we are happy.

Having passed Crawfie's inspection, we leave the nursery and pass by the lines of our toy horses that are very neatly stabled outside the door, under the enormous glass dome of the roof, as we're on the top floor. Our stuffed horses are all different breeds and colors, with reins that I like to keep polished so I can ride them around the top floor of the house before bedtime. I have been known to attach a pair of cherry-red reins to the end of my bed so that I can pretend to be taking my horse for an evening trot around Hyde Park. I keep all of the toy horses nicely, though, so no one can complain about the amount that litter the landings.

We race down the stairs right to the bottom step and then stop ourselves running into the drawing room, where we can hear our parents laughing with each other. We don't want to get scolded for running inside the house. The drawing room doors are slightly ajar as if our parents are waiting for us to enter, and so we do. My father's face beams at the sight of us, and the card table is already set up in front of the sofa for us to play several rounds of racing demon before supper. Mummy looks beautiful in a pale gray dress with a lovely fur collar, but she always looks very nice whatever she's wearing. Our parents are quite the handsomest of all the parents who I've met so far.

"Ah, here you are," my father says, and I take my place on the sofa, ready for our card game to begin. Margaret hops straight onto my father's lap and wraps her arms around his neck.

"Papa, do you know what Cousin Halifax did today? He was terribly naughty, and I do believe that he might have broken one of the little china dogs in our nursery."

I raise my eyebrows at this news, as the only china dogs in

our nursery belong to me. On the shelves to the side of the fireplace there are our books and games, and in pride of place stand two small black china dogs that were a Christmas present from my nursery maid, Bobo. One has a tiny red ribbon tied around its neck and the other a tiny blue ribbon. Both have friendly faces and pink tongues that poke out of their mouths, giving them quite a comical air. I like them very much but they are quite delicate.

"Margaret!" I cry. "Those dogs are mine!"

"It wasn't my fault." My sister has that look on her face—a sort of innocent wickedness that is very much her specialty.

"You aren't allowed to touch my things." I glare at Margaret, feeling quite cross now. I do wish sometimes that I had remained an only child or at least had a baby brother who I'm sure would be less trouble than my sister.

"I just wanted to feel the ribbon, but then Cousin Halifax grabbed it and it fell on the floor." Her wide blue eyes are filled with a sort of guilty shame, yet she is smiling as if she's not sorry at all.

"You always want what I have. Leave my things alone."

"Hush now, girls. I'm sure it was just an accident, Lilibet. Now, Margaret, please apologize to your sister and do be more careful in future." My mother's calm voice settles us down again and Margaret begrudgingly apologizes, before sliding off my father's lap and taking her place on the sofa next to me. My mother is shuffling the cards and getting ready to play.

Margaret grins at me wickedly and then says, "I'll tell Cousin Halifax to be more careful next time."

The next hour is spent with numerous games of racing demon, which get us both rather excited as it's played at top speed and you have to be very quick to win. Margaret is really too young and too slow to play, so she is often allowed to win a round just to stop her crying. It's very unfair, but that's how it is. When she gets older, she will have to play by the same rules as the rest of us. Eventually Mummy sweeps the cards up and places them back in the pack and signals that our games are over for the day.

We kiss my mother and father good-night, and off we go back up the stairs to have supper and then our bath. If I eat quickly, I can have time to ride my toy horses around the park once or twice before bedtime.

Friday is my favorite day of the week. Of course, we have to suffer arithmetic, writing, and then history before we are allowed to go out and play, but after lunch we all bundle into the car and set off for Royal Lodge. Over breakfast, Crawfie tells us that Uncle David is coming to visit us tomorrow with one of his friends, and we are to have tea with him. We used to see him quite often, but lately he's been very busy being the King and so we don't see him much at all. It was the same with our grandfather, as he rarely had time to play with us. On his last visit Uncle David brought us a Doctor Dolittle book, so I am secretly hopeful that he might bring us another to read. He's always good fun and loves to play games with us.

I am sitting in the window watching the goings-on down below in Piccadilly before our lessons begin. There is a riding school just down the road, and I like to watch the horses trotting in and out with their riders, all ready for a gallop across the park. I have to wait until we get to Windsor to ride my pony, so I make do with giving each rider marks for their dress and posture as they proceed down the street.

All of a sudden, I hear a crash behind me, and as I turn around, I see that Margaret is standing over the shattered remains of the second china dog.

"It really wasn't my fault, Lilibet." She stares up at me, her eyes wide with horror. "It wasn't even Cousin Halifax this time. It fell off the shelf. Honestly, it must have been a gust of wind coming down the chimney or something. But it definitely was not my fault."

A bubble of rage begins in the pit of my stomach and rises all the way to the top of my head. I don't say a word. I don't cry or scream or pout. Instead, I stand up and walk over to our sideboard where we keep our inkpots and pick up the nearest one. It's filled to the brim with dark blue ink and has a silver lid, which I remove with one hand. All the while Margaret is standing there as if frozen to the spot, waiting for me to say something. I can see her watching me with a mixture of curiosity and then—as it gradually occurs to her what I intend to do—a growing horror.

A cold wild fury spurts out of me, and before I can reason with myself, the entire pot of dark blue ink has been tipped upside down, and my sister is standing there with blobs of ink dripping down her cheeks.

"Oh dear. Look what Cousin Halifax did," I say icily, but my words are drowned out by the sound of Margaret wailing.

Later that evening at Royal Lodge, Margaret slips quietly into my bed. "I am sorry about your little dogs." And with that she lays her still damp hair on my shoulder.

"And I'm sorry about your hair. Has it all washed out now?" We hold hands under the covers, and for a moment I feel glad to have a sister, for even when we fight, we always make up again.

"Yes, but they had to shampoo it at least ten times to get all the ink out. It would have been funny to have blue hair for a while, but it's all gone now. Do you think Uncle David will bring us anything nice?" Margaret whispers hopefully.

"Maybe a new book. Do you want to ride my horse around the park for a bit?" My cherry-red reins are tied to the bottom of my bed as usual, but I have not yet begun riding my imaginary pony, since Margaret interrupted me.

"Shall we both ride it together?" she says with her usual impish smile.

"All right. Here, you take one rein and I'll take the other." And so we spend a happy few minutes peacefully trotting and galloping, although at one point I was galloping and Margaret was trotting, which wouldn't work at all if you had a real horse.

Uncle David and his guest arrive just in time for tea. It's a terribly rainy day, and we spent the whole of Saturday morning doing our usual lessons and trying to remember what we had learned that week—without much success, I'm afraid. The lesson seems very fresh at the time and one does think it's gone in, but by the time we get to Saturday, it's very difficult to remember our arithmetic or history. Eventually Crawfie let us read our books as long as we were quiet. Margaret and I were very well behaved, as we didn't want to risk further punishment (having already lost our pocket money for the week), but whenever we got the chance, we were peeking out of the windows watching for Uncle David's car. We always know which one is his because he has his little flag on top of it.

We must have become far too engrossed in our books, for suddenly we heard voices and Crawfie told us to make sure our hands were washed and we were "shipshape" for our visitors.

It's very gray and wet, so I don't expect we will go outside to play, but at least there will be tea with Mummy and Papa and then games with Uncle David.

As we arrive in the Octagonal Room downstairs, I can see that Mummy is standing by the fire while Papa, Uncle David, and a woman I don't recognize are all sitting together. Uncle David and the woman are side by side on the sofa while Papa is in his usual armchair.

"Ah, here are the girls," says Mummy with a smile, but she doesn't look particularly happy, and I wonder if she's still cross with us after yesterday. I vowed to be extra good today, and so has Margaret. Uncle David gets to his feet, and after we've done our curtsies, he sweeps us up into his arms and seems delighted that we are there.

"I brought you a new book to read, but first of all, I want you to meet a very special friend of mine. Lilibet . . . Margaret . . . this is Mrs. Simpson." He beams down at us and I see that he wants us to like his friend very much.

"Do call me Wallis," the woman says in a quiet drawl. She has an accent, and I think she may be an American. I don't believe that I've ever met an American before, and I inspect her closely when she's not looking at me. Her lips form a rigid smile, and although her voice is friendly, she doesn't seem particularly pleased to meet us.

Mummy nods toward the other sofa to indicate that Margaret and I should sit down. As the footman enters the room with the tea things, I crane my neck to try to work out what flavor of sandwiches and cake we have, and I'm delighted to find that it's a chocolate cake. I'd like Uncle David to visit more often, as they always bring out the very best cake when he comes to see us.

Mummy and Papa seem quite serious, and even Uncle David is not his usual happy self today.

"What a lovely room," Mrs. Simpson says as her little violet eyes flit from corner to corner taking it all in.

"Yes, we are very happy here," Mummy replies, but her voice sounds quite peculiar and not at all her usual lovely way of speaking to people. Margaret and I are allowed to help ourselves to a sandwich, and we sit quietly side by side watching the grown-ups talking to one another. From time to time, Uncle David gives us a beaming smile, but he doesn't ask what we've been doing or how we are. My father is smoking one cigarette after another, which Mummy normally tells him off about, but today she doesn't say a word, and we all sit silently staring at our teacups and saucers rather than one another.

"I am sorry that I haven't been to see you girls. I'm afraid that

I've been too busy to play," Uncle David says, but instead of looking at us, he is peeking out at Mrs. Simpson from under his lashes, and she seems quite uncomfortable. I very much suspect that we won't be playing this afternoon since there is a terrible atmosphere in the room as if somebody has died. Margaret and I sit very still trying our best not to fidget because something feels very wrong. Of course, Margaret chooses that moment to wriggle closer to me, and I give her a scolding look.

A great heaviness fills the air as there was when our grandfather, the King, passed away and we were all very serious and sad. As far as I know, nobody has died, but you wouldn't think it to look at us. Nobody is talking normally or even looking at the other in a kindly way.

Margaret and I have our sandwiches and a slice of chocolate cake each, but then we are given our new book and sent back upstairs to the nursery, which is quite disappointing. We were hoping for our usual card games or some other fun, but they don't seem as if they want to play anything. All the time we were eating our cake, I was watching Mrs. Simpson quite curiously. She picked at her sandwich and refused a slice of cake, choosing instead to sit there with a teacup and saucer in her hand and a cool smile on her face. Whenever she saw me looking, her smile disappeared and she gave me a frosty glare. I've decided that I don't like her one bit. From time to time, she glanced over at Uncle David, and they exchanged a little look between them that made me feel as if they didn't like Mummy or Papa and wanted to leave. It was really most peculiar, as Daddy and Uncle David are always having fun together or talking loudly about politics and other things. Yet today they have hardly said a word to each other. Uncle David only seems to care about what Mrs. Simpson has to say, and since she has barely said a word, it's all been very awkward and silent.

Everyone seems quite cross about something, yet I can't

think why Uncle David and Mrs. Simpson might be cross with us. After all, they've chosen to visit us and had our best chocolate cake—so it's rather a puzzle.

Margaret and I go back upstairs to the nursery, and I am pleased to find that our new book is a lovely illustrated copy of *Black Beauty.* We begin to read it straightaway. Some time passes as Margaret and I sit quietly reading with the fire crackling away while the icy late-November rain lashes against the windowpanes. Then we hear the sound of a car door slamming, and we rush to the window to see that our visitors are leaving already.

"It's not fair that we didn't get to play any games," Margaret says, and for once I agree with her. We've been cooped up inside all day as it was too wet to go riding and we were all waiting for Uncle David's visit. I'm afraid I blame Mrs. Simpson for our lack of fun because she didn't seem as if she wanted to play games with us, and I know that Uncle David would have played even if he was feeling tired from being the King all week.

"We could play hide-and-seek before supper," I whisper to Margaret.

"Shall we?" she whispers back, and I nod. We make our excuses to Crawfie and she says it's all right to play for a little while, but we must be quiet and not make a fuss. Well, there couldn't be a quieter game than hide-and-seek and so off we go.

Margaret is the first to hide but she always uses the same hiding place and so is rather too easy to find. I know she's in the cupboard at the top of the stairs because that's always her spot, but I pretend to be looking in our bedrooms and around the nursery until I finally fling open the cupboard door and discover her. Then it's my turn and Margaret stands there with her hands covering her eyes counting to twenty while I race off down the stairs as quietly as I can manage, determined to find the perfect hiding place.

I reach the bottom step just as I hear Margaret's voice clear as a bell shouting, "Ready or not, I'm coming to find you, Lilibet." And I squeeze myself behind a rather large vase just outside the drawing room. I have to fold my arms right onto my lap and kneel down in the most uncomfortable way so as not to be seen. I expect that Margaret will begin her search upstairs so I may be here some time.

A few moments pass, and I am beginning to get a little bored, plus my legs are feeling quite cramped. Margaret hasn't even made it down the stairs yet, and I wonder how long I can hold out in this most uncomfortable position. I am considering dashing down the hallway to find a different hiding place when I hear Mummy and Papa coming out of the drawing room. I try to keep a little giggle to myself as I imagine their surprise if I were to jump out on them, and I'm waiting for the perfect moment when I hear Mummy say, "Oh, Bertie, what are we going to do?" in such a sad, weary voice that I squeeze myself even tighter behind the vase in case they see me.

"I r-r-r-really don't know. He can't go through with this. S-s-s-someone will talk him around," Papa says with his little stutter that always comes out when he's upset about something. I'm straining to hear what they're saying, and my foot is beginning to tingle with pins and needles, but I don't dare move a muscle. They must be talking about Uncle David, but I don't know why they are upset with him. Mummy and Papa are always so happy together, so this must be very grave indeed, but what on earth could it be?

"It's the children I worry about . . . and you, of course, my darling," Mummy says with a little sniff, and for a horrible moment I think that she may be crying. I feel awful in my hiding place hearing things that I'm perfectly sure they wouldn't want me to be listening to, but it's too late now.

"Yes, it will be a great burden for all of us," Papa says. "If only David would find someone else. Someone suitable. He could m-m-marry and have children of his own. A boy perhaps to be K-King and we could all carry on with our peaceful lives. I can't bear to think of Lilibet having to t-take all this on someday."

My mind is racing. Take what on? I don't understand what I have to do with this. For a second, I wonder if my silly fight with Margaret yesterday has caused some dreadful problem, but I don't believe a couple of smashed ornaments and a few too many shampoos would lead my parents to sound so upset. They are normally very calm about things. My heart is racing, and I have the most terrible guilty feeling inside, as if I've overheard some desperate secret that I shouldn't know.

"I want us to have our ordinary happy life. He's the King. It's his duty to find a suitable wife and to take care of the country. He can't just walk away from it and let everything fall on your shoulders, Bertie. He can't do that to our children—to Lilibet especially."

"Well, unless he changes his mind or there is a male child, that will be her future, I'm afraid. I feel quite despairing at the thought of it. How can my brother give up the throne? It's unthinkable."

I feel rather sick as the meaning of their words begins to take shape in my mind. Uncle David means to stop being the King. Their voices fade as they walk up the stairs to their rooms, and I let my body go limp and stretch out my legs so they won't cramp up. I spy Margaret peeking through the banisters and I reach out my foot farther to let her find me.

"Lilibet, I can see you!" she cries, and I, with some relief, crawl out of my hiding place. My face must look stricken because Margaret says, "What's wrong, Lil? Are you feeling ill?"

"No. Come along, let's go back upstairs." I grab her hand and we rush back to our nursery. Margaret's little legs can't take the steps as quickly as mine, so I have to slow down and let her catch up.

"Why are we rushing?" she says, huffing and puffing all the way up.

"Because I don't want to play anymore," I say without further explanation. A ball of worry fizzes away inside me. I don't want to be Queen. I don't want Uncle David to give up being the King and I don't want Mummy to cry anymore.

It's a rather somber weekend at Royal Lodge, and by the time Sunday evening arrives we all head back to 145 Piccadilly with some relief. I am almost happy to begin our weekly lessons, and even the prospect of Monday-morning Bible study followed by history is better than the awful strained silence that hangs over us all. To try to cheer us up, Crawfie asks if she can take us to the Bath Club for swimming lessons, and it is agreed that we can start the following week. It's lovely to be out and about in London, as the Christmas lights are up and the shop windows are filled with all sorts of quite magical displays with little toy reindeers or nativity scenes.

We all set off for our lesson with new swimming costumes and hats, and although we are both perfectly awful on our first try, eventually we do manage to float around a bit; but moving our arms and legs in the right order and remembering to breathe prove to be quite tricky. The water is freezing cold and smells quite strongly of some sort of chemical. Everyone is shivering on the edge of the pool, but once you get in and your body is working, you soon warm up.

Margaret keeps going off balance and half of her body looks as if she might sink to the bottom at any moment. In the end, thankfully, nobody does sink and we survive our very first attempts at swimming. After our lesson we are allowed hot cocoa and a ginger biscuit, which we accept gratefully, being quite hungry.

When we return home to 145 Piccadilly, we find that Mummy is sick with a bad chest cold and unable to leave her bed, while Papa is shut away in his study holding a great many meetings. There are a lot of whispered conversations going on around us, and something must be wrong because everyone is being very nice and letting us do things that we wouldn't normally be allowed to do, such as read our books instead of having our arithmetic lesson.

The afternoon goes slowly, and by the time we are thinking about our tea and what cake there might be today, Crawfie tells us that we must get changed into our nice velvet dresses with our little cardigans and go downstairs to greet Papa.

"Aren't we going to have tea?" I ask.

"You can have tea a little later today. It's important that you go downstairs now. When you see your father today, you must curtsy before you kiss him. Do you understand?"

"Why?" Margaret says a little sulkily, as she doesn't like change.

My heart sinks at the news because the worst thing must have happened.

"Your father will explain it all to you. Now off we go and don't forget a nice deep curtsy."

We do as we're told and walk very quietly downstairs to the drawing room of 145 Piccadilly. Papa is standing in the middle of the room quite alone, smoking a cigarette. As we stand in the doorway, Crawfie gives us a little tap on our shoulders to remind us, and Margaret and I sweep into our best curtsies before we run to him. As he greets us in his usual fashion, I see Crawfie curtsy behind us, and I hear her say, "Your Majesty . . ."

Papa looks very serious, but when he sees my worried face he smiles. "Now, girls, there will be some very great changes, I'm afraid. Uncle David has decided that he can no longer be the King, and so I have to take on that role." He pauses and waits for us to take in the news. My stomach feels strange and queasy. I nod, trying to keep my face completely calm, but inside I feel as if I'm a tiny boat that's been cut adrift. My father kneels down and puts his arms around us. "I'm sorry, my darling girls, but it does mean that we will have to move from our little home here at 145 Piccadilly and go to live in Buckingham Palace very soon. And you will no longer be known as York, but rather just Windsor, as befits the children of the King."

Margaret looks most indignant, and her face is sharply upturned, glaring at my father. "But I've only just learned to write York."

He pats her head once and smiles wearily. "I know there will be many new things to get used to, but we four are together . . . and together we can manage it all. I expect you girls to help your mother and make me p-proud. Now come and give me a kiss, and then Crawfie will take you off to have your tea."

And with that we are dismissed back to our nursery, where even the sight of my favorite chocolate cake can't raise my spirits. My heart is still racing with the shock of it all, and I can't think of anything to say. Even Margaret is unusually quiet, and we leave half our sandwiches and cake uneaten, which is very unlike us.

That night after our bath, we slip into our white flannel nightgowns, ready for bed. I don't ride my toy horses, leaving them neatly stabled outside our bedroom door. Instead, I get down on my knees by the side of my bed to say my prayers. Within a second, I'm aware of Margaret slipping into position beside me as her tiny hand reaches for my own. We kneel side by side, holding hands, and I feel a terrible sense of sadness come over me.

"Does this mean that you'll be the Queen one day?" she whispers softly.

"Maybe . . ." I reply, not really knowing what will happen or how I should feel about it. The future seems unknowable and far away from our ordinary lives here at 145 Piccadilly.

"Oh, that's bad luck," she says as I release a deep sigh.

"Come on, let's say a prayer," I say firmly, for nothing else can help us.

"What are we praying for?" Margaret whispers gravely while giving my hand a gentle squeeze of support.

"A brother," I reply.

PART THREE

The Daily Sparkle

BY IDA LAPINE

The Duke of Soho?

Regular readers will know that I love a good lunch as much as the next person—unless that person is a duke with very royal connections. That little Thursday lunch club in Soho must have an interesting menu.

"Friends" of a certain duke appear to have quite the appetite for "dessert," it seems, and you know what they say about judging a man by the company he keeps.

Rumors abound, but my lips are sealed.

Blondes Are Not More Fun

We had such high hopes when we heard that Marilyn Monroe was going to be working with Sir Laurence Olivier. However, a little birdie tells us that all is not well on the set of *The Sleeping Prince*.

We could have guessed that the problem would be a certain blonde who is making her mark and not in a good way. She is constantly late to set and driving Sir Larry crazy with her antics. Sources close to the action tell us, "Poor Larry is at his wits' end. She can't act and she can't even turn up on time."

What a pity, but honestly is anyone even a bit surprised?

Stay tuned because there are months of this to go . . . and something has got to give.

NORMA JEANE

1956

"I wish people could see you this way." Arthur's voice is warm as honey as he stands in our bedroom doorway looking at me.

"I'm just reading my book, that's all," I say with a laugh, but I know that he means people might be surprised to see Marilyn Monroe sitting around with no makeup on, wearing an old shirt, with a well-worn copy of *Anna Karenina* on her lap. Some of the pages are turned down at the corner where I like to re-read the love scenes between Anna and Vronsky, and of course the tragic ending. It makes me cry every single time. That poor woman—loving somebody so much that without them you just want to die.

"What do you think of Tolstoy?" Arthur moves across to our bed and flops down beside me, burying his face in my stomach and planting kisses there.

"Stop it." I giggle. "Oh, he's a wonderful writer. I think he knew great love and great sadness both at the same time. . . . Don't you think?" My fingers smooth back Arthur's hair, which is slick with his hair oil.

"Yes, I think you're right. You have to know great pain to

write that depth of emotion. You should read *Madame Bovary* next. . . . It's Flaubert and I think you'll really enjoy it."

"*Madame Bovary*? I'll buy a copy next time we go into London." I sigh. "I'd love to be able to conjure up all those feelings in just a few words. It's a great gift. You're lucky that you get to do that too. . . ." I barely finish my sentence before Arthur wraps me up in his arms, and for a moment everything in my life is perfect. Then I let out a long sigh as I remember that I'm due back on set tomorrow. If Larry thinks he can just order me around again like I'm some kind of a doll, then he has another think coming. "Act sexy . . ." indeed. Why, I'll show him.

"What's that sigh for?" Arthur raises himself up on one elbow, his deep brown eyes suddenly full of concern.

"Oh, nothing. Things aren't going so well with Larry. We have very different ways of working. I don't think he approves of movie actors. . . ." My voice trails off, as I'm not sure how to explain it exactly.

"There are bound to be creative differences, but you two really hit it off when we all had dinner in New York that night." Arthur goes back to planting kisses along my stomach.

"We really did. . . . Pa, I know this might seem silly, but would you come to the set with me tomorrow? Maybe if you were there, it might defuse things a little? And I'd feel better having someone who is completely on my side." I feel stupid asking, but I'd like to see another friendly face when I look around.

"Sure, if you think it will help. Anything for you, Mrs. Miller. . . ." His kisses grow more urgent across my belly, moving up toward my breasts.

"Call me that again," I whisper, but there's no need for words now.

The bad dreams begin just before dawn. This time I am trapped and screaming to be let out of somewhere, but the words are all stuck in my throat, and I can't make a sound. There are faces in my dreams, but they aren't human—just monster faces, like devils'. I can't get away from them no matter how hard I try.

I wake up with a loud cry and my face wet with tears. Poor Arthur sits up in bed, startled out of his sleep. "What is it, baby? What's wrong? Did you have a bad dream?"

"Yes. I'm sorry I woke you, Papa." I'm trembling all over and my heart is racing as Arthur sweeps an arm over me.

"It's okay. I'm here, honey. I'm right here. Get some rest now," he moans sleepily. Within seconds his breathing slows, and his arm goes limp. I don't want to disturb him again, so I just lie there not moving until, through a crack where the drapes have parted, I see daylight coming over the horizon.

My body feels heavy, and I have that dragging pain in my stomach again. My head is woozy like I've been drinking, which I haven't—well, except a little champagne with my dinner last night. I just want the pain to go away and to get some proper sleep, but I can't take another pill now or I'll be late, and Larry will be angry with me.

Slipping out of bed, I wrap Arthur's blue cotton shirt around me. I'll find my script and read through it—maybe I'll even take a bath. That should clear all the fog from my brain.

Peeking out of the window, I can see it's another misty English morning. Yesterday we took another bicycle ride around Windsor, and on the way back a smart black car whipped past us, and it had the Queen's tiny flag flying on the hood. It went by us too quickly for me to catch a glimpse, but it must have been her. I would very much like to have seen her so I could wave or something. I'm still writing "arrange tea with the Queen" on Alan's list every day, but so far, no luck. I guess she's pretty busy with her day job.

Standing there wrapped in a soft peach-colored towel, I inspect my face in the bathroom mirror. There comes a time in every girl's life when you can begin to see the kind of old lady you're going to turn into. It's like a ghost face that is taking shape right under your girlish looks. I'm thirty now. It won't be long before I start to see that ghost face become my everyday look. I peer hard at my reflection, but I don't think there are more wrinkles than yesterday. I hope I still look okay on camera. I should check with Jack.

I drop the peach towel and take a long look at myself. My body is softer than it was, and it's bound to get worse as I get older. It's not like I'm going to be able to pour myself into these tight dresses forever. That's why I need to get where I'm going.

Oh, I've got a good plan. First there's Arthur and our babies—I want to be a mama more than anything in the whole world—and after that I want to do serious parts so that I don't have to look a certain way. Of course, every girl wants to look her best, but more than anything I want to be a great actress.

I wonder if the Queen thinks about getting older. I guess it doesn't matter so much in her job, although I'll bet people have plenty to say about what she wears and how she looks. It's the same with women the world over—everyone has an opinion about us. We're too fat or too thin, too dowdy or too trashy. You can't win. . . .

My fingertips are all wrinkled from being in the bathwater for so long. Once I get in, it's hard to persuade myself to get out. The bath hasn't helped at all with the fog in my brain. I just feel so exhausted all the time these days and my mind feels cloudy.

We're filming the dinner party scene today. That caused another row in rehearsals, as I told Larry straight: it will work better if there's real caviar and champagne for me to eat and drink. It's not that I want to eat caviar or drink champagne all day long—as a matter of fact I don't at all. But I know it will make the scene better. Elsie has to be silly and a little drunk, toasting President Taft with her champagne, while Larry's character is trying to make telephone calls in the background. Then of course he tries to seduce her. I have to be funny and bright, then look sweet . . . but sexy. It's sort of a slapstick scene, but all the time you have to think this girl is beautiful and deserves the best things in life. She's Cinderella, only Elsie has all her shoes accounted for. She's the kind of girl you should want to look after, but also make love to. It's important to get her just right so the audience is rooting for her. Without that, the whole picture will fall apart.

I sigh at the thought of going back to work, but at least with Arthur there, Larry wouldn't dare behave like he did the other day. All I need to do now is fix this face. The mirror glares back at me. I look like death. My face is puffy in this light and my eyes are dull. It's going to be quite the challenge for Whitey this morning.

"My dear, you pour yourself a glass of champagne and then you make an excited noise—like a child. Can you do that?"

The champagne has made me a little tipsy, as we've done so many takes of this scene already, but I just need to get this one part right and we can reset for the close-ups. The caviar is making me feel sick, and all I can taste is sour fish in my mouth.

It's been a difficult morning so far. First I spilled food down the front of my dress, and we had to cut so that I could change. Then I fluffed my lines a couple of times, and the first time I got the damn line right, the caviar fell straight off my fork and landed splat on my beautiful white dress again. Eventually the wardrobe girls had the idea to put a false front on the dress so we could whip that off if I dropped anything. I am trying to be as careful as can be, but now my stomach is beginning to churn, and if we don't get through this soon, I'll spoil the take by vomiting all over the pink couch.

I can feel Elsie Marina, though—the way she would be giddy with excitement and not used to champagne at all. Lifting the bottle, I pour the champagne until it fizzes over the top of my glass and then squeal as loud as I can. I sound like a kid going down a ride in the fairground, and Larry nods approvingly. Once we wrap the scene, I have to run back to my dressing room to use the bathroom, but we got it damn straight, although I overheard Larry complaining about the cost of all that booze and caviar. I'll bet, though, when we watch it back, he'll see it's all worth it. I don't say so, but I think I've really captured this girl on-screen. She's like a glass of champagne, fizzy and light but also sharp and funny. There's no heaviness to her at all. She glides and dances and smiles, but she's nobody's fool.

Yet when I look at Larry in his tuxedo with his monocle in one eye, I don't believe him. He's playing dress-up with his silly accent. It's not real, and I can see it. In my mind the Prince Regent of Carpathia is an elegant and dignified man, but underneath he's kind of lonely and in search of love. That's how I see him. Yet Larry is stomping around the place most days with his fake accent and a chest full of medals, and any fool can see that he's not real. There's no depth to his character, no life beneath the lines.

I would never mention it, though. He can be so rude to me, but if Marilyn Monroe started telling Laurence Olivier how to improve his performance, I guess everyone would have plenty to say about it.

It's so funny that, before we started working together, he was my idol. I thought he was just the greatest. When he played Heathcliff, he was so natural that I believed every single word that came out of his mouth. Whenever I've seen him on-screen, he looks so handsome and romantic, his character feels real and filled with life, but with *our* movie—the one I need him to get right—it's all wrong. I don't get it.

I button my lip, though, and say I think it all looks fine. It's an uneasy truce, and I don't want to have another fight about it. All I can do is concentrate on my own performance. I'm trying so hard to get things right on set and not be a nuisance to anyone. It's hard, though, because Larry does tend to place the camera where it works for his good side, and that usually makes me look worse. Then every other scene is a close-up on him, where I'm always in the background somewhere, or if the camera comes close it's usually on my ass.

I thought we'd be partners, talking through creative decisions and having fun with it. But instead, every day is another battle.

. . .

When we stop to reset the camera for my close-up, I turn to smile at Arthur, but he's standing to one side deep in conversation with Larry. The two of them are laughing and joking—at one point, Arthur pats Larry on his shoulder like they're old friends, and I feel betrayed. I wanted him to come to the set to support me, and here he is making nice with Olivier. He's not even watching me.

I feel so alone here. Everyone else has worked together before, or they know all the same people. They don't know what to say to me, so whenever they see me coming, they scurry away or speak to me in that strange too-polite way that English people have. I thought it meant they wanted to be friends, but it really doesn't.

When we broke for lunch on the very first day, I walked into the studio canteen at Pinewood and the whole place went quiet. There were hundreds and hundreds of people there, but you could have heard a pin drop.

It was like one of those scenes in westerns where someone walks into a saloon and everyone is watching to see what will happen next. I felt so self-conscious that I ran straight back to my dressing room and ate lunch all by myself. It just makes me so nervous to be stared at like that—everyone here looks at me like I'm a statue they can talk about. Oh, this is right or this is wrong. Sometimes I overhear the crew discussing my face or my hair, talking about my dress or the way I'm standing, like I'm nothing but a piece of marble for them to gaze at all day long.

Larry calls "ACTION," and I do the scene again for my close-up. The champagne is making me even more woozy, and suddenly the exhaustion kicks in and all the lines that I'd delivered perfectly well earlier won't come out of my mouth.

"To President Traft . . ." I say instead of "President Taft." It's such a stupid mistake, and I see Larry raise his eyebrows. We cut and I smooth down the front of my dress and rehearse my lines again, raising the champagne glass and saying, "To President Taft." I get it just right, and when Larry calls for "ACTION," I feel confident.

I deliver the line crisply and note perfect, but the champagne spills down the front of my dress and I could cry. We break again to swap out the front of my gown, and then I get ready for my close-up once more. A horrible rippling cramp almost makes me double over with pain, but I bite down on my lip a little until it passes and look around for Arthur.

I'd hoped having him on set would make Larry treat me better, but he's just as rude as before. Every time I get irritated over something, I can see Arthur standing to the side, laughing and joking with him.

When we take a break, I get mad about it. "Pa, how can you stand around joking with Larry when you hear how he speaks to me on set. He treats me like I'm a model that he can make do silly poses for him, rather than an actress putting in her performance just the same as he's doing."

Arthur hushes me with his kisses and says sweetly, "Baby, I'm just trying to smooth things along. He's your director, though, so maybe he has a point at times."

"You're taking *his* side?" I say sharply, turning away from Arthur.

"Hey . . . I'm not on his side. I'm just saying that maybe Larry isn't the enemy. You all want the same thing here, honey." He pulls me back to him and kisses me on my cheek while I bite down on my bottom lip, not wanting to argue with him.

I let it go for now, but I don't understand it—the way Larry talks down to me, yet Arthur can still be perfectly nice to him and see his point of view? Shouldn't he want to punch him on the nose or something? Not that I want him to go around punching people, but I just want to feel that he's truly on my side.

After a short break we go back on set and try the scene again for a close-up, but it doesn't work. I get my part right, but this time there's a problem with the lights.

"Let's take five minutes while we get the lights fixed." Larry frowns at me as if I was the one who broke them.

"Yes, Mr. Sir," I whisper to myself. I've started calling Larry "Mr. Sir" behind his back. It's childish, I know, but he treats me like a child, so I respond that way. That Norma Jeane stubbornness comes out, and there's nothing I can do about it. I go back to my dressing room and slam the door on them all. When the boy comes to tell me they're ready, I sit there for a full ten minutes before I move just for the hell of it. After all, it's my damn production and I won't be treated like I'm the "hired help" around here.

Eventually we get the scene finished, and there's not much more left to shoot today, which is a good thing, as I'm running out of patience. My stomach hurts real bad, and I'm so exhausted I could just lie down on the floor and sleep.

"Let's take a quick break and then reset for the final close-ups," Larry says in his booming voice that I'm sick of hearing. Arthur gives me an encouraging smile from across the set, but he's perfectly happy chatting away with Larry, and I'm beginning to wish I hadn't asked him to come, so I head back to my dressing room alone and in a furious mood.

My head is splitting, and I'm so tired right now that I could just curl up and cry. But I have to get the close-ups right, especially as we paid out for all this real champagne and caviar. We can't afford to waste it. I've had so much of it already that I feel sick to my stomach.

I've barely sat down when there's a tap on my dressing room door and a voice yells, "We're ready for you on set, Miss Monroe."

Tears prickle behind my eyes and I take a long look at myself in the dressing room mirror and put my head in my hands. I can't do this anymore. I'm just worn out and I want to go home.

I don't know where Arthur has got to—still making nice with Larry, I expect, while I'm in here falling apart. I wish we'd never come here. I should have stayed in New York.

Paula stands in a corner of the room, her face pinched with worry. "Is there anything I can do? Do you want to try another exercise to find your character?" she says earnestly.

"No . . ." Tears spill down my cheeks, and I look up at her in the reflection of the mirror. "I can't do it. I can't go back out there. . . . What am I going to do?"

I don't feel like Elsie Marina—all light and full of life—and I don't know how to make things better. I've tried working with Paula on my character between takes, but I'm so exhausted right now that nothing is helping.

I can't go back out there like this, and I can't stand to be talked down to, or scolded, or humiliated in front of the crew again. I don't know what to do. . . . A wave of horrible panic starts to flow over me, and suddenly I can't catch my breath and my eyes go funny. I feel sick and dizzy, and I start to shake.

The next thing I know there's another knock on the door, but it opens before I can say anything, and my business partner, Milton, comes in. "Hey, honey. They're ready for you. . . ."

I can't even look at him, but he knows me so well. Standing back, he sees instantly that I'm in trouble.

"What's wrong?" he asks. "What is it? Do you need me to fetch Arthur?"

"I can't do it! I can't go back out there. I really don't feel well and I didn't sleep at all last night and now I can't remember my lines. I just can't do it, Milton. Don't make me go out there again. . . . Please don't make me do it." Tears are blinding my eyes, and I want to run away from all of this and never come back.

Milton kneels down by the side of my chair and puts a hand on my arm. "Baby, listen to me—you *have* to go back out there. We have to finish this picture. If we can just get this movie done, then we're made. The studio will know that Marilyn Monroe Productions is a real thing. We talked about this. C'mon, honey. I know you're tired, but it's just a few close-ups, that's all; then you'll be done for the day. You can do this. You can do anything. You're Marilyn Monroe! Come on now!"

I want to believe him, but I know this time he's wrong. I really can't go back out there. My voice is trembling and my stomach churns with the combination of too much caviar and the worry of it all. I fix Milton with a teary gaze. "I'm worn out. I've gone straight from making *Bus Stop* to getting married and now working on this. I need a break. I can't work like this. My mind is all foggy. I can't remember my lines or where I'm supposed to stand even. . . . Please, Milton. . . ."

"I tell you what. How about you take a little rest now—I'll tell them you need more time, okay? And then we'll get the shots later today? Please, honey?" He shoots a sharp glance at Paula. "See if you can do something to help her . . ." he says, and with that Milton is gone.

I know he's probably right that we need to get these shots done, but the pain in my stomach is getting much worse—like a red-hot clawing inside me every time I get a cramp. My head is in my hands and my fingers keep pulling at my hair. I just want this to be over.

Suddenly Paula is standing behind my chair, patting me on my shoulder.

"Help me. . . . I don't know what to do!" I cry. Tears spill down my cheeks. I feel so desperate that I'd try anything that might just get me through these scenes.

"I have something that might help. . . ." Paula moves away and begins rooting through her enormous suede handbag. After a long moment, she pulls out a small brown bottle and hands it to me. "Here . . . take two of these."

"What are they?" I ask as I take the bottle of pills from her hand.

"They're your 'break glass in case of emergency' pills, honey. They will pep you right up. You can't take too many of them, but they really work." Paula pats at my shoulder again and begins pouring water from a jug on the dressing table.

I unscrew the cap of the brown bottle and tip a couple of the tiny purple pills into the palm of my hand and stare at them for a second.

"You'll feel better, I promise! Now swallow and you'll feel fine." She hands me a glass of water and I take a long cool drink. Then I wait for the little purple pills to kick in because Marilyn has to sparkle.

A girl's gotta do what a girl's gotta do in this world.

LILIBET

1956

"Do you remember the first time you came to stay with us at Balmoral?" I ask Philip quietly as the car sweeps through the Scottish hills. I don't know why I felt the need to ask that question, but suddenly I could picture him quite clearly in his naval uniform—both of us so very young and full of plans for the future.

"Yes, of course I remember. I was fresh from the war and your family was quite keen to inspect my table manners." Philip chuckles to himself at the thought of it.

"They weren't inspecting you. . . . They were merely trying to make sure that I was making the right choice," I say with an inviting smile, for I so want us to have a lovely summer before he goes off on his tour for four months. I shall miss him dreadfully, and I do know that underneath it all, he is still a little cross with me for suspecting him of poor behavior.

"Ha! The right choice indeed." He looks at me with an enormous grin on his face and throws his head back in delight. "Well, it felt very much as if I was being given the once-over and found lacking in many areas. A homeless prince with a mother locked away in a sanatorium and a father living with his mistress—not to mention my sisters having married German officers. I'm sure they all agreed that I was a complete disaster, and you would be much better off with some nice English duke."

"They did not, and luckily for you neither did I."

"Yes, I suppose that's true. You were always on my side," he says with a sigh. Neither of us could have known that on his very first visit to Balmoral, for all our excitement at being together, that only six years later my dear papa would be dead, and our lives changed in an instant. We thought we had so much more time to explore each other and make our family strong.

"I'm still on your side, Philip," I say softly, but he merely shrugs his shoulders and stares gloomily out of the car window.

In the distance, I can see the turrets and towers of Balmoral Castle, and I feel a sense of anticipation for what the summer might bring us. I turn to look out of the rear window at the car traveling behind, which contains Mummy and Margaret and our two very excited children, Charles and Anne. I can't pretend there haven't been tensions between us all the past few weeks, but hopefully some good Scottish air and outdoor pursuits will sort us out and bring a fresh perspective. Margaret can barely bring herself to speak to me at the moment, and the way we left things still stings when I think about it. I do hope we can find a way forward over the coming days.

There is something quite liberating about the moment we all pile out of the cars and into the entrance of Balmoral Castle. It has none of the rather stiff and serious entrances of the London palaces, but rather a doorway crowded with a good supply of Wellington boots and waders, complete with a grand assortment of fishing rods and stout walking sticks. It reminds us all that we are free to wander—spending hours on the Scottish hills or on the banks of the River Dee.

I go to take hold of Charles's hand, but he shrugs off my attempt and grabs hold of Philip's arm. "Papa, may we have a picnic tomorrow if the weather is good?" he says, racing around

Philip's legs and almost tumbling over in his haste to get inside the castle.

"Yes, I should think so. And if it's a calm day, I'll take you both out in the little rowing boat. Would you like that?"

"Yes!" both children cry out, for this is what they love. Philip is quite natural at making everything an adventure for them, and it's a skill that I envy.

"I'll come up and read you both a story in a bit. Would you like that?" I offer them with a guilty heart, as I seem to have to make excuses to them most days.

"No, Mummy, we're going to play with the go-carts. Papa promised us," Anne says adamantly.

"Oh . . . well, that will be fun, I'm sure. Papa is very good at playing." I feel a tiny twinge of sadness at her words. More and more these days the children seem to turn to Philip or my mother whereas they always used to cry for me.

"Hurry, Papa!" Charles shouts, and the two children race ahead, giddy with excitement.

Philip gives me a rueful glance and an apologetic shrug of his shoulders as he follows behind them. Then all I can hear is the sound of squealing and childish giggles from a distance. He does love to tease them and race around the place. He has a seemingly infinite amount of energy for playing games with the children, and they adore him for it. I, on the other hand, always appear to be too busy for them, constantly having to tell them that I can't play now and to come back later. A pang of regret surfaces from deep inside as I think back to those happy days as a naval officer's wife in Malta, where I could spend hours with our children doing jigsaw puzzles or playing on the beach. Having friends over for lunch and spending long lazy afternoons chatting. Those carefree days with no red boxes or official engagements were all too brief. The problem with an idyllic life is that often one doesn't realize it is until it's taken away from you. The degree of happiness seemed perfectly natural to us all, and it is only now when everything has changed that we understand how fortunate we all were. I miss that life so very much.

As I walk along the corridor of red carpet, I feel watched over by the dozens of stag heads that adorn the wall—with their glassy staring eyes and enormous great antlers—each one a hunting trophy from times gone by. My father shot the one at the end of the corridor, and Philip has two trophies up on the wall now. There's even one that I bagged many years ago. And very proud of it I was too.

Pausing at the bottom of the staircase, I glance up at the white marble statue of Prince Albert. It is said that Queen Victoria would have the servants turn it slowly as she walked upstairs to bed so that her beloved husband could watch her go. She missed him terribly, and her heart was quite broken when he died.

"That thing gives me the creeps." Philip appears at my shoulder. "He's always watching me."

"I wonder what he would think of us all now," I murmur almost to myself, as I am suddenly distracted by thinking of my great-great-grandparents and their lives that seem so far removed from my own.

"What are you two looking at?" Margaret hurries along the corridor and comes to a halt by the side of us. She is wearing a pale blue skirt with matching jacket with a pearl brooch on the lapel that suits her beautifully. I am about to say how nice she looks, but her gaze is cool and she doesn't smile at all, so I am definitely not forgiven.

"Oh, nothing. Philip feels a little haunted by Prince Albert, I fear. Happy birthday, you!" I smile brightly, hoping to encourage a reconciliation, and I plant a friendly kiss on my sister's cheek.

"Please don't mention it. Twenty-six is so very old. I'm nearly thirty and that's positively ancient," Margaret says with a grimace. "I shan't be celebrating this birthday at all."

"I'm thirty . . . and if you don't mind, I'd like to believe that

I'm not quite ancient just yet." I doubt that her words were entirely accidental, and the barb was certainly intended for its target. It will be a very long summer break if this behavior is going to continue.

"Oh, so you are. Bad luck," she says with a sullen pout, and runs up the stairs away from us.

"Problem?" Philip asks warily as we are left alone again.

I let out a small sigh and shake my head with exasperation. I have no wish to tell Philip what my sister and I have fallen out about and dredge that whole conversation up again. "I've upset Margaret. It's nothing—I'll deal with it later. Anyway, I'd better get on with my papers. What are you going to do with yourself this afternoon?"

"I thought I might take an ax to this statue. We could replace it with one of me so that you can remember what I look like when I'm away." Philip grins at the thought of it.

"Don't you dare touch Prince Albert," I say with a mock sternness, and am surprised when he kisses me rather fondly on my cheek.

"You'll just have to do your best to remember me without a bloody great statue watching over you." His eyes twinkle with laughter at the thought of it, and I am still giggling as I walk away toward my study, where the red box will be waiting for me.

Papers to read and sign—the latest briefings on the happenings over the Suez Canal. That particular situation seems to be getting worse by the day, and I'm not sure that Mr. Eden knows how to extricate us without the risk of a full-blown conflict. I do sometimes wonder if he wants a war so that he can prove himself the equal of Winston Churchill in some way. I hope not, for this country has suffered enough and we very much need peace and stability for a good long time.

My desk is placed close to the window so that in a rare break from work I can look out at the rolling hills and imagine myself walking on them all alone and perfectly peaceful. There is something quite transcendent about the grandness of the natural world in this area, and one can quite understand why the Romantic poets fell in love with immense hills and mountains, a wide rolling sky and the sense of something much greater than yourself at play. There is very little that cannot be made better by a good long walk, I find.

Unlocking the red leather box, I take out a pile of brown cardboard folders and stack them neatly on my desk. It takes quite some time to work my way through each folder and read the official papers that are contained within. Some of the folders contain top secret briefings from the Foreign Office, which are interesting but also worrying. I do wonder whether having access to so much information is a good thing for one's mind, but there is no other choice. I am the keeper of all the country's secrets and unable to say a word about them to anyone. Not even Philip can be told what is in the red boxes. It's the most difficult part of the job, I find, and the part that makes it such a lonely burden some days. There is nobody to confide in, and I am required to remain impartial and not speak out on anything. History is littered with kings and queens who have not taken that lesson to heart, and it has often cost them their lives.

Of course, most days the brown cardboard folders contain bundles of very dull dispatches about things that I don't fully understand. New laws, couched in legal language that makes them terribly difficult to read and even harder to grasp with their endless paragraphs and subsections. I sign where necessary and package them all back up, locking the box, ready for my private secretary, Michael, to return them safely to the government offices.

Leaning back in my wooden chair, I gaze out at the view of the hills for a moment. Outside my window I can see Philip and the children racing some go-cart-like contraptions along the garden path. They are shouting and giggling as the little carts speed down the pathway. Philip looks quite comical seated astride one of the things, as it was built for a child to use, and I can't help but smile at the sight of him. My happy little family, I think, and hope that they are and remain so. I could go outside and join in with their games now, yet part of me likes to sit here and watch them having fun.

Next to my red box is a selection of the daily newspapers that have been laid out for me to look at, and I glance quickly through the main news items, flicking through the pages. Endless reports and speculation on what may or may not happen with the Suez crisis. Will we take military action, and if so, when? The tension seems to be spilling over the entire country as people wait to see if there will be another war.

On one or two of the front pages there are some rather lovely photographs of Margaret taken in Clarence House to celebrate her birthday. She's wearing her favorite pink tulle evening dress with embroidered flowers and sequins trailing down the front of the skirt. She looks entirely lovely, but to my eyes there is a loneliness etched into her face that makes me feel terribly guilty. I vow to make things up with her.

I carry on flicking through the pages of the newspapers when my heart suddenly skips a beat as I see the words that are splashed across the top of the page: THE DUKE OF SOHO?

A gossip columnist has got hold of that same silly rumor that Margaret was peddling and has splashed a nasty little story out of it, designed to sting.

As I read the horrible sniping words, I feel a hot flush of humiliation. The article accuses my husband of nothing in particular, but the implication is obvious. There is specific mention of his lunch club and the goings-on in Soho on Thursday afternoons, plus an obvious reference to Mike Parker as his accomplice, as it were. Yet apart from the fact of Philip's attendance at lunch, there is nothing substantial to the story.

I want to stop myself from reading on, but something compels me to keep on going. The story is designed to tantalize and imply all kinds of knowledge without actually relaying any of it. It's a spiteful piece of writing, and I feel quite bitter and furious about it. How dare they write these things about my husband. . . . I can feel a terrible anger burning inside me at the injustice of it all. My lips tremble, and I blow out tiny exasperated breaths to calm myself down.

A shriek from outside in the garden distracts me from the nasty little story for a moment, and I glance out of the window just in time to see Philip picking up Charles and throwing our darling little boy over his shoulder, wriggling and squealing with delight, while he carries our daughter Anne with his other arm. They are all laughing and having such a jolly time that I immediately want to rip the newspaper into tiny shreds and bury it somewhere where nobody will ever read it, but it's much too late for that. Spiteful words are like flames on dry wood. If one is not careful, they may set everything ablaze.

Philip was so very cross with me for daring to raise this matter after my conversation with Margaret, but now that it's printed in a gossip column, I fear it won't be long before questions are being asked about the state of *our* marriage. After all, he is about to go off to the other side of the world for four months. Much as I want to bundle up this newspaper and use it for the fire, I know that I will have to do something.

I sigh, a long slow exhale of misery as I realize that I will have to speak to Philip again and this time we must formulate a proper response to quash these rumors before they get worse. A feeling of dread sinks into the pit of my stomach as I try to think of how I might raise this matter delicately—without us having an argument over it. It seems so ridiculous that people can make up complete nonsense about us, and we should have to confront that nonsense as if it's reality. If these people could only understand the harm they do gossiping as if we are barely human and therefore cannot be hurt by their spite and venom. I feel furious about it, yet at the same time, if I am being perfectly honest, there is a small part of me that believes in that old saying: "There is no smoke without fire."

I'm about to crush the offending page of the newspaper into a ball and throw it into the wastepaper basket when I notice that underneath that particular piece of literary venom is another paragraph hinting that all is not well on the set of Laurence Olivier's new film. It accuses the actress Marilyn Monroe of turning up late and causing them endless problems with her inability to act. I cannot help but read to the end of the story and feel quite ashamed of myself for doing so. Next to the column is a photograph of her smiling rather shyly into the camera, which was taken somewhere in Windsor, and for a moment I wonder if this glamorous actress is reading about herself and also feeling quite furious. I don't expect that I have very much in common with a Hollywood star, but at this moment I do feel a sort of kinship, as we two share the same experience at the hands of this gossip columnist. I wonder how her husband copes with all the press attention. It's a difficult life being married to a woman always in the public eye, although I believe that Mr. Miller has a certain celebrity of his own.

The gossip is quite awful, though, and my lips purse in a tight grimace as I fold up the newspaper carefully and try to decide what action to take. As I sit there chewing on the inside of my bottom lip and contemplating what to do next, I am suddenly aware that I am no longer alone.

"Oh, Michael . . . it's you."

My private secretary comes fully into view and stands to the side of my desk. "Ma'am, would you like me to take the box if you've quite finished? There's nothing else for you today except Mr. Eden and his wife have confirmed their visit for the week after next."

"Yes, Michael . . . and could you get rid of this, please?" He looks puzzled for a moment as I hand him the newspaper, but he's too polite and well trained to question anything that I might ask of him.

"Yes, ma'am." He gives a little bow and begins to move toward the door.

The gossip column has infuriated me, and I feel quite incensed about it, not only on Philip's behalf but also on Miss Monroe's. I have no idea if the problems being alluded to on the film set are true or not, but I do feel a flash of righteous indignation that even if they are, it is her private business and not to be repeated as some awful tittle-tattle. Before I can stop myself, I find myself saying, "That charity film premiere in October . . . could we add Miss Marilyn Monroe to the list of invitees? I believe that she's currently filming in England."

I'm not sure what I hope to achieve by inviting her, as she may be perfectly awful, yet I feel sorry for her being a stranger in this country and having nasty gossip written without a care. The photographs I've seen of her so far show her being very beguiling, but also a little shy, I thought. I imagine she must find all the attention quite overwhelming at times. Anyway, I shall invite her to the premiere and see for myself.

Michael's eyebrows shoot up to the top of his head, but he merely nods and says, "Of course, ma'am. I'll send the appropriate communications today."

"Good . . . and maybe this week we might watch one of Miss Monroe's films, as I don't believe that I've ever seen her work. Have you?"

"Yes, one or two of them are rather amusing." Poor Michael is staring at me as if I've gone quite mad, but the invitation will be sent out to her, and we shall have our film night this week. In the meantime, I have to get ready to celebrate Margaret's birthday, and at some point, I will have to choose the right moment to speak to Philip about that newspaper story however much I dread doing so.

Some people have nothing better to do than gossip and invent complete nonsense. Part of me is completely sure that it's all fabricated to sell newspapers or to make an amusing story at dinner.

Yet as I watch Philip walking back toward the house with our children hanging off him, I can't help but wonder. . . .

NORMA JEANE

1956

Another day is over, and honestly the sooner I can get this movie done with the better. I really don't feel at all well, and my stomach hurts all the time now. Every day is just one long exhausting scene after another, and I really wish we could finish up and go home to New York.

Since we landed in England, Arthur is finding my moods difficult, and I know that I can be a monster to live with when I get like this. It's just that I'm under so much pressure and I feel so alone here. I'm going to make it up to him, you'll see. Starting tonight . . .

We're going out to a dinner party, and I'll just be Mrs. Arthur Miller for the evening and let him shine. They're all his friends anyway. Theater people who adore him and hang on his every word. He's a genius, though, and deserves all the praise. Imagine being able to write a whole play, and then actors bringing it to life on a stage, and you can sit there and think: *I did that*. That's how smart my husband is. He can just make up things out of nothing. He's always scribbling away his important thoughts in his notebook. I bet it's filled with clever ideas and beautiful words like poetry—not like my little poems that I scribble down on napkins and receipts for things. They're all sad, and what can you say about sadness? Not much. It's not very interesting.

I get out of that damn white dress and back into my cigarette pants and shirt. Alan, my publicist, has brought my mail to the studio for me, and I flick through it for anything interesting. It's mostly fan mail and business stuff that can wait.

Suddenly I notice a bulky white envelope that seems like it might be important. Inside are a number of folded-up pages and an elegant white card with dark blue writing on it. It's an invitation from the Empire Theatre to the Royal Film Performance to be held on October 29 at 8:30 p.m., and someone has written my name, MISS MARILYN MONROE, while underneath is printed in large letters: FOR PRESENTATION TO HER MAJESTY THE QUEEN IN THE CIRCLE LOUNGE.

Letting out a tiny squeal, I dance around in a whirl of excitement until my dresser comes in to see if I'm all right. The other pages in the envelope are lists of events in the run-up, but the Queen will be there only on that one day, so that's the only thing I care about. There's a long list of instructions for how to dress—"Ladies should dress modestly and should not wear decorations." The way they talk, it makes me sound like a Christmas tree. I guess they don't want people wearing more jewels than the Queen—although it's pretty unlikely, I'd say.

It's nearly the end of August, and the premiere is only two months away. I have to find a dress to wear, and not just any dress, but a dress fit for a queen. I can probably get one made in time if I get right on it. What do you wear to meet a royal? I don't know, but someone will tell me. I have to look perfect—not a hair out of place. The entire world will see these pictures of Marilyn meeting Queen Elizabeth. I have no idea what to say to her, but I'll think of something. The gossip columns are all full of stories about her husband, and I know what it's like to have nasty things written about you, so maybe we'd have a lot to talk about if we got the chance.

I have to look the best that I've ever looked because I want everyone who's ever treated me badly to see a picture of me shaking hands with the Queen of England.

Look what Marilyn can do—and you ain't seen nuthin' yet. . . .

The invitation to the royal premiere has made me happier than I thought possible, but I still feel so weak and tired that I just want to crawl back into bed. I took a long soak in the bath with plenty of bubbles, just the way I like it, and then I began to get ready. It's quite the job putting Marilyn together for a night out, and I want Arthur to feel especially proud of me this evening. He doesn't say so, but I think he wants his friends to be a little jealous of him.

Arthur brings me up a martini, and suddenly another wave of exhaustion hits me. My stomach is still cramping badly and the last thing I feel like doing is going to a party with a load of strangers. I know Pa will be disappointed if I say that I don't want to go out this evening, as he's been counting on me to meet his friends here.

"Here you are, baby." Arthur hands me my cocktail and wraps his arms around me. "I'm glad to have you all to myself for a night. Seems like it's all been about your movie these past few weeks," he says softly, and although he doesn't mean to be nasty, I feel a little scolded.

"Well, this evening is all about you and your friends. I'm just plain old Mrs. Arthur Miller. I want to make you proud of me, Pa." I plant kisses along his jawline as we stand there folded into each other.

"Mmm . . . you smell good enough to eat," he whispers in my ear as the martini fizzes around my blood, and I smile back at him. "I can't wait to show you off, Mrs. Miller. And we're going to be late, so I'd better let you get ready." He gives me a long lingering kiss and then reluctantly lets me go. I hear his footsteps going back downstairs as I take a long slug of the martini and fix my lipstick.

He's right. We have been spending all our time on my movie, so this evening I owe it to Arthur to make a good impression on his friends. Inside I feel so dog-tired that I'd honestly like to curl up in that soft white bed right now, but I can't let Pa down. Reaching into my makeup case, I fish out the little brown bottle of Paula's "break glass in case of emergency" pills. Tipping the tiny purple pills out into the palm of my hand, I swallow them down with the last of the martini. Then I wait for a few moments. . . .

Here she comes. . . .

I feel like the old Marilyn again—full of laughter and joy. I look like her too. My favorite black silk slip dress with its spaghetti straps, long diamond earrings, and a pop of my favorite red lipstick. I've bought some Floris London perfume in rose geranium. I heard that it's the same brand that the Queen wears, so I had to try it, and on one of my days off I went to London and bought the most elegant suede gloves from the store that she uses. Maybe I'm turning into a royal person. The thought makes me giggle out loud again. Honestly, just one little invitation has changed my whole mood. Even Sir Larry couldn't annoy me this evening. I practice a curtsy in the mirror and say, "Your Majesty . . ." as if she's right there in the room with me.

I've noticed that everyone here talks about her like she's a country and not a woman made out of flesh and blood, like the rest of us. It's a strange thing to be a queen, I guess. A bit like being a movie star—in the end, it's all costumes and performances, isn't it? Maybe I'll end up playing a queen in a movie some day and this will be my research.

I dab a little Floris perfume behind my ears and then between my breasts. You need just the smallest amount—I like men to smell my perfume only when they get close enough. All I needed was a martini and a couple of little purple pills to make the pain and tiredness go away, and here we are. Even the British weather is cooperating this evening, as a warm scented breeze drifts in through the open window. It's a perfect moment.

I slip my feet into a pair of black suede Ferragamo shoes, and suddenly I stand straighter. There she is in the mirror, staring back at me. Hair like white cotton candy, Elizabeth Arden lips, and sparkling eyes. You can't imagine the effort that goes into it. Layers of Erno Laszlo cream, sometimes Vaseline to keep my foundation from drying out. All sealed in with a dab of a Max Factor Crème Puff to stop any trace of a shiny nose or a sweaty forehead. Then eyelash curlers and a cake of mascara. The little brush painting my lashes: it's like painting a picture. Filling in the eyes and the cheeks. Last of all the mouth—bright red lipstick—and there she is: *Hello, Marilyn, my old friend and protector.*

She's so brave and ready to take on the world. Not a worry about meeting new people or whether Arthur's friends will like her. I feel suddenly nervous about Pa's theater friends—some of them are very important people who pay to have plays put on, and I don't want to say the wrong thing. I had planned to be just plain old Mrs. Arthur Miller this evening and fade into the background, but Marilyn is here now, and it would be a shame to waste her. I just hope she stays around a bit longer so we can all get through this movie shoot and go home. When I get scared or I'm in pain, it's hard—on those days I can only find Norma Jeane, and she's too little and frightened to do anything. Lately Marilyn has been kind of flickering on and off when I reach for her. I guess it all comes down to how much sleep I get.

The martini and pills have gone straight to my head. I haven't eaten much of anything today, but before I left work, I saw the rushes of our champagne and caviar scene, and it was everything I'd hoped it would be.

When you see Elsie up there on-screen, you should believe this girl is a little tipsy and playful. She's helping herself to food and champagne, but all the time she's performing for herself and giggling. The audience has to love her being a fish out of water in that great palace. I'd love to ask the Queen what it's like living in a palace—she would have been a great help with my research for this movie. I was right about that scene, and Larry didn't give me any credit for it.

Arthur suddenly appears in the doorway of our bedroom to hurry me along. "The car is here, honey."

"I'm ready." I blow him a kiss from across the room as I lean over our bed to pick up my wrap, and off we go down the stairs.

I can feel the eyes of strangers watching us leave. The staff all try to be invisible, but I always know when someone is watching me. I guess I'm a good story to tell. Which me is in the story, though? That's the question. Who do they see when they bring me breakfast in bed, or serve us dinner in the evening? Which me are they spying on, especially in the case of Mr. Hunt, our security guard? I make sure I draw all the drapes in the house so he can't look inside and see what I'm doing. It makes no difference, and tiny details seem to end up in the newspapers every day. I wish they'd found us the cottage I had dreamed about. I like my privacy too much, and people always gossip about me.

Just the other day some mean columnist wrote a whole piece about how awful I was, turning up late for work and driving Sir Larry crazy. I hate that kind of spiteful chatter. It's just so nasty, and most of the time it's completely made-up. I try to brush it off, but I'd be lying if I said that it didn't hurt my feelings or make me mad when it's all a pack of lies. Now I just think to myself: *Well, honey, you try to do my job with no sleep and the worst period in the world.* I was bleeding so bad and I had to stand there in that damn white dress all day long. People can be so mean, but I try not to let it bother me. Anyway, I deserve to have some fun tonight and let my hair down a little. I'm sure Arthur's friends are as nice as he is.

The car pulls out of the driveway of Parkside House and we are on our way to London. Since we arrived, we really haven't done that much socializing. I've either been busy working or just wanted to stay home quietly with Arthur, having dinner and playing music. I glance up at Windsor Castle as the car turns the corner, but there's no little flag on the tower. She's not at home, and I wonder what she's doing right now.

Leaning back in my seat, my fingers threaded through Arthur's, everything feels so fine. I love being with my husband and spending quiet evenings together, but now those little purple pills have worked their magic, I'm in the mood for a party. I hope that there are fun people there because I'd like to dance the night away.

We drive for what seems like an age, before the car glides to a halt outside one of those fancy houses somewhere in London. I never know where anything is here. The areas all sound very grand to me, and I repeat them to myself under my breath. KENsington. MAYfair. BelGRAvia. I can never pronounce them the same way that English people do, but I'm trying. I could ask where we are, but it hardly matters, as we probably won't ever come back here.

The house itself is all white with two stone pillars standing guard over a glossy black front door. It's in a row of houses, and the entire street kind of curves around like a horseshoe. I think that's so elegant—the way they have houses all joined together like that. I'd like to walk along the street and look at them all—to see the ways in which they're different—but Arthur is already ringing the doorbell so I slip my hand inside his and wait.

The woman who opens the door is older than I am, I would guess. Probably closer to Arthur's age. She's tall, kind of willowy, with no bust to speak of, and very little makeup that I can see.

"Darling . . . how lovely to see you," the woman says as she kisses my husband on both cheeks, before turning to me and smiling for a beat too long. "And, Marilyn, welcome to London." Her name is Mary but I don't catch the rest of it. I don't know who she is, other than she obviously knows Arthur.

"It's very nice to be here. You have a lovely home," I say, and she laughs.

"Oh, this isn't my home. Nigel's my cousin. . . ." I recognize the name as the guy who backs a lot of plays here, and who is also a good friend of Arthur's. I just smile that full Marilyn dazzle at her as we move inside.

Mary is wearing a lilac silk evening dress that covers her arms and comes right up to her neck. It suits her, although I've seen nuns wear less clothing. When I slip off my wrap, she takes in my black slip dress with its little spaghetti straps, and I see a particular look cross her face. "That's a beautiful dress, Marilyn. Only you could get away with that." Then she giggles like a schoolgirl. Her teeth are bunched together—crowded in her mouth—and it makes her smile seem a little lopsided. They'd sort that out for her in Hollywood straightaway, I think to myself, but of course I'd never say such a thing.

"Come in, you two—I'll introduce you to everyone." Mary leads the way into an elegant drawing room. It's got a very high ceiling and enormous glass windows. There's a lovely fireplace in the center of one wall with logs piled in it, but of course the fire isn't lit. On the opposite wall is a long green couch with some low tables on either side. There's music playing in the background, but I don't recognize the song. There are six or seven people standing around in the center of the room, smoking cigarettes and drinking cocktails. A young girl in a waitress outfit is flitting between them, collecting empty glasses. I feel like I'm dressed all wrong. The women here are all covered up and wearing very little makeup. I'm kind of wishing that Marilyn had stayed home tonight, but it's too late now. The men seem glad of her appearance, though, and there's nothing for it but to plaster that big old smile on my face and stand tall—well, as tall as I can manage, which is around five feet four inches, although I can look these men right in the eye wearing my Ferragamo heels. In fact, I look down on the bald spots of one or two of them, which I don't expect they'd like at all if they knew about it.

"We're just having a drink, and then we'll go through for dinner. Martinis all right?" I nod at Mary, but she's already walking away. A man on the far side of the room suddenly spots Arthur, and the room erupts in a lot of backslapping and handshaking. I say hello to them and stand there politely, on my best behavior. Arthur rattles off names as the men lean in a little too close to kiss me on the cheek. They're his friends, I guess, so I give them the full Marilyn treatment. I want him to feel proud of me. Some men like it if other men find their wife attractive as long as they don't cross the line, you know.

Pa puts a protective arm around my waist as we stand there in the middle of a group of men.

"How's the play coming along?" one of them asks Arthur.

"Oh, you know how it is. Last-minute hitches, but we'll be ready. It's been a busy time with the opening, and of course my wife is making a movie here . . ." Pa accepts a light for his cigarette from one of the guys so he doesn't have to let go of my waist. I feel a tiny thrill at him describing me as his wife. I like feeling as if I belong to him.

They envy him, I can tell, and he enjoys this envy. But these men can't begin to imagine being woken up in the middle of the night because my dreams are so bad I can't stop crying. And they wouldn't want that reality, either. They only want fantasy Marilyn, where I always look like this, smiling and available to them. Never aging or getting cranky. Well, Arthur could certainly tell them a thing or two about my moods some days. If I haven't slept well, there's no living with me.

I'm introduced to their wives and girlfriends. I smile and smile, but the only words I speak are "hello" and "thank you." Mary returns carrying two martinis for us. There are three other women apart from Mary. They're small and thin with sallow complexions and mousy brown hair. They could sure use a little help from Whitey. One of them laughs in a peculiar way—she makes a loud braying noise like a mule or something. Nobody seems to notice except me, or maybe they are all being polite. I can't tell with English people whether it's good manners or they just aren't very observant. Everyone is talking to me at the same time, asking the same questions about how I like England and of course the weather.

People come and go, but I don't catch the names. They float by me so quickly that I can't grasp them, so I just stand there smiling and feeling stupid. I'm grateful to have a cocktail glass to hold as Arthur releases my waist, leaving me stranded and all alone. He's talking about theater and his latest play. People are hanging on to his every word because he's so clever and brilliant, and I'm so proud of him.

A long few seconds go by before a handsome young man plants himself right by my side and offers me a cigarette, which I gratefully accept. "Hello, Marilyn," he says, as if we're old friends, although I'm pretty sure that we've never met. "Aren't you a sight for sore eyes?"

He's standing a little closer than I'd like, and I can smell the sourness of his breath. I think he may be a little drunk, but I don't mind it. He's very good-looking. Black hair and bright blue eyes with a little twinkle in them.

"Sorry, I didn't introduce myself, which is frightfully rude of me." He stands back a little and gives me a little bow like I'm the Queen or something. "I'm Nigel," he says, smiling right at me.

"Oh, it's nice to meet you. I met your cousin earlier," I say, gesturing toward Mary, who has her arm threaded through Arthur's and is leading him toward the dining room. "You have a lovely home."

"Thank you. Shall we go in to dinner?" Nigel offers me his arm, and I take it. I know he's important to Arthur, so I want to make a good impression.

The dining room is an elegant, square room with crimson wallpaper featuring tiny birds in gold cages. It's kind of embossed, and I'd like to run my fingers over it, tracing the outline of the cages, but I don't dare. In the center of the room is a long dining table covered in a white tablecloth with two silver candelabras placed on either side of a bowl of white roses. The candles are lit, and it all looks beautiful—very classy. These people have some money, I guess—I mean old money. They seem to talk in a code that I can't understand, although Arthur has no problem at all and, by the looks of it, is enjoying himself.

Nigel sits down at the head of the table and he pulls me into a chair right next to him. "There must be some perks to hosting a dinner party, and choosing who sits next to me is one of them." His eyes are twinkling away at me, and I look down the table at Arthur, but he doesn't seem to mind. From time to time, I see him glancing over, but I'm all right here, and I just want him to enjoy talking to his friends for a change. So much in our lives revolves around Marilyn—her movies, her studio rows, her management, her needs. It's a lot for a man to put up with, although there are perks to his job too. . . .

Nigel insists on pouring me a glass of white wine as the food is served. It tastes delicious, although I barely recognize anything that's on my plate. It's all French cuisine, he tells me, cooked by a chef who used to work in the finest restaurant in Paris. I don't know why that chef is here in London cooking when he could be in Paris, but the food tastes good.

The wine gives me a warm, fuzzy feeling right down to my toes, and I find myself just gazing at Nigel's blue eyes. I like people's eyes . . . they tell you who they really are. Some people can't look you right in the eye, but I like it when someone can do that—as if you're really seeing who they are and they don't mind you knowing about them. He's making me laugh and flirting a little, but in that way that men do when they know there is nothing to it. It's like scoring points to make me laugh, or to make me interested in what they're saying.

I'm laughing a lot tonight and it feels so good. I don't think I've laughed very much since we landed in England. Everyone has been so very serious.

"I hear you and Arthur have settled in New York. I've spent quite a bit of time there myself. It's a great city, isn't it?" He leans in a little closer.

Immediately I start describing the wonderful art and museums that I love, but we quickly move on to people we might know.

"Do you know Truman Capote?" I ask. "He's a great friend and used to take me to see so many wonderful things there. We would have the longest lunches and he would make me laugh so hard. His stories are always wicked but so funny," I say, suddenly getting a real pang of homesickness for those carefree days when I was having so much fun exploring the city.

Nigel shakes his head. "No, we've never met."

I'm about to ask him what his favorite things to do in New York are, but then I notice that he's sitting so close to me that he's practically looking right down my dress. I realize that Nigel isn't all that interested in who I know in New York. His blue eyes are sparkling away, and he leans in to whisper in my ear: "Oh, Marilyn, if only we'd met before you married Arthur. I could take you around England and show you all the lovely things here."

My fingers are playing with the dessert fork, and suddenly he places his hand over the top of mine. The warmth of it shocks me, and I quickly pull my hand away. This guy is an important backer, though, and I really don't want Arthur to suffer, so I take a long sip of my wine. If this guy wants to flirt with Marilyn, then I guess it's pretty harmless as long as I don't let him cross the line. He just wants a good story to tell his friends.

At the other end of the table, Mary gets to her feet and begins shepherding guests back toward the drawing room. My head is starting to ache a little, and I try to catch Arthur's eye to signal that it's time to leave, but he doesn't look up at me. He is deep in conversation with two gray-haired men about the staging of his new play, *A View from the Bridge,* which is opening here in October. As we all return to the drawing room, I see that the rug has been rolled up and the chairs are all pushed against the walls.

"I thought rather than brandy and cigars, we'd have some dancing to work off our dinner." Nigel places a record on the turntable, and the needle crackles for a second before a Cole Porter tune begins to play. Grabbing hold of my hand, he whirls me around as we cross the floor. He is a very good dancer—light on his feet but with a firm grip. I like it when a gentleman takes charge of a dance. Before I know it, I'm dancing with another man and then another. It seems like the whole world is lining up to grab the chance to have Marilyn in their arms for a few minutes. Then Nigel puts on a Sinatra song that I love. It's the saddest love song in the world—pure heartbreak. He pulls me close and we dance cheek to cheek. I'm really not thinking about the dance very much. I'm thinking about Frank and New York—and the lonely nights I've spent listening to this song. Loneliness is a funny thing. It's like an ache inside that never goes away—or at least that's true for me: no matter how many people are in the room, I'm always lonely.

The music stops quite abruptly as one of the men is midway through saying something about me posing for a calendar:

"From what I saw, she had nothing on at all." Of course, he wasn't expecting the music to stop when it did or that I would hear him. The air turns hot with embarrassment.

From across the room, I can see Arthur's face darken. Quick as a flash, I swing around to face this guy. "Well, it's not true that I had nothing on. . . . I had the radio on."

Everyone bursts out laughing. Everyone except Arthur.

LILIBET

1956

It's so very quiet here at night that it's easy to imagine we are all alone in the world. Although it's still summer, there is a distinct chill in the air, and one can feel autumn approaching. There is always a day in the middle of every season where one can sense the change coming. The vacation, such as it is, will be over before we know it and we'll be back in the midst of the parade of visitors and appointments.

The house has fallen silent. The children are tucked in their beds sleeping sweetly, and I am finishing off some last-minute papers before turning in. Parliament is not sitting at the moment, so there is a little respite in the amount of government papers to sign and read, but the Suez problem is rumbling on, and some kind of armed conflict feels inevitable. I do hope it won't come to that, but both Mr. Eden and Colonel Nasser seem very stubborn and not given to negotiation.

I sit back in my chair, put down my pen, and look around me. Papers are scattered across my desk. The Scottish hills outside my window have disappeared into the inky darkness, and I am quite alone. It is only at times like these that I think about the woman I might have been had Uncle David not given up the throne. I wonder why he couldn't carry on. Of course, there is the matter of love for another person, but there is also your country and your duty. He chose Wallis Simpson over his own brother. He must have known that the Crown would be a terrible burden for my father and indeed for me, yet he still followed his heart. My grandmother, Queen Mary, called him self-indulgent, and there is no doubt that he was, yet some part of me understands the urge to throw it all away and live an ordinary life with the person you love.

I miss the girl that I was, but more than that I miss the woman that I could have been. Every part of me has been given over to the job of Queen. It is only in the deep silence of these rare moments of solitude that I can feel her stir deep inside me.

I would have liked to breed horses, I think, if life had gone a different way. A large stable somewhere close to a racetrack. Of course, Philip would still want to be in the Navy, but maybe we could have lived the Navy life while the children were young, had some more babies as we'd originally planned, and then, after Philip's retirement, I could have run my stables. Spending all day watching horses and planning their breeding would be a rather marvelous way to fill one's time, I think.

I'd have liked to travel too, but not as we do at present—I mean private travels, seeing things that you really wish to see instead of politely eating local delicacies and sitting through endless welcome ceremonies. That's the life that Lilibet would have loved and thrived in, I feel. Not this stuffy existence of duty and ceremony. I take a deep sniff and exhale a long sigh before picking up my pen again. No point daydreaming about things that one can't have.

My mind wanders back to my sister and her birthday dinner earlier this evening.

It was a jolly affair, with everyone making their very best efforts to celebrate Margaret, but at the same time it felt draining, underpinned with a sense of time passing and things slipping away. Everyone was trying almost too hard to be amusing as we served slices of our traditional chocolate birthday cake, before playing rounds of charades in the drawing room until everyone was too tired to carry on.

As we sat there playing our games, I couldn't help but look at them all. Mummy and Margaret with their broken hearts, and of course Philip, who seems to grow more frustrated with every passing day. Tomorrow I will sit down with him and ask about these silly rumors, both to reassure myself and so that we can form a joint strategy. I can understand curiosity at how we live and such, but this is the first time I've ever had completely hurtful things written about someone I love so dearly. Why do people become so incensed over the lives of perfect strangers? It's puzzling to me but no less upsetting when it happens.

Suddenly I become aware of a gentle tapping sound on my study door, which I've left open because I wasn't expecting company. As I turn my head, I see my sister swaying slightly in the doorway, and I suspect she's had a little too much birthday champagne.

"Am I disturbing you?" whispers Margaret from across the room.

"Of course not. I was just finishing up and about to call it a night," I reply while gesturing for her to join me.

"I'm not tired at all. If this were London I'd try to find a party to go to. I hate feeling so bored and alone." Margaret sits down in the armchair and stares forlornly into the unlit fire.

"You're not alone. You have a family who love you very much. Oh, Margaret, I hate to see you feeling so miserable—and on your birthday too. You have so much to look forward to. I'm sure of it." I keep my tone deliberately bright and cheerful, but the truth is I'm not sure of it. "You seem to get bored very easily these days, especially when you meet new people. Maybe you should give them a bit more of a chance. You never know when somebody could become very special."

Margaret leans back against the armchair and closes her eyes. The combination of her birthday and a generous amount of champagne appears to have softened her anger toward me, but her sadness remains and is so very hard to witness.

"I do try to give people a chance. I want to meet someone else—I really do. But at the same time, they're not Peter. I do want to feel happy. More than anything in the world I want that, but everything feels so very bleak. I don't know why I can't be more like you. You're always on an even keel and I'm always thrashing around trying to find my way. I feel terribly inadequate in comparison."

"Like me? Goodness, I wouldn't wish that on you." I try to sound lighthearted, but it doesn't quite come off. "We all have our problems and our challenges."

"What problems do you have?" Margaret asks quite sharply as if she couldn't possibly envisage them.

"Well, as it happens the newspapers have picked up on that horrible piece of gossip you were sharing. So there's that. . . ."

"Oh . . . I see. I'm sorry, Lil. What did Philip say?" She eyes me keenly as her fingers pick at the stitching on the armchair.

"I haven't spoken to him about it yet. There hasn't been the right moment to raise it." I mumble slightly, as I am a little embarrassed by the delay in talking to Philip, but the truth is that I just want to ignore this whole matter until it goes away. I couldn't stand for it to be true.

"Well . . . I'm sure he'll clear things up as it were." There is a long moment of silence as my sister appears to forget my predicament; she is obviously wallowing in her own pool of self-pity this evening.

Margaret's face is so unbearably wretched that I can't stand to see it. "Do you ever hear from Peter?" I ask tentatively. If they are still in touch, it might explain why she has so much trouble mending her poor heart.

"No, we made our decision, and part of it was that we would

never contact each other again. Clean break and all that." She lights a cigarette and exhales a tiny cloud of smoke.

There is part of me that wants to fix things—to make people feel better, all the while knowing that of course one can't fix anyone and often only time will do the trick.

"What would help? If there's anything I can do . . ." I ask as warmly as I can manage, although I am biting back a sigh.

"There's nothing to be done. Maybe the African tour will take my mind off things and give me something more interesting to do."

"Yes, I often find keeping busy is the answer." The words sound so incredibly trite that I feel quite ashamed of having offered them to her, but what else can I say?

"Don't you ever miss how things used to be, with the four of us in our happy little home? You and me—Mummy and Papa. Of course, when you married Philip things were different, but at least I had them both. Once Papa died, everything changed and all I had to lean on was Peter, don't you see? Without him I feel as if I've lost everything over the past few years."

"But you still have your family, Margaret. All of us who care about you. We all miss Papa, of course."

"I know that's true, but you're always so busy now. It's not the same as when we were girls together . . . and you have your own family. I'm twenty-six—you were already married with two children by the time you were my age. I don't know what will become of me if I can't get over Peter, and yet part of me doesn't want to let him go. I'm stuck in this life—a spare part. I'm so lonely, Lil." Her voice becomes thick with emotion and her eyes brim with tears.

"I do know it's been difficult, and I will try to make more time for us. It's just this job—my time is not my own and every twenty minutes or so there's someone else waiting to see me, or another ribbon to be cut, or papers to be signed. Papa was exactly the same if you remember."

"Papa always made time for us," Margaret says a little too sharply for my liking.

"I make time for you. I'm making time for you right now."

Margaret fixes me with a watery glare and crushes out her cigarette in the ashtray. "Yes, of course you are. Well, I won't take up any more of your time. It's getting late. Good night, Lilibet. And good luck with Philip," she says a little pointedly, getting to her feet and offering a reluctant kiss on my cheek.

"Good night," I say softly, and watch her as she walks away.

Absentmindedly I move around the photographs of my family that sit on my desk. A wave of sadness washes over me as I pick up a silver frame.

It's a picture of my father leaning over to explain something to me—I am very young, only four or five years old, and he is smiling so lovingly at me. I keep it on my desk as I find it comforting to see his face as I try to do the same job that he did. It's as if he's urging me on and always completely on my side. "You can do this, Lilibet," I hear him say, but some days I am really not sure that I can. Margaret talks as if she's the only one who grieves his loss, but I miss him too. I put the photograph back down and a memory comes back to me, as clear as day.

My father was at this very desk, smoking his cigarette, with his hand placed flat against his cheek as he went through his papers. He often allowed me to sit quietly in the armchair and watch him while he worked, as he liked me to keep him company.

That day I asked my father what it was like to be the King, and he looked at me very seriously and said, "It's a hard burden to bear some days but also the most wonderful thing to know that you've been chosen for this role. It's a great honor, Lilibet, and I want you to remember that always." I nodded, but I never completely understood why he felt that way when he so obviously struggled. Most days still, I find it difficult to feel the great honor rather than the burden.

Getting to my feet, I walk wearily toward the door. On the wall of my study in between the many paintings by Edwin Landseer is a portrait of my great-great-grandmother, Queen Victoria, in her later years. Her face is both sad and furious, as if life had not turned out the way she wanted it to.

For a moment I stand in front of it and gaze into her wise old eyes. I cannot imagine being a queen for so many years. Turning from a bright young woman filled with hopes for the future into someone at the end of their days. What will I be like when I'm sixty years old or seventy and beyond? I can't imagine it, and yet neither can one imagine not existing at that age. How will the world change in that time and what will be my role in it? There is a great insecurity in being the monarch, for at any given time people could suddenly decide that they don't want you any longer, and that will be that. I wonder what Queen Victoria would say if she were here now?

As I walk up the stairs, I look at the statue of her beloved husband and feel a pang of sorrow for her, having nothing except a lump of marble to look at her as she made her way upstairs.

The next morning is one of those cloudless August days that are so very rare here. The sky is a deep blue and, apart from the terrible midges, all is peaceful. We have set out to have our family picnic in two Land Rovers packed with everything we could possibly need to eat or want to do. Wicker hampers of meats and cheeses, loaves of bread and a slab of butter, jars of chutney and pickles, plus some sausages for Philip to cook over a campfire. There are warm tartan rugs to sit on or wrap around us, should the weather take a turn for the worse, and several flasks of drinks, both hot and cold.

As we pile out of the cars, I pick a good spot on the banks of the river and begin laying out the rugs, while Philip organizes the children into finding the perfect sticks to cook their sausages with. They need to be thin enough to spear the thing, but firm enough to withstand their task. We've had many lost in the past as the poor stick collapsed and a child wailed as their sausage turned to ash in the fire.

Charles and Anne excitedly start to pick up sticks and reject them as too short or too thick as Philip builds his little fire carefully and thoroughly. Mummy, Margaret, and I unpack the picnic table and begin buttering bread and cutting slices of cheese while pouring drinks for everyone out of the flasks.

The afternoon passes in a peaceful haze of sunshine as we all eat heartily—the sausages are scorched but consumed nevertheless, and the children exhaust themselves by running around. Then Philip baits his fishing rod and stands there trying to get a bite while Charles watches eagerly for any signs of movement in the water.

"Do you remember that time your father thought he'd caught an enormous fish and it turned out to be an old Wellington boot?" Mummy says wistfully.

"Oh yes," I say. "He was quite cross about it too." Margaret and I laugh but I can't help but notice that when Mummy mentions my father her voice cracks, and her eyes turn misty. It's as if a secret door opens in her mind and she disappears into a room that we can't enter. Her face clouds over and she falls silent.

Anne tucks in at my side and leans her sleepy head on my shoulder. She's becoming quite her own little person now—fiercely stubborn and very independent. She reminds me of Philip so much.

"Are you having a lovely time, darling?" I put my arm around Anne and draw her to me.

"Yes, but I'm tired of playing now," she says, and her eyes begin to flicker shut for a moment as I sweep her hair back off her face with my fingers.

For a brief moment there are no official duties, and we can all be together like any other family enjoying their summer holiday.

"And what's on the agenda for this evening?" Margaret asks. She's probably hoping for some company, as she must be quite bored with us by now, but sadly I have nobody to offer her.

"We're having a film night," I say with a bright smile as if it's the answer to everything.

"And what are we watching?" she asks in a tone that implies she won't be impressed with whatever I've chosen for us.

"Well, I thought we'd watch something with Marilyn Monroe, as she's our new neighbor in Windsor. It's called *Gentlemen Prefer Blondes*. So that should be fun."

I can tell by Margaret's face that she can't decide whether to be bored by this information or not. She shrugs and purses her lips as if she's about to comment on it but then decides not to. I do hope we aren't going to argue about every little thing this summer, as it's so very wearing.

"Anyway, that's for later. Is everything ready for your African trip?" I ask, changing the subject to indulge my sister since she likes nothing more than talking about her plans.

"Yes, it should be fun. We're going all over the place—right down East Africa and on to Mauritius. I have to admit that some time away from my family will be most welcome." She announces this in such a haughty tone that I roll my eyes.

"Margaret!" I exclaim, and she gives me a rather chilly stare.

"I'm teasing. Although I will be glad to get away for a while. I'm so bored seeing the same faces, and who knows, some dazzling man might sweep me off my feet on my travels."

"The change will do you good, I'm sure," Mummy interjects, trying—as ever—to humor Margaret. "But there are plenty of very nice men here for you to meet if that's what you want," she adds hopefully.

"I've met them all and they're deathly dull. I want someone interesting . . . someone completely different to my usual set," Margaret says with a pout.

"You need a good man, not a dazzling one. I wasn't dazzled by your father when we first met, yet as I came to know him, I found that he was quite the best man I'd ever known." My mother's eyes fill with tears again. Poor Mummy. She is so very sad without him.

We're interrupted by Philip and Charles shouting that they've caught something. Philip begins reeling in his fish, and for a moment everyone watches to see what he's managed to catch. It turns out to be quite small, and he swiftly unhooks the line from the fish's mouth and throws it back into the water. "Not worth the effort," he mutters.

I turn my face upward toward the sun for a moment and feel the warmth on my skin. Anne shifts her little body away from me and leans against my mother, who delights in having her grandchild next to her.

My limbs feel itchy and restless as I get to my feet. I'm tired of going around in circles, bouncing between my mother's sadness and my sister's anger. "I think I'll take a little walk. Anyone care to join me?" I ask, and am thankful when they refuse. The children are too sleepy and the adults lulled into that kind of gentle laziness that happens after a good hearty picnic, so I leave them to it and set off along the riverbank.

I like to walk, for it helps me think. There is a bend up ahead and I quicken my pace, feeling more carefree with each step. When I reach the bend, I settle down on a patch of grass and amuse myself by throwing tiny pebbles as the river rushes and whirls past me. Lying back on the grassy bank, I close my eyes for a second and let the sound of the burbling water fill my mind. I am completely alone, and for a brief moment, I don't have to perform the role of Queen for anyone. A delicious sense of peacefulness comes over me, and I am tempted to take off my walking shoes and stockings and dip my toes in the cool water.

I pick a long blade of grass and thread it between my fingers. Part of me is suddenly transported back to our long summer holidays as children. My father in his kilt trying to catch a fish while Margaret and I threaded daisy chains around my mother's neck. In my imagination I can see the four of us sitting on the riverbank as clearly as if I am back there now. I can smell the warm tobacco scent that always surrounded my dear papa, and it is almost as if he is here beside me.

"Everything all right?" Philip's voice startles me, and I sit up quickly, caught between two worlds.

"Yes, I'm fine," I say breezily.

"You disappeared. . . ." Philip flops down beside me on the grass and hugs his knees to his chest.

"I just wanted a stroll."

"Family driving you mad again?" He grins at me, and I want to reach out my hand to stroke his face, but I don't move.

"Oh, just the usual." I should say something about the newspaper story, but I can't bring myself to raise it. The sun beats down on us, and I lean my head against Philip's shoulder for a moment. "Do you remember that little club we used to go dancing in when we lived in Malta?" I say.

"Ah . . . the one with the trumpet player who only had one leg." Philip smiles, but his face looks suddenly wistful as if he misses those days too.

"Yes, that's the one. I was just thinking about all the lovely times we spent there."

"They were happy days, weren't they? Just the two of us with our children. . . ." His curious eyes fix upon my face. As our eyes meet, I suddenly feel tears welling up inside me. I won't be able to bear it if these ghastly rumors are true. If I can't rely on Philip, then I don't know what I shall do.

"You seem a bit down. Are you all right?" Philip asks softly.

"Do I? I'm just a bit tired, I expect. There was something that I wanted to talk to you about. . . ." The words have barely left my mouth when I hear the excited cries of Charles and Anne coming closer, calling us. "Oh well—it will keep. It's not important." I swallow my questions and get to my feet. "Shall we get back?" I ask, allowing Philip to take my hand and leaving our difficult conversations for another day.

The screen has been set up and we are all ready for the film to begin. Everyone has their post-dinner drink and the lights are turned off. Philip is sitting in one armchair while I have the other, leaving Mummy and Margaret to share the sofa. The children are tucked between them, but I'm sure they will fall asleep long before the film ends.

Marilyn Monroe and Jane Russell are wearing the tightest

costumes that I think I've ever seen. They certainly leave nothing to the imagination. Both of them are dressed in red sequined dresses with large slits up the side, so we can see their legs all the way up to their thighs. I study Miss Monroe for a moment—her voluptuous figure, her blond hair, and her bright red lipstick. I know very little about her, but she seems like the kind of woman who has a particular impact on men.

We are complete opposites and, as I watch Philip laughing across the room, I wonder: am I merely a dull and dutiful person, rather than a woman with the capacity to entice? Margaret has always been the more glamorous sister, while I am a mother of two and thirty years old now. It's ridiculous to worry over such things, but the rumors about Philip bother me more than I have let on, and I do need to speak to him frankly, for we cannot allow any hint of scandal. Gossip columnists today could become front-page news tomorrow. I tell myself that I will speak to Michael first thing in the morning, ask him whether he thinks there's anything to these rumors. I need to get all my facts together before I approach Philip again.

A tiny sigh escapes me, but nobody notices and I try to focus on Miss Monroe, who is trying to climb out through a small porthole. She's very amusing in the film, and I wonder what she's like in real life. I imagine her to be permanently tantalizing and confident in her ability to get her own way. Because we appear to be so very different on the surface, I am curious as to what life is like for her. Yet at the same time, I am very aware that often I'm performing my role behind a mask, so it would make sense to consider that others are doing exactly the same.

The film comes to a close and the lights are put back on. Nanny arrives to take our two sleepy children to their beds, and Philip busies himself refreshing everyone's drinks.

"By the way, I've invited Miss Monroe to the charity film premiere in October," I offer tentatively.

"Really?" Margaret says, puffing away on her usual cigarette.

"I wonder what she's like. I mean, she can't be the dumb blonde that we see on film, can she?"

"You waited until I was away to invite her. You did that deliberately." Philip laughs, but I think underneath he really is slightly irritated that he will miss out. There is something about her that certainly fascinates everyone.

"I expect she's just a perfectly ordinary person like the rest of us. After all, being an actress is her job, isn't it? She's performing for us. She may be very different in her real life. Anyway, I shall report back on how she seems, although I imagine our meeting will be quite brief. These things are usually a quick handshake and 'lovely to meet you' then move on to the next person."

For the life of me I am unable to understand why someone would choose to be famous if they didn't have it thrust upon them from birth. If I'd been born an anonymous person, I can't imagine why I would want to throw myself into the public eye.

"She's certainly going to stand out in the crowd. You couldn't miss her—she is very obvious, in a vulgar sort of a way," Mummy says. She has very strict rules for how women should present themselves in public, and is not overly enamored with performers of any kind.

"I think it's just the fashion these days," I say kindly, trying to be fair to this actress whom I've never met.

"Well, as long as we're not expected to turn up looking like that. I prefer a more classic and elegant way. An English rose—that's what I've always encouraged in both of my daughters." Mummy eyes us proudly.

"I think she looks perfectly fine. A lot of women dress like that these days and the world is brighter for it," Philip says with a little gleam in his eye that makes me uncomfortable. It tells me that he spends too much of his time in Soho, and it also manages to remind me that I am not a woman who dresses to dazzle.

"Don't worry," Margaret says. "I can't imagine Lilibet turning up in red sequins to open Parliament." She giggles at the idea of it, and the prospect makes me laugh too.

It's been a peaceful day for a change, but tomorrow I know that I will have to speak to Philip. I simply can't put it off any longer.

NORMA JEANE

1956

"Are you all right? You're very quiet," I whisper to Arthur so the driver can't hear me. He's barely spoken a word to me since we left Nigel's house.

"I'm fine. Just tired, that's all." His jaw is set in that determined way, and a tiny muscle is twitching in his cheek. I curl up next to him, watching the streetlamps get farther and farther apart, until we swing back into the driveway of Parkside House.

Arthur throws his jacket over the back of an armchair and sits down at the dining table, where he begins pulling out his notebooks. "I'm going to write for a while. You go on up," he says without even looking at me.

"Papa—why don't you come to bed with me?" I stand close to him, my hands tousling his hair, until he brushes me away. "Please, Pa . . ." I whisper in that breathy voice he likes so much.

"I'm not tired yet. Go to bed. You're on set early tomorrow and you need to sleep." His hand grazes my thigh in a half-hearted patting motion, and I feel crushed. He seems so cold. Earlier on he was all over me, but now he's behaving like I'm of no interest to him at all.

"Pa—have I done something wrong?" I whisper as I kiss him good-night.

"I want to work—you go on up." He doesn't return my kisses, and I can't tell if he's mad at me or just in that place where writers go sometimes. They get an idea and often you can't reach them. I know that his work is very serious and important, but I really wanted us to be together this evening. For the first time in a long while, I felt great, thanks to the little purple pills—like I could dance all night long. The pain was gone, and I mostly had fun at the party. It reminded me of being back in New York, where I could dance or spend hours in conversation with people who made me laugh. Yes, that rude guy was a jerk, but overall, I had a really good time.

Standing in the doorway, I watch Arthur's back curve over the notebooks on the table. He leans on his elbow with his chin resting in the palm of his left hand.

"Good night, then, Papa," I call from the doorway, but he doesn't hear me . . . or he doesn't care to respond. I hate it when I can't reach him. The minute someone goes cold on me, it gives me a funny panicky feeling like I'm left alone again. It reminds me of that first night in the orphanage when I didn't know a single soul and there was nobody I could call to come and get me. It was the loneliest place in the world.

In our bedroom, I kick off my black suede heels, scattering them across the room. Then I unclip my diamond earrings and put them on the dressing table. The black slip dress lies in a pool at my feet, and a moment later I am naked. Raking my fingers through my hair, I head to the bathroom.

Pulling on my satin robe, I cream my face with layers of Erno Laszlo to get rid of all my makeup. I carefully apply all my face lotions because you have to take care of your skin no matter what happens in your life. I'm a great believer in that. By the time I've stripped away every trace of Marilyn, it's late and there's still no sign of Arthur. He must be writing something really important—maybe ideas for a new play. When he first gets an idea, he doesn't like to talk about it with me, although later on, he will ask for my opinion of things or even read through something that he's working on. I always feel honored to be his first reader like that.

Part of me wants to go back downstairs and try to get him to quit working, but I decide against it—after all, I hate to be interrupted for no reason when I'm working. Crawling into our bed, I gulp down two Nembutal with some water, and close my eyes.

The clock on the bedside table says it's a little after 2:00 a.m. when my eyes open wide. I wake up in a terrible panic with my throat choking. I can't breathe, and I have that awful suffocating feeling of being trapped again. A terrible devilish face looms right over me, and I'm screaming, but the words won't leave my mouth. There are beads of sweat on my forehead, and my heart is slamming against my ribs.

I don't know why I keep having these dreams. I've tried everything known to man. Therapy, pills, enough booze to knock a person out, yet almost every night I wake up in a cold sweat. Some nights, I'm crying so hard that I've woken Arthur with my sobs.

Tonight, I wake up with a gasp like I've been drowning and have just found my way back to the surface.

I sit up in bed and realize that Arthur is here. He must have crept in beside me while I was asleep. Watching the shadowy outline of his face in the darkness of our bedroom, I feel a burst of love for him sleeping next to me.

I think of Anna and her Vronsky, feeling so much love that she would rather die than lose him, and I wonder if I'd rather watch him die, or watch his love for me die.

Oh, I couldn't bear it. I hope I die before him when we're very old. I know he loves me more than anything, but he's stronger than I am, and I think he could cope without me. I just don't know what I would do if anything happened to him.

There's no chance of sleep now, and I can't take any more pills. I don't know why they don't work for me all the time. I guess those dreams just cut through everything. There are hours of darkness left to lie here all alone. I know that Arthur is lying next to me, but when a person can't sleep, it's as if they're the only one who is left alive in a world filled with dead people. That's how it feels some nights—like I'm the loneliest girl in the world.

I can't stand to just lie here listening to Arthur sleeping so peacefully, breathing as though he doesn't have a care in the world. I don't know what to do. It's a long time until daylight, but I don't want to wake him up. Maybe I'll just creep downstairs and drink some scotch until I feel sleepy again. Either way, I can't just lie here in the darkness, wide awake, with nothing but lonely thoughts to keep me company. Thoughts are always bad in the middle of the night. All the things you can ignore during daylight come back to haunt you, and they seem so bright and loud at night.

Slipping quietly out of our bed, I pull on my robe, tying the satin belt tightly around my waist. The door to our bedroom opens softly, but the stairs and floors of this house are quite creepy after dark. Everything creaks and the pipes make a weird gurgling noise. The whole house is filled with strange noises, and I wouldn't be at all surprised if the entire place was haunted by the ghost of some old movie star who once stayed here.

All the staff have gone home or are fast asleep, and the place is silent apart from the ghost noises. I let out a long breath. It feels like I've been keeping it inside me since we got here, unable to really relax or feel at home. This is the first time in the house I've truly felt that no one is watching me. It's a nice feeling.

I switch on the small lamp by the side of the dining table and fill a glass with a generous slug of scotch. Maybe the whisky will make me drowsy, and if I can just get back to sleep, then things will look better in the morning.

These sure are the lonely hours. I feel like the last woman alive, and I just need someone to hold me tight and tell me that it's going to be all right.

Sitting down at the dining table, I cradle my glass between the palms of my hands. I have no idea how long Arthur was writing for, but he's just abandoned his notebooks all over the table. They are black with hard covers, and the one closest to me has been left open. The pages are covered in Arthur's writing. All those words scribbled down—some of them underlined as if they're important and must not be forgotten. He told me once that he can get an idea just from one sentence. Imagine that! Thinking idle thoughts and turning them into plays with real actors performing them in front of audiences. I know how to change those words into characters with feelings, but I don't think that I could ever come up with them in the first place. Changing people's lives with your words and making them think about things differently, or feel something they haven't felt before. That's a great artist. I want to do that with my acting—really make people feel something when they look at me up there.

The pages covered in Arthur's words are just calling to me. I shouldn't read them—after all, it's his work, and if he wanted to share it with me, then he would. But he knows so many things that I want to crawl inside his mind and feel what he feels and think what he thinks.

Maybe it's the scotch, or the nighttime blues, but I can't resist taking one little peek. Just one look won't hurt, and he won't know.

The whisky feels cool on my tongue, and it settles my mind. Gently, I pull the notebook toward me and smooth the palm of my hand across the page.

His writing is urgent—scrawled across the paper—and it takes me a moment to decipher it. Thoughts and feelings; bright wild ideas. Notes to himself to remember things. Different themes he could play with. Loneliness and masculinity. He's scrawled stuff about characters—a woman waiting for a divorce meets two losers out West. My fingers chase the ink across the page. My brilliant love. I'm so very proud of him. The smartest guy I know, and out of all the women in the world, he chose me. He's my everything. I love him like the rain and the sun all rolled together.

Then I see it.

At the bottom of the page, the very last paragraph is double-underlined in dark blue ink. I put down my glass of scotch and hold the pages up to the light to get a better look at it. The pen has been pushed down so hard, it's almost torn the page where Arthur has written: "I've done it again. I thought I was marrying an angel, and find I've married a whore."

I let out a gasp of shock as if I've been punched in my stomach. For a moment, I can't catch my breath—it's like I've forgotten how. I want to scream, but my throat has closed tight and my head is swimming. We've been married only seven weeks . . .

WHORE! I feel like I've been stabbed straight through my heart.

I'm shaking as I get to my feet. We swore we'd love each other until death do us part, but in just a few weeks his love has turned to regret.

He thinks I'm a whore.

A feeling like a tidal wave comes rushing through me. I can't get divorced one more time. I can't do it. Men never get the blame for it; it's always the woman. Nobody will ask Arthur why he couldn't stay married to Marilyn Monroe. They'll all ask her why she can't keep a man happy.

The pain feels so big and sharp, I don't think I can stand it. It's like a big black bear with claws that will cut me to pieces. I don't want to feel it. I don't want to feel anything ever again. I want to die. It would be better for everyone if I wasn't here.

I race upstairs with my blood pulsing in my ears. I can't think straight.

Scrambling around in the bathroom, I find the bottle of sleeping pills and I begin pushing them into my mouth, swallowing them down with handfuls of water. I don't want to feel anything. I want nothing but darkness to sweep me away. I want to sleep until all the pain is gone.

Tears are pouring down my face. "*A whore . . .*" I sob.

Not even my own mama loved me enough to protect me, and my daddy never cared enough to stick around and didn't want to get to know me later on, even when he found out I was Marilyn Monroe.

Somewhere inside, a wound tears open that's so deep I could never heal it. And I finally understand that nobody will ever love me. Nobody will ever care about Norma Jeane. They will only ever love Marilyn.

I swallow another pill. I can't breathe. . . .

Arthur is still sleeping without a care in the world. The pain shifts suddenly, and the sight of him lying there causes an atom of fury to explode inside me, and I jump onto the bed and start pounding my fists on his chest.

Arthur wakes in a panic, struggling to sit up. "What the hell—Marilyn, what are you doing?" He's gripping my wrists tightly to stop me from hitting him.

I can't get the words out. That old stutter comes back from when I was a kid, while my breath comes in great shuddering bursts. "A wh-whore? Arthur . . . th-that's what you think of me? I d-di-disappoint you . . ." My head is spinning, but I keep on trying to wriggle free of his grasp. His face looks guilty and pained.

"You read my notebook . . . I didn't mean it. . . ." He sounds panic-stricken, but his voice fades away to silence as he tries desperately to think of some way to defend what he wrote.

"You left those pages open. You wanted me to see them. You *hate* me." I am sobbing so hard that I'm trembling all over, but my head feels woozy as the pills kick in.

"No. NO! I was just mad at you for flirting with Nigel and those guys at the party. That's all. I didn't mean to write them. They're just words. It doesn't mean a thing. You *weren't* supposed to read them." He's trying to reach for me—to calm me down—but I feel wild and crazy like a trapped animal.

"You don't love me . . ." I cry out as I wrestle free of his grip and stumble off the bed.

"No, Mazzie, that's not true, honey. I *do* love you."

"It's too late. I don't believe you. Nobody cares about me. You'll be better off without me. That's all I am to people—a dumb blonde . . . a whore . . . a freak. . . ."

"Don't say that. I worship you. There's nobody else that comes close to you. Come to bed, honey . . . please." Arthur sits on the edge of the bed wearing just his pajama bottoms. His voice is pleading with me, but his eyes can't meet mine.

"I just want to die if you don't love me. Why can't anyone love me, Pa?" My voice cracks.

Maybe nobody can ever love me because I'm so bad.

I curl up on the floor just outside the bedroom door, rocking back and forth, feeling the pills begin to take away the pain. Arthur seems to be fading away, and the pain is getting smaller. I start to laugh because it's all going to stop now. My eyelids flicker and I'm falling through clouds.

The palm of my hand uncurls and the rest of the pills scatter across the landing.

Then Arthur is kneeling by my side, yelling, "What did you take? Marilyn! For the love of God, what did you take?"

It doesn't matter anymore. Nothing matters anymore.

LILIBET

1956

"Michael, there is something that I wish to discuss with you. It's . . . a delicate matter concerning the Duke of Edinburgh."

I can tell by the look in Michael's eyes that he has been waiting for me to raise the subject of the newspaper story, and now the moment has arrived, I sense a slight panic as he stares back at me with a tight smile on his face.

"Certainly, ma'am." He shuffles his feet for a brief second while waiting for me to continue. It's so terribly awkward for both of us, but I need to have all the facts before I speak to Philip again.

"It has come to my attention that some newspaper columnists are writing gossip about the Duke of Edinburgh and Lieutenant-Commander Parker, suggesting certain activities with the members of his lunch club. Parties with . . . women. Are you aware of this, Michael?"

His mouth flaps open and closes again before he bows to the inevitable and nods. "Yes, ma'am, I am aware of the gossip."

I eye him with a steely glare; as awkward as this moment is, I need to know.

"Please tell me what you know . . . *everything* you know." And I straighten my spine and wait for the worst.

"Only that the Duke of Edinburgh and his private secretary have a habit of socializing together at certain clubs and private houses . . . parties and such. They have a code that they use with the staff at the palace—it's a sort of joke, ma'am."

"What is it?" I ask warily, for the idea of everyone in the palace sharing this joke is too awful to contemplate.

"That if anyone asks for them, the staff is to say that 'Murgatroyd and Winterbottom have popped out for a stroll.' That's all I know, ma'am. I certainly have no reason to think that any particular piece of gossip is true or I would have brought it directly to your attention." Michael cannot meet my gaze; he seems to find a particular part of the tartan rug completely fascinating at this moment, for his eyes are firmly fixed to it.

"Murgatroyd and Winterbottom?" Repeating the silly names doesn't make the situation any better.

"Yes, ma'am. I believe that's how they refer to themselves when they're about to go out for the evening." Michael lifts his gaze from the rug in a brief flicker, and for a moment we stand there, both of us wanting to end this conversation immediately but seemingly unable to do so.

I clear my throat. "Thank you, Michael, that will be all."

As my private secretary escapes the room with an obvious air of relief, I stand at the window staring out over the Scottish hills with a terrible sinking feeling in the pit of my stomach.

"Do you have a moment?" I ask gently, observing the back of my husband as he wields his watercolor brush over his sketchpad. There is something rather delicious about his concentration, which reminds me of a small boy's, and I can see the curious and focused child that he must have been once upon a time.

"Depends what for . . . I'm trying to finish this." He's scowling at having been interrupted, but what I have to say won't wait any longer.

"It is rather important, Philip, otherwise I'd let you get on," I say with a determined tone in my voice. I have thought long and hard about raising this matter, or rather how to raise this matter and what outcome we could possibly achieve by talking about it, and indeed what possibility there is of stopping the press from indulging in such awful baseless gossip. At least I very much hope that it is baseless gossip. After all, I don't know what they do at this "gentlemen's lunch club." I understand they meet once a week in Soho, and I presume there's drinking and chatting over lunch, but the newspaper implied there were other less savory activities. The way Michael described their little nicknames, it's as if this is all some sort of game to them, but I must make Philip see that it has real consequences for us. I have always liked Mike Parker and his wife, Eileen, but I do now see that it might be better all round if Philip had a more serious companion to work with him.

There is a long moment of silence before he finally looks up, his paintbrush hovering in the air and an impatient look on his face. "Well . . . what is it?" he says.

"There was a rather nasty piece of gossip printed in the newspaper the other day concerning . . ." My mouth feels dry as I notice his eyes are narrow and fierce.

"What?" Philip says angrily.

"Well . . . concerning your gentlemen's lunch club. The article implied there was rather more to it than lunch and drinking. It was suggesting you might be engaged in other less savory activities." There—I've said it. A wave of nervousness floods through me for a brief second as I wait for him to respond.

"Bloody ridiculous."

That's all he says, and now I am standing here feeling rather foolish and quite unsure as to how to proceed.

"I'm afraid that we need to formulate some kind of plan to

deal with these rumors. We cannot allow them to percolate. Philip . . . we need to have a serious conversation about this. Are there any grounds for these rumors?" I am trying to be as diplomatic as possible so as not to cause more upset, but I can feel my own frustration beginning to boil.

"I won't be cross-questioned as if I am on trial. The gutter press likes to print all kinds of nonsense to fill up their pages, and today it's my turn to be served up. Ignore it or, if it bothers you that much, get one of your palace courtiers to have a quiet word with the editors of Fleet Street."

"I can't do that. Philip, we have to do something. We must take this kind of thing seriously. I understand from the staff that you and Mike Parker go out together quite often . . . socializing and such. In fact, I am given to understand that you even have some kind of little code for your departures. 'Murgatroyd and Winterbottom have popped out for a stroll. . . .'"

"Oh, for goodness' sake. Am I being spied on now?" A burst of impatience flashes across his face. "Are you going to have reports of every little joke I make sent directly to you? Are you my wife or my headmistress?"

His voice is raised, but I can't back down without resolving this situation once and for all. He must see that we cannot allow anything that endangers the reputation of the monarchy. This isn't a game. I had hoped to resolve this between us as husband and wife, but it does very much seem as if I shall have to pull rank, which is always my last resort with Philip, as it does tend to inflame things between us.

"I think you should consider replacing Mike Parker as your private secretary. You're going away soon on this very long and arduous tour, and it's important that it goes well. Maybe it's time to consider someone else to accompany you." Fleetingly, I feel a sense of relief that the words have been spoken, as if we are halfway to some kind of mutually acceptable solution.

"Replace my private secretary . . ." The paintbrush is thrown down on to his desk leaving a tiny trail of sky-blue paint dotted across the wood.

"You can still be friends . . . but maybe a little time apart would allow these rumors to die down. Clearly, as these goings-on have made the papers that will likely mean more journalists will be interested." His face darkens and I don't know how to make him see this might be for the best. "We can find Mike Parker another role—but I do think it would be better to cool your friendship for a little while, until this all goes away."

Philip glowers at me and shakes his head. "So you want me to fire my private secretary and friend because of some stupid rumors?" The icy tone startles me as he slowly gets to his feet. Then he raises his voice. "I won't do it!" Flecks of spittle land on his painting as he yells; I really hope the servants are far enough away so they can't overhear us.

"There's no need to shout at me. This isn't my fault. I told you even Margaret has heard these rumors. They're all over town, and you know full well that however innocent these activities, they cannot be allowed to reflect badly on the monarchy." I draw myself up to my full five feet two inches as he towers over me. I won't be intimidated, and he should know me better than that by now.

"Reflect badly on the monarchy . . . or the monarch?" Philip says bitterly.

"What is that supposed to mean? It's my job to secure the Crown in this country—not to allow anything that may damage its future. I can't have newspapers printing stories about my own husband—you must see that, surely?" My voice is raised in anger now and Philip is being so infuriating that I really don't care who hears us. He's the most stubborn, pigheaded man sometimes, and I feel utterly exasperated with him.

"I won't fire him and that's that," he says emphatically, and then promptly sits back down and picks up his paintbrush. His lips are tightly pursed as he focuses on the painting, and I feel as if I'm being dismissed.

"But the newspapers . . . Philip, for goodness' sake, you can't just pretend these rumors aren't happening!"

"Oh, but I can, and so should you. I won't give up one more damn thing for you."

The words strike me so violently that I am slightly stunned by the impact. "What do you mean?"

"I have no proper role here. I have given up my naval career—my former life—and dedicated it *all* to you. My children don't even have my name. You have left me with nothing, and so the answer is NO. I will not surrender one more thing." Philip's face reddens with anger, and I cannot believe what I'm hearing.

"Is that how you consider our life together? The family we have built? . . . A terrible sacrifice?" I can feel a wave of emotion rushing through me, but I won't give him the satisfaction of seeing me cry. "You knew what the life would be when you married me. It wasn't a secret that I would become Queen. You chose me and all that I am and would become." My voice cracks slightly as my throat thickens.

Philip remains unmoved by my words. He clings to his paintbrush although he hasn't touched the paper with it in quite some time. Staring directly at his watercolor of the Scottish hills as if his life depends upon it, he is perfectly silent.

"I'm sorry that your life is so very miserable; however, that is not my doing. If you insist on going to this lunch club and continuing your relationship with Mike Parker, then the rumors have to stop. I will not allow you to make a mockery of us because you want something of your own to do.

"You have everything you could ever want right here. A wife who loves you very much and children who adore you. And while I know it hasn't been easy for you—or any of us, come to that—you can carve out a role for yourself and make a real difference in the world. You have an important tour coming up very soon, and rather than sulking about all the things that you've lost, perhaps you should count your very many blessings." A tight ball of fury uncurls inside me, and I am in no mood to back down.

"You don't understand the first thing about my life or what life is like for any of us. Those of us forced to live in *your* shadow." His sharp blue eyes meet mine. There's hurt behind the anger, but he's gone too far for me to make peace for now.

"None of you live in my shadow. I am just an ordinary human being trying my best. It is the shadow of the Crown . . . not me. I'm still Lilibet—the same person that I've always been. It's not my fault that I happen to have this job, and I am so very tired of being blamed for your unhappiness. All of you hold me responsible for your particular brand of misery, and I'm sick of it. I'm asking that you look for better ways to spend your time instead of carousing around Soho with your so-called friend."

Not bothering to wait for his response, I walk briskly out of the room, the dogs scattering in all directions as I go.

A weak band of sunshine spreads slowly across the wall in my bedroom as the mournful wail of the bagpipes announces a new day. The piper, dressed in his tartan kilt, parades back and forth beneath my window in his traditional morning greeting. I lie back against my pillows, peaceful for a moment, relishing the solitude of an early morning before the inevitable scurrying of servants and family and dogs that always surrounds me.

There is barely time for a moment of contemplation before I hear a gentle tap on my bedroom door. The door opens and the morning bustle begins. "Good morning, Your Majesty." Curtains are flung open and a most-welcome cup of tea is brought to me. The radio is turned on so that I can listen to the BBC news.

As I lie there sipping my tea, listening to the announcer talking gravely about the latest from Egypt, my heart sinks. The Russians have rather thwarted Mr. Eden's plan to hold Egypt to ransom by removing the expertise of the boat pilots—those men who are skilled in navigating the difficult twists and turns of the Suez Canal. Mr. Eden hoped to bring Colonel Nasser to the negotiating table—or rather more likely hoped that he would merely give up his fight and normality would resume. However, the Russians have sent skilled men to replace the boat pilots and now it looks as if we are rather stuck for a new plan. Military conflict of some kind would seem inevitable and, judging by the tone of the radio announcer, the experts in such matters apparently agree that this standoff cannot continue for much longer without action.

I shall make a point of asking Mr. Eden what he intends to do at our next meeting, even though he does have a very annoying way of dismissing any concerns I might raise, and I do sometimes feel that he views me as having no right to question his decisions because I am a young woman. It's very difficult when one is expected never to have an opinion, or to try to force a different line upon the government. My role is to support and remain impartial. I can advise, but it's not my job to tell the prime minister what to do, even if I think he is getting it wrong. I am surrounded by the most stubborn men—all of whom take great delight in ignoring my concerns when it suits them.

After draining my teacup, I get out of bed and shuffle my feet into my slippers. It's a fine day with a glimpse of some cloudless sunshine beginning to roll across the hills. I shall go for a good walk with the dogs and then see about making up with Philip. His bedroom door remained firmly closed last night, and we haven't spoken since our terrible row. I shall try to make things up with him today, as it's always best not to let anger settle into something hard and cold with time. Yes, that's the plan—we'll meet at breakfast as usual and hopefully we can both talk about this situation without losing our tempers.

An hour later I am bathed and sitting at my dressing table rubbing cold cream into my cheeks. My dressing room at Balmoral is a cozy cluttered little room with a bright tartan carpet and a large window covered in cream curtains with a floral pattern embroidered on them. The same fabric has been used to cover the two armchairs that sit either side of my dressing table. Next to the window are two wooden chests of drawers, while across the room is a fine old mantelpiece with a large mirror hung over it and some glass clocks ringing out the hour. There are hundreds of clocks in each palace and castle, all kept going by two members of staff who we inevitably christen "Tick" and "Tock." A fire is kept burning on cold days, making this a warm and inviting place in which to get dressed.

Bobo bustles about, unrolling my stockings and brushing down my tweed skirt, getting them ready for me to put on. Eventually buttons are fastened and zips done up. I take a look at myself in the mirror and see a pinched, rather dour-looking scowl on my face, but the rest of me is passable. A good waist even after two children, sturdy legs, although ankles a little thicker than I would like, and hair neatly curled. I dab on a smear of my favorite Elizabeth Arden red lipstick just to give my face some color and take a final look. "Hmm, that will have to do," I say, although Bobo has scurried away somewhere with an armful of laundry, so I am talking to myself.

The breakfast table is laid out, but there is no sign of anyone. From the delicious smell coming from the silver dishes on the sideboard, I deduce that the kitchen has sent up kippers, which I simply adore. Margaret and I discovered them while walking around Windsor Castle one day during the war. We had never smelled anything so enticing and followed the scent until we found where it was coming from. On discovering one of the servants cooking up some kippers for his breakfast, we were invited to try a bite, and so began a long love affair with the dish. It puts me in a good mood instantly, and I help myself to a small bronze-colored fish, hardly able to wait to place a forkful into my mouth.

"Good morning, Your Majesty," the footman says as he brings a fresh pot of tea to the table for me.

"Good morning. Am I the first?" I ask, slightly puzzled that Philip is not already up. My mother is no doubt taking breakfast in her room as usual, but Philip is an early riser and we usually meet at the breakfast table each morning.

"Yes, ma'am. The Duke of Edinburgh took breakfast in his room just before he left." The footman stands there awkwardly, trying not to look at me.

"Left? To go where?" His tour doesn't start for another week, so I can't imagine where he has got to . . . unless he's gone out shooting.

"London, ma'am." The footman's mouth clamps shut, and he nods his head, ready to beat a hasty retreat.

"Did he say when he might be back?" I ask.

The footman clears his throat. "No, ma'am."

"I see." But I don't see at all. This is our last week together before he goes on tour for four months to open the Olympics in Australia and to visit dozens of other countries. Although we exchanged harsh words, I didn't think for one moment things were so bad that Philip wouldn't want to spend his final week with me.

Yet that is precisely what has happened.

PART FOUR

NORMA JEANE

1946

The minute I saw my first modeling picture in a magazine, a little spark inside me started burning, and in the end, I guess it burned my old life down to the ground.

Schwab's Pharmacy is where everyone comes to hang out. People on their way to becoming stars and people who are all washed up. Hollywood is like that. It eats you up and spits you right back out again. Sitting at the counter trying to make a soda last most of the day, practicing my smile on anyone who looked like they might be going places, it occurred to me there must be a million pretty girls right here in Los Angeles. I need something to stand out, but I don't know what yet.

"Hey, Norma, you hear this?" Carol waves at me from the other end of the counter. She's a long-legged, tall, black-haired girl who once got to do a scene with Clark Gable. That's her claim to fame, which is more than I have to shout about right now.

"Hear what?" I yell back.

"There's a big fancy party tonight in West Hollywood. They're looking for girls to go along. You interested?"

"Sure . . ."

That's the other thing about this town—there's always a party to go to if you're a pretty girl. Rich men never get tired of looking at a cute face, especially if their wives are out of town. If I like someone, then I don't mind keeping them company over dinner, but I won't be bought. I pay my own bills in this town.

"Pick you up at eight?" Carol mouths at me, and I nod back at her. The other good thing about a fancy party is there's usually plenty of food there. A girl can live on party food if she does it right.

I finish my soda and slide off the stool that I've been keeping warm for way too long. I need to make myself look like something special tonight—after all, you never know who you might meet at one of these shindigs.

When I get home there's a letter for me propped up on the kitchen table, and I can tell by the handwriting that it's from Jim. He hasn't signed the divorce papers yet, and this envelope isn't thick enough to be full of legal documents, so I leave it right where it is. Poor Jim. He's a good guy, and if it hadn't been for him, I'd have ended up back in the orphanage because I was only sixteen and my foster family couldn't look after me anymore. Getting married at that age is way too young, but I tried to be a good wife. I guess you can't marry someone to stay out of a place. You have to really love the guy, and the truth is I want more out of life than to be a wife. I mean, I do want to be a wife one day—just not right now. Every time I drive past those film studio gates, I know that's the place for me. I want to be somebody.

I run up the stairs, go straight into my bedroom, and pull open the closet doors. I've got two good evening dresses that I alternate for Hollywood parties: a long white satin gown and a pink taffeta number. The pink one is the nicer of the two, as it fits in all the right places, but it picked up a cigarette burn the other week, and I have to hope nobody notices it. My bedroom is small, but I don't mind that. It's got nothing but a single bed, a dressing table, and a full-length mirror next to the closet, so I try not to spend too long in it. Most of my days I'm either at modeling jobs or hanging out in Schwab's trying to catch a break. I mostly only come home to change clothes and sleep.

I fix my face and hair before inspecting myself in the mirror. I just can't get a break no matter how hard I try, and I worry maybe it's my face that's all wrong. It's like a class I take—my personal studies. Some people study literature, but I study Norma Jeane's face and its very many flaws. My eyes are nice, but my chin is a little soft, that nose is too close to my lips, and my face still has a kind of childish quality about it, so no real cheekbones to speak of. My hair is light brown, nice and wavy. People keep saying I should dye it blond if I want to get on, but I don't know. There are a million blondes in this town, and I don't want to be just another golden-haired girl smiling sweetly at a producer. You have to offer something different from all the rest—but what? That's the question.

I go to classes as often as I can afford to—all kinds: acting, singing, dance, you name it. And of course the movies are my college. Every week I sit there studying the women on that screen. How they look. How they move. How they speak. I'm getting reborn as a whole new person once I make it to Hollywood. I just don't know who yet.

A car horn blasts three times outside, and I'm not even dressed. Throwing open my bedroom window I lean out so that Carol can see me. "I'll be right down," I cry. Finishing off my makeup and hair, I slide into the pink dress and zip it up. I look good. Elegant and classy, which is what I aim for these days. Dabbing perfume on my neck, I take a final look in the mirror and declare myself ready.

Carol drives like a crazy person, and I am hanging on to the door with one hand as she checks her look in the mirror. Suddenly a tiny critter runs right out into the road, and Carol slams the brakes on so hard that I almost hit the glass of the windshield.

"Hey . . . not so hard on the brakes! You'll ruin our careers before we even get started!" I cry, and then we laugh with relief that we're both fine.

"I'm sorry, Norma. I didn't want to hit that thing. That's bad luck to kill something." Carol turns to me with her big, black eyes.

"Yeah, well, it would be bad luck to kill us instead of that little thing, whatever it was."

"I guess you're right. I'll go slower. I promise." And with that she manages a whole twenty feet before her foot hits the gas like a hammer.

I swear I'm never getting in the car with her again, but as we abandon it outside one of those grand Spanish-style houses that rich people like to live in, I am still very much alive—and hungry as hell. My stomach is making little grumbling noises, and it crosses my mind that I haven't eaten anything since a party in Beverly Hills the night before.

The path leading to the front door is lit up with a long series of orange lights, and the brown wooden front door has been left half open. Probably someone got tired of people ringing the bell. Carol is wearing a dark green silk dress that leaves her shoulders bare. It looks good, but I think my old pink taffeta holds up in comparison. The lights are dim inside the house, so nobody is likely to notice the tiny cigarette burn, which is practically on my ass. I don't even want to think about how that got there. I'll just keep my back to the wall and hope everyone is too busy looking at the front of me to care.

We walk into the hallway, which is about three times the size of my bedroom. I can't imagine being so rich that you get to have all this space to yourself. Everything is fresh and clean with enormous vases filled with exotic flowers in deep pinks and oranges. I can see a bunch of women I recognize from auditions and modeling jobs standing around holding cocktail glasses with that look on their faces. It's a kind of vacant smile—well practiced, as if the man you're listening to is the most interesting person who ever lived. Nobody ever looks like that when they listen to the girls talk, though. Some of these women must have money from somewhere because their dresses are the latest fashion and fresh out of the box.

It must be nice to have everything new and not hand-me-downs, but I don't know what they have to do to get those nice dresses. It's probably more than listening with that vacant smile on their faces.

"Hey, aren't you a sight for sore eyes. What's your name, cutie?" The man is old enough to be my father. His face has deep grooves in his skin like someone carved the wrinkles right into him, and he has tufts of black hair coming out of his ears, which I really don't like the look of. His suit jacket is straining at the button, and his neck is too big for his shirt collar. He has nice teeth, though, and was probably handsome when he was young, which was a long time ago by the looks of it.

"Well, hello . . . I'm Norma. Norma Jeane Dougherty." He already has my hand in his, and I'm glad of my evening gloves because his palms seem kind of sweaty.

"Would you like some champagne, Norma Jeane Dougherty?" The way he repeats my name seems almost like he's mocking me, but if I say yes to the champagne, he'll have to leave my side to go fetch it, so I nod sweetly and off he goes.

Once the man who never bothered to introduce himself has gone in search of my drink, I quickly shift from my spot and move deeper into the crowd. Spying a waiter carrying a tray of salmon puffs, I make a beeline for the food, taking two at a time to stop my stomach from grumbling.

Outside in the garden is a large swimming pool surrounded by dancing girls who are wearing grass skirts and nothing except garlands to cover their breasts. The crowd of men in their tuxedos and women in all kinds of evening gowns spill out over the lawn. It's noisy with laughter, and in one corner an orchestra is playing dance tunes.

Standing there, cramming another salmon puff into my mouth, I suddenly notice a dark-haired man watching me from the other side of a potted plant. He's leaning against the wall and smoking a cigar with what looks like a glass of scotch in his hand. I can see Champagne Guy making his way through the crowd, carrying two glasses, his eyes searching for me, so I take a step to the side of the potted plant, and swallow the last of my salmon puff.

"You in hiding too?" The guy drains his glass of scotch and extends a hand toward me. "Harry Clifton. And you are . . . ?"

"Norma Jeane Dougherty." I smile and place my palm in his.

"Actress?" Harry speaks quite brusquely—no nonsense, like he needs to get to the point of everything and has no time to waste.

"I want to be . . . I'm doing some modeling right now, though." It's always awkward when people ask what you do. I'm an actress inasmuch as I go to class and put on a performance, but I've never had a role of any kind. My job title may as well be "audition girl."

"You've got something about you." Harry laughs, but not in an unkind way. "Oh, don't worry, I'm not trying to pick you up, Norma. I'm way past that game. It's my job to notice girls who stand out from the crowd."

"What do you do with them when you find them? Some kind of circus act?"

He laughs at my joke and finishes off his cigar, crushing the stump of it under his shiny black shoe. "You could say that. I work over at Twentieth Century-Fox. You've heard of them, I suppose."

My shoulders straighten right up, and I lift my chin to smile broadly. "Yes, I've heard of them. What do you do there?"

"I look for girls to put in my circus act. No guarantees, but you might get an audition at least." He's kind of fresh, but I like him, and the idea of an audition at the Fox studios makes me giddy with excitement. I move a little closer and smile a little sweeter.

All of a sudden, Champagne Guy shoves his way through the crowd and plants himself right by my side. "There you are, Norma. You disappeared on me. Here you go."

I take the glass of champagne from him and sip it for a second while I figure out how to get rid of him and focus on Mr. Fox Studio. The two men eye each other for a long moment until I figure that I've got nothing to lose and—just maybe—everything to gain. "Thank you for the drink. That's so sweet of you," I say with a bright smile. "And this is my husband, Harry. I'm sorry, I didn't catch your name?"

Champagne Guy splutters a little before shaking hands with Harry, who is trying his best to stifle a laugh.

"Thank you for taking care of my wife. She gets pretty thirsty if I leave her alone too long," Harry says, playing along. I am finding it hard to keep a straight face myself, but Champagne Guy doesn't seem to notice at all. His face reddens, and he looks like he can't wait to get away from us.

"Well, it was very nice to meet you both. You make a fine couple. Enjoy the party." And with that he heads right across the lawn toward the half-naked dancing girls.

Harry lets out a roar of laughter. "I like you, Norma Jeane. You're funny. Funny is good."

"Why, thank you. . . ." I take a gulp of my champagne and work up my nerve. "So can you put me in front of someone at Fox? I just need a shot." My words all tumble over one another in my eagerness to impress him. I don't know what he expects in return for this favor, and right now I don't care. I just want a chance to shine, and this could be it. "I'm a hard worker and a real fast learner."

"I'll bet you are. I tell you what, you call this number first thing tomorrow and mention my name." He takes out an expensive-looking brown leather wallet and plucks a white card from one of the pockets. For a moment he doesn't let go, and I'm holding the edge of the card with two fingers while he looks me up and down: "Good luck, Norma Jeane. I hope it works out for you."

"You won't regret it."

"I already regret it. Be lucky," he says with a smile.

I tuck the calling card away in my purse, making sure it's as safe as can be, but when I turn back to thank him, Harry is gone.

"This is Whitey Snyder. He'll do your makeup, and then we'll start shooting." Mr. Lyons is all about business, even though it's barely five-thirty in the morning and I'm half-asleep.

"Oh . . . but I did my own makeup, just like I do for my modeling pictures."

Whitey shakes his head. "That won't work on camera. Film is a different thing. You're gonna have to trust me on this."

He has a real nice manner, and something about the way that he speaks to me makes me feel like I should just let him do what he wants. So I give him a nod and say, "Okay, I'll trust you. But make me look good . . . please. I've got a lot riding on this."

"I'm going to make you look so good that you won't even recognize yourself in the mirror. Now let's wash all this off and see what we can do." Whitey gives me a little smile and I grin right back at him.

Once my makeup is all washed off, Whitey sets to work on my face. I can feel my nerves kick in at the thought of being in front of a movie camera. I've never had to say lines before, and my mind has gone all fuzzy, so I know I won't remember anything. My skin is breaking out in red blotches, like it does when I get upset, and I can feel tears welling up. I want this so badly, but now that I'm here, I just want to run away.

"Hey, don't worry! It's just like modeling. You don't have to say a word. You just look straight into that camera and do what Mr. Lyons tells you," Whitey says, as if he's read my mind. I guess he deals with nervous girls all the time in this place, but I'm still touched by his kindness.

I can feel the light pressure of his brushes painting me as if I am a picture, and then before I know it, he's done and there I am—only better than ever. My face has a kind of glow about it that wasn't there before.

"Wow . . . how do you make me look like that?" I ask.

"Vaseline . . ." Whitey smiles at me. "And a few other tricks I keep up my sleeve. It's not difficult to make you look good."

I reach a finger to my cheek and smile. "Thank you, Whitey."

"You're welcome. Good luck," he says just as a short fair-haired woman appears in the doorway of the dressing room, carrying a bright red sequined gown across her arms like a precious child.

The dresser zips me up, and we stand back to look at the finished effect. The gown shows off my figure nicely and pulls me right in. I feel a burst of excitement and a tremble of nerves all mixed up together. I cling to Whitey's words.

All I have to do is look straight into the camera.

I walk onto the movie set, and at first it's hard to stay focused, as there are people gathered around setting up great big lights that are so bright my eyes can't stand to look at them. Next to them is the camera, and I can see Mr. Lyons standing there talking.

"You look fine, Norma. Now, I need you to sit on that stool right there and smoke a cigarette. Can you do that for me?" Mr. Lyons gives me a little nod of encouragement, and I head over to a tall wooden stool that's been placed right in the middle of the movie set. It's tricky trying to slide onto it because the dress is tight, but I do my best. As soon as I'm seated, a young man appears with a cigarette and lights it for me.

Mr. Lyons calls for the lighting to be set, and the stool is bathed in a soft yellow glow.

"Okay, Norma, I want you to smoke the cigarette, then stub it out and walk over to the window. Got it?"

I glance over my shoulder to check where the window is. It's just a hole cut out of a wooden wall, and another light has been set up to shine through it like sunshine. "Okay."

"And ACTION!" Mr. Lyons calls.

I'm so nervous and dazzled by the lights that I forget everything he just told me, but then I take a deep breath. This is my chance to change everything. I think back to poor little Norma Jeane with the crazy mama, being passed around foster families or washing dishes in the orphanage until her hands were red and raw.

I'm going to be somebody.

I am getting reborn right here, right now. It's only a camera, and I gaze at it for a beat, trying to work out what to do. Then I see how it is. It's the same as taking pictures for modeling. The camera can be my friend, if I want it to be. I can make it love me, even if I haven't figured out how to do that with people yet.

I raise the cigarette to my mouth and inhale. Then I exhale slowly, and all the time I look straight down that lens as if I just want to take off all my clothes and make love to whoever is watching me. I slide myself off the stool and crush out the cigarette as the sequined dress falls into place around me, and I head for the window. Walking slowly—letting my body do the talking. Then I breathe deeply, turn right back to the camera and give it one last lingering gaze.

"CUT!" The shout snaps me back to reality, and all the nerves start tumbling over me again. "Okay, honey. That was great," Mr. Lyons says, and I hear the guy behind the camera give a low whistle, which makes me feel like it was a home run. "We'll call you . . ."

Mr. Lyons already explained to me that they need to show my test to Mr. Darryl Zanuck, the head of the studio, as he's the guy who makes the decisions. I only hope that he likes what he sees.

"Morning, Joe." I see Joe every morning when I arrive at the 20th Century-Fox studios, and he's always nice to me. He's one of those big bearlike guys who works security here, but every single day he has a smile and a wave for us girls. It's as much part of my day as breathing now.

Mr. Lyons said that my screen test went well, but it was up to Mr. Zanuck to offer me a contract. He and some other people at the studio told me I had a "luminous quality" on-screen, and I could tell that I'd done all right in the test, just from the way the men were all grouped together chattering away about me at the end.

A couple of days later, Mr. Zanuck called me into his office, which was all expensive-looking wood, with a big desk that he sat behind, reminding me of a headmaster in a school. He is a short guy with a way of looking at me like he's found some gum on the bottom of his shoe. I didn't like the way he talked down to me at all, as if I was some naughty kid, but I'll put up with pretty much anything if he lets me make pictures for Fox.

So I bit my lip, and smiled sweetly. "I really want to learn everything you can teach me here," I pleaded.

Eventually he turned to Mr. Lyons, without even a glance in my direction, and said, "One year . . ."

I'm going to be a movie star! I have a studio deal for a whole year, and if I do well then that could turn into a permanent contract.

Me—Norma Jeane Dougherty—will be right up there on that screen for the whole world to look at. Oh, I could have hugged both Mr. Zanuck and Mr. Lyons, but of course I just smiled and said thank you, like a good girl.

I want to be a great actress, and I'm learning so much just from hanging around the Fox studio all day long. I'm learning how to stand and move as I'm speaking the lines. How a tiny gesture makes all the difference to the shot. The camera doesn't need you to do that much. It needs you to feel things inside and, like magic, it will show what you're feeling to the audience. When I get it right, it makes me glow, bright and warm, and I feel like I've come home . . . as if this is where I was always meant to be.

And the things the studio can do to make you look better! Anything you need, from fixing your face to doing your hair and makeup. Already I look more grown up and womanly, although I'm only just twenty. I'm still taking all kinds of classes too, from acting to singing and dancing, rushing from one class to another and watching everyone to see what I need to do to put myself out there. I don't ever want them to turn me away because of something that I can't do. If they need someone to sing a song riding bareback on a horse, then I'll find a way.

This morning, I put on my lucky dress—it's pale blue cotton with a white collar, which I pair with some white open-toed slingbacks. It's the same outfit that I was wearing the day Carol told me about that Hollywood party that changed everything for me. I figure that went well, so I should wear it again, as I've got a big meeting with Mr. Lyons today. There's a lot riding on it, and as I greet Joe at the studio gate, my stomach does a funny little flip that makes me feel queasy. I send up a little prayer to whoever watches over me, because somebody must be doing that job.

I want this so bad . . . more than I've ever wanted anything in my whole life.

I'm going to show them all how good I can be.

. . .

Mr. Lyons's office is much smaller than Mr. Zanuck's. He has two comfortable brown leather chairs in there, and his desk is pushed back against the wall, so it doesn't feel like a schoolroom. He invites me to take a seat, and so I position myself carefully at my best angle—back straight and legs crossed at the knee—while he sits down opposite me, smiling broadly. His white shirtsleeves are rolled up, and his jacket hangs on the back of his chair, like he's a man always involved in *doing* things, not just standing around looking important. Although he is important.

"It's good to see you again, Norma. I've been thinking a lot about you, and where we go from here. Of course, you'll start off doing background stuff—you know, walk-ons—but if you work hard and it goes well, then we could find you a speaking part. It's a long road and you've got a lot to learn."

"I know, and I really want to learn. Like I told Mr. Zanuck, I am ready to learn everything you can teach me." My voice sounds girlish and eager, but I mean it. It's like finding a new world, and now you just want to explore every single part of it, until it becomes *your* world.

Mr. Lyons looks at me intently. "Are you a determined kind of gal, Norma? Because it's going to be hard work to break through. I need to know that you've got what it takes to keep working at it."

My eyes widen and I stare right back at him, "Mr. Lyons . . . you need a certain kind of stubbornness to get yourself out of the orphanage and away from foster families, and to make a career in this town . . . especially as a girl with a certain look. Some men have tried to take advantage of that, but I know how to take care of myself. To go from working in a factory . . . to modeling and now making movies—that takes some gumption, and I've got plenty of that."

Mr. Lyons sits back in his chair and smiles like I've managed to impress him.

"Okay, Norma, let's get to work. Now, you've got a sweet look, but it's kind of a girl-next-door thing, and we've already got a lot of girls like that. We need to make you sexier. Starting with your name . . ."

"What's wrong with my name?" I ask.

"There's nothing wrong with it. It's just . . . I don't think Norma is a very sexy name. It's not a movie star name . . . not for the kind of roles I see you playing, anyway."

He looks at me as if I'm going to start bawling over changing my name. As if I haven't always had a new name attached to me. I've gone from Mortenson to Baker to Dougherty, and none of them means a thing.

"I don't mind changing my name, Mr. Lyons. In fact, I think it's a good idea. What did you have in mind?" I say, hoping that whatever he comes up with is a good trade.

"Well . . . this is just my first thought, so you can say if you really don't like it, but I think you look like a . . . Marilyn. There's something about you that reminds me of that great Broadway star Marilyn Miller, and *that's* a movie star name."

I imagine stepping outside of myself—saying good-bye to Norma Jeane. All the loneliness and the pain that she has in her memories . . . they won't be in Marilyn's mind at all. I like that idea. I can be a whole new person—I can be anything that I choose. Marilyn is a newborn. I see myself stepping right into her, and she feels like a suit of armor.

I uncross my legs and shift back a little in my seat as I try the name out. Rolling it around my tongue. *Marilyn . . . Marilyn.*

"Sure, that's a nice name. I'd like to be called Marilyn. But Marilyn Dougherty . . . ?" It doesn't sound right. It reminds me of someone who works in a factory, and not a woman who is going to be a great actress shining up there on the big screen.

Mr. Lyons frowns and shakes his head. "No, we need to think of another name that goes with Marilyn."

I do like the sound of Marilyn, but it doesn't belong to me. If

I'm going to be called a different name by strangers, then I want something that really does belong to me. The name needs to feel truthful, like it was always mine. I think for a moment about what Mr. Lyons said about Marilyn Miller, and then the name just flashes right into my mind.

"My grandmother's name was Monroe—how about Marilyn Monroe?"

Mr. Lyons's face lights right up. "I like that . . . yes—Marilyn Monroe. Now *that* is a movie star name if ever I heard one." He sits forward in his chair, grinning at me.

Naming a person is a strange thing, but of course movie studios do it all the time. Cary Grant was Archie Leach, and Judy Garland was Frances Gumm. You can take any old name and make that person have an ordinary life, because what else are they going to become with an awful name? Yet when you change it, something begins to fit together inside you differently.

A second ago, I was Norma. An orphan. A girl who nobody wanted, who was always getting knocked back. But *Marilyn* . . . even saying the name makes me sit differently. I could be anyone now, a whole new me, without all those wounds to tend. Marilyn is strong, and she isn't afraid of anything. She would take you on and spit in your eye if you tried to stop her becoming what she's meant to be.

I practice saying it out loud and it makes me giggle. It's a happy-sounding name.

Marilyn, Marilyn . . . Marilyn Monroe.

"Great. Then I'll get all your details changed to Marilyn Monroe, and we'll let the press office know so they can begin putting that name around town."

"Thank you, Mr. Lyons." I stand up and offer him my hand, which he grasps nicely. I like him. He's been good to me so far, fighting in my corner and giving me a brand-new name. Maybe a brand-new life.

As I walk out of his office and back toward where Joe the security guy is standing in his usual spot at the studio gates, I find I'm walking with more purpose, like my body fits together differently.

"Good day to you, Miss Dougherty," Joe says as I pass him. He's the kind of guy who takes pride in remembering the name of everyone on the lot.

"My name is Marilyn now . . . Marilyn Monroe," I say, and start giggling again because it still sounds strange to me.

"That's a good name." Joe grins back at me. "I'll be sure to remember that name—Marilyn Monroe. It's a lucky name, I'd say."

As I walk away from the studio I whisper under my breath, "I sure hope so. . . ."

LILIBET

1946

Philip is coming to stay with us for a month at Balmoral Castle, and now I am so nervous I can barely eat a thing. Suppose it all goes wrong—suppose we don't like each other as much after spending an entire month together? Suppose he doesn't ask me . . . suppose my father won't allow it. . . .

There are so many complications, but all I can think of is that this afternoon he'll be here and we'll have endless days of summer, without the shadow of the war or anything else to distract us. We can talk properly and have fun together. These past few years have been so starved of fun, especially for poor Philip, who's been serving on a ship for the entire time. He's been so very brave, and I prayed every single night for him to be safe and come home to me.

I find myself humming as I wander around the strange little rooms and winding staircases of Balmoral, wondering how we shall take to each other. I feel as if I know him deeply, as we wrote to each other all through the war, and of course there have been visits to the palace and occasional nights out dancing. Most of the time Margaret has been with us, and I'm so pleased my sister and Philip seem to like each other tremendously. We three have such good times together, although I would like to spend some time alone with him so we can really see whether there's something lasting waiting for us.

The clock-winder man is doing his rounds, and part of me would very much like it if he could move the clock hands on an hour or so and make time go faster. There are a great many clocks at the castle—and they all require winding by hand. It seems a strange job for someone to solely be employed to walk through the rooms carefully winding them all, but that's what he does. Of course, he also fixes the clocks and keeps them ticking, so I imagine that's quite satisfying work, as they are very old and lovely things.

The train from London takes an age, and then there's the drive from the railway station. It feels as if Philip will never get here, and I am trying my best to be patient.

It's very funny how things have turned out. I have such high hopes for this summer, but if it hadn't been for a case of the mumps, things might have taken a very different course in my life—and the mumps weren't even mine.

It's the smallest things that can change your entire life without you even knowing about it at the time. Rather like a tiny boat setting sail on the ocean and you alter course by a fraction, only to find you've ended up in a new and foreign land.

So it was with Philip and me when we first met.

My parents had asked Margaret and me to accompany them on a visit to Dartmouth Royal Naval College. I remember that I was wearing a lovely blue dress, which felt quite grown up, having just turned thirteen years old. Of course, at that age I had no wish to be inspected in any particular way, being quite shy by nature.

It was a beautiful day with a deep blue sky and the sun shining down on us. The cadets all looked so very smart in their uniforms, with their white hats glinting in the sunlight. At first it did not seem so very different from the many other royal visits to schools or chapels or other places where I was required to dress nicely and comb my hair so that people could see a neat and suitable princess.

We were supposed to go to a special service in the chapel, but suddenly we were interrupted by the college doctor, who informed us that two of the boys had come down with the mumps, which are very infectious, and neither Margaret nor I had had them. It was decided that the cadets would be allowed to enter the chapel and the service would take place as planned, but that Margaret and I would go with our governess to the captain's house, where the Dalrymple-Hamiltons live with their children. It was a lovely old house—the kind anyone would be very happy in. The children greeted us nicely, and we were taken to a large, sunny nursery where they had a clockwork train set running all over the floor.

Margaret and I thought it great fun and played for a long time. Then the door to the nursery opened and in walked a tall, fair-haired boy with fiercely blue eyes. He was a few years older than us, at least sixteen or seventeen, I thought, and very striking. He'd been sent to amuse us presumably, and he took on the task with great relish, kneeling down on the floor to play with the trains. I remember meeting his bright blue eyes as he said, "How do you do?" and I felt some strange sensation fizzing through my veins—an excitement racing around inside that wasn't there before.

My cheeks began to flush pink, and I could do nothing to control it however embarrassed I felt. Philip soon got bored with the trains and suggested we all go outside and try jumping over the nets in the tennis court, so we did. He was very good at it and able to jump much higher than Margaret and I. We spent most of the day and evening with him, and I was pleased to find that he was allowed to come back again to have lunch with us the next day, even though the threat of mumps had receded, with the poor invalids having been taken to the infirmary to recover.

Philip spent quite a lot of our lunch teasing Margaret, but he sat next to me, and so I was able to study the line of his jaw, the way his hair curled slightly around his ear, and the length of his neck and broadness of his shoulders. It was quite a lopsided view of him, being taken from one side only, but I imprinted each detail onto my memory, as if I were sitting for some sort of test.

As we sailed out of Dartmouth, the cadets were allowed to follow us for a while in whatever boat they might get their hands on. Margaret and I stood on deck watching all the cadets in boats, both large and small, rowing after us for all they were worth. Eventually they all stopped and sat back, resting their oars and waving us good-bye. We waved back furiously, very excited by the sight of them, and then Margaret nudged me: "Look, Lilibet, isn't that Philip?"

And there he was, the last cadet to be rowing after us. I do believe he wanted to catch up and say a proper good-bye, but the water was full of dangerous currents, so everyone shouted at him to stop and go back.

My eyes fastened on him, wanting him to be safe and return to the harbor, yet at the same time wishing he would carry on. It was the most thrilling thing and made the feeling inside me spark and fizz all the more. I'd certainly never met anyone like him before. Prince Philip of Greece certainly made quite the impression, and from that day on my heart was set on him.

The clock strikes the hour for lunch, but I really couldn't eat a bite. My stomach makes a nervous little flip inside, and I keep running to the window to look for a car. I just can't settle, and it would probably be the best thing if I went for a walk to get rid of this feeling so that when poor Philip does finally arrive, I can stop behaving in this silly giddy way and greet him warmly.

"No sign yet?" Margaret appears in the doorway, and I'm sure she knows instantly why I'm at the window staring longingly down the driveway.

"No . . . he's taking an age. I do hope he didn't miss the train, or he won't get here at all today." Up until that moment it hadn't occurred to me that he would miss the train, but now the thought has lodged itself inside my mind, I can't release it. "You don't think he would have missed it, do you?" I turn to face Margaret, searching her face for comfort.

"No, of course not. He would have telephoned from the railway station to let us know," she says, and the knowledge that she's right gives me a brief respite from my nerves. "You look very nice," Margaret adds, smiling in that encouraging way sisters do for each other.

I'm wearing a dark wool skirt with a rather pretty peach-colored cardigan—what Margaret thinks of as my headmistress look. "Not too serious?" I ask, and my hand pats at my hair.

"Just right," she says. "Are you coming to lunch?"

"I really couldn't eat a bite. Anyway, I'll wait for Philip because if he misses lunch, then he'll need to eat something later, and I'd like to keep him company should that happen."

Margaret squeezes my arm and plants a kiss on my cheek, "Good luck, Lil. He's so very nice and obviously quite mad about you. Fingers crossed." She holds up her crossed fingers, and I feel touched, almost emotional. Without us ever speaking about the situation, she has understood what this summer means to Philip and me.

"Thank you, I shall do the same for you someday. Then we shall both have the men we love." I surprise myself at the words coming out of my mouth. Ever since that day in Dartmouth seven years ago, I've loved Philip and only Philip. The thought of it makes me slightly breathless, as Margaret grins at me on her way out of the door.

I've been waiting for Philip for what feels like a lifetime. All through the war years, when he was serving on a ship in the Far East, I would wait impatiently for the post to arrive. I can still remember his very first letter to me after we met at Dartmouth, which was excruciatingly polite, saying how pleased he had been to meet me. The letter itself actually said very little, but the fact that he'd written at all seemed to say quite a lot. Of course, we are distant cousins, so after that we occasionally ran into each other at family gatherings and formed a friendship. At first, we wrote infrequently, but then, as war broke out and we both got older, our letters became warmer and more personal, as if each of us were relying on the other.

My heart would leap at the sight of his letters and that familiar determined handwriting. Inside the envelopes, his words spoke of his hopes and dreams for the future. A future without war, where we could just do ordinary things. We talked of taking picnics out into the Scottish hills, or places he might take me dancing in London when he got leave. Happy plans for a world we hoped might arrive, if the war ever ended.

I have kept every single one of his letters in a large wooden box, the pages slightly thinned by reading and rereading them. There are tiny blotches from tearstains from when, some lonely evenings when the news was particularly bad, I imagined what might happen to my life if Philip were to be killed. The thought of losing him—of never seeing those fierce blue eyes or his mischievous grin again—reduced me to terrible sobs on more than one occasion.

The crunch of tires on gravel makes me inhale an enormous gasp as the car rolls into sight, and I can barely contain myself from running to the front door, which wouldn't do at all. I can see Philip in the rear of the car—his face searching the windows of the castle, until his eyes meet mine and we smile at each other. I give a brief wave and smooth down my skirt, pat my hair again, and otherwise try to calm myself. I hope that spending so much time together this summer doesn't make him reconsider our attachment. Part of me hopes desperately that he will propose while he's here, but that brings its own worry, as my father would have to give his permission for us to marry. Oh . . . I so want everything to go well.

"Ah, there you are," my father says as Philip gives him a polite bow before shaking his hand. Papa's eyes seem stern as he looks Philip up and down, but then they turn to mischief as he sees me hesitating in the doorway. "Welcome, young man. Good to see you again. They'll take your things up, and I'm sure that Lilibet and Margaret will show you where everything is, won't you?"

"Yes . . . of course." Although mysteriously my sister seems to be missing at this precise moment. Silently, I thank her for giving us time to greet each other privately before her chaperoning duties begin in earnest.

"We're about to have lunch, so do come down when you're ready. Lilibet, I'm sure the poor boy is starving, so don't keep him away too long showing him the house." My father winks at me as he leaves for the dining room, making me flush crimson.

Philip's bags are collected and taken up the stairs by a succession of servants scurrying past us, until eventually it's just the two of us glancing shyly at each other.

"Goodness, he looks as if I've kept him waiting." Philip points to the marble statue of Prince Albert and begins to chuckle.

"Your room is this way," I say, and I'm about to climb the stairs, when I feel an arm slip around my waist, and my feet practically leave the floor, as Philip pulls me to the rear of the statue of Prince Albert and kisses me.

"There . . . that's better. Missed me?" He has that devilish look on his face that I find so attractive.

"Yes . . . I mean . . . I . . ." I am rambling, unable to get a sensible word out.

"Well, aren't you going to show me my room? After all, we're holding up lunch for everyone." Philip's face breaks into a wicked grin, and the sight of him finally being here—standing so close to me that I can smell the warmth of his skin—is doing quite peculiar things to my ability to think straight or speak.

"This way . . ." I manage eventually, and race up the stairs as quickly as I can, still feeling his kiss lingering on my lips.

"I think this is my favorite place in the entire world." I am showing Philip the grounds of Balmoral, and every part of me wishes for him to love it as I do. The peaceful silence and the rolling mists across the hills: there is simply nothing like it. Given the choice, I should like to live my life here surrounded by such beauty.

"It's very lovely, but not nearly as lovely as you." Philip takes my hand and toys nervously with my fingers.

"I am sorry that we've had so little time to spend alone." It seems that every day since he arrived here has been shooting parties or picnics or some such thing organized for us. We have had to make do with long, lingering glances across a crowded room or snatched moments when Margaret made an excuse to let us have a few minutes to ourselves.

"Your family is very keen to inspect me. But I don't blame them for it. After all, apart from being a distant relative, what do I have to offer the King of England and his family? A homeless sailor . . ."

"Not quite . . . You are a prince, and that counts for something." I do worry that my family doesn't think Philip is quite suitable for me. His family has no throne to offer any longer, and his sisters married high-ranking German officers before the war, which makes things terribly awkward—to say the least.

"They want better for you." He stands quite still for a moment, staring out at the distant rain clouds rolling in.

"They want me to be happy." I can't say what I feel, which is that Philip is the only man for me, and however hard they searched, it would not be possible to find a better match. I don't want to be married to some dull English duke. I want to feel that electricity sparking inside me when those fierce blue eyes fasten upon me. I want him to ask me . . . but there are so many considerations. It's not just me that he'd be taking on—for one day the Crown will rest on my head, and that will be a great responsibility for both of us. I wouldn't wish it on him. In many ways, I would rather he was free to live his life completely as he wishes—and yet I cannot let him go.

"And I want you to be happy, so on that we are agreed." He smiles somewhat wistfully, and there's a sadness to it that puzzles me.

"What is it?" I say softly.

"It's a serious business. It's not just the two of us, is it? I love you, Lilibet . . . very much. You know that . . . and I want us to be together, but I do want to be up to the task, as it were." Philip's face is so earnest and serious that I could reach out and kiss him right here, where anyone could see us.

"I'm sorry that it's so complicated. I know it's rather like taking religious orders, joining this family. Your life will never be your own, but my father is a young man and we would have a long time to ease ourselves into the job," I say hopefully, and I'm sure that we will.

"Yes, that's true. I'm sure we'll both feel very differently about the challenge ahead of us in twenty or even thirty years. We're still young with so much to look forward to before you become Queen, and I become . . . what? Your loyal servant." He chuckles a little to himself.

"Yes, a lot can happen in twenty or thirty years. We have so much time ahead of us." I mean it: as I say the words, I can picture our lives so long and seemingly endless. Our future so bright together.

Philip puts his hands on my shoulders and gazes at me with such seriousness that I could cry. "I want a proper home with children. A life together that's secure and stable. It's something that I've never had. After the revolution that took my father from his throne, my family disintegrated and scattered in all directions. My mother spent years in a sanatorium, while my father entertained his mistress in the South of France. My sisters went to Germany to marry, and I was left all alone. I've got used to doing things my own way and taking care of myself, and I know that I may not be the easiest person to deal with at times, but family is very important to me. I suppose that's why I've always loved the Navy—it's become a sort of surrogate family. But now with you . . . I'd like to have a real family again . . . to belong somewhere. To belong with you . . . if you'll have me."

My breath catches in my throat as my heart leaps. A current of electricity sparks through my blood, and all I can think about is that finally we can be together. He's all that I've ever wanted, since that first day I set eyes on him at Dartmouth. He seems so brash and sure of himself at times, but I see his softer side. The bit of him that missed out on a proper family life and desperately wants to be part of one again. We would be a good team, and I know he will always be completely on my side.

"I'd like that very much," I whisper softly, perfectly sure that he must be able to hear my heart beating hard in my chest.

"I should do my best to support you . . . and look after you completely and utterly." He takes my hand and holds it to his lips, kissing the back of it and not relinquishing it for a moment.

"I know you will." I reach my hand up to touch his cheek, gently stroking it, and then, just as great fat raindrops begin to fall all around us, we kiss for the longest time. . . .

Dinner is a jolly affair with my family, although my mother seems to be questioning Philip on all manner of things, as if testing his mettle in some way.

"And do you still visit your sisters in Germany?" she asks, her beady eyes glaring at him.

"No, not since the war broke out. It's been quite difficult, as

I'm sure you can imagine." Philip answers her directly and without avoiding her stare.

My father has been out shooting, which always puts him in a good mood. It's the perfect time to speak to him, and I try my best to telegraph this information across the dining table to Philip, who seems to catch my intention and nods back at me. My family usually plays games after dinner, or sometimes has a film to watch, but there is always a moment when my father likes to go off and smoke by himself. And that might be the perfect time for Philip to broach the subject of our engagement. I am praying that Papa agrees to a wedding next spring, which should give us plenty of time to organize everything.

It's going to be complicated, of course, as the country still has rationing and I don't even know how we could get enough silk for a wedding dress, or whether we can hold such a large royal occasion in the current climate. It's only a year since the war ended, and people might think it inappropriate. Yet everyone loves weddings—they're such hopeful, cheery occasions, and ours is sure to be filled with joy. Anyway, if my father doesn't say yes, there won't be a wedding. He must surely know that I won't marry anyone else. I shall live alone like the first Queen Elizabeth if I can't have Philip.

Dinner is venison, and I play with my food, all the while wondering if I should speak to my father before Philip does—before deciding that might undermine Philip. They have to sort it out between them.

Suppose Papa says no . . . ? I couldn't bear it.

"You're very quiet, Lil," Margaret whispers to me. She is sitting next to me, chattering away, being the usual life and soul of the party, so I'm surprised she has noticed.

"Am I? I must have a lot on my mind, I expect," I say, longing to confide in her but not daring to say a word until it's all settled.

Finally, dinner is over, and we all make our way back to the drawing room to play parlor games until it's bedtime. My father takes the opportunity to wander off into the garden to smoke in peace and quiet, and I catch sight of Philip following him out of the door. I can't hear what they're saying, but both of them walk outside together, and all I can do is hold my nerve and pray.

A little while later, Philip reappears and settles himself beside me on the sofa in the drawing room, as a rather intense game of charades is under way. The room is filled with the noise and chatter of my extended family, as various cousins have arrived to stay with us, and for this evening I am very glad of the distraction so that Philip and I can whisper to each other without anyone noticing.

"Well? What did he say?" I ask urgently, barely able to contain myself, for everything in my life rests on what comes next.

"He said, 'I see.' And went on smoking his cigarette." Philip grimaces back at me.

"Is that all? Just 'I see'? What good is that?" I feel a desperate sense of panic and long to run to my father, demanding that he give us an answer right this minute, but I know it would be useless to do so. My father is a stubborn man.

"I suppose we shall have to wait to see what he says. I made my case very clearly, and as politely as I could. I promised him that I would take the very best care of you and do my best to honor this family, and my country. It was quite the speech, if I do say so myself." Philip gives me a weary smile. I can see that, like me, he is also terribly disappointed to have to wait for my father's response, and I hope that it doesn't mean that he will refuse us permission. He can't do that, surely? I tell myself that he merely wants a little time to get used to the idea; after all, he'll be losing a daughter. Yes . . . that's it. Tomorrow my father will say yes, and we'll drink champagne to celebrate and draft the engagement announcement.

"He probably just wants to sleep on it. Tomorrow will be our day, I'm sure. And then we can tell everyone."

"Do you really think so? Suppose I got it wrong and I've turned him against me?" he says, trying to work out the worst-case scenario we may have to face.

"You haven't got it wrong. He probably just needs a little time to get used to the idea. We should see what tomorrow brings. Under normal circumstances, Papa would say yes immediately. It's the job, you see. He has to think about the Crown and that sort of thing. I'm sure it will all work out."

I try to keep my voice hopeful, but part of me worries that it is perfectly possible that my father sees only the negative things about Philip—no real home, and a family that is complicated to say the least. He will think about the prospects for the monarchy as much as for my future happiness, and I do understand that duty is a very necessary thing, but I won't give Philip up under any circumstances.

The night seems endless, but dawn eventually breaks, and before too long the piper is playing his bagpipes signaling the start of a new day, one that will bring immense happiness—I hope and pray.

My father doesn't appear at breakfast, and so Philip and I spend the morning playing cards with Margaret. We're terribly distracted, and she eyes us both with some concern but wisely says nothing. As the clock ticks away, Philip and I sink into a deeper misery. He is staring gloomily out of the window without meeting my gaze. Both of us are rather twitchy and fidgeting in our seats.

Then, just as we are losing all hope, my father appears in the doorway, beaming at us in his kindly way, and I could run into his arms, for I can see from his face that he will say yes.

"Margaret, I'd l-l-like to t-t-talk to your sister and this young man in private, please," my father says, and she is quick to leap to her feet, leaving us alone. In the doorway, she hesitates for a moment and gives me an encouraging smile.

My father waits for her to depart before settling himself into the armchair opposite us. He looks first at Philip and then at me before starting to speak.

"I'm sorry to have made you both wait. It's such an important decision, you see, and you are my precious daughter. Your happiness is as important to me as my own. Now, I know you are both young and in love. I'm not so old that I don't remember that feeling myself, and a good marriage is the strongest foundation. Through all my d-d-difficulties, my life was made much easier by knowing that I had the constant love of the Queen, and I want the same for you, Lilibet. To be assured that when you are in my position . . . many years from now . . . that Philip will be the rock on which you can stand. T-t-to that end, I have to inform you both that I have made my decision."

Philip and I exchange nervous glances, and I hardly dare breathe. My eyes fasten on my father's face, imploring him to put us out of our misery.

"My d-d-decision is that you should both wait until next year. My suggestion is this—you have an informal understanding between you that can be considered binding, if that's what you both wish. However, Lilibet, the four of us will leave for South Africa next February for three months, traveling as a royal family, and when we conclude that tour, if you and Philip still wish to marry . . . then I won't stand in your way."

"But that's almost a year to wait. And we'd be apart for all those months." My voice sounds shrill to my ears. Three whole months apart. He can't do this to us. Almost a whole year to wait after we've already spent most of the war apart, relying on letters and occasional meetings. I wouldn't blame Philip if he wanted to change his mind. I can't bring myself to look at him.

"I understand, sir," Philip says quietly.

"Do you, lad? I hope so. Lilibet is not twenty-one until next April. After that she is of age and can make her own decisions, although her position necessitates that she have my blessing. Youth makes us see only possibilities, so it's up to those of us who are older to temper that enthusiasm, not out of cruelty, b-but out of love."

"But, Papa, it's such a long time to wait!" I plead a little, even though it's hopeless. He won't change his mind.

"My dear, if you and Philip marry then, you will have very many years of happiness to look forward to, and this will be a tiny moment on your journey together. I'm not standing in your way because I don't approve. On the contrary, I think Philip has shown himself to be a remarkable young man, and I see how dear he is to you. I want only happiness for you both, but this is my decision as your father, and as the King." With that he gets to his feet and walks out of the room, leaving Philip and me completely shell-shocked and staring wildly at each other.

"I'll speak to him—" I begin, but Philip puts his hand over mine.

"He's right, Lilibet. I forget that you are younger than I am—not even twenty-one yet. I'll wait for you, and if we're meant to be together . . . then we both have to be sure of it."

His arms wrap around me, pulling me close to him, and for a moment I could cry in his embrace. How can we wait a whole year when we've already waited so long? It doesn't seem fair. . . .

PART FIVE

The Daily Sparkle

BY IDA LAPINE

The Duke Is Out to Lunch

A certain duke may be missing from Soho over the coming months, as he's being packed off to far-flung places, presumably to keep him out of trouble.

He and his friends are certainly getting quite the reputation, carrying on like bachelors, and rumor has it they're seen around town more often than party-loving Princess Margaret these days.

Will absence make the heart grow fonder, at least as far as their wives are concerned? A little birdie tells us the wives are most displeased and that we should stay tuned for further developments over the coming weeks. . . .

Monroe Is "Off Sick" Again

Speaking of unhappy wives, news reaches us that once again all is not well on the set of *The Sleeping Prince*, due to the indisposition of one Miss Marilyn Monroe. Honestly, is this woman ever well enough to work?

We hear that her husband is returning to the USA to visit his children and leaving his new bride, who by all accounts has taken to her sickbed.

Sources tell us that poor Sir Larry is trying to coax her back to work. If she carries on like this, who could blame people if they stopped employing her?

After all, blondes are ten a penny in Hollywood, and they must be able to find one of them who will turn up on time? Sir Larry certainly hopes so. . . .

NORMA JEANE

1956

Click . . . smile . . . click and smile. The grass feels damp and cold, but the photographers asked us to sit, and so we do. The *Daily Mirror* newspaper is taking pictures of Arthur and me in our garden—the happy couple here in England.

Little do they know . . . You certainly couldn't tell by looking at us. This may be my greatest ever acting performance.

After I took the pills, I was rushed to a local hospital under the name "Miss Baker" to have my stomach pumped out. Pa was so frightened he would lose me that he actually cried at my bedside when I came home. He got on his knees and sobbed like a little boy—swearing all the time that he was just mad at me and he would never write such a thing again. He must have said he was sorry a hundred times. But I don't know if I'll be able to trust what he says to me now. I can't tell whether he is sorry for the thoughts in his head or just the fact that I ended up in the emergency room.

"Could you turn toward Arthur, Marilyn?" one of the photographers asks. "Great big smile . . . that's it. A little more . . ."

I curl my legs under me and smile wider and brighter, but Marilyn isn't here.

It's just me now—a broken glass that someone stuck back together again. Sometimes I feel like some of the pieces got lost and I can never replace them. I didn't want to die when I took those pills, but there was a moment when I was drifting away on that black tide and I felt nothing at all. There was no pain, nobody could hurt me, and I wanted to stay in that space forever.

The morning after they pumped my stomach, I felt so exhausted that I took a couple of the little purple pills to keep me going. I called in sick so at least I didn't have to face Larry. I can't do it anymore. I had to get away from them all. Arthur swore he'd stay right by my side all day long, but then a problem came up with the opening of his play, *A View from the Bridge,* and he was on the telephone for the entire morning trying to sort things out while I took a bath.

I sat in that bathtub for so long that the water turned cold and I didn't even notice. Then I fixed my face and slipped on a simple black dress with matching shoes. My wedding ring lay there at the side of the sink, and I walked away feeling that lightness on my finger. The ring is inscribed with the words NOW IS FOREVER. But I slammed the bathroom door on it, wishing I could leave heartbreak behind me so easily.

Covering my hair with a white silk headscarf and without saying a word to anyone, I slipped out of the house and asked John, our driver, to take me to London. The purple pills kicked in and I felt my eyes widen. A kind of buzzy feeling was running through me like a current, and in a flash I turned from this exhausted cloud of misery to a person who could walk for miles or dance all night long. I couldn't feel anything—not the pain in my heart or the constant pain in my belly.

John dropped me off on Regent Street, and I quickly blended into the crowd. I can do that when I'm not being Marilyn—you'd be surprised how soon you become just another blond woman going about her business. Thanks to Marilyn, there are a lot more blond women on the streets than before. Alan told me last week that there was even a fake Marilyn going around England arranging appointments with dressmakers or making reservations at restaurants, and then not showing up. All those people got giddy at the thought of meeting me and then thought I'd let them down.

I put on a pair of black sunglasses and decided to head off to lunch. I just wanted to sit quietly and read a book or watch people go by. I love to do that—making up stories about the tall man with the folded newspaper under his arm, or the sparrow-like woman with the tiny dog. I give them whole lives and families as if they are characters in a book.

At the end of Regent Street, I strolled across Piccadilly and saw the statue of Eros with his tiny bow in his hand. I've always wanted to see him in real life, and Piccadilly Circus looked just like it does in photographs—full of brightly colored signs advertising things. It reminded me a little of Times Square and, for a second, I felt a pang of sadness—kind of homesick, but not for any building. Instead, I felt a terrible sense of longing for the Marilyn who slipped on a black wig and fur coat and ran away from 20th Century-Fox—calling herself Zelda Zonk—to the airplane that took her to a new life in New York. The woman who told them she wouldn't stand for it anymore and she wanted control over her own destiny. I miss her. I wish she'd come back to me because I was so sure of myself at that moment. When I landed in New York, I felt happy for the first time in a long time. Maybe I should have stayed there. . . .

It feels disloyal to think that I was happier before I started seeing Arthur. Was I, though? It's true that I didn't have a great love in my life, but when I look back on it, my days in New York seem like a whirl of museums and galleries, of working all day on my acting skills at the Studio and then going to see wonderful plays in the evening. Spending long nights talking with incredible actors like Brando, or brilliant writers like Carson McCullers. Parties at El Morocco and the 21 Club. I felt like I belonged everywhere I went.

New York for me was a world of ideas, and when I started dating Arthur, who is so cultured and refined, I thought he would complete that part of me.

Arthur told me that he could only see the best of me, and if I saw myself through his eyes, I'd really believe that I was a woman with all these hidden depths waiting to be explored. He would share his work with me and help me prepare my scenes for the Actors Studio, and we would talk for hours on end about music and theater and books.

He made me feel as if only he could see that person inside me. And for the first time in my life, I felt like I was unfolding my wings and getting ready to fly.

But now I feel just as lonely as I did before.

As I walked across Piccadilly, I realized that someone was watching me. I always have a sixth sense for people seeing Marilyn. It usually takes a couple of beats before I'll hear a timid voice say, "Excuse me . . ." Sometimes they'll kind of hedge their bets and tell me that I look like her. I glanced over quickly and saw that I was right. It was a young man—about twenty years old, I would say. He was wearing a navy blue suit that was too small for him, and his trousers were flapping around his ankles in a way that appeared quite comical. As I looked at him, the young man saw his chance.

"Excuse me, aren't you Marilyn Monroe?" he asked.

Quick as a flash, I pulled a face—a sort of sneery mocking smile planted itself on my lips—and in the most outrageous London accent I could manage, I said, "Oh no, my love . . . my name is Elsie. Marilyn . . . well, I never." And I walked away before he could argue about it.

Loneliness wrapped itself around me like an invisible cloud of expensive perfume, but at the same time, I didn't want company, so I slipped quietly into a restaurant on Coventry Street. The waiter didn't recognize me, or care about any of his customers particularly, so I took the table in the corner, far away from the window, and ordered a bowl of soup.

I took out my book, opened it, and smoothed a page with my fingers. Walt Whitman's *Leaves of Grass*. It's one of my favorites, and I keep it by my bedside. There's something about poetry that goes straight past your brain and into your heart. On the page, I saw the words *Resist much, obey little,* and somewhere deep inside I felt a spark, as if a little flame had been reignited.

The waiter placed a small white bowl of chicken soup on the table, and I took a mouthful. It scalded my tongue a little and didn't taste of chicken at all. I left it to cool and carried on reading the poems, letting them work their magic on me. As I was beginning to relax, a sudden noise made me look up, and I realized that I'd been spotted. A group of young girls were standing outside the restaurant window, giggling and pointing at me. I knew it wouldn't be long before a crowd gathered, and then I'd need some help getting out of there. It's like a tide rushing in, and you can find yourself stranded on the shore if you're not careful. I called the waiter over and whispered softly, "I don't want to be a problem or anything, but I'm Marilyn Monroe and you may want to call somebody."

As I said the words, I pointed toward the window where there was a sea of faces all staring inside the restaurant. One of the young women knocked on the glass and screamed, "Marilyn . . . we love you."

I stared back at her blankly and thought to myself: *You don't love me. You don't know me.*

All those people wanted was a glimpse of Marilyn—they wanted to measure her up and see what she's really like. Except Marilyn wasn't there. There was only me, Norma Jeane.

By the time I got back to Parkside, everyone was mad at me for disappearing like that. The word had even spread back to

Larry that I'd been in London having lunch when I was supposed to be off sick, so he probably thinks that I'm faking illness. If only they knew . . .

There are all kinds of crazy rumors about what happened the other night, and the only way to shut them down is to do what I always do. You know what they say—a picture is worth a thousand words. The world needs to see Marilyn Monroe smiling and looking lovingly at her brilliant husband. She has it all. They have it all.

Just look at them—the King and his Queen together.

So here we are sitting on the damp grass in the garden at Parkside House, while I stare lovingly at Arthur and the cameras go click. What does he see when he looks at me? A woman he loves or a woman he loves to possess? An angel to put on a pedestal or someone who will never be his equal?

"Just one more, Marilyn—could you smile again? That's it, nice big smile now . . . lovely." The photographers continue to shout their instructions at me: it's business as usual. Tomorrow I will accompany my husband to the airport and kiss him goodbye for ten days . . . or maybe forever.

Then I'll go back to work. "'Resist much, obey little,'" I mutter to myself.

Nobody will ever know that Norma Jeane nearly died. Marilyn can never die, only Norma can do that . . . because only one of us is real.

LILIBET

1956

Outside the window of the train, the yellowing leaves of autumn hang damp and forlorn from their windswept trees as we pass through small villages and towns whose names I barely remember. Possibly I've visited them at some point—cutting ribbons to open new buildings or watching a display of some courage or skill. The visits become a blur of sameness after a bit, and one only really remembers the times when things went horribly wrong or something stood out to make it memorable. Raindrops run lazily down the outside of the window, and the warmth of the carriage is making the glass mist over.

"Your tea, ma'am." The train steward delicately places a cup and saucer on the table in front of me.

"Thank you," I say, eyeing my children across the aisle. They are a little grumpy today. The end of summer for them is a return to school and an end to the fun of fishing or picnics, camping or long afternoons playing games. They are pinching each other when they think I'm not watching them, and I know this is bound to end in tears at some point, so I give them a stern look. Anne shuffles about in her seat under my gaze, while Charles turns away and stares out of the window.

"Won't be long now," I say to them.

The rhythm of the train is slow enough to lull one to sleep on the long journey from Scotland to London, but it does give one a chance to think about things and make plans.

Philip and I shared the briefest of telephone calls last night. Underneath the polite enquiries about the family and our arrangements to see him off at London Airport lies a furious rage. We are both equally angry with the other, I should think, and quite how we resolve it I don't really know—yet resolve it we must.

I take a small sip of my tea and consider passing the time by doing my paperwork. Once we are back at Buckingham Palace, the full schedule of investitures and meetings and royal visits begins all over again. The endless parade of people waiting to shake hands. Only time for the briefest of chats: "And what do you do? How lovely . . ." and then on to the next person. I can see the nervousness in their eyes, and I do try to make them feel comfortable, even though I know they've probably been practicing their bow or curtsy for days and hanging their best dress or suit so that it will look just right. And then I'm gone, and they all return to their normal lives. Yet for me that is my normal life . . . or at least part of it.

The landscape becomes much more industrial, and suddenly we are at the outskirts of London. I give a small sigh and prepare myself for whatever lies ahead. A difficult reunion with Philip, and then the endless rounds of duties.

"Ma'am, would now be a convenient time to go over your schedule?" Michael is eager to prepare me for the coming weeks.

"Very well," I say reluctantly. I'm not quite ready to face it while my mind is full of what Philip and I are going to say to each other when we come face to face this evening. But I must.

"Not too much this week. You're due to go to the Horse of

the Year Show tomorrow, and then of course you'll be seeing the Duke of Edinburgh off on his tour. Next week is quite a busy one, ma'am. There's the visit to Dumfries on Tuesday, then on to Sellafield for Wednesday. We'll take the train to London from Keswick so that you're back at the palace on Thursday for your weekly audience with the prime minister that evening. Then you're giving a lunch at Buckingham Palace for the Costa Ricans on Friday."

"It does seem rather poor planning to come all the way back from Scotland only to return to Dumfries for a visit, but I suppose it couldn't be helped."

"No, ma'am. I'm afraid not." He looks at me apologetically, and I give a brief nod to indicate that our discussion has ended. He gathers up his papers and the large leather-bound diary containing every single plan we have for the rest of the year and beyond, before giving a bow and walking away.

I finish drinking my tea as the more familiar sights of the houses and businesses of London flash past the windows. The train trundles into St. Pancras station, letting out a gasp of steam as it comes to a halt, and we all spill out onto the platform, walking briskly to the cars that will whisk us back to the palace.

"Hello. Good trip down?" Philip looks tired, and underneath the politeness, I sense a reluctance to open up a conversation about our argument. He kisses me briefly on both cheeks, and the warmth of his lips is quite at odds with the coolness of his tone.

"Yes. The usual, really. We got on the train. We got off the train. And here we are." I try to keep my voice light and cheery, but there's a rather obvious strain to our conversation, and our eyes don't meet as we make polite chatter with each other.

"Right . . . well . . . I'll see you at dinner," Philip says before retreating to the comfort of his own study.

For a moment, I am completely alone. The staff, sensing a

strange electricity in the air, have all found something to do that doesn't involve standing in proximity to us. The dogs have been taken out for their walk, and so I sit down in a comfortable armchair, running my fingers along the green stems of the embroidered flowers on the arms. Tomorrow Philip will be leaving for four months, and if we don't clear the air this evening, then who knows when our next opportunity will arise. I cast my mind back to those endless days of the tour to South Africa, when my father was testing our resolve to marry. Each day seemed to last twice its proper length, and I couldn't think of anything except whether or not Philip and I would stand the test. As soon as we docked back in England, Philip arrived at Buckingham Palace to greet me. The two of us were a little shy and awkward at first—waiting on the other for confirmation that all was the same between us. He stood by the fireplace, his eyes wary as we made polite conversation about the merits of South Africa and the beauty of that country. Until I couldn't stand it any longer.

"I haven't changed my mind, Philip, so if you have, then it's best if you tell me now." I could hardly breathe as I stared longingly at his face, praying for the right response.

His smile became so broad and happy. "I feel exactly the same way, and if you'll have me . . . then I would very much like you to become my wife."

He took a step toward me, and I fell into his arms. "Yes, I would like that very much." The burst of happiness rushing through me was almost too much to bear.

We survived that separation, and in the end, even my father could see that nothing would stop us and there was absolutely no point in trying to talk me out of it. My heart was fully set on Philip.

And here we are after nearly nine years of marriage and two wonderful children about to be faced with a similar test of character under very different circumstances.

As I get to my feet, I know that I need answers, for I cannot allow him to leave me for months on end without some kind of resolution to this gossip.

"Can we talk without fighting . . . please?" I watch the bones of his back stiffen at the sound of my voice.

"That depends on what you're about to say, I imagine," Philip says gruffly, although I note that he at least looks up. His eyes contain a dull fury that I can only imagine is solely aimed at me.

"I don't want us to part on bad terms. You're going away for quite a while—almost half a year. It would be nice if we could resolve some of our issues before you go." I move closer to his desk and place a hand on his shoulder, willing him to respond.

"I don't know what you want me to say. I haven't done anything to apologize for." He looks hurt, as if the thought of being accused of something has pierced him.

"Philip, when you married me, you knew that one day I would become Queen. And although it's of great regret that this job fell to us much sooner than we had anticipated, we both know that there's nothing to be done about it. If we were a private married couple living a quiet life somewhere, we could do as we pleased with only the other person to consider. But you know that's not how this works for us. Please don't treat me as if I'm making up some problem where none exists. . . ." I find myself pleading somewhat, and his face appears to soften, but quite how successful I've been is hard to tell.

"I don't see that we should jump to attention whenever some bored journalist writes some untruth about us. If it were true . . . if I *were* squiring a succession of 'party girls' around London and the Home Counties, then I might agree with you that our issues are not private, but to respond to gossip and nonsense seems to me completely unfair."

I draw myself up to my full height, which admittedly is not that tall, and stick out my chin. "So you are saying that these rumors are not true in any way?" A beat of silence goes past, and I find that I am holding my breath a little, waiting to be put out of my misery.

"For goodness' sake, I can't go to the lavatory without somebody watching and waiting outside the door. How on earth do you imagine I could be conducting the kind of life painted in such lurid colors by our friends in the press?"

"I see. . . ." I don't know why he couldn't have just said so right at the beginning. I presume his stubborn pride stopped him—but he has said it now, and the relief runs through me so strongly that I could cry. How ridiculous. I wasn't aware that these emotions had been building themselves inside me, but I suppose that's how gossip works, isn't it? A snakebite. A poison that drips quite slowly through your veins until none of your previous joy or hopefulness is left inside you. I brush a tear from my cheek before Philip should see it, but I'm too late.

"Oh, Lilibet . . ." he says sadly.

"I don't want to take anything away from you that you need to make you happy. I want you to know that, Philip. I do understand how hard this job is for you, and how very much you've given up for me. I feel completely torn in two between my duty as Queen and my duty as your wife, and I do want you to understand that however difficult things may be for you . . . well . . . they are also difficult for me." I manage to make my little speech without giving in to the well of tears I can feel brimming inside me. I feel quite desperate at the thought of him going away, as I shall be even more alone than before.

Philip looks at me for a long moment without saying a word, and then he clears his throat. "I am sorry."

"Thank you. Please can we try to work out some kind of strategy to deal with this situation?" I smile weakly, willing him—this stubborn man whom I love so very much—to see things my way.

"If we must—but I tell you now, I will not under any circumstances fire my private secretary. Mike Parker stays on the tour." And with those defiant words, our fragile truce ends.

"Oh, for goodness' sake, Philip." I exhale a long and exasperated sigh and shake my head. "You really are the most infuriating man."

And with that I turn on my heel and walk out of the room.

NORMA JEANE

1956

"Okay, Marilyn . . . you walk to the window and hear the music coming from the street, and then you do your little dance right here." Larry points out the space at the back of the pink couch where two points have been marked out on the carpet. I have to dance between them.

I stand on my mark and wait.

"And ACTION!" he shouts as the music begins, and I walk over to the window and start to hum along with the song before moving to the closest point to begin my dance.

"CUT! No, Marilyn, your bag should be in your other hand, and this hand is on your shoulder. Got it?" Larry sighs as he walks away, and I feel stupid. For some reason, in my mind I had it the other way around.

The music begins once again, and he calls, "ACTION!" I walk to the window and begin humming the song, and then I start my little dance, but halfway through my foot gets caught in the mermaid tail of my dress and we have to stop again.

"Try kicking it out of the way with your foot, Marilyn!" Larry snaps at me as if I'd designed the damn dress. "Let's do it again. Places, everybody, and ACTION!"

I walk to the window and hum along with the music before going into my little dance, but before I can dance a full step, a lightbulb explodes to the side of me and we have to stop again.

"Take a break, everyone," Larry says with a sigh, and I walk back to my dressing room and sit with my head in my hands, trying to keep it together.

Arthur left yesterday. He's going back home to visit his children. The two of us drove through the empty streets saying very little to each other. Since it was a Sunday, most things were closed, but as the car sped along, I stared at all the little houses with their lights on—filled with families. Some people never close their drapes at all, so you can see their entire lives all laid out inside their rooms. People having dinner together or doing laundry. There was a woman just staring out of the window like she was carrying the world on her shoulders, and I wanted to ask her what was wrong. Too many things probably. Thankfully there weren't many people about when we reached London Airport except the usual photographers.

As we sat in the back of the car, I remembered the dreams I had when we first landed here—the two of us in our tiny honeymoon cottage eating dinner on our laps by the fire or taking long walks in the rain. Now Arthur's face was turned away from me, and I could tell that all he wanted was to get on that plane. In some ways, I feel sorry for Arthur that I'm not what he expected. I always turn out to be just another human being after all.

Nothing has turned out like I thought it would. But I can't deal with it right now. All I can do is keep going, finish this movie, and then see what is left of Arthur and me once it's done.

Arthur leaned in close. "Remember that I love you," he whispered. I could smell that sweet earthy scent of his skin, and for a moment I just wanted to throw myself into his arms, but I didn't.

I *know* he loves me, but I'm not sure that he likes me very much sometimes.

We got out of the car and kind of stood there, shifting from foot to foot. Then, just as he turned away to board his flight, I touched him lightly on his shoulder. I didn't know what to say or how to make things right between us, so I just kissed him hard on his mouth and said, "Come back to me."

Arthur nodded and then he was gone.

As I was driven back through the empty streets, I pressed my face to the window. In the distance I could see the castle, and I looked for the Queen's flag, but it wasn't there. It sounds silly, but I kind of miss having her around—not that I've really seen her, except that one time when her car went past us. I like to think of the little flag as a kind of secret message that she's trapped in the castle and she needs me to set her free. See, I told you I like to make up stories about people. As the car approached Parkside, I started laughing at the thought of it. I've seen too many movies about women kept prisoner in a tower, I guess, or read way too many paperbacks.

I've asked Paula to stay at the house with me until Arthur comes back. I hate to be alone at night, and this place is especially creepy after dark. I think Arthur has given Paula instructions to keep an eye on me. Everyone seems very concerned that I take the right amount of sleeping pills, but I'm not going to do anything silly.

I don't want to die. I just want to be happy again.

There's a tap on my dressing room door, and it's time to go back out there and face them all, but I just can't do it. The minutes tick by, and still I sit there unable to move. I feel so alone here. There's nobody on my side—not even Arthur anymore. There's another tap on the door, and an impatient voice calls out, "Sir Laurence is ready for you on set, Miss Monroe." Taking a deep breath, I think about when I was sitting in that restaurant reading my book, and Whitman's words come to mind: "Resist much, obey little." And I get to my feet. . . .

There are nasty stories in the papers about me keeping people waiting, but there's something about the walk from the safety of my little room to the set where there are so many people watching me that still makes me nervous after all these years. I'm not very good in groups—I like being with just one or two people, where you can really talk and look right into their eyes to understand what they're about. In large groups, I just get so scared and my stutter comes back—then I get worried about stammering and fluff my line, or end up in the wrong place entirely.

The set has a little buzz of chatter as I walk in, and I can see Larry in the far corner deep in conversation with Jack. They're leaning over the camera, pointing and gesticulating, so I guess they're working out the shot. Larry sees me and lifts his hand, but it's not so much a welcoming wave as a gesture of recognition. I give him an ice-cold stare in return.

"Ah, you're finally here," he says with a grimace.

"I am finally here, Mr. Sir," I reply, and then I walk away across the set before he can say another word. I don't apologize for being late because he has never apologized to me for his rudeness. It's a petty little war, and there can be only one winner.

I find my chair eventually, as someone has moved it right to the edge of the set. It has my name written across the back of it in white letters—MARILYN MONROE—and I can see that someone has left a magazine on the seat. As I lean down to pick it up, I realize that it's an old theater program with a photograph of Larry and Vivien on the front cover. It takes me a second or two before I recognize the way she's dressed, and my heart begins to pitter-patter. It's a picture from the opening night of the stage play of *The Sleeping Prince,* with Vivien playing my part. She looks so elegant and sophisticated all dressed up as the showgirl. I just look like Marilyn Monroe . . . no matter what I do.

Glancing around I wonder who put it there and whether it was Larry. The crew are all busy setting things up, and nobody pays any attention to me, but somebody put this magazine here deliberately to make their point. I'm sure they would all have preferred Vivien to play this role so they could be one big happy family. They have no time for me at all. I drop the magazine back down on the seat and pretend that I didn't see it. Instead, I take out my script and focus on the scene.

It's too late, though, as a wave of panic sweeps right through me, and my hands begin to tremble. I can't stand here and recite my lines or do a dance knowing that someone hates me so much they left this magazine here for me to find. It's just so spiteful.

I look up to find that Larry is walking toward me, but my feet make up their own mind, and I start running across the set and back along the corridor to the safety of my dressing room.

Paula follows behind me, and I can hear her calling, "But what's wrong, Marilyn? Wait . . ."

But I can't wait.

I don't leave my room for the next two hours because I'm too upset about everything. I need something to make me feel better. I know that I shouldn't do it, but I take one of the tiny purple pills and pour a slug of vodka into a glass. Acting has to be truthful, and if I'm trembling and crying, how can I film scenes where I'm dancing and singing?

There's a knock on my door, and before I can say a word, Larry walks in. "Darling, we're all waiting for you. It's just a little dance, that's all. Could you come back and try?"

"I need a minute . . ." I say, and my voice is frosty.

"A minute . . . very well."

His face is fixed with that smarmy smile that I've come to hate, but he turns his back on me and walks out of the door.

I didn't mention the magazine, and anyway maybe he already knows. I would never have come to this country if I'd known people would be so cruel. Just because the newspapers reported that I was having lunch in Coventry Street when I was supposed to be on set, they think that I wasn't sick. That it was all a lie.

They don't know a thing about me and everything I've been through. These men can't imagine the pain I've been in. . . . Even if they wouldn't care about my marital problems, they should at least know that I've been really sick.

There have been days that I've stood here in agony, yet I've plastered that smile all over my face and I've fizzed and bubbled like Elsie Marina because that's how good an actress I am and that is who Marilyn Monroe is. They think I'm some dumb blonde, when all I needed was a friendly face and some kindness, which they don't seem to be able to manage. I'll show them what I'm made of. I feel so mad now that all the fear goes away and I stop shaking. I check my face in Whitey's mirror and then I walk straight past Larry and say, "I'm ready now." When I pass by my chair, I notice that the magazine has vanished.

After thirty takes I still can't get the damn dance right, but we keep going. Then out of the blue I do the most perfect take where everything flows together: the way my body moves and I laugh, the young king enters the room, then the line just falls out of my mouth. It's exactly right. It's perfect, and I could shout with joy except that the actor playing King Nicholas seems so surprised that he fluffs his line. I could cry. So we do it again and again until eventually, just as we're both too exhausted to care, we finally get it right and that's a wrap for the day.

Arthur didn't telephone when he said he would, and I barely managed an hour of sleep before the horrible dreams woke me up. I crave the blankness of a dreamless sleep, but I was wide awake and it wasn't even dawn.

This morning I'm blurry around the edges, and my brain is

like mush: so tired it won't think straight. I can't face any more trouble on set today or the way they all look so disappointed with me, so I gulp down two little purple pills with a mouthful of vodka.

It's the only way I'm going to be able to face them all. . . .

LILIBET

1956

My mother breezes into my drawing room, managing the briefest of kisses and a curtsy on the same breath as she says wearily, "Lilibet, have you *seen* this?"

To my surprise she appears to be brandishing the very same newspaper that contains the gossip column about Philip, although it is now weeks old and I can't imagine how she has got hold of a copy. Without bothering to sit down in her favorite cream armchair, my mother remains standing in front of the fireplace, all the while holding up the offending article as if protesting something. I half expect her to start marching suffragette-like through the palace, carrying a placard made up entirely of this old newspaper.

A flush of humiliation colors my cheeks pink, and I sigh silently. My mother has always been perfectly polite to Philip, but I am only too aware she has always held her own reservations about his suitability. My heart races a little at the thought of having to defend him against her attack, especially when I've been quite cross with him myself.

Wearing her soft lilac dress with its neat little ruffles around the collar and her usual pearl necklace, she looks every inch a queen, but of course since the death of my father she is no longer *the* Queen. It's a fact that irks her tremendously: her irritation is made obvious every single time she curtsies to her own daughter with such great reluctance. All the people who once obeyed her now serve me, although, to be perfectly honest, I can't be sure they're not all reporting back to her. Indeed, her possession of this newspaper article does seem to be evidence that somebody has brought it to her attention quite deliberately.

I manage what I hope is a gracious smile and say calmly, "Yes, I have read it, and of course it's complete nonsense. Philip's lunch club is not some den of iniquity but rather a place where he and his friends can let off a little steam. I have of course discussed this with him, and we both feel the best course of action is to ignore it. They'll find someone else to gossip about very soon, I'm sure."

It's a half-truth, but I really cannot face the prospect of marital advice from my mother at the moment. Philip is leaving this afternoon on his tour, and then I have a meeting with Mr. Eden, my prime minister, this evening to discuss the extremely serious situation in the Suez Canal. I have neither the time nor the inclination to discuss this gossip with my mother.

"Do you know how we first found out that your uncle David was infatuated with Mrs. Simpson?" My mother's face has taken on the stern look she likes to adopt when telling off her children. It's a rare sight and not one I relish.

Sighing inwardly, I try to compose myself for I know only too well how this conversation will unfold.

"It was in a gossip column and the subject of wild rumor and speculation for months, and look where that got us. . . ." Her lips are pursed as she taps the offending newspaper article with her index finger.

"Mummy, it's not the same thing at all. Philip's little club is not a threat to the future of the monarchy. This is merely silly gossip. Please don't worry about it."

"But I am going to worry about it and about you. Lilibet . . . he's your husband and you . . . are the Queen."

"I am only too aware of that situation, and I have dealt with it." I am trying to remain calm and unflustered, but it's quite tricky to reassure my mother when I cannot even reassure myself that the situation has been completely resolved. Another flush of humiliation envelops me, and I silently curse whoever has seen fit to hand my mother this newspaper.

"You *must* do something to stamp out this kind of gossip—and the behavior that leads to this type of thing landing in the newspapers. Philip must see—"

"Philip *does* see!" My voice has taken on a sharp edge, and I am trying to keep my temper, but honestly the whole world seems to have nothing better to do than to interfere in my marriage. The truth is I'm not sure that he does understand the seriousness of this situation, but I am so very tired of fighting about it.

"You really need to make sure that he surrounds himself with more suitable people, as clearly he is spinning about like an unguided missile." She gives me a long-suffering and somewhat icy glare, and for a long moment we stand there, each woman preparing her next move as if this is a chess game.

Then, surprisingly, my mother softens and sinks into her favorite armchair, abandoning the newspaper on a low table at the side of her. Placing her hands together in her lap, she casts her eyes downward and takes a deep breath.

"You know how close we came to disaster with your uncle David and his selfishness. He was a man given over to impulsive behavior—to overwhelming passions. Spending his evenings and weekends at parties with any number of unsuitable companions, until he found Mrs. Simpson. A divorced American of all things . . . *divorced*." My mother repeats the word as if she can barely believe that anyone could do such a thing, and then, after drawing a long breath, continues. "A country needs stability above all else. They need a monarch who is calm and reassuring. The entire point of a royal family is to provide a Christian example of duty and sacrifice—to show others that such a life may be possible. Your uncle David was not capable of that, as he proved on multiple occasions. Your late father was completely the opposite—a man so given over to his duty and love for his country that he sacrificed his own health and well-being. Your first responsibility must be to this country—you cannot be a fair-weather queen. You have to be unequivocal on this matter. And you cannot and must not put anything before your role. . . . The marriage must fit the duty, Lilibet, and not the other way around. I understood that fact perfectly, and you know how happy your father and I were together. Even Margaret's situation—as unhappy as it has made her—was absolutely the right decision. This is a life of public service, and duty must always come first." Her pale blue eyes search my face—her expression so earnest that for a moment I don't know how to respond.

"I'm not a fair-weather Queen. I am dedicated to my country and my duty, but I am learning the job. It's only been four years since Papa died, and it's not easy. I cannot stop the press printing silly stories. What would you have me do? Send them to the Tower of London?"

Her implied criticism stings and is further confirmation, if any is needed, that I am failing on every front at the moment: failing to please and support my husband, my sister, and now my mother. Yet this is the first time any of them have suggested that I am not doing my duty as Queen in the right way, and given our personal relationships at the present time, I really cannot think of any area in which I am succeeding.

My mother shakes her head, and her voice takes on an exasperated tone. "You must talk to Philip and make him understand that we cannot allow any tiny chink in the armor of this family to be exploited. It's not about *our* personal reputations—it's about the country and ensuring proper leadership. We must be faultless. It's our duty." Then, satisfied that she has made her point, my mother gets to her feet. "Promise me that you'll speak to him . . ." she says, not unkindly.

"Very well. I'll talk to him. Will you be staying to lunch?" I am very much hoping that the answer will be no, but one has to ask.

"No . . . thank you for the invitation, but I'm hosting a lunch party at Clarence House, so I should be going. Do think about what I've said, Lilibet. It's our responsibility to make sure we provide an example—the right example. . . ."

Feeling quite chastised, I watch my mother getting into her car from the window. I do understand the importance of stability in the country; after all, nobody wants a queen whose personal life is splashed across the *News of the World* every Sunday. But on the other hand, is it really necessary to react to every little murmur and whisper from the press? Is monarchy such an endangered species that we all have to have a fit of the vapors every time somebody in the family goes to a nightclub or is seen in public with a friend? After all, we are human beings. Are we to sacrifice any semblance of a normal life?

I don't know what the answer is.

Philip and I are perfectly silent as the car takes us on the short journey to London Airport, where he will board his flight to Mombasa to join the royal yacht *Britannia* and begin his tour. I want to say something to him—to make things better—but I find that I can't quite come up with the right words. We haven't been apart for such a long time—not since the run-up to our engagement—but my father designed that as a test of character and the strength of our love for each other. I suppose in many ways this is the same.

"We shall miss you very much," I say softly, trying to break the rigid silence between us.

"And I shall miss all of you. I may not miss your scolding

quite so much," he says. There's a little bitterness in his tone, but I can also see a tiny smirk playing at the corner of his mouth.

"Am I so very terrible? I do rather feel as if I am letting everyone down at the moment." The words spill out of me in spite of myself. I hadn't wanted to pick this moment to have any kind of emotional conversation, but four months is such a long time to be apart, and we have been at odds with each other for far too long.

Philip gives me one of his looks. A mixture of tenderness and slight irritation. "Not so terrible . . ." There is a proper smile behind his words now, and I reach for his hand, squeezing it firmly.

"If there was something that I should know . . . you would tell me, wouldn't you?" I don't quite know what I'm asking of him. He's about to board a plane, and this is hardly the time for a heart-to-heart, and yet I can't let him go without asking. All my unanswered questions are racing through my mind. *Do you still love me as you once did? Can we be happy in this life?* What am I really saying? *That I love you with all my heart and I couldn't bear to be humiliated in the press—to be the brunt of jokes, as happened to Uncle David and Mrs. Simpson . . . and I suppose my own sister in some ways.*

For a moment a brief flicker of annoyance crosses Philip's face, but the thought of us parting for such a long time has made him softer too. "Do you remember that summer we spent in Balmoral before we got engaged . . . all those years ago?"

"Of course I remember. It's ten years almost exactly."

"I told you then how important it was to me that we have a happy family life. It was something I hadn't experienced as a boy, and I wanted to be part of something like that more than anything. My father spent a great deal of my childhood pretending that he no longer had a family. It hurt me greatly, and I would never want that for you or my own family. You are the only person in the world who I've ever confided that to. Oh, I know what the rest of them think of me, but I've always wanted you to see the best of me . . . to believe the best of me. I still want that. . . ."

The car sweeps onto the tarmac and comes to a smooth halt by the steps of the airplane, where a small parade of dignitaries are waiting to see him off.

"I do believe the best of you. I want to do that . . . always," I whisper to him, and I mean every word.

"Good . . . then I will do *my* best to live up to it." He nods firmly, as if we've come to some agreement—and maybe we have. Maybe it is really that simple.

"I don't care what anyone says about me or what they write. I do very much care what you think, Lilibet. Now come along: I've got a plane to catch. . . ."

His words make my heart quite full—or maybe it's the thought of not seeing him or being able to talk quietly like this for the next four months.

I shall miss him so very much.

NORMA JEANE

1956

It was late in the afternoon when I first felt the pain again. The same old fist gripping my insides, signaling that my period is on its way, but this pain seemed worse than usual. I borrowed a couple of aspirin from one of the costume girls and tried not to screw my face up on camera when the cramping hit. We wrapped for the day, and I didn't stick around to look at the dailies. My head felt hot, and the pain was getting much worse. The studio doctors here won't give you strong enough painkillers, so the best I can get is a kind of fading feeling.

When I get back to the house with Paula, she pours me a vodka to try to take the edge off the pain, and I carry the glass up to my bedroom. Once I get undressed, I find that I've started bleeding and it's pretty heavy. After downing the vodka and whatever pain pills I have left, I lie between the sheets and a stabbing cramp ripples through me.

I hug Arthur's pillow, and for a moment there's a trace of him—the faint scent of his hair cream. It makes me miss him so bad that I almost start crying. Curling up into a ball, I hug my knees to my chest until the pain begins to dissolve a little at the edges. I feel just awful, but I don't want to be alone.

Paula sits on the edge of my bed and tries to distract me with amusing stories of people that she's worked with over the years, but I'm not really listening. I feel so sick, and I miss Arthur so much. At least I miss the Arthur I thought was in love with me. I still haven't spoken to him, although he has called and left me sweet messages saying that he loves me. The time difference is making it difficult for us to connect, and he's traveling again. I can't help thinking about the words he wrote about me and I can't seem to forgive him.

There's a light tapping noise on the bedroom door and Paula gets up to answer it. I don't want any of the staff to see me like this. Nobody wants to see Marilyn bleeding and cursing with the pain, and I don't have the energy to put on a show for them. Whenever I'm caught off guard, things have a habit of ending up in the newspapers. Everyone has their price, I guess—whether that's money or it makes people feel good to say, "Here's something I know and you don't." I hate it that I can't keep anything to myself for long. Someone will always sell you out for something they want—eventually.

"It's the housekeeper. She wants to know if you're hungry—would you like a tray brought upstairs?" Paula asks, but I shake my head and mumble something in return. I'm in such agony that I can't form proper sentences.

"It hurts . . ." is all I can manage to say. I can see by her face that she's getting worried about me. We're in a strange country, and neither of us knows how to get hold of the kind of pills that might make a difference. There's a studio doctor, but I don't want him. I don't want anything that is linked to Larry and that damn movie. I just want the pain to stop.

I try rubbing my hand across my abdomen, then curling and uncurling my legs. I hug my knees back up to my chest and roll onto my back. The pain is so bad, it's making me feel sick and I think I'm going to throw up. Stumbling out of bed, I run to the bathroom and only just make it as my stomach heaves out my lunchtime sandwich and glass of milk, plus the vodka I downed earlier. My face feels clammy to the touch and nothing seems to be helping. As I lie there shivering on the cold tiles of my bathroom floor, Paula gently strokes my arm and whispers that she's going to call someone to help us.

An hour later, I've made it back between my sheets as Paula darts in and out of the room, fetching things to help me. On one trip she returns with some pills, which I greedily swallow down with a glass of water. "These are stronger," she says with a comforting smile. "There's a doctor at one of the London hospitals who specializes in endometriosis, and he's going to call on you tomorrow. He sent these over. There may be a small procedure they can do to help you without you going to the hospital. He understands the need for privacy."

I don't even want to know how Paula found out about this doctor, but I hope it wasn't connected to Larry. I don't need him knowing about my period problems on top of everything else. He'd probably announce it to the entire crew if he knew. Another flaw I have, along with my yellow teeth and stupid acting method. A spark of anger flares inside me as I sink back against my pillow. Paula allows me two Nembutal and eventually sleep comes to take me away.

Thankfully the dreams don't come, and I wake the next morning with the pain softened a little and feeling ravenously hungry. Paula has already told the studio that I won't be in today, as I'm sick. The doctor will be here this afternoon, and I hope there's something he can do for me because this pain is too much to bear on top of everything else.

I manage to eat some eggs and drink a glass of milk, which makes me feel much better. Then I bathe and get dressed before swallowing down two more of the pain pills the doctor has sent over. At least they give me some relief. I lie back in my bed and try to read, but my eyes skim over the words in the morning papers, and nothing makes sense to me. Then I see that someone has slipped in a nasty little story about me from the movie set. Vicious and spiteful stuff about how I'm a diva who can't act at all. I hurl the newspapers across the room in a temper. Why can't these people just leave me alone? I'm trying my best.

The doctor seems like a nice man. Tall, kind of wiry, with dark hair. Not handsome but with a good strong face, the kind you can trust. I like that in a doctor—I think it's important. He asks me the usual questions about my symptoms and how long this has been going on, so I tell him everything. The years of cramping, the awful, awful pain, the vomiting and fever. He asks about the bleeding and I feel embarrassed to tell him, but it's so heavy and I feel so weak and tired all the time. Sometimes I can't even think straight. The doctor doesn't say much, but he writes it all down in his notebook and says there is a procedure he can carry out that might bring me some temporary relief. He's done it on other women, and they've felt better for a little while. It's kind of like cleaning things up, I guess. I am willing to try anything at this point.

There are tiny drops of rain racing down my bedroom window. I see the doctor's nice smile as he gives me a shot in my arm. I feel woozy and warm. The doctor puts on his rubber gloves and I feel my eyelashes close.

As I open my eyes again, Paula is fussing around me, straightening the covers and listening intently to the doctor's instructions. He prescribes me some more pills to take, but I can already tell that the pain feels much better, and when I eventually manage to get to the bathroom, I see that the bleeding is lighter than it was. The doctor fastens his raincoat and pats me on my arm. "You're to take it easy for the next twenty-four hours, and I'll be back tomorrow to check on you, but of course if you have any issues before then, do call me. I would recommend a course of iron tablets, as they might help with the tiredness."

I mumble good-bye, as my mouth feels furry and my lips

won't move properly, and all I want to do is sleep until Arthur comes back. I wish he was here. I want to be in his arms and hear his voice whispering in my ear all the things he loves about me.

I hope this procedure makes the bleeding more bearable for a while—at least until this movie is over. It won't be long now, and that means I'm pretty close to the day when I'll meet the Queen. As my eyes flicker closed again, I feel a small burst of happiness. I'm not in pain right now and as soon as I'm well enough, I'm going to find a dressmaker and get the perfect gown for the occasion.

This has to be the most beautiful gown that anyone ever saw. After all, those pictures will go right around the world. I wonder what Queen Elizabeth will wear? I don't suppose they tell you that kind of thing. I've seen photographs of her wearing so many jewels that she was practically sparkling as she walked in, so my dress will need to compete with all the diamonds in the kingdom. We've all been told that we are expected to follow the rules for meeting royalty. There's a long list of the proper things to wear—the English are very keen for things to be "proper," I've noticed. For ladies, the colors should be conservative, and the style should be elegant but sufficiently covered up.

I listened to all the advice and read the guidance, but here's the thing: this is my one chance in life to meet a real queen and I am going to wear what makes me feel good.

Norma Jeane is like Cinderella and she is going to the ball, or at least the Queen's movie premiere. I tried sketching out some ideas for the kind of thing I'd like, so we'll see what a dressmaker can come up with. People keep trying to persuade me to wear black, but I wear too much black as it is and it's not a funeral. I know exactly the look I am going for. I want to look like a precious gem—like the *most* precious gem in the world.

Marilyn is going to shine like only Marilyn can.

. . .

The doctor came to the house to check on me this morning and I am feeling a little better. There are things he doesn't know, though. The fact that I feel so scared and worn out every single day that I take two little purple pills just to wake me up. And I've started adding vodka to my morning tea to give me some Dutch courage. It's the only combination that keeps the fear at bay for long enough to do my job.

Whitey finishes off my face and I get to my feet, but I stumble a little. "Are you okay?" he asks, his eyes filled with concern.

"Me? I'm just peachy. . . ." I laugh and head straight out the door to the set. My head feels woozy, and it's perfectly possible that I was a little heavy-handed with the vodka in my morning tea. The thought makes me giggle, and I put a hand across my mouth so nobody sees it.

Standing on the edge of the set, I take a long look at them all as I lean against the wall. I can see them watching me: Larry and Sybil . . . the crew . . . even Jack is giving me a strange look today.

It's too hard to be surrounded by people who don't value you or are always looking for any opportunity to mock you. I know that I've frustrated them by being late or taking sick days, and if I could help it, then I would. Having said that, I have been late some days just to annoy Larry when he's been a pompous ass to me—which, in my defense, happens a lot.

I exhale loudly, shaking my head and giggling a little to myself. Even though I was late again, I was pretty quick to get ready, and here I am. . . .

Today I have to do a scene where I sing to Larry, and the thought of it is making me feel sick, although right now I may be too drunk to sing a note. A giggle bubbles up from inside me and I kind of dance into the center of the set.

Suddenly there's a loud noise like firecrackers going off, and I realize that the beads on my dress are popping off and hitting the hard floor. "Oh dear . . ." I say, and then I start laughing while Larry looks as if he could kill me right there in front of everyone.

The costume girls rush to my side, and I have to go and get changed so they can sew the beads back on again.

By the time we get that fixed, all the lights have gone out as there's an electrical fault and nobody can shoot anything.

While the lights are out, I sit in my dressing room trembling like a leaf over the thought of singing to Larry. I suddenly feel like I've never acted before in my entire life—I mean, I've stood up there in front of the entire crew at the Actors Studio with guys like Brando watching me and felt fine, and you know why? Because they wanted me to succeed. They were interested in our craft and watching people dig deep to get there. It was a safe place to strip away all the layers of protection and show people the real you.

This is a very different experience, and I just feel that I can't do it. There's nothing for it but to take another purple pill. They are little confidence boosters—kind of like a best friend telling you that you're gonna be great. Well, I don't have one of those, so I use pills and booze, I suppose.

I can sense when I walk on set that they think I'm going to be terrible or take all day about it. Their faces are grumpy and sneering, except Jack, who always has a smile for me, which I appreciate. I've heard that some of the guys take bets on how many takes I'll ruin before we get something we can use. I can't even feel the humiliation of that, because the pills and vodka have kicked in, so I straighten up and smile like I know exactly what I'm doing.

Marilyn is here—watch this, boys!

I begin to sing and the air around me shifts. I can tell by their faces that I've finally impressed them. The scene surprises them all. I sing it really well with a soaring melody because I don't feel afraid. I feel light and full of fun, which is how I see Elsie Marina. The whole thing is beautiful, and we get it wrapped in five takes, which is something else that surprises everyone. As I walk back to my dressing room, I can hear them all talking about how nicely I'd sung the song and I feel proud.

All the way home in the car, I feel good about it and hope that maybe the tide is finally turning in my favor. The late sun is making the leaves golden, and I'm reminded that it's fall already. Seems like yesterday we arrived, but we're only weeks away from going back home. Tomorrow I'm going to take my blue-and-white bicycle out for a ride around Windsor Great Park. It's one of the things that I really love about living here. The wind blowing fresh in my face and my wheels spinning over the path. I feel like I'm flying and I'm free of everything.

As the car drives along the now-familiar road to Windsor, I notice the Queen's little flag is waving at us from the castle, and I feel happy that she is back—as if she's an old friend who's been away.

LILIBET

1956

My heart is leaping a little out of nervousness as I press the buzzer on the table next to my chair. Outside the door, the prime minister is waiting for my equerry to hear the buzzer and show him in for his weekly audience. I don't know why, but I always feel a little anxious in the moment before the door opens and the prime minister enters. It's the same sort of nervousness I get at state banquets or important lunches or great occasions, as if I'll suddenly let the side down and say the wrong thing. It's a lot of responsibility to represent an entire country, and the past four years I have mostly felt as if I was ill prepared for it. My parents were quite wonderful, yet they didn't deem it important that I be given a thorough education in history or literature, or something that would prove useful in my work.

As it is, I really do try to say as little as possible that might offend or, worse, make me appear to be stupid, which I most certainly am not. It's hardly my fault if I wasn't given a university education to be on a par with many of the men I have to deal with on a daily basis. The vast majority of my government ministers have come through the usual channels at Eton and then

Oxford or Cambridge universities. They've all studied the same subjects from the same kind of tutors. Of course, the downside to this is that they all think the same way, but naturally I don't say that to them.

I keep to quite rigid and safe topics of dogs and horses, as I find most people are animal lovers, or have a passing interest in such things. Either way, they are subjects that I know I won't make a fool of myself with, and that counts for something. One really doesn't want to cause some awful diplomatic incident by putting one's foot in it.

There is something about Mr. Eden that makes me feel more nervous in our weekly meetings than I did with Winston Churchill, and surely that situation should be the reverse. Winston was such a towering figure yet always so kind and supportive, and he talked to me as if I were a young queen who was yet to find out how the world worked, which in some ways was most comforting in the aftermath of my father's death and my accession to the throne. But Mr. Eden is a different character altogether. He's a striking man—or certainly he was in his youth—and he seems to react with a whiff of disdain whenever I ask a simple question, which I'm ashamed to say makes me feel quite irritated.

I clear my throat and smooth down the front of my skirt with my fingers. My trusty black leather handbag sits on the floor by the side of my chair. There's not very much inside it, to be honest—a handkerchief, a compact, and a lipstick. I'm very fond of a good lipstick, as my face appears quite washed-out and pale without a spot of color on my lips. The handbag is mostly good for signaling to other people that our time is up or I'm about to move on from them. I can also use it as a form of semaphore, making tiny signals to my staff to rescue me from some of the more tedious guests we invite to the palace.

There is little need of it today, however, as the tiny buzzer to my side will do the job beautifully.

The door opens, and my moment of nervousness is replaced with a sort of dread in the pit of my stomach as Mr. Eden enters the room and bows an overly deep, meaningful bow, which seems quite unnecessary since it's only the two of us. I stifle an uncharitable thought as he is bowing for so long that I am reminded of Sir Walter Raleigh or some other great explorer returning after many months at sea to his queen. Of course, Mr. Eden has only been driven in the back of a government car for the entire ten-minute journey from Downing Street to Buckingham Palace.

He stands just inside the door. "Your Majesty," he says before straightening himself back up again, and walking the few paces over to where I am now standing to receive him.

"Do sit down, Prime Minister." I gesture to the empty seat as he waits somewhat impatiently for me to be seated. I take my place in the dark cream chair just opposite his so that we can talk quietly and frankly if need be. Once I am settled in my chair, he sits down rather gingerly as if his knees are bothering him.

"Thank you, ma'am." Mr. Eden cocks his head to one side and smiles in that calm, rather patronizing way of his, waiting for me to say something . . . so I do.

"I wondered if this week we might talk a little more about your plan for resolving the situation in the Suez Canal." I stare at him quite glacially until his smile freezes on his face.

"My plan, ma'am?" he says, as if not quite grasping the words I've used, although I am very sure they were formed in the Queen's English.

"Yes. I read the briefing notes concerning the removal of the British and French pilots that navigate the shipping along the trickier parts of the canal, and it appears that your plan to bring Colonel Nasser to his senses hasn't worked." This time it is I who leans her head to one side as I beam my most practiced and benign smile at him.

"There . . . well . . . there have been some difficulties due to, um, well . . . the Soviets having replaced the pilots, ensuring that the impact of *our* plan was unfortunately minimal."

I may not be Oxford-educated, but I can read people instantly, and in this case, I can see how my prime minister believes he is cleverer than everyone else. His thoughts regarding my impudence flicker across his face. *How dare this slip of a girl question me?* A young woman demanding answers from the prime minister of this country . . . and a decorated war hero at that. The most brilliant man of his generation . . .

Well, he is quite a brilliant man, but nobody is so clever that they shouldn't have to justify their actions.

There is a beat of silence between us as we each regard the other, and so I take a deep breath and speak, although my confidence is fading a little.

"And what happens now?" I ask, more timidly this time. I was never educated to understand international politics or to question Oxford scholars, yet I feel an instinct that I can't explain over this situation. My fingers begin to fiddle with the skirt of my navy blue wool dress, smoothing and straightening, although it's quite perfect as it is.

"There are talks going on . . . with interested parties. I attended a meeting in Paris a few days ago, and we are thrashing out our next moves. These things take time, ma'am." His lips clamp shut and the calm smile then returns to his face. He lingers over the word *ma'am* as if I need to be reminded that I am merely a woman and couldn't hope to understand the complicated nature of these discussions. Maybe they teach them this in Oxford and Cambridge—how to deflect or be deliberately vague.

"And who was at this meeting in Paris, Prime Minister?" I ask quietly.

"The French . . . obviously ourselves . . . and the Israelis, ma'am." Mr. Eden gives a quiet sniff as he reels off the list of attendees.

"I see. And what are the Israelis offering to do?" I ask with an icy smile on my lips.

"Do, ma'am?" Mr. Eden gives me a startled look as if I've asked a rather uncomfortable question.

"Yes . . . I mean, I presume there was talk of things that you might do together or separately?"

This time the silence between us is long and ominous, but then he gathers himself and says, "We haven't decided on any outcomes. It was more a general discussion on the problem." His lips are stuck in a rather rigid smile, which I find satisfying, as if I've scored a point with my question.

"Very well. I shall look forward to hearing the outcome of these 'discussions.'" I bring the matter to a close as it's very clear to me that he won't give me any more information.

I can feel a tension inside my chest as his eyes refuse to meet mine. There is something about this man that I don't quite trust.

Just over his shoulder, I can see silver-framed photographs of our family, including my darling papa, and I wonder how he might have dealt with this prime minister. I imagine him swearing like a sailor and pouring them a whisky each as Mr. Eden explained the many intricacies of the delicate situation in the Suez Canal. Anyway, it's far too late for such imaginings. Mr. Eden is stuck with me. A mere woman . . .

The rest of our audience is taken up with inconsequential issues until I cut him off in mid flow with a full ten minutes left of our allotted time.

"Well, I won't take up any more of your precious time, Prime Minister. I'm sure you have a lot to be getting on with."

He looks quite startled at being interrupted, and for a second my finger hesitates over the buzzer on the table as I try to think whether there is something else that I should ask, but in the end, I press it firmly and wait for my equerry to show Mr. Eden out.

They would have much preferred to have a king. All of these men. There is something about them that can only really look up to a man the same age as they are. Any younger, and the men are seen as mere boys, fools, and hotheads; any older, and they are viewed as having lost their competence; and as for women . . . well, don't even presume to expect anything other than the usual courtesies.

Mr. Eden stops to bow again just before he leaves the room, but this time it's a brief nod in my general direction, and I find myself sighing as he disappears through the open door.

Picking up my handbag from the side of the chair, I get to my feet. There's a little time before my next appointment so I might go and play with the dogs for a bit to calm myself down. Mr. Eden is a perfectly polite man—indeed some might say a charming man—but I always come away from our interactions feeling annoyed, as if I've been vaguely insulted in some fashion. There is nothing that I can put my finger on precisely, just a sort of female intuition, as it were.

Just as I get to my feet my private secretary, Michael, appears in the doorway. "Could I have a moment, ma'am?"

"Does it have to be right now, Michael? I've just got enough time to have ten minutes with the dogs if I hurry." I've had quite enough for one week between being told off by my mother and accused of being a fair-weather queen, and having my own prime minister being far too coy over plans that very much impact this country . . . and I haven't heard a word from Philip since he embarked on his tour, although the newspapers are full of it.

"I'm afraid this won't keep . . ." His face has that grave look that always means trouble, so I sit back down in my chair with an impatient sigh, placing my handbag on the floor beside me and folding my hands in my lap. I look up at Michael and wait for the bad news that is surely forthcoming.

Michael doesn't sit, and I don't invite him to. For a long moment, we each stare at the other in anticipation of whatever is coming. He gives a slight cough and then clears his throat to speak. The news must be very bad if it requires this amount of preparation to get the words out, I think to myself. He attempts a brief smile, which I don't return.

"It has come to my attention that there is some speculation over the state of Lieutenant-Commander Parker's marriage. It seems that, um . . . his wife, Eileen, intends to seek a divorce." Michael says the word *divorce* as if it physically pains him to offer it to me. Our eyes meet and he continues, but this time his words tumble over one another to exit his mouth. "There are some worries that this might reflect on the royal marriage at this time, given the . . . recent press coverage." Michael's lips purse, and he swallows nervously.

A divorce in royal circles is the last thing we all need. There would be a scandal and no doubt endless stories about Mike Parker's poor behavior. It seems selfish, as I've always liked Eileen—indeed, we spent many happy hours together, the four of us, in Malta—but all I can think about is the awful gossip columnists and the wicked spiteful things they might write now.

"I see . . ." My voice trembles a little, and I gaze up at Michael, hoping he is about to offer me a solution to this problem. I say a silent prayer to myself, wishing for some divine intervention; failing that, the diplomacy of the Buckingham Palace courtiers would do. A divorce this close to the monarch or, to be more accurate, her husband, can only be disastrous in terms of its impact. I feel a burning flash of anger toward Philip for not listening to me and stubbornly trying to hang on to his friend in spite of all the evidence that it wouldn't be good for him.

"What do you suggest, Michael? Should we say something? What should the Queen do in times like this?" I say, waiting and hoping that there is something to be done.

"Oh no, ma'am. *No.*" Michael vehemently shakes his head. "I don't think we need to be offering the press any comment at this time. I don't believe there's anything official for the monarch to get involved with. But I would suggest that you inform the

Duke of Edinburgh as soon as is possible given the time difference that Lieutenant-Commander Parker should leave the royal tour in order to deal with his private business. That way we can hopefully distance ourselves from his marital problems and come out of this unsullied, as it were."

The idea that I should say something has clearly horrified him, yet part of me knows this can't be contained. It's too close to us, and there are too many instances of Philip and Mike Parker going around town together. "Murgatroyd and Winterbottom" out for their evening strolls, indeed. "Very well. I'll endeavor to make contact with my husband first thing tomorrow morning, and we'll take it from there. Thank you, Michael."

Michael offers a relieved nod of his head. "Ma'am," he says as he scurries out of the room, leaving me sitting alone with my thoughts. Although there is really only one thought that keeps racing around inside my mind . . .

What will Philip say when he finds out?

NORMA JEANE

1956

"You're back . . ." The minute I see Arthur come through the front door, I want to fling myself into his arms and plant kisses all over his face, but I can't seem to move from the couch that I'm curled up on. He drops his case right by the front door, and I can see in his eyes that he's missed me as much as I've missed him.

"It's so good to see you, baby . . ." His voice is thick with emotion, but I still can't forget what he wrote on that page.

"We need to talk, Arthur. I need to understand why you wrote those words about me. What did I do?" The question is a whisper, and part of me doesn't want the answer, but I need to be able to trust him again or this marriage is over.

Suddenly he's by my side and I can smell the dusty scent of his skin and the damp raindrops on his jacket. "You didn't do anything. I was jealous. That's all. Crazy jealous. You were shining at that dinner party like the star that you are, and I got all messed up about it. I'm sorry . . . I really am." Our hands are touching, our fingers threading in their old familiar ways, and it feels good to have the warmth of his palm against mine.

"Pa . . . do you really love me, or did you just want to marry

Marilyn Monroe?" My eyes search his face for the answer. He looks puzzled at my question, as if he'd never thought of it that way.

"I love *you*. I love our life together, but I don't love the goldfish bowl that comes with Marilyn the movie star."

"I don't love the goldfish bowl either, Pa—but I can't help it. You knew who I was when you married me." I bury my face in his neck and hug him as tight as I can. It's all been wrong and strange since we arrived here, like we're wearing shoes in the wrong size for us, but underneath it all we're still crazy about each other and that's all that matters.

"We'll make it work, baby . . . I swear we will." Arthur stands up and pulls me to my feet, wrapping me up in his arms and kissing me so intensely that I can't say another word.

We go upstairs and spend a sweet hour together in our bedroom. It's only there, where we are truly alone, that Arthur shows me exactly what I mean to him. His kisses are like a fever all over my body. They're the kisses of a man who knows he came too close to losing something precious, and I love him beyond all reason. Just the way he touches me makes me wild for him. My "Pa" is all I want.

As we snuggle under the sheets, I feel the heat of his body next to mine—our legs are all tangled together and his mouth is resting on my skin. Everything is forgiven and I'm so happy that we're like this once again. Like Anna and Vronsky, or Cathy and Heathcliff, we're a classic love story—except we won't have a tragic ending. When two people love each other as we do, you can't help but be happy.

At least I like to think that. No . . . I'm sure of it.

Afterward we lie in each other's arms and talk for a very long time about what we will do once this movie wraps, and how we are going to make this marriage work for us. As long lazy shadows fall across our bed, we don't even bother to go down for dinner. I just feel so soft and safe in his arms that I never want to move. He's so wise.

Arthur thinks that we should stay clear of Hollywood, and I agree. We need to get out of the goldfish bowl once and for all. I don't want to go back to Los Angeles and have that studio life again. I thought that we might live in New York together. I was so happy there last year, but Arthur suggests that we could make his house in Connecticut our permanent home.

It makes a lot of sense, as he has a lovely house there and we can be private, which is something that he prizes above all else. After all, he's a great writer and he needs peace and quiet to work. We don't need a pack of photographers following us around. Also, Connecticut is a good place to raise our kids, and that's what we will do. Maybe we'll split our time between the two places.

I promise Pa that in future I will only make one movie every couple of years, and the rest of the time I'll just be plain Mrs. Arthur Miller sitting in a rocking chair on the porch with her babies. Doesn't that sound fine?

Of course, should I get offered a great part—I mean the kind that's too good to turn down or one of those roles that I've always dreamed of playing—then we'd have to think again, but for now we have our future plans all set.

When it's just the two of us like this, we slot together so perfectly. It's all the movie stuff that gets in the way. Fame can do that to you. It either makes you crazy or makes the people around you crazy. Arthur is quiet, and he hates the circus that travels with Marilyn. I've just got used to it, I guess, but he's my priority now.

I'm going to love him forever. He knows that I've got this darkness inside me sometimes, and I fight against it on a daily basis. Pa says that I put up a valiant fight, and I feel so brave when he says that. I do try so hard not to let little Norma take over. She's the one who can't feel enough love sometimes, or she gets stubborn and wants to pay people back for hurting her.

Norma is just a kid who needs a lot of love, not like Marilyn, who doesn't care about stuff like that because she knows how good she is.

The trouble is that Marilyn doesn't stick around for long enough, and then little Norma acts up because she's feeling scared. I hate feeling so fearful that my mind won't work properly. I can never think of anything hopeful or even one good thing about me. Then other times it's like this, when Arthur has both arms wrapped around me and I feel loved to pieces just lying here beside him.

These are better days for us, and I'm not in so much pain anymore. Whatever the doctor did seems to have worked—but mostly I'm so very happy that my love is home with me.

I'm back on set tomorrow and, quite honestly, I'm dreading it. There are so many leaked stories now, and most of them are nasty about me. They've come from Larry's people or someone on set who takes his side, or wants him to notice them. I just want this movie to be over with now. And I have to get a good night's sleep every night to do that.

Pa says he couldn't bear for me to get mixed up with my pills again, so I ask him if he will measure them out and make sure I only take the right amount. He says he'll do it, and I hand over all my sleeping pills. I don't care anyhow as long as I get some rest. I curl up right next to Arthur, and he gives me two Nembutal to help me sleep.

Two pills are better than one. One pill means bad dreams and waking up crying in the night, but two pills can mean out like a light. Sleep like blankness—like death—and then the next thing I know it's morning and my eyes open to the world.

So far, it's working well. You can tell how much Arthur loves me that he would do that for me. Doling out my little pills and kissing me good-night on my forehead like I'm his little girl. I think my "accident" gave him such a scare that it's made him love me all the more.

. . .

We're shooting the coronation scene today, which I'm happy about, as all I have to do is stand around looking very solemn and moved by the occasion. There's no dialogue at all, just the music. It all looks very beautiful on set, and I think it will impress people when they see it on the screen. I am playing the queen's lady-in-waiting during the coronation, and I began to wonder what it's like working for the real Queen. I mean, they must know her as well as anybody and see all the little private moments behind the scenes. However glamorous the woman, there are always times when you kick your shoes off and rub your feet. Trust me, I know the difference between what the public sees and what happens at home. I'd like a day being a lady-in-waiting just watching everything the Queen does and seeing what she's like when she's off duty.

I've never seen a real-life coronation, but of course, a lot of people in this country saw one just a few years ago. I mentioned it to the costume girls on set, and the next day one of them brought in a magazine that they'd kept as a souvenir. She showed me pictures of the Queen wearing a gold cape and a crown in the abbey and riding through the streets of London in a gold carriage. It looked like something out of a fairy tale, and I tried to keep that same look on my face during the scenes today—a sort of reverence, like it's your solemn duty.

We are filming some close-ups, so there are a lot of stoppages, but it's technical problems rather than my fault. Once or twice, we needed Whitey to step in and fix some shine on my face, or for Jack to change the camera setup for the reverse shots. Larry was very quiet today and barely muttered a word to me. We both have our own teams of people now, and sometimes I'll hear things and get upset, but it turns out it's just the way that British people talk to each other. Stuff gets lost in translation, I guess.

One thing for sure is that I love Dame Sybil. Whenever I have scenes with her, I look forward to them enormously. She's incredibly wise but always so very kind to me. I asked her today how she always seems to be so happy, and she puts it down to having a loving marriage. That brought me to tears, thinking of all the hopes I have for Arthur and me.

As there was no dialogue in today's scenes, I asked if we could play some music. I like listening to something when I work—it cuts out the part of your brain that's always trying to make logic out of things, and goes right to your heart. I brought my record player to the set and we played the "Londonderry Air" as we worked. I felt it really helped me to focus, but some people looked as if they didn't care for it. You can't please everyone, that's what I always think.

As we were wrapping up, Larry was standing in the middle of a small group of actors and I heard him say, "Oh yes, it will be good to get this movie finished. It's been quite the burden being both the director and the producer."

Technically he is both those things, but I couldn't resist trying to prick his ego a bit, so as I walked by, I stopped right next to him and with a bright smile I said, "Co-producer, Larry. I'm the other producer . . . and of course the owner, as I bought the rights to the play."

Well, the looks they gave me were worth it.

I went away humming the "Londonderry Air" and left all those men to stew over it. It's true anyway. It's my production too. Larry seems to think he just hired me to look pretty, and he quite likes to give people that impression—as if he's a god of acting, slumming it with some trashy blonde.

I mean, he is a great actor, but we are very different in our styles. It was a childish thing to do . . . but I'm done letting people treat me like I'm nothing. It's time to stand up for myself and let these guys know who they're dealing with—whether it's Marilyn or Norma Jeane. I'm not gonna let anybody walk over me.

The gown is finally ready, and the staff at Madame de Rachelle's are bringing it to Parkside on the weekend for the final fitting. She had some ideas to add to my rough sketch, and between us I think we've come up with the perfect dress.

It's a long column that is exquisitely tailored to my body, going in and out in all the right places and held up with two thin spaghetti straps. It's very low-cut in the front with a length of cloth forming a kind of fold that drapes down from the bust. It's quite daring, but I think we've solved the problem of modesty by making a matching cape and purse. At first, Madame suggested making the entire outfit in an elegant black velvet, but I really wanted something so stunning that the minute those pictures flash around the world, everyone will see the Queen and me glittering together.

I am going to shake hands with the Queen of England, and I've been practicing my curtsy every single day. You have to be really careful not to get caught in the hem of your dress or you might tumble right over and fall on your ass in front of her. Wouldn't that make a picture?

They showed me a lot of different fabrics—all the colors you can imagine, from coal-black velvet to silvery blues, the color of the ocean. The minute I looked at those pictures of the Queen's coronation, I knew only one color would do for this meeting.

The dress has to be gold.

At Madame de Rachelle's, they had everything, from a kind of brassy silk to a stiff brocade with silver embroidery running through it, but they weren't quite right for this particular style of gown. Then they brought out a length of the most beautiful gold lamé, and the moment my fingers touched the fabric, I fell instantly in love with it. That gold fabric moves with your body, gliding over your hips and washing around your legs. We decided that if I'm feeling too nervous on the night, then I can just keep the gold cape on, but if I feel . . . well, if Marilyn wants to shine, then I can take off the cape and let them have it. It's nice to have the choice because this night is so special to me and I won't be able to bear it if things go wrong.

The gown has been laid carefully across our bed, and it's even more wonderful than I thought it would be. The gold glitters under the light, and I can't wait to try it on. I've promised Arthur a peek as, when I do the final fitting, I need to make sure that everything is perfect.

The staff from Madame de Rachelle's fuss around me as I slip out of my satin robe and into the dress. It trickles down my body like liquid gold, and I carefully place the spaghetti straps into position on my shoulders. I can see even before they zip it up that the gold lamé falls perfectly, and the fold hanging from the bust drapes so elegantly that I can't help smiling at my own reflection. It's the most beautiful dress I've ever worn—it truly is fit for a queen.

I can't wait to show Pa. I want him to feel so proud of me. So much of this summer has been hard and not what we'd planned, but this is a night for him to take his wife to meet the Queen of England. I want him to feel like the luckiest man in the world, and when I gaze into his beautiful brown eyes, I hope very much to see that pride looking back at me.

In just a few weeks now, we'll be going home to the States, and this is my big chance to show him that all our problems are behind us. I've promised Arthur that he will come first—our life together, and our babies when they come, will take priority over everything else. I'll even learn how to bake those pies, and the minute we get back to Connecticut, I will lay off the pills and booze. I just need to get through the final scenes of this movie. Once I'm home again, then all our problems will go away and I won't need them anymore. You'll see . . .

Marilyn will be in control again, and little Norma Jeane . . . well, she'll be so loved and safe that the pills won't be necessary.

One of the women finishes zipping up my dress while the other gently places the gold cape around my shoulders so that it covers my bust. They both stand back and smile admiringly. The whole effect is so beautiful that I can hardly believe it's really me. I look different—not like a movie star but like another being. This dress is everything. . . .

When I think of poor little Norma Jeane with her hand-me-downs, I could weep with joy looking at my reflection. The gown makes me look as if I'm the most elegant gold statue, but when I move the dress ripples around me. I twirl around in front of the mirror, this way and that, looking at myself, smiling as I bite my bottom lip because I want to squeal with joy. Then I gather up the bottom of the dress and cape with both hands and run downstairs to Arthur's study, where he's writing. I wouldn't normally disturb him, but he wants to see me all dressed up, and he's as excited as I am about me meeting the Queen and what I'm going to wear.

I tap gently on the door and whisper, "Hey—can I come in?" because I don't want the staff to hear me or come out to stare. I hear Pa call back to me to come in, and so I do.

I stand right in front of him as he leans back behind his desk, smiling at me like I'm a kid who's come to entertain him.

Then I let the handfuls of gold lamé drip onto the floor so that both the dress and cape take their proper shape. I see Pa look me up and down like he is so very proud of me, his dark eyes drinking me in. His lips purse together, and he raises his eyebrows and gives a low whistle.

"Wow—look at you," he says with a broad smile on his face.

I knew this dress was the perfect gown, and everything is going to be fine now. I do a silly little dance for him, wiggling my backside around, because I know that he likes that, and then I slide the golden cape off my shoulders to reveal the dress in all her glory.

Then I see it—that look flickering right across his face. It was only there for a split second, but that was long enough, and I say, "What's wrong, Pa? Don't you like it?"

His mouth opens and closes again. A little muscle in his cheek twitches once or twice, and he frowns.

Suddenly it feels as if everything is unraveling, and just as I've worked so hard to make this perfect for us. My smile fades to nothing, and my shoulders sag a little.

Pa looks up at me with those sad brown eyes and says, "Isn't it a little . . . I mean it's very . . . well, you know what I mean. You are meeting the Queen, after all. . . ."

And just like that his voice tails off, and in my mind all I can see are those words he scrawled in dark blue ink across the page: *I've married a whore.*

LILIBET

1956

As the car draws closer to Windsor, I keep thinking back to the day of my coronation and that long procession in a very uncomfortable gold coach toward Westminster Abbey, where every English king or queen has been crowned since William the Conqueror. It's all a lot of pomp and tradition, yet the most sacred part of it is still so very precious to me: the moment, as "Zadok the Priest" was sung, when I was hidden from public view so that nobody should see me except the Archbishop of Canterbury as he anointed me God's faithful servant. That day I made promises to fulfill my duty, regardless of what I want or whether it would make me happy. I vowed to put God and the country first. Then, when the ceremony was over and all the sacred promises were made, I was a queen anointed before God. My life, given over to a noble purpose.

I can still recall the feeling of my gold embroidered cloak brushing against my skin, and the crushing weight of the bejeweled crown upon my head, and my hands full with the orb and scepter. And in that moment, Lilibet Windsor was no more. Yet since that moment, I'm not entirely sure that I have managed to live up to those vows, as it's been so very hard to cast her off and take on the mantle of Queen Elizabeth.

I feel torn in two between my duty and my family most days, and part of me still longs to be just an ordinary woman with a simple life. Yet I cannot undo what has been done. It's a vow I take seriously, and I have sworn to dedicate my life to the service of the British people.

The royal standard flutters over the tower of Windsor Castle to indicate my presence, and I exit the car as soon as it draws to a halt at the front door.

"Have you managed to track down the Duke of Edinburgh yet?" I ask Michael as I walk briskly through the familiar corridors, my private secretary scurrying behind me as we go.

"No, ma'am, I'm afraid not. With the time difference it's proved a little tricky, although we have left numerous messages saying that you need to speak with him urgently." Michael tries to keep pace with me but finds himself tripped up by two of the corgis suddenly changing direction without warning, as they are prone to do.

So far, the news of Mike Parker's impending divorce has not reached the press, but I'm certain that it will, and probably soon. I prefer we acted before the press get hold of this story, rather than once again be caught on the back foot, as it were.

"Do try again, Michael. Leave messages telling him to call me day or night—never mind the time difference. I won't rest until I speak to him about this."

"Very well, ma'am."

Michael disentangles himself from a pair of my more boisterous dogs and walks quickly back down the stairs toward his office. I do hope that Philip heeds his messages and telephones as soon as he can. He must know about the divorce proceedings by now. I'm sure that Mike Parker would have confided in him. It's such a mess. I don't know why people can't keep to the vows that they make, as difficult as that may be. A promise is a promise, after all, and one made before God is something to be considered sacred.

As I turn the corner, a footman stands to attention and bows his head. "Your Majesty, Her Royal Highness the Princess Margaret is waiting for you in the drawing room."

"Oh, thank you. What luck," I reply somewhat sarcastically. With everything else going on, I've been avoiding any long conversations with my sister, but as the door to the drawing room is opened for me, I catch a glimpse of the back of Margaret's head as she sits on the sofa reading a magazine, with a glass of what looks like gin and tonic in her hand. The room smells of cigarette smoke, and no doubt she has been indulging herself while waiting for me.

"Hello, you . . ." I say cheerily, although I can't avoid the sinking feeling that is flooding through me. I really cannot bear any more family drama today.

Margaret looks startled, as if I've caught her doing something she shouldn't have been. She stands, casts her magazine to one side, and bobs her reluctant little curtsy before offering a brief kiss to my cheek. "I've been waiting for you."

Glancing down at the abandoned magazine, I notice that there is a photograph of Marilyn Monroe on the front cover wearing a most funereal-looking black dress that in daylight looks quite harsh against her white-blond hair. Her face carries a sort of haunted expression, as if she is being hunted like a sort of prey, and I feel a rush of pity for her, although there's no reason why I should interest myself in her affairs at all. Goodness knows I have quite enough going on in my own life.

"Well, here I am," I reply as Margaret settles herself back down on the sofa, crossing and uncrossing her legs a little nervously.

"And how was Africa?" I ask as I settle myself into the armchair opposite her.

"It was lovely, actually. It made me think about the future, and that's why I wanted to talk to you," she says with a shy smile, which is unlike her.

"Oh . . . and what can I do for you?"

"The thing is . . . the whole trip made me realize that I want to *do* more . . . take more of a leading role." Margaret eyes me nervously and swallows before continuing. "When I was in Africa, it felt good to be the star of the show for a change, and I'm sure you need the help, so I'm volunteering. . . ." She places both of her feet on the floor and sits forward a little as her pale blue eyes inspect me. Her gaze is as sharp and clear-eyed as ever, and it is quite obvious to me that she has been rehearsing this little speech.

"That's . . . nice. Doing what exactly?" I try to keep my tone calm and friendly because, the Lord only knows, Margaret can be quick to flare up in anger sometimes.

"I don't know. Whatever it is that you do—that you might need a hand with?" Her face returns to its usual petulant expression, and I'm really not sure whether she is asking me to help her in some way or demanding that I let her be a sort of part-time queen.

"Well, you already *do* things . . . you have your charities to take care of. There really isn't much more that I can share with you. Some things can only be done by the actual Queen, sadly." I smile as warmly as I can, but my sister's face looks distinctly unamused. "I'm sure there can be other royal tours in the future if that's what you'd like. Always plenty of countries that need visiting," I add to try to smooth things along.

I'm really not sure what more she wants from me—perhaps a tiny replica of my crown to wear around town? The thought is a mean one, and I bite my lip slightly to try to keep the peace.

Margaret leans back against the cushions on the sofa and sighs with displeasure. "Lilibet, you really are impossible. I'm offering to help, and you just want to do everything yourself. I thought that I could do more of the tours and the investitures, public occasions and that sort of thing—leaving you free for your paperwork and meetings. Sometimes I think you worry that I'll outshine you in some way." Her lips purse slightly and, as she frowns, a deep furrow appears between her eyes.

Ah . . . by the sound of it, Margaret wants me to do all the dull parts of this job while she does the more glamorous public role. Honestly, this family is quite impossible.

I exhale sharply and say, "This isn't a beauty contest or some kind of West End musical. I don't have an understudy. Honestly, Margaret, sometimes I don't think you understand my position at all." I can barely keep the irritation out of my voice. What is wrong with this family that every single member of it believes that they could do a better job or that I'm doing everything wrong? It makes me feel like a complete failure as a queen, as a daughter, and as a wife . . . and, yes, probably as a mother too. *What do they all want from me?*

"And I don't think you understand *my* position. . . ." Margaret's voice cracks with emotion, and for a second, I regret my irritation with her and soften my tone.

"I do understand . . . I really do, but that's the life we have. I have this job with all that it entails, and I can't change it to make the rest of you feel better." I am pleading with her to understand the situation.

"And I am the *spare* sister, I suppose. Not even the spare now that you have a son. A nothing then. A nobody. What am I supposed to do with my life?" Her startling blue eyes well up with tears suddenly, and I am quite knocked off my guard.

"Margaret, darling . . . you're my only sister. You're not a spare anything. I don't know what you expect me to do. I'm bound by the rules and traditions—by my coronation vows that I swore before God. Anointed with holy oil in an abbey. This isn't some role I applied for. I know it's hard, but you have to make a life for yourself filled with purpose and joy. I can't do that for you. If I could, then I absolutely would." I lean across and place my hand on top of hers, squeezing it gently. We have always been the closest of companions, but with the death of our dear papa came a rupture between us that is so very difficult to fix. Being Queen is a lonely job because nobody can possibly understand how it feels to be selected without any say in the matter, and given a role that you have to carry out to the best of your ability until death. I mean, even priests and nuns get a say in their roles. I was told as a child that this was to be my life, and I've never questioned that this was how it had to be.

Margaret's face is a picture of anguish. "But how? Nobody ever tells you how to make a life of purpose and joy, do they? They all say the same thing. *You're a princess.* As if that's enough for a human being to feel happy and fulfilled . . . and it's not, Lilibet. It's really not." I watch as the tears begin to trickle down her cheeks. Poor Margo is so sad and heartbroken, but what can I do to fix it? Nothing that will help her.

"Well, start by looking at the things that you love, and see how you could get involved and help." I am nothing if not practical, and sometimes it is the only solution.

"Like what?" She brushes away her tears and stares back at me defiantly now.

"I don't know—maybe ballet? You love the ballet far more than I do. You could get involved with that in some way."

"And that's it? I shall live my entire life in your shadow trying not to cause embarrassment to the Queen, and if I'm good I'll get to attend a few ballet fundraisers. Is that your idea of a worthwhile life?" A flash of anger crosses Margaret's face. "Why does it have to be like this for the rest of us? It's all right for you. Everything revolves around the Queen."

It's not often that I retaliate in anger, but suddenly without any warning, a burst of rage explodes out of me, taking both of us by surprise.

"If the whole show didn't revolve around me, then what? If I turned around tomorrow and said: That's quite enough attention, I'm off—what do you think would happen, Margaret? The monarchy doesn't just stop because one human being fails or dies or runs away. It goes on and on to my children and their children—and if I should take them away with me, it would land on your shoulders, and you would have even less freedom and choice than you do now.

"I am living this life so the rest of you don't have to do it, because *it's my duty*!" Blinking back my own tears, I take a deep breath and look across at Margaret. Here we are, two sisters fighting because of a destiny neither of us wanted, but it has to be somebody's destiny, and I have to carry it to the end of my life as best I can.

My sister takes a long sip of her gin and sniffs back her tears. "Do you think we would bicker as much if we were just plain Betty and Marge from Hackney? If life had gone that way and not this. . . ."

The thought of it makes me chuckle for a moment. "I don't know. I expect all brothers and sisters argue, no matter where they're born. Everyone seems to think that they have the hardest time or the most problems, when in fact they're likely to be equally shared. I'd quite like to be Betty from Hackney some days, although I'm sure her life isn't at all easy. It is at least private, or maybe there are just as many awful gossips in Hackney as in Fleet Street—who knows?"

Margaret smiles wearily. "You don't seem to need anything or anyone—except perhaps Philip—but I'm not like you. I need to feel that I matter, Lilibet. Some people don't need that or they don't seem to. If I was Marge from Hackney, then I'd still need that feeling, I think, whereas I imagine you . . . Betty . . . being perfectly content to spend her days walking dogs and washing dishes. That's not me. That's why I couldn't marry Peter in the end and settle for an ordinary private life. . . ." Her words hang in the air between us: the admission that it was her decision not to marry Peter—not because of anything I did, but rather that my sister could not bear to be ordinary.

Her face crumples in despair, and for a moment I hesitate, unsure of what to say or do to help. It all feels so hopeless. Margaret blinks up at me with a tearful gaze. "I have this need to make a difference, yet I don't seem to matter to anyone, and I find that the hardest thing of all."

My heart simply aches for her, but with this realization I do hope that she can finally stop blaming me for her misfortune.

"You do matter very much. I'll do all that I can to help you, Margaret, but in the end it is up to you to find a life that you love and to make the best of things as we all have to do. But never doubt how much I love you. I care deeply what happens to you and that will never change."

Margaret's lips part as if she is about to speak, but a footman suddenly enters the room. "Your Majesty, the Duke of Edinburgh is on the telephone for you."

"Hello . . . hello . . . can you hear me?" I twist the black telephone cord between my fingers and wait to hear his voice, but there is only a crackling silence at the other end. "Philip, are you there?" I try again, and then to my relief he answers.

"Hello, Lilibet . . . I'm here. How are you?" He sounds remarkably cheery, considering the nature of this call. He must have been informed about Mike Parker's impending divorce, and I was rather expecting that he would be upset or annoyed at being proven wrong, as it were.

"Yes, I can hear you. Are you well? How's everything going?" Beginning with polite chatter and trying to lead up to a more serious conversation is not the easiest thing with my husband.

"I'm fine—well, I haven't put my foot in it yet, if that's what you're asking." He chuckles, and I feel relieved to hear him sounding happy.

"We've all been keeping up with your travels in the press, and it does seem to be going over splendidly. Well done, you!" I take a breath and offer up a silent prayer that we can maintain this good humor during what is sure to become a much more delicate conversation.

"Where are you?" I ask, suddenly realizing that I have no idea which country he's calling me from.

"On my way to Malaya. We might have to skip Singapore because there are riots going on."

"Oh, what a shame. Well, you're doing a wonderful job. Everyone says so. . . ."

"Do they? Ha, I've finally done something right for the men in gray suits. Seriously, Lilibet, I'm rather enjoying it. I feel as if

I'm making a difference being here—spreading the word, as it were. It does make one think about what we do and why it matters, in ways that are much harder to fathom wandering around that stuffed mausoleum we call a palace. It's given me quite a lot of ideas actually, about things we can do to adjust or modernize for the future." He's excited about this change of perspective, and I feel a tiny note of dread, knowing that he will come back full of new ideas, and the old guard in the palace—those men in gray suits—will resist him at every turn. Change happens slowly or not at all within these walls.

"Well, I'm very glad to hear it's going so well . . ." There is a pause, and I wish he were here in this room, as the sound of his voice so full of good cheer makes me miss him all the more. "There is something that we need to discuss, however. I'm sure you've heard by now that Eileen Parker is talking to her solicitors with regard to a divorce."

"Nothing is definite yet." Philip exhales softly as if he's been expecting this moment and then continues. "Mike thinks this will all blow over and she won't go through with it. Eileen is probably just making a point. He's been trying to get hold of her, but communications are not the best from this side of the world, as you know." Philip sounds wary, tiptoeing around a great bear trap of a situation.

"I'm afraid that's not what I've been led to believe. She's quite made up her mind, and this won't remain their private business for much longer. Once the word *divorce* is out there, you know what will happen next. There will be endless speculation and gossip, particularly if there are stories regarding his infidelity . . . and it won't stop with the Parkers. You must see that it's quite impossible for him to remain with you on this tour." I can hear the crackling static on the line again, and for a moment I wonder if he has heard what I said, as there is nothing but silence on the other end of the telephone. "Philip . . . are you still there?"

"I'm here," he says, but all the good cheer has left his voice.

"So that's decided then?" I say, hopeful of a resolution without an argument.

"No!" he shouts. "Nothing needs to be decided at this moment. Look, we're having a very successful tour, and I need Mike with me. He's my friend, and I trust him implicitly. If he says he can talk Eileen around, then I'm sure that he can. There's no need for any of this to reach the press, and I don't think you can just remove a chap from his job because of speculation. Let's give him a bit more time and see how this unfolds."

I cast my eyes to the heavens in exasperation. I had thought that this news of an impending divorce so close to us would shake Philip out of his misplaced loyalty. Clearly, I was wrong. "If we wait until the press are printing stories about the Parkers, then we will have a much bigger problem. The advice is to let him go now so that when the news breaks, we can say quite truthfully that he no longer works for you, and that it is entirely a private matter for the Parkers. Don't you see?"

"No, I don't see. I don't know what's got into you lately. Jumping on every little bit of rumor and gossip as if it's all fact. For goodness' sake, Lilibet, tell them all to bugger off and mind their own business. I mean, it's the twentieth century and people do get divorced. Times are changing, and we can't allow ourselves to be trapped in the old ways of doing things. Why can't we all just grow up and carry on? It's none of our business." The telephone connection is slowly getting worse, and he is positively shouting down the line at me now.

"You know why? If it were up to me, then I wouldn't care a bit for what people might say. And as your wife, of course I want you to have the support of the staff you trust, but I am also head of the Church of England, whose teachings on divorce I must follow. I cannot—*we* cannot—be seen to endorse it in any way."

"We're not endorsing it. We're minding our own bloody business. I don't want to tell Mike that he has to leave this tour, not when he's doing such a good job."

The depth of his sigh down the telephone speaks of his frustration, but I simply cannot take the chance on this story blowing up into a terrible scandal that envelops the monarchy. We have to be beyond reproach. Or, more importantly, we have to be *seen* to be beyond reproach.

"I can tell you from the other side of the world, surrounded by your loyal subjects, that nobody would care. Outside Buckingham Palace, the world is becoming modern, and we are in danger of looking stuffy and old-fashioned."

"You mean I am stuffy and old-fashioned . . ." I don't understand why every single time I have to uphold the required standard, people assume it's some kind of character flaw, as if I don't possess the wit or imagination to live in the modern world.

"I didn't say that, but you always take the more conservative approach in these matters. Let's wait and see how this plays out. That's all I'm saying." Philip has calmed down a little, and I can tell that he is trying his best to get me on side.

"I'm sorry, Philip, but we can't wait. We can't take the chance."

"So, as my wife, you would leave me on this tour with no proper support that I can rely on. What good is that?"

"As your wife I would wish you to have whatever makes you happy, but I believe that Mike Parker should leave the tour right now, before this situation gets worse. You must know if there's any truth to these rumors of his infidelity. This could cause us maximum embarrassment when this is dragged through a divorce court. You could even be asked to give evidence. Maybe you can't see how damaging this will be because you're on the other side of the world." I purse my lips together tightly as I have nothing more to add.

The telephone crackles once again into my ear, and I release the cord from my fingers, allowing it to hang limply over the desk. There is silence again, but this time it is unbroken.

"Philip . . . are you still there?" I ask . . . but there is no answer.

I cannot be sure if he has hung up on me or we got cut off, and I feel so annoyed with him that I don't really care.

"That man is absolutely infuriating. . . ." I mutter to myself as I hang up the telephone and call the dogs to my side. Walking briskly out of the room, I almost collide with Michael, who was obviously on his way to track me down.

"Ma'am, would it be possible to have a quick word about the arrangements for the film premiere on Monday evening?" He offers me an apologetic half smile, but I carry on walking away.

"Not now, Michael. I am taking the dogs out for a walk, and if any of my family wishes to speak to me for the rest of the day, please tell them that I am unavailable."

Giving an exasperated sigh, I rush down the stairs and pause by the door to slip on my olive-green rain jacket, while feeling around in the pocket for my blue headscarf, which I proceed to tie firmly under my chin. "Come on, *tch tch,*" I say to the dogs, who obediently fall into step with me.

I shall walk off my temper until I am calm again, but it could very well take quite some time. *What am I to do with them all?* This family who I love, who are all so very disappointed in me.

Stuffing my hands deep into my pockets, I put my head down and set off across the park at such an angry pace that my poor detective struggles to keep up.

NORMA JEANE

1956

The dress lies in a gold lamé pool on our bedroom floor as I race wildly down the footpaths of Windsor Great Park on my blue-and-white bicycle, inhaling great gulps of air with tears streaming down my cheeks. I'm crying so hard that I can hardly see where I'm going. All I can see is Arthur's face looking at me in my beautiful gold dress as if I was a disappointment to him once again. Not classy or elegant enough to be Mrs. Arthur Miller. A trashy blonde about to embarrass him in front of the Queen of England.

All my life people have wanted me to be somebody else. When I was a baby, they wanted me to be a quiet child so that I could fit in and not be a nuisance for whoever was taking care of me that week. The girl with no daddy to claim her. The child who nobody cared about—at least not for very long. That's the truth . . . nobody has ever loved me for very long. It really doesn't matter how quiet or good or well-behaved you are, if people don't care for you, then they don't care. There's nothing you can do about it.

So I turned myself into Marilyn . . . the woman who everyone loves, and nobody stays with.

But Arthur . . . I really thought he was a man so cultured and refined that he would rise above the "Hollywood stuff" and love the *real* me. I thought he would let me be everything I was capable of being. And he will, as long as the "real me" meets his standards—and I don't. . . . He wants a Marilyn he can keep in a bottle and only take out for his own personal use. A doll who can talk about Tolstoy with his friends and look sexy—but not too sexy, just the right amount, so that all the guys can envy him, but not so much that they think his wife is a whore.

The trees with their yellowing coppery leaves all rush by me in a blur as my wheels spin across the dirt track. Wiping the back of my hand across my face, I lose balance for a moment before righting myself. I want to ride faster and faster until I can fly away from all the pain, and the bad feelings go away. You can't ride fast enough for that to happen, though.

I thought I looked beautiful in my gold dress. I imagined how I would look shaking hands with the Queen, and the whole world would finally see how little Norma Jeane turned out.

Look at me, Daddy! Watch me, Daddy! Can you see me now?

I thought I had it all—a career I could finally control for myself and a man who was crazy about me . . . but you can't have it all.

Somebody always wants you to act like you're someone else. I *hate* him for not loving me the way that I am. I *hate* them all for not caring about the real me. I'm just another blonde to everyone. A freak show. Someone to stare at, but nobody cares about how I feel inside.

I've got so much to offer this world, but nobody wants it. They want me to pose and preen and "act sexy" for them. I'm sick of it. Why can't anyone love me for the real me? Why can't they see me?

The pathway narrows, and I don't recognize this part of it. I've been crying so hard and riding so fast that I've gotten myself a little lost.

Well, ain't that the truth?

Everything is a blur as my wheels are spinning so fast that the air rushes into my lungs and stings my cheeks. Suddenly the tire hits some loose stones on the path and I find myself sliding to the left and heading toward a tall old tree. I try to stop, but I guess I try too hard, because the bicycle stops moving and I keep right on going, tumbling off the side of the handlebars and landing smack on my ass.

The force of the landing knocks the breath right out of my body. For a split second, I lie there flat on my back, feeling stupid. I could laugh it's so ridiculous, but instead I try to sit up quite carefully in case I've broken anything, and then I put my head in my hands and weep.

I came to England with such high hopes. I felt on top of the world, and now look at me: lying here on some old dirt track, covered in bits of twigs and gravel, with my backside hurting like hell—what a sight for sore eyes. The thought of it makes me cry even harder, when suddenly a strange voice says, "Are you all right? You took quite the tumble."

It's a young woman, wearing one of those olive-green waxed rain jackets and a bright blue headscarf. She's peering down at me with such great concern that it makes me feel more stupid than ever that somebody witnessed my fall and, even worse, my crying like a baby. I just hope she doesn't recognize me. I'd hate for this to end up splashed all over the newspapers. A girl can't even cry or fall on her ass without somebody using it for entertainment.

Gulping back my tears, I manage the weakest of smiles. "Yes . . . at least I think so. It's my fault. I was going too fast, and then my wheels skidded back there. I tried to brake too hard, I guess, and here I am. . . ." I shrug my shoulders and try to sound like I'm not a crazy sobbing idiot in the middle of an old park in England, but the woman doesn't seem at all bothered by me.

"Take a minute. I always find with these things, one can't

know the extent of the damage until the shock has worn off. I've often taken a tumble from a horse, and it does take a moment before all parts report in, as it were." Her blue eyes are warm and friendly, and I'm grateful for her concern, but also part of me wishes she would leave me alone.

We're about the same age, I would guess, and when I look at her closely, I see there's a weariness in her face that I recognize and feel familiar with.

"Thank you. I think I'm okay now," I say softly.

She doesn't leave, though. The woman stands with her legs slightly apart and her hands dug deep in her jacket pockets, looking at me quite carefully as I pick bits of leaf and dirt out of my hair and clothes. "Oh, my goodness, of course—aren't you Miss Monroe? I thought you looked familiar. I never forget a face." The woman smiles in her nice, concerned way.

"Some days I am. . . ." I answer, because right now I don't feel much like Marilyn would. What was I thinking, racing around on this stupid bicycle? The woman looks slightly puzzled at my answer and purses her lips, as if she's thinking of what to say next. Brushing my hair back off my face, I set about wiping all the traces of my tears away and try to stick on that old bright smile, but it won't come. "I'm sorry. I am having a bad day," I say shyly.

"Ah, me too, as it happens. Things can get a bit too much at times, can't they? Do you feel well enough to try to stand up?"

She offers her hand and carefully, gently but firmly, helps me to my feet. Leaves scatter off my clothes as I try to think of some polite conversation so I can say my good-byes now and make my escape, although not on my bicycle, that's for sure. I'll walk back to Parkside from here—wherever here is; I don't recognize it at all. I look around for a long moment, trying to think of how to get back to the main path.

"I think I got lost. Which way is Englefield Green from here?" I ask.

"If you go back that way and take the path to the left, you'll be there in no time. It's not too far, but you have rather wandered off the track."

As she speaks, I notice for the first time there are four or five small coffee-colored dogs with little white paws chasing one another around the bushes. I've never seen this kind of dog before, and it makes me smile. "Oh, your dogs are so cute."

"Thank you. They are very mischievous creatures, but I adore them all," the woman says, and her whole face lights up.

I smile back at her, but a real smile this time. If she hadn't come along, I probably would have just sat there in the dirt bawling. "They must love walking in this big park. It's so nice. I love dogs . . . but in a city it's so hard to take them on long walks like you can in England. You must love living around here."

"I do—very much." The woman eyes me curiously, but doesn't say any more. I get the impression that she's sizing me up in some way. Probably comparing me to how Marilyn looks on the movie screen or in a magazine. "It's none of my business, of course, but you seemed quite upset. . . . It must be difficult being so far from home?" She has very gentle eyes, I decide, with a distinct twinkle in them. I'm usually quite guarded around strangers, but there is something about this woman that makes me feel as if I can trust her. Even though she recognized me, it didn't change the way she behaved at all. She seems very warmhearted.

"Oh, it's stupid, I guess. You see, I've been invited to meet your Queen, and I got this fancy gold dress because I want to look really special. I mean, it's a big thing for me to meet an actual queen. And I want to look the best that I've ever looked, but . . . some people think it's not suitable. Anyway, I got upset. . . . I guess there's some kind of rule that I'm not following, but it's the perfect dress. Of course, I wouldn't want to offend anyone or upset the Queen. I just wanted it to be a nice evening." The words all rush out, and I don't know why I'm telling this woman all this, except that she seems like the kind of person you can tell things to.

"I'm sure the Queen would love you to wear your beautiful dress. I'd go so far as to say that I'm fairly certain she wouldn't mind a bit." The woman bends down to pat one of the dogs before rifling around in her pockets and pulling out some treats for them. The dogs start yapping and leaping around her knees to take them from her hands, and the sight of them makes me giggle.

"Do you really think so?" I ask. "She wouldn't be offended if I broke the rules a little bit?"

"I think it would probably brighten up her evening. I imagine a lot of these events are quite dull, and anyway, you shouldn't listen to other people. Everyone has to follow their own path in life, don't they? If you love the dress, then you should wear it." The dogs all settle down at her feet, and the woman fixes me with a friendly gaze.

"I would normally. . . . I mean, I can be stubborn about these things, but I want my husband to be proud of me. . . ." My voice fades away, as I can't say that I'm thinking about Arthur writing down those words to describe me. I feel a flush of red-hot humiliation run right through me.

"Ah, I see. Husbands can be quite stubborn, I find. I'm sure he is very proud of you, but more importantly, I think you need to feel proud of yourself and let him see that. It doesn't do to base one's opinions on what everyone else needs or thinks, I find. Although it is certainly easier said than done when it's your family, of course." Her words are spoken quietly, and for a moment her voice sounds quite sad and wistful, as if she's not really thinking about me and my gold dress at all. In the distance, I catch a glimpse of the castle and that tiny flag fluttering over the tower.

"I guess so. Oh, look over there. . . . The little flag is flying! You know that means the Queen is home. Say . . . have you ever met her? I bet she has a real nice life. What I wouldn't give to be in charge of everyone so they all had to be good to me!"

The woman seems delighted by what I've said and laughs in a way that makes her whole face light up. "I'm not sure it works like that. I expect she has a lot of people trying to tell her what to do."

"Do you really think so? I didn't think it was allowed to tell queens what to do. If I was her, I'd tell them all to leave me alone or I'd . . . I don't know what queens can do if they get mad at someone. . . . Maybe I'd lock them up in that tower like in fairy stories." I'm being silly, I know, but suddenly my whole mood feels brighter now, and I'm glad this lady came along, as she's really cheered me up.

"If only one could. . . ." she says, and we both stand there for a moment, smiling at each other.

"Well, you've been so kind. Thank you. I should get going." I pick up my bicycle from where it's lying on its side and look toward the path that the nice lady pointed at earlier. "So it's that way?" I ask, just to check, as I really don't want to get lost again. That's the trouble with Great Parks—they go on forever.

"Yes, that's the quickest way if you can manage the walk. I could arrange for someone to give you a lift back if you can't?"

"Oh no, please don't bother. I hate to be a nuisance. I'm fine now . . . really I am. I'll have a bruise on my backside tomorrow, I expect, but no real harm done. Thank you again. You've been very kind." I hesitate for a brief second, unsure of what the etiquette is for saying good-bye to nice strangers, before I start wheeling my bicycle away.

"Good-bye, and do wear your lovely dress. I'm sure it will be a big hit," the woman calls after me.

It's only as I reach the end of the path that I realize I never asked her name.

LILIBET

1956

"Everything all right, ma'am?" Richard, my detective, appears by my side as I walk away.

"Yes. It was nothing—just someone wandered off the track a bit. Right, let's go, shall we?"

All the way back to the castle I think of nothing else except how terribly sad Miss Monroe seemed with her tearstained face. Her husband has obviously upset her quite dreadfully. It is so terribly easy to undermine someone so that they lose confidence in their abilities, and even their own judgment. I count my blessings that for all his stubbornness, Philip wouldn't dare try to tell me what to wear.

How strange to see her in such a vulnerable state, almost childlike in many ways, when every newspaper and magazine has nothing but the most alluring images of her. I don't think she had any idea who I was, and I didn't want to embarrass the poor woman by telling her—although it does mean she's going to get rather a shock when she arrives at the film premiere in her pretty dress. She looked so distressed sitting there on the path crying, and I do hope that she's all right.

I wonder what the dress is like to have provoked such a reaction. We women are completely human but often dressed up to appear less so. Once one appears in full costume, as it were, then others are bound to let loose with their opinions. It can hurt one's feelings if someone is callous with their views, rather than kind. And so many people consider their opinions to be a matter of fact, when of course it is no such thing. We all have opinions on every aspect of life, but it doesn't mean that we are always correct.

The dogs have slowed their pace a little, as have I, becoming lost in thought about women in the public eye and how tricky it can be to maintain one's self intact and not be blown about like an autumn leaf in order to be liked or approved of.

Eventually I reach the door of the castle, greeting the soldier in his sentry box with a polite nod as he stands to attention. The dogs playfully pester him for a moment until I call them away to have their paws wiped before we head back up the stairs.

My mind is a whirl of small worries and, as I sit back down at my desk trying to focus on my paperwork, I can't help but think about the situation with my sister, and of course the issues surrounding Philip and Mike Parker. I don't know what to do for the best, as I feel quite split in two between what Queen Elizabeth should do and what Lilibet wants to do. I only want my family to be happy, but I cannot go on living as two separate people trying to keep the peace. It makes me feel as if I'm an impostor rather than a queen.

As I stare idly around the room, my eye comes to rest on a portrait of my great-great-grandmother, Queen Victoria. "What would you do?" I whisper softly to her. I'm sure that she wouldn't take any nonsense from anyone, as she was by all accounts quite formidable, and I am anything but that. Although, of course, most of those reports are of her as a much older woman—she may have been very different at my age. For a moment, I try to imagine what advice she might offer me, but there is only silence in response to my question.

I can't stop thinking about poor Miss Monroe—who is surely the most sought-after woman in the entire world—sitting there on the pathway, crying over the fact that somebody didn't approve of her choice. Are we all doomed to make ourselves miserable trying to please other people, no matter how wealthy or famous one might be? Yet in my own case, if I were to do as I pleased and not care if others were upset or disappointed, how would that make for a happy life?

Does one always have to choose a side? And what if I have no choice but to take up the side of the Queen and play that part for all I'm worth? This halfway house has very little happiness attached, as I constantly feel as if I am failing, and just for once I would like to feel as if I were doing something right.

I sign the last of my papers and lock the box with a sense of relief. There is something still bothering me about the way Mr. Eden responded when I asked him about that meeting in Paris . . . something that I don't quite trust, yet I can't put my finger on what exactly. Maybe it's a feminine intuition, but I feel that he's not being entirely truthful with me.

Sighing, I get to my feet. It's all a bit of a mess. As I walk back to my drawing room, I think about Philip and wonder what time it is in Malaya. I'd like to hear his voice, as I do miss him very much, but I don't want us to have another argument over the telephone. He's the kind of man who deserves to be in charge of his own household, so his is a most difficult position; I fully realize this, and do try my best not to pull rank, as it were. Although, sadly, it is often unavoidable.

The whole royal setup is like wearing a badly fitted costume that doesn't leave much room for you to breathe freely. Perhaps his absence will give us the chance to redefine our relationship so that we can both feel equally valued. I only hope that Philip will discover that he loves me enough to want to accept more of the constraints of this life without us having this constant battle of wills.

Anyway, I shall ask Margaret if she'd like to have dinner with me. I do so hope that we can be proper sisters once more. We've always managed to make up after our little rows, but this time she is so very unhappy, and I have no way to change it. Maybe I should make an effort to give her more things to do—keeping busy would probably benefit her at the moment. At least it might take her mind off her troubles.

Then I shall speak to Bobo about what to wear to the premiere, as I can't have all these Hollywood stars thinking that I'm a frump. One can't let the side down.

Monday morning brings a chilly wet start to the day. I am back at Buckingham Palace meeting ambassadors as they present their credentials. It's a tradition that dates back centuries—sometimes I imagine what it must have been like for all those kings and queens who came before me, doing exactly the same things. There's a lot to be said for tradition and stability, I think, and it's always nice to welcome people to our country. Ambassadors are generally very easy to make conversation with, thank goodness. It's been a very busy start to the week, and of course with the film premiere this evening it will be a late night too. No rest for the wicked . . . although I would hope that God doesn't consider me too wicked.

I have just enough time to take a short walk with the dogs before lunch, but then I must attend to my red box before getting ready for this evening's entertainment. I'm just about to set off with the dogs when Michael appears by my side.

"I'm afraid there's an urgent issue, ma'am." He has the good grace to look apologetic.

"Michael, I am honestly beginning to dread the sight of you lately, as there's always a problem." I laugh to lighten the mood, but truthfully part of me does feel this way.

"I know, ma'am, and it can't be helped, sadly." He waits for me to lead the way back into my office and, once I am comfortably seated behind my desk, begins to speak. "It seems that the press has got hold of the story concerning the Parkers' impending divorce. I had a call from a journalist in Fleet Street just now, and although I tried my very best to stall him, we do need to act quickly, ma'am. The thing is . . . Lieutenant-Commander Parker has a close association with His Royal Highness the Duke of Edinburgh, and the reporters are asking questions about . . . um . . . well, about the royal marriage, ma'am. No smoke without fire—that sort of thing. A man being known by the company he keeps, et cetera." His face looks grave and distinctly embarrassed, and now I can fully appreciate why, as this will soon turn into a nasty scandal if we're not careful.

I have always been a cautious sort of a person who would never dream of rushing into situations impulsively. But something inside me begins to shift now that it is faced with a decision that will upset a great many people—including my husband. If it were left to me, Lilibet, I would ignore this situation, or take a calm approach, letting it play out.

As Elizabeth, I simply cannot do that.

One cannot stay on the sidelines trying to keep the peace. In the end we all have to choose and act in line with our own inner wisdom. I look around the room and see the family portraits, and I think of all the kings and queens that have come before me.

Suddenly I am ten years old again, sitting in an armchair, watching my father smoking his cigarette and studying the papers in his red box. His face smiling at me as he explained that, even though this job could be a great burden at times, it was without doubt a great honor to be chosen.

Then I think of my great-great-grandmother, Queen Victoria, who dedicated her entire life to this country from such a young age, and suddenly I know what I must do. The future of this institution is my responsibility now.

No matter what the cost, I must follow in their footsteps and do my duty.

"What do you want to do, ma'am?" Michael looks at me earnestly and waits for my decision. He knows what this will cost me, but there is nothing else for it.

I get to my feet and take a deep breath. "Tell my husband that I have given instructions for Lieutenant-Commander Parker to leave the royal tour at once. Then I'd like you to issue a statement saying that he no longer works for the Duke of Edinburgh and any impending divorce is the Parkers' own private business. Furthermore, you should add that there is absolutely no rift in the royal marriage, and as head of the Church of England, I believe marriage to be a sacred vow taken before God. No further comment will be made on this matter. Is that clear?"

Michael's eyes widen slightly with shock as he says, "Crystal clear, ma'am. I'll do that right away."

"Thank you, Michael. That will be all."

I know Philip will be cross about this, but there really is no alternative now the press has the story. Going forward we will have to make changes to find Philip the kind of role that will make him feel valued, but in return I shall lay down conditions about the kind of behavior that's expected and the sort of people he associates with.

I cannot and will not be the only person in this family who considers how our actions affect others or who worries about the dignity of the Crown. I cannot allow my beloved family to protest their unhappiness—at least not in public. It is simply too damaging. And if my family doesn't like my decisions, then I won't apologize for it.

I cannot be all things to all people.

PART SIX

NORMA JEANE

1956

I've never met a queen before, and the thought of it is making me so scared I keep licking my lipstick right off my mouth. Whitey has put it back on twice already this evening, and we have to leave the house pretty soon. I keep blowing out little nervous puffs of breath, imagining all the very many ways that I could embarrass myself. I just want it to go well and for her to like me—at least a little bit. I don't expect we will have more than a few seconds to talk, but I'd like to get the impression that she thought I was more than just some blonde.

When I was washing dishes for nickels back in the orphanage, there wasn't one part of me that imagined I'd be a famous movie star, never mind shaking hands with an actual queen. I guess life throws things your way sometimes, both good and bad.

"Stop licking your lips, Marilyn. I'm begging you," Whitey says with a frown. I'm ruining his creation and I clamp my tongue to the roof of my mouth, trying to resist.

"I know . . . I'm sorry. I don't want to make a fool of myself in front of everyone," I whisper.

"You're gonna be fine. Trust me!" Whitey says with his usual calm look on his face.

My hair and makeup are done, and now it's time to get dressed. The gold lamé dress is hanging on the back of my bedroom door, while Arthur is waiting for me downstairs.

We haven't talked about the dress again since that day I showed Arthur what I was wearing. When I came home from my bicycle ride, he could tell I was upset and was sweet as anything, but I knew that, deep down, he still wished I would wear something different tonight.

And I thought about it for a little while, and then I thought about what that nice lady said to me when I fell off my bicycle. *Everyone has to follow their own path in life,* and that's right. I believe that. I can only be me, otherwise what's the point?

The two thoughts went round and round in my mind all day, but the minute I woke up this morning with a big purple bruise on my ass as a memento, I knew exactly what to do.

"You look beautiful, Marilyn. Fit for a queen. Knock 'em dead," Whitey says as he leaves me to get dressed. One of the girls from Madame de Rachelle's salon has come to make sure there are no last-minute problems with the gown, and she stands there in her neat white coat, nodding in agreement with Whitey.

Slipping off my satin robe, I step into the gold dress, feeling it glide up over my hips and waist, allowing the girl to arrange the thin straps and then to fasten it at the back. I slide my feet into my platform heels and instantly stand taller as the dress flows over them. The girl fusses around me, arranging the golden folds, and then I take a look in the mirror.

Oh, Marilyn—look at you! Fit for a queen, like Whitey said.

Reaching over to my dressing table, I grab the bottle of Floris perfume and apply a tiny spritz here and there. Then the girl helps me into a pair of long cream evening gloves before finally arranging the golden cape across my shoulders and pinning it at my throat.

The sight of the gown and cape takes my breath away. I look

so elegant. At this moment I couldn't be further away from little Norma Jeane in that orphanage.

This is who I was meant to be. This is Marilyn as I want the world to see her.

I pick up my matching gold purse and turn to the girl. "Will I do?" I ask eagerly, because I so want to get this right. I think it looks beautiful, but I need someone to tell me so.

"Oh, Miss Monroe, you look wonderful," the girl says with a beaming smile.

"Thank you. Look at me—I'm shaking like a leaf." I hold out my trembling hands to show her and take a deep breath. My lipstick is still on my mouth—for now at least . . . and I'm ready.

Arthur is standing by the fireplace in the drawing room, smoking a cigarette, as I make my entrance. He turns to look at me as I put my shoulders back and lift my chin in a determined fashion, daring him to criticize me. Waiting for his look of disappointment—but it doesn't come.

"You look incredible, baby. Now we should get going or we'll be late for the Queen of England and that will never do." He looks so handsome with his dark hair slicked right back and his black tux—I like a man in a tuxedo. It always makes a fellow look taller and more dignified, I think. As he comes toward me and kisses me softly on my cheek, I can feel his body so lean and hard underneath his jacket, and I want to hold on to him forever.

A feeling of relief floods right through me. Nothing can go wrong now. I'm going to have the most wonderful evening, and tomorrow everyone in the world will know that Marilyn Monroe met the Queen of England.

Little Norma Jeane, whose daddy didn't want to know her, whose mama wouldn't look after her—she's got it all now.

John, our driver, helps me into the car, making sure every bit of the gown is safely inside before slamming the door shut. Arthur slides into the seat next to me as my tongue finds its way to my lips. Quickly I try to stop myself licking off my lipstick, clenching my teeth as I shiver a little. The car is chilly and this dress doesn't offer a whole heap of warmth, so I snuggle a little closer to Arthur, feeling the heat of his body next to mine.

We'll be done in England soon. The movie will wrap, and we have our whole lives ahead of us, just me and Pa. Then a baby, maybe even two, and in a few years I might consider bringing Marilyn out of retirement for another movie—but only if I find a great script. No more junk parts for me. I might even do a stage play—star on Broadway in something. I've always wanted to play Grushenka in *The Brothers Karamazov*, and I could do it too.

I mean, if a girl can get all the way from an orphanage in Los Angeles to meeting the Queen of England, then who knows what she's capable of achieving? None of it happened by accident. I did it all.

I made it happen. . . .

Out of the window I catch a glimpse of the dark outline of Windsor Castle as we head for the road to London. The little flag isn't flying, and so the Queen is at Buckingham Palace getting ready to meet me! The thought of that races through my veins, fizzing like that first mouthful of champagne.

The dark streets fly past us and, before I know it, I see a huge crowd of people all standing around waiting in Leicester Square. They must be getting cold out there, as there's a bitter wind blowing this evening. Or maybe British people are just used to it. I don't think I've been warm for one day, and it rains all the time—although I like walking in the rain.

The car glides to a halt, and to one side I can see photographers everywhere I look. Arthur frowns at the sight of them. Their flashbulbs poised, ready to fire as soon as I step out of this car. I lick my lips nervously and smooth down the front of my dress.

Suddenly my confidence begins to trickle away. Suppose the dress *is* all wrong and tomorrow the whole world is laughing at me or thinking that I've insulted the Queen of England?

Arthur steps out of the car and offers me his hand.

It's now or never. Come on, little orphan girl, what are you going to do? Are you going to chicken out? I close my eyes for a long moment and take a breath. *Marilyn will take care of you just like she always has. Walk tall and let them all see who you are.*

I grasp hold of Arthur, feeling the pressure of his hand through my gloved fingers, and then the next thing I know, I'm giving those photographers the full Marilyn smile.

A gust of wind blows my cape back off my shoulders and everyone gets their first glimpse of the gold dress. Flashbulbs explode around me with blinding white lights as I smile and smile, waving to the crowd of spectators who are going crazy at the sight of me.

Arthur tries to help get my cape back onto my shoulders. I guess he's keen to cover me up again, but I won't have it. After a few moments of waving and smiling, we head inside the theater, where we're guided to the circle lounge. I just have time to fix my lipstick one more time when outside we hear a huge cheer go up and someone tells us all to get in a line, as the Queen has arrived with her sister, Princess Margaret.

"Go on, honey. You'll do great." Arthur is not being presented to Her Majesty, so he will watch on the screen they've put up and meet me afterward.

I put my hands to my throat and unpin my cape so that there's just Marilyn and her beautiful golden dress, fitted tight at the waist and low-cut across the bust. Arthur swallows hard as I hand him the cape, but I give him a steely glare and he doesn't say a word.

We all file out into a long corridor with a plush red carpet under our feet. It's a long line of who's who in Hollywood and London. I can see Joan Crawford dressed in white satin, and, thank God, I'm nowhere near her as she's always hated me. Instead, I slot in with Victor Mature on one side of me and Anthony Quayle on the other. Two handsome guys in their black tuxedos and me like a gold statue between them. I'm about halfway down the line so there's a little time to wait.

Then a buzz of excitement shoots right through everyone as a young woman in a beautiful black velvet gown steps into the room. We're all pretty dazzled by the light glittering off her jewels, and suddenly I feel the nerves kick in and my tongue keeps reaching for my lips.

Whitey will be so mad at me, but I can't seem to stop myself. Victor was making me laugh with his jokes, but now he goes quiet, as we're all feeling the same thing.

Nobody wants to be the one who messes up meeting the Queen of England.

Suddenly she's right there in front of me, and I can't even look at her. Our hands touch, and my eyes sweep the floor as I dip into the deepest curtsy I can manage. Fear swirls around inside me, and I'm pretty sure my lipstick is all but gone now.

Then, taking a deep breath, I allow myself to straighten up and look at her for the first time.

"Good evening, Miss Monroe, I understand we're neighbors," she says.

Her blue eyes smile at me as if we're old friends.

LILIBET

1956

"My goodness, look at you in full battle dress. You look different somehow." My sister has a way of delivering a compliment that makes it sound like an insult. Margaret offers a brief kiss to my cheek and then stands back to take another look at me. As she turns her head, taking in the front and side of my dress, I feel rather like a prize cow being measured at a farmers' market.

"As a matter of fact, I rather like this look. I've upped the glamour for the occasion," I reply as I allow myself to be inspected. Margaret takes in my black velvet evening gown and long white gloves and nods approvingly.

The dress is quite a heavy velvet, but it falls beautifully, and the sleeves drape nicely off my shoulders. I've brought out the big guns in terms of jewelry, as I'm wearing the Vladimir Tiara that belonged to my grandmother, Queen Mary, who had it altered so that one could wear it either with pearls or, as in this case, fifteen enormous emeralds inserted inside the diamond-encrusted circles.

I've chosen an emerald necklace and a pair of matching earrings to complete the ensemble. The combination of the inky-black velvet and the sparkling green of the emeralds is very acceptable, if I do say so myself. I've scrubbed up rather well. Certainly, Margaret thinks so, as her face is a picture. It has run the complete range of emotions, from a slight look of jealousy to a fleeting admiration.

I reach across to turn off my little radio, but just as I do so, there is a news bulletin and I hesitate for a moment to listen to the headlines. The announcer in clear, crisp tones says that Israeli armed forces have tonight invaded Egypt with the intention of taking back the Suez Canal. Suddenly Mr. Eden's behavior and his avoidance of telling me everything about his meeting in Paris becomes only too clear, and I feel an absolute fury at being treated so disrespectfully both as a woman and as a queen.

I turn and stare at my equerry, who is hovering by the door. "Tell the prime minister I wish to see him first thing tomorrow morning . . . without fail. He has some explaining to do."

"Oh dear, someone's in trouble," Margaret says.

"Yes, indeed. I am very tired of being treated like a fool by that man. I won't tolerate it." My tone is sharp, but I soften it with a smile. "Come along, you. Let's go and look at the Hollywood stars, shall we?"

I can see Miss Monroe waiting nervously about halfway down the presentation line, and she's wearing the most dazzling gold dress. It is very low-cut and fitted quite tightly, but she does look every inch the Hollywood star. As I draw closer, I notice that she keeps licking at her lips in a nervous fashion. If she carries on, there won't be a spot of lipstick left on her mouth. I feel a little dash of pity for her, being so scared at the prospect of meeting me—when we have already met and spoken quite easily. I do hope she won't be embarrassed by that meeting—maybe I should have introduced myself at the time, but that might have made her feel worse. Sitting there as she was, quite alone, and in floods of tears.

"Lovely to meet you," I say over and over again as I shake hands with the great and the good. They're all wearing their most sensational outfits, silks and satins in elegant colors, glittering under the lights. Everyone is giving a well-practiced bow or curtsy, and then I see Miss Monroe getting closer, and I can tell even from this distance that she's trembling a little. I carry on smiling and making polite noises about being delighted to meet them and asking them some small question about themselves, as I find it relaxes them. Then I'm shaking hands with Victor Mature, who seems very nice, and Miss Monroe is next in line.

I say my good-byes to Mr. Mature and move along to stand in front of her, holding out my white gloved hand to take hers.

Miss Monroe's eyes are fixed to the floor as if she doesn't dare look at me, and then she sweeps into a deep curtsy just as I take her hand. I'm waiting for her to glance up, but she doesn't, so I give her gloved hand a tiny squeeze with my fingers.

Suddenly her wide blue eyes flicker upward and I say, "Good evening, Miss Monroe. I understand we're neighbors?"

I see the shock of recognition cross her face, and her mouth falls open slightly as she replies, "What?" in that very American way.

I smile, not wanting her to feel at all awkward, but rather as if we two are sharing in a private joke. For a second there is no reaction, but then her face lights up with sheer delight, and our smiles broaden.

"And how are you enjoying Windsor?" I ask, my eyes twinkling with pleasure at her reaction to seeing me, for now she is in on the joke, as it were.

"We love it. As we have a permit, my husband and I go for

bicycle rides in the Great Park. Sometimes I even go there on my own . . ." she says with some excitement.

"Ah, how lovely. It's a very good place for that. Although you do have to be careful to stick to the proper pathways," I say as I take in her beautiful golden dress and give a tiny nod of my head to show my approval. She does look quite stunning, and I don't know why anyone would have thought otherwise, although I'm sure there was probably some comment about its suitability.

"Yes . . . I'll be careful to do that," Miss Monroe says with a shy, knowing smile. For a long second the two of us stand there with bright smiles on our faces, enjoying our secret moment of recognition. If only everyone knew about our meeting, they'd be quite surprised. Certainly the woman I encountered crying looks very different from this exquisite creature standing in front of me in her golden gown.

I suppose that nobody really knows anyone—particularly if all you see are the expensive dresses and glittering jewels—for everyone has their private sorrows.

"It was lovely to meet you," I say with a final nod of my head, before releasing her hand and moving on to Mr. Quayle, who is waiting patiently beside her.

"That went well?" I say as Margaret and I settle ourselves into the back of the car.

"Yes. What did you think of Miss Monroe? That was quite the gown she was wearing and not entirely suitable for meeting members of the royal family." My sister is beginning to sound very much like Mummy in her opinions about how women should dress.

"I thought it brightened up the evening. She seems like a very sweet person, but so nervous that she'd licked off all her lipstick. I think we might have another of her movies for our film night. That might be fun?" I say with a smile.

Margaret smiles back at me, and sitting there, as the car crawls through the damp, chilly streets of London, I remember all the happy times when the two of us have been side by side. Our blissful childhood in Piccadilly, until the abdication forced our father to become King; the dreary war years in Windsor worrying about our parents in Buckingham Palace with bombs falling on them; and of course my first and only love with Philip, when Margaret was my chief supporter and confidante. We have always been together, playing on the same team, supporting each other through thick and thin—until Peter came along and changed everything.

Turning to her I say, "Do you remember back in Piccadilly that time we said a little prayer for a brother?"

Margaret laughs a little. "Yes, I do. You were quite horrified at the prospect of becoming Queen as I remember."

"You know I never wanted this job. I'm not really the kind of woman who enjoys the spotlight. You would have been better at that part of it, I'm sure. Yet I am a steady sort of person, and I do very much believe that this country needs that sort of stability. We've all been through such a lot of heartbreak—losing people so very dear to us—but when people get spun around in a whirl of problems, I like to think that they can look to me as a sort of lighthouse in a storm."

"I've never really thought of you as a lighthouse, Lil." Margaret laughs but not unkindly.

"Oh, you know what I mean. I want to be something constant for people—beaming out a little ray of light that provides a sort of normality. A kind of 'if she's still there doing her duty, then all will be well.' At least I hope that's what I'm providing.

"Anyway, I want you to know that I love you all so very much—you, Mummy, Philip of course, and my children, but just as a lighthouse can't ever switch off its beam, so a queen can't choose not to accept her role. You do see that, don't you?" I place my hand over my sister's and squeeze it gently, waiting for her to respond as I hope she will.

"Yes, I do see. I really do. I know you have a very difficult job and I will do my best to support you however I can. It's just been so very hard when you're all that I've got left, apart from Mummy. I miss Papa so much—and you have Philip, so it's not the same." As she speaks her blue eyes brim with tears, and I feel so desperately sorry for her.

"I know it's harder for you being alone, and I will try to do what I can to help. Can we make up, please? I do so hate it when we fall out with each other." I can feel my own tears catching at the back of my throat as it becomes thick with emotion.

"Yes, I'd like that," Margaret says, wrapping her gloved fingers through mine, just as we used to do when we were tiny children.

"By the way, I was rather hoping that you might stand in for me next week, as I've been invited to the ballet, and it's much more your kind of thing. Dame Margot Fonteyn is dancing, and I think you'd enjoy that. It's on Wednesday evening if you're free?" I watch my sister's face soften as she realizes that I am trying my best to help her make a new life.

"Yes, I'm free. Thank you . . . I won't let you down," Margaret says gently.

"I know you won't. And if you do, I shall send for a pot of dark blue ink, and you know what will happen then!"

There is a brief silence, before we both burst out laughing, which feels very nice. Then Margaret squeezes my hand. "I'm sorry for being beastly to you—about Philip. I didn't mean to hurt you, Lil. I would never do that. . . ."

"I know. Thank you for the apology," I say quietly.

Families are such complicated things. We love each other so dearly and yet also hurt each other, often without thinking. Our family in particular has its own unique way of doing things, and we all have to play our roles for public consumption. I cannot be a proper sister or daughter or even a wife at times because the job will always come first in some ways. But I do have great faith that the love we have for one another will stand the test of time, even if I cannot be the same Lilibet as before.

I am a queen . . . I am *the* Queen.

London, November 20, 1956

LILIBET

BUCKINGHAM PALACE

Nine years ago today, I walked down the aisle of Westminster Abbey on my father's arm, in my beautiful silk dress, to marry the only man who I've ever loved. I can still recall the swish of silk along the abbey floor and the scent of my bouquet—white orchids and a sprig of myrtle hidden away among the flowers. If I close my eyes, I can feel the warm steadiness of my father's arm as we arrived at the altar and that spark of joy when I saw Philip's loving gaze.

Time has flown by in the blink of an eye, and here we are nine years later. Our brief telephone conversations lately have been friendly but not exactly loving. I'm sure he's still quite cross at losing Mike Parker from his staff, but it really couldn't be helped, and I do hope he understands that.

I miss Philip terribly and want us to make up, especially today of all days, but he's so very far away.

The dogs skitter around my feet as I walk briskly along the palace corridor to my office to begin my day's work. I can see my private secretary hovering outside the door—lying in wait for me to go through the diary and begin our day.

"Good morning, Michael. And what do we have today?" I ask with a brief smile.

"Good morning, Your Majesty. We have the reception with military veterans and their families. They'll be presented to you, and then we'll give them lunch with a couple of government ministers."

"Ah, of course." As I walk into my office, the first thing I see is the most beautiful bouquet of white roses sitting in a crystal vase on top of my desk. Each rose gleaming bright white against its dark green stem. "Oh . . . where did they come from?"

"They're from the Duke of Edinburgh, ma'am. Happy anniversary!" Michael says, offering me a white envelope. "There's a card."

"How lovely! Thank you." My face beams with delight as I sit down at my desk and slice the envelope with my trusty silver letter opener. Teasing the card out of its envelope, I see a picture of two iguanas embracing fondly—presumably meant to represent us as a pair. For a moment I laugh out loud, as I wonder if he thinks of me as resembling an iguana. One hopes not. It's a very sweet picture, though, and funny. So typical of Philip.

Michael clears his throat and stands back for a moment to allow me some privacy. The scent of the white roses is quite intoxicating, and I feel a rush of happiness at the sight of them.

I open Philip's card and read his words. In his usual determined hand, with navy blue ink, he has written:

Happy Anniversary to my darling Lilibet,
All my love, now and forever.
Philip

A single tear glides onto my cheek so softly that I barely notice it. My sailor husband . . . who is thousands of miles away but thinking of me on this special day.

Our little ship has weathered a number of storms, and here we are marking another milestone in our life together. It will soon be Christmas . . . and then before we know it, Philip will be home again.

There will be other anniversaries to celebrate together—a lifetime of them. . . .

"I believe they're ready for you now, ma'am," Michael says, and I get to my feet and begin the long walk from my private office along the corridors of Buckingham Palace, surrounded by the portraits of all those who came before me.

As we reach the Bow Room, the doors are flung open and a voice pronounces loudly, "Her Majesty the Queen."

NORMA JEANE

LONDON AIRPORT

It's certainly a lot quieter to leave a place than to arrive in it. London Airport seems pretty deserted this evening as I answer the final few questions from the press. Dressed in a coal-black mink coat with a dark wool dress, I say my final good-byes to England. It feels like it rained every single day while I was here, or maybe that was just me. Either way, I'll be glad to get home to New York and start my real married life with Arthur—just the two of us.

"What did you enjoy the most about England, Marilyn?" one of the reporters shouts out as he sits there, chewing on his pencil, poised to take down my answer.

"The biggest thrills for me were meeting your Queen . . . and seeing my husband's new play," I say, and then I make my little rehearsed speech about thanking the British people for their warmth and support these past few months.

"And what's next for you, Marilyn? Another movie?" a stout fellow at the back of the room yells out at me.

"Well, I have nothing lined up for me right now . . . except being a wife. We are going home to New York, where I want to be a wife . . . where I will be Mrs. Miller." I gaze lovingly at Arthur as I speak, and he smiles back at me. He's waited all summer for this moment. We both need some time away from the goldfish bowl to see what we really need from our marriage.

The press guys seem a little disappointed with my answer. They want the carnival to continue, but this carnival ride is over . . . for now.

"I'll take one more question," I say, and a short, dark-haired woman with black eyes suddenly stands up.

"Marilyn . . . it's Ida Lapine from the 'Daily Sparkle' column. Could you tell our readers what you thought of the Queen?" The woman stares quite sternly at me.

"Sure . . . the Queen is very warmhearted. She radiates sweetness . . . and I liked her very much."

The woman opens her mouth to ask another question, but before she can say a word, the officials jump right in to say we have to leave or we'll miss our flight. And that's the end of that.

Climbing the steps to the Pan Am flight that will take us home, we stop at the top to wave a final farewell to everyone. I can feel the strange busy electricity of the little purple pills, working their magic inside me. I'm going to stop taking them as soon as we land. Everything will be different when I get back home. No more pills. No more booze. I'm going to live on love from now on. It will all be different when we're back in New York, you'll see. . . .

I'm going to be the best wife to Arthur that he could ever want. If I can meet the Queen of England, then I can do anything in this life.

And we're going to have such beautiful babies—a girl for me and a boy for him. Our babies are going to be so loved. They will never go a day without someone telling them how loved they are, because people should do that for their kids.

This summer has really taken it out of me, but the movie is all wrapped now and Arthur and me, for all our troubles . . . we're still here. We've made it through.

Goodbye, England! I glance down at the guys loading the plane and notice them putting my little bicycle into the hold. "Hey, you guys better be careful with that!" I yell, and they wave back at me. Every time I look at that bicycle, I'm going to remember the day I met the Queen and she was so very kind.

I think of poor little Norma Jeane in that orphanage wanting to be somebody, and then I remember the night of the premiere standing there in my gold lamé gown, chatting to the Queen of England as if we were old friends.

There's nothing Marilyn can't do when she sets her mind to it. You wait and see. . . .

Marilyn Monroe won two international Best Actress awards for her role in *The Prince and the Showgirl* (formerly *The Sleeping Prince*). She and Arthur Miller filed for divorce in November 1960 on grounds of incompatibility. She never returned to England, although she kept her bicycle as a souvenir for the rest of her life.

On August 4, 1962, Marilyn Monroe died from a suspected overdose. She was just thirty-six years old.

Queen Elizabeth was married to Prince Philip for seventy-three years until his death on April 9, 2021. She reigned for more than seventy years and died on September 8, 2022, at Balmoral Castle, at the age of ninety-six.

She was the longest-reigning monarch in British history.

Elizabeth and Marilyn met on October 29, 1956, at the film premiere of *The Battle of the River Plate.*

It was their only meeting . . . that we know of.

ACKNOWLEDGMENTS

It is a tricky thing to write about real people and to reimagine events in their lives. Timelines have to be shifted, as fiction cannot wait for real life to catch up—sometimes things have to be manufactured in order to display what you see as a greater truth. I hope that I have done both Lilibet and Norma Jeane justice while trying to show the women I believed them to be.

There are many wonderful factual accounts of the summer of 1956, and I am particularly grateful to the following works for allowing me to glean more insight into the characters of these two women: *When Marilyn Met the Queen* by Michelle Morgan (2022), *Marilyn: The Passion and the Paradox* by Lois Banner (2012), and *Marilyn in Manhattan: Her Year of Joy* by Elizabeth Winder (2017). For Queen Elizabeth, I am indebted to the following works: *The Little Princesses* by Marion Crawford (1950), *Elizabeth: An Intimate Portrait* by Gyles Brandreth (2022), and *Elizabeth & Philip* by Tessa Dunlop (2022).

Elizabeth and Marilyn is a work of fiction wrapped around some real events, but I hope that it shows what I believe was a very significant summer in the lives of both of these women.

This book started with a lie. Somebody posted on social media that Elizabeth and Marilyn shared a birthday. That turned out not to be true, but the idea of these two women being born just weeks apart stayed with me. They seemed such different characters . . . and yet there was something in each of them I felt that spoke to the experiences of the other woman. And indeed, they were slightly fascinated with each other. Marilyn really did want to have tea with the Queen and shopped at the same stores, while the Queen watched Marilyn's movies in private. I owe a debt of thanks to whoever posted that incorrect information about their birth date because it led me to write this book.

Thanks as always to my UK editor, Clio Cornish, for taking my rambling suggestion over lunch and encouraging me to make it real in time to celebrate the centenary of their births in 2026. Huge thanks as always to my team at Penguin Michael Joseph in the UK: Clio, Maddy, Kat, and Frankie. To Nick and Richenda for their careful work and constant checking. Many thanks to Sarah and the rights team at Penguin Books, to the audio team for their great work in casting our narrators, and to my US editor, Susanna Porter, and Anusha Khan and the whole team at Ballantine Books in the US for all their help and support, and thanks to Sophia Chunn for the beautiful US cover.

It takes a village to make a book, and I'm grateful to everyone who has played a part in bringing this to you.

Early readers are like Santa's little helpers to an author, and I am so thankful to Georgina Moore and Charmaine Wilkerson for reading early copies of this book and giving such lovely feedback. I'd also like to send huge thanks to all my readers and the many wonderful book bloggers who shout about my work. Virtual bouquets of flowers to you all!

Finally, all my love and thanks to Sean for his endless support of me and my work. Behind every woman writing books is someone making sure they are suitably caffeinated to face the world.

Jx

SIAN TRENBERTH PHOTOGRAPHY

JULIE OWEN MOYLAN is the critically acclaimed author of three previous novels, *That Green Eyed Girl, 73 Dove Street,* and *Circus of Mirrors*. Her writing and short stories have appeared in a variety of publications, including *Sunday Express*, *The Independent*, *New Welsh Review,* and *Good Housekeeping*. She has a master's in filmmaking and an additional degree in creative writing and English literature.

www.julieowenmoylan.com
IG: @JulieOwenMoylan

RANDOM HOUSE BOOK CLUB

ELIZABETH AND MARILYN

BY JULIE OWEN MOYLAN

DEAR READER,

This book began with a lie. I was scrolling through social media one day when I saw a post suggesting that Queen Elizabeth and Marilyn Monroe were born on the same day. It was completely false, but that post led me to the discovery that they were in fact born just weeks apart. I found this surprising because I think of the late Queen as being a very old lady and of Marilyn as being forever young. Yet the idea of them living parallel lives on different sides of the Atlantic Ocean just wouldn't leave me alone. Ideas tug at authors, and this is how most books get started.

I began to imagine Elizabeth and Marilyn as girls of ten years old and then as young women of twenty. What were they like? How did they live? Eventually I discovered that during the summer of 1956, these two incredibly famous women were living practically next door to each other in Windsor, and I knew that I wanted to write this novel.

Like many of you, I thought I understood who these women were, but my research surprised me. Marilyn was so much more than a blond-bombshell actress, and I also came to appreciate how difficult it must have been for Elizabeth to lose her beloved father and step into the role of Queen. The public faces of Elizabeth and Marilyn seemed very different from the private women, Lilibet and Norma Jeane, who were often struggling to cope with their celebrity, their work, and their homelife. I wanted to write about them as women, not merely as celebrities, and I hope you find plenty to discuss in my portrayal of them.

I think at its best reading helps us to empathize with people who live completely different lives with completely different circumstances from our own. In the pages of a book, for a brief period, we can be a Queen or a famous movie star and imagine what that must be like. I hope your book club enjoys this read and has fun with the discussion points I've provided, although do feel free of course to talk about anything that comes up with regard to these women. They are truly fascinating characters living extraordinary lives.

I have also included a recipe for jam penny sandwiches, which were much loved by Queen Elizabeth as a child and which she continued to enjoy with a cup of Earl Grey tea every afternoon. I hope some readers will enjoy a passionate debate about this book while drinking tea and sharing a plate of jam pennies.

Thank you for choosing *Elizabeth and Marilyn* for your book club. I hope it provides much food for thought!

Julie Owen Moylan

QUESTIONS & TOPICS FOR DISCUSSION

1. In what ways do you think Elizabeth and Marilyn were different from Lilibet and Norma Jeane?

2. Did reading this book change your opinion of either of these women? Did they surprise you in any way?

3. Do you believe these women would have been happier if they had not been famous at that time? In what ways might they have been happier?

4. Can you see any parallels between Elizabeth and Marilyn and any celebrities today?

5. How would Elizabeth and Marilyn have behaved differently if they were young women in 2026 rather than 1956?

6. In what way does gossip/tabloid culture affect our view of famous women? Have you been influenced by newspaper or magazine stories about celebrities?

7. How were these women affected/supported/*not* supported by the men in their lives? What were your opinions about Philip and Arthur and the roles they played in this book?

8. What would you have done differently if you had been Elizabeth or Marilyn?

9. In what way did the summer of 1956 change these women?

10. Why do you think Elizabeth and Marilyn were so fascinated by each other?

11. If you could ask either of these women a question, what would it be?

12. If you could ask the author one question about this book, what would it be?

RECIPE FOR JAM PENNY SANDWICHES

INGREDIENTS (MAKES FOUR JAM PENNIES):

Two slices of good quality sliced white bread (medium cut)

Unsalted butter, slightly softened

Strawberry jam/preserves (although you can use any flavor)

DIRECTIONS:

Butter one slice of white bread and add a generous layer of strawberry jam on top of the butter.

Take another slice of white bread and place on top of the jam.

Press gently together and then remove the crusts from the bread.

Using a round cookie cutter, cut the sandwich into small circular shapes. I use a two-inch cutter.

Enjoy with a cup of Earl Grey tea (or a beverage of your choice)!